ROOKED

Wall Street Never Saw It Coming

Disclaimer

Names, places, characters and incidents, whether of actual persons or locations or persons or locations invented by the author, are used fictionally. Any similarities between people, places, incidents, or organizations to the fictional characters, incidents or settings in this story are purely unintentional and/or coincidental. While associations are made in this story to actual events surrounding the global financial collapse of 2008, too many creative liberties have been applied to take anything in this story as factual. This story was created for entertainment only.

Joyce, Susan.
    Rooked

Published by Susan Joyce Carlson

ISBN 978-1-7343230-0-9

Cover Image by Susan Joyce Carlson

Edited by Quinn Editing

Copyright © 2020 by Susan Joyce Carlson

    All rights reserved

No part of this publication may be reproduced, stored in a retrieval system, or transmitted in any form or by any means (electronic, photocopying, recording, or otherwise) without the prior written permission of the author and publisher.

This book is dedicated to my children:

Ty, Rachel, and Toby

ROOKED

by

Susan Joyce

CHAPTER 1: DEAD END
FIDDLERS PARK, MINNESOTA

Friday, May 4, 2007: 2:35 P.M. (CDT)

Is fate a cause or a symptom? In the case of a caterpillar—when it devours itself to become a butterfly—is it both? I stand like a jerk in front of the whole company and wonder how much more trite my life can possibly become. My co-workers sing as sincerely as possible on a Friday afternoon in May "... for he's a jolly good fel-ehl-ooh, which nobody can deny." I've just been promoted to assistant sales director for a department of three, which includes the director and myself.

"Thank you," I say, hoping no one expects a speech.

"Speech, speech, speech," they all begin chanting.

Durkee Box Manufacturing is the only claim to industry in Fiddlers Park, a virtually invisible village located between St. Paul and Minneapolis. Residents in St. Paul refer to the area as Minneapolis. People from Minneapolis refer to it as St. Paul. The Park, as we locals call it, is the abyss between these two metropolises from which I, David Daniel Yates, cannot seem to escape.

I live in a converted storeroom above a stinking hair salon called the Curl Up and Dye, and I do mean stinking as in perm solutions and hairspray. Between paying off student loans and trying to get my truck fixed I'm having about as much luck finding my fortune as I am finding the perfect woman. This isn't how I had expected my life to turn out and yet here it is, my momentous occasion!

There are exactly nineteen people crammed in the tiny lunchroom for this "celebration" as Walter Durkee had put it a second ago. I have either eaten lunch or peed next to every one of them during the past eight years.

Durkee is a tight group—"family" as Walter usually puts it. "We take care of our own," he likes to say, as though it is Durkee against the world. Walter psychologically adopts everyone as kin. The primary reason I am being promoted today is because I am a kid from a broken home. Walter took me under his wing when I was sixteen and gave me a job in the mailroom when they didn't have a mailroom. He kept me on the payroll all during high school and college more to put an honest jingle in my pocket than because he needed another employee. By the time I graduated from the University of Minnesota with a bachelor's degree in business I had six years' experience with the company, which looks good on my résumé, but I still can't land a job at Medtronic or General Mills where the pay is bigger and the bonuses better. So, I had taken Walter up on his offer of a sales position while I continued to search for greater opportunity elsewhere. That was more than a year ago. Haven't made it out of the box yet, no pun intended.

Walter is standing next to me, eyes wide in anticipation of wonderful words to flow from my mouth about how Durkee is the best place in the whole world to work and how he is the best boss ever. Walter Durkee had been a top sales rep for Brown and Bigelow before striking off on his own in 1958. He is a tall, husky, lumbering man who looks like he could carry the world on his shoulders, and he tries hard to live up to that image. For as large as he is, his voice is remarkably soft and kindly, unless he is giving a speech in which case his diaphragm expands and contracts in the same manner it does every Sunday in the Our Savior's Lutheran Church Choir. His first two years in business for himself he worked an average of ninety-five hours a week that he has since scaled back to sixty hours in more recent years. "Learning to give up the reins," he tells people. But that will never happen so long as he's alive.

The cake reads "Congratulations to the Best Box Broker"—which is what it says every quarter—but today another line has been squeezed into the space between 'congratulations' and 'best box broker' by a nervous baker and reads: 'Assistant Sales Manager.'

I clear my throat. "As you all know, Durkee is the place to be and Walter is the man," I say holding my hands out to pass the attention to Walter. Walter chomps on it like a northern pike on a frog. I step back into Walter's shadow and let him ramble on about how Durkee Box Manufacturing produces more than boxes—"We produce leaders!" He pats me on the back a couple more times for effect before everyone disperses to their cubicles, cake in hand.

"Way to go, buddy," someone shouts.

"You're the man," someone else belts out.

They all stumble up and slap me on the back on their way out the door. Before I know it, I am alone in the lunchroom with the remains of the cake, listening to the faucet drip. I better put on another pot of coffee if we're going to make it through the afternoon. I've been here long enough to know the entire office will be battling a sugar low in less than an hour.

Friday, May 4, 2007: 5:35 p.m. (CDT)

Nothing in Fiddlers Park goes by its original name. The original Snyder Rexall Drug on the corner of Commons Street and Paine Avenue was known as Nick's before I was born and has since become Rick's Nick's since the '80s when Nick's son, Rick, inherited it from Nick.

Everyone born and raised in the Park refers to the Carnegie Library as 'the steps' because the structure has a unique exterior two-way stairwell upon which every kid in the Park first earns his or her wings learning to jump, and from which several received the real badge of courage—a cast everyone else signs with magic markers and crayons. Teens meet there on summer evenings and 'the steps' become 'the *big* step,' which adds a whole new meaning to a first kiss. So, it is no surprise that the establishment serving the village's tired and thirsty—which was named The Lady Slipper in 1932 by its original owner, Thomas Schmitt—is known as Schmitty's. No matter who owns the joint, anyone who stands behind the bar eventually comes when called Schmitty.

It's the place where the locals hang out. Now and again some sightseers wander through the door and marvel at the quaintness, like the place is an antique or something. "A page from the past," I heard someone comment once. But it's *today's* page for us. The same old page.

Schmitty's starts hopping about four-thirty on Friday afternoons when people cut out early from work. By nine it's a sea of heads. Its success rate for pairing up is notable, so nearly every single person in the Park winds up at Schmitty's most Fridays. I grab a stool next to Petie Skoog who I've been hanging tighter with since my best buddy, Maynard, got married four years ago.

I dubbed Maynard 'the Mayo' in second grade and even his wife Ruthie calls him that now. Mayo got a job digging dirt and carrying nails for Twin City Construction, and he and Ruthie are having their second kid. I'm happy for him and all, but I miss the good old days when us guys hung out and chased skirts and knew all the answers to everything. Right now, listening to Petie, I realize he doesn't know a damned thing about anything. Petie is starting to get on my nerves. I grab my beer and swivel around on the stool until my back is against the bar, then prop both elbows behind me. Petie turns toward me but remains facing the bar. I toss him a couple affirmative grunts as I check out the room. Nothing. Nothing. Maybe. Nah.

Incoming left, periscope up. It's Sally Weatherstrom—all bouncing boobs and ruby lips. She cracks her gum and winks as she saunters up to me and bumps my knee with a gentle swing of her hip as she passes. Sally's a regular and this is her watering hole. We did it two months ago and are done with each other but she likes to keep her options open.

I had heard Sally's cousin was in town and what followed behind her was clearly Weatherstrom genes, only much more refined ... soft flowing sandy hair that spills over her shoulders and frames a set of hooters that could stop an offensive lineman in the middle of an overtime play. Smoky painted eyelids drop immediately when our eyes engage. My primal pursuit instincts kick into full gear. I purse my lips and let out a whisper of a whistle. By the time she passes me, she's felt my eyeballs all over her. She looks back over her shoulder with a real poker face but her eyes say, "Come and get it."

Petie is staring into my chin by now. "Why don't girls like me?" he mumbles through lips that no longer work effectively. "And tell me straight, man, 'cause I gotta know," he drools as he falls further into my chest. I heave my chest with enough force to push Petie back onto his stool and take off after the Weatherstrom bait.

Her name is Sydney, but close friends call her Sy, she tells me, then adds, "Which is what I make men do." Her tongue slowly rolls over her lips before she puckers and blows me a kiss.

"Honey, you just bought a ticket to the big show," I say with a wink. She's all smiles and the rest of the world fades into the background as we start the ol' mating game ... coy smiles, teasing talk, a few accidental bumps and rubs. All I need now is a slow dance and we can make our exit to my place. It's all coming together except for one thing—a nagging sensation that I'm just not interested. How can that be? I'm a guy. It's Friday. Why am I not acting like it?

"Hey, buddy," Mayo says as he slaps me on the back and leans close to whisper in my ear. "Am I intruding? ... because if I am, I'm outta here, man." It's a gentleman's agreement: never interrupt when a buddy is trying to score.

"Naw, naw," I say as I jump off the stool, excited to see him. "Where's Ruthie?" I ask, looking around. She's home with Mayo Jr., he tells me, rubbing a bulge they already named Bruno—short for Bronson Edward after both their fathers. I invite him to sit with us. The mood changes immediately when I introduce Mayo to Sydney with the story about how Mayo got suspended from school in tenth grade when he flushed a lit cherry bomb down the toilet in the boy's locker room and blew it to bits. Mayo and I laugh and shake our heads over the fun we had in high school but Sydney starts looking around the room.

I ignore Mayo's look that begs to know why I'm not all over Sydney like a four-wheeler on sand dunes and instead dive into another tale about how the Ol' Mayo came to be known throughout the annals of our alma mater as "Kid Ketchup." By the time I finish recalling how Mayo could squirt ketchup from a plastic bottle concealed beneath the lunchroom table with such aim and accuracy as to nail any unsuspecting student without getting caught, Sy has retreated into the crowd, never to be seen again.

"There was that one time you nailed old man Wiley and you nearly got caught, but Alison Bly stepped up and took the rap for you, saying she had accidentally squeezed the ketchup too hard," I say, finishing the story.

"Whatever happened to Alison?" Mayo asks after a hearty chuckle over the ketchup caper.

"I don't know," I reply, wondering why I don't know. The three of us had grown up together, but Alison and I had been a twosome since we were toddlers. She and I dated all through high school and I can't recall how or when we drifted so far apart that I no longer knew anything about her. I used to know everything about her. "Huh," I shrug.

With Petie being three sheets to the wind and Sy looking for greener pastures, Mayo and I are able to have a private conversation for a change—something we haven't done since before he was married. I realize I'd never even asked him how married life was. Just took it for granted that it must be good, judging from the look on Mayo's face whenever Ruthie is around and his general demeanor when she isn't. "So how's it going?" I ask seriously.

Mayo doesn't pick up on it immediately and responds with the expected glance around the room in a male-like hooter check and nods with a smile. "Not bad for a Friday night in the Park," he says.

I smile and shake my head. "Naw," I say, "I mean married life and all."

He just looks at me, trying to decide if I'm serious.

I am.

He leans on his elbows as though he's about to give me some fatherly advice, but when he looks up it's like looking into the eyes of a twelve-year-old boy who has just been handed tickets to a Super Bowl game.

"Fine as frog's hair," he gushes with a wink.

"Yeah? Really?"

"Yeah."

We sit there smirking at each other for a few minutes, each trying to decide if the other is on the level. Once each of us is convinced the other is genuine, Mayo begins to spill his innards like a party piñata. It is like he's been itching to tell someone just how great married life is, and when he starts talking about his kid takes it to a whole new level. I just sit and listen, wondering how it might feel to love someone that much, and what it might be like to look into some kid's face and see your own nose and things like that. I am happy for him. I really am. As much as I wish things had never changed between us, I am sincerely happy he's found his place in life. But looking at him now, expressing the same eagerness over his family as he once had over the band of kids we'd pull together every summer for fast pitch softball known as the Mop Squad, causes a tinge of regret or something that doesn't sit right deep in my gut. I miss him. I just plain miss him.

"Been looking at houses now with the second one coming," he says with hope that quickly changes to despair. Mayo and Ruthie moved into the basement of his parents' home when they first got married. It's what most guys do here in the Park until they can afford to move out. Some never move out. Like my folks. Like Mayo's folks. We're third-generation Parkites. He takes a long pull on his beer. I can tell this is eating at him. He wants out of here as much as I do.

Mayo and I have one more brew before he bugs out. I walk him out the door, intending to go back in—or at least insinuating to him I will—but as I watch Mayo drive off I just stand there listening to the muffled conversations intertwine with country music as it wafts from Schmitty's and find myself straining against it all to listen to the croaking toads instead. I walk down the block to an opening in the canopy of trees and stare up at the stars. As I strain to find the big dipper, the night sounds come alive. Nothing is ever silent, even on such a still night as this, I think to myself. Everything seems to be moving and shaking only I can't see a thing.

I walk the five blocks to my efficiency, climb the stairs and, without turning on the lights, flop on the bed and throw my hands behind my head. I lie staring at the light from the blue blinking neon sign outside my window as it sprays across my ceiling until sleep overcomes me.

Saturday, May 5, 2007: 8:55 am (CDT)

It's Saturday and I wake with a clear head and an empty bed for a change. It feels sort of good, actually. I'm glad not to have to disentangle myself from some lovely I'd dragged home the night before. I feel the need to be alone, on my own, clear for takeoff—if I only knew for where.

Walter had given me one of the Durkee season passes to a Twins game for this afternoon as gift for my promotion to assistant sales manager. Even though I'll be sitting among forty-thousand or so fans it isn't likely anyone else from Durkee will show up to fill the other three seats today, which is fine with me. I just want to be alone with my thoughts. Trouble is, I don't have any thoughts.

By the time I get out of the shower my place reeks of perm solution. I'd tolerated the smell over the past four years in exchange for cheap rent, but this morning it irritates me fiercely. The stench is enough to gag a maggot. While growing up, I remember when my sisters Barb and Julie would come home from getting their hair done and smelling like a new paint job; as a kid I even sort of liked the smell. But after five years of living in this stinking hole, I taste the stuff even when I'm not here, as though I gargled with it or something.

This building is owned by Maggie Swenson, who also operates the salon below me where Mom has had her hair done ever since her high school prom. Maggie hasn't changed a bit from how I remembered her as a kid. She is always cloaked in an aqua smock with imprints of black scissors and pink combs on it. She dyes her hair so black it sometimes shines blue. Her lips are fire engine red. Her eyelashes reach to her eyebrows and her blue powdered eyelids resemble window shades whenever she blinks, flashing blue from inside and out. She stands about five-foot-three and is just about as wide.

She had fixed up the room above her shop as a favor to Mom once I was accepted at the U of M. Mom didn't want my kid sister, Julie, warped by me bringing girls home, so she talked Maggie into letting out the upstairs of her salon. It's close to both campuses, within walking distance to Mom's for food, and to Schmitty's for a brew, and private most evenings past six p.m. Ideal for a college guy working part-time at Durkee and messing with girls between studying—but it all seems a bit pathetic now.

I don a pair of jeans and a plain white t-shirt, slip into loafers, and grab my wallet. I bolt down the stairs, hearing the door slam shut behind me, but Maggie meets me in an alcove too small for the both of us. The door to her shop is still swinging shut as I hit the last step. She's wearing rubber gloves and holding a bowl of brownish goop in one hand and something that looks like a basting brush in the other. My immediate thought is how she got the door open but she's standing there with the same look in her eyes that I'd seen for the past four days.

"Monday," I tell her. "I'll have the rent to you by Monday." She's heard it all before. She purses her lips and does something with her butt that opens the door to the shop and struts back to her draped captive, bowl and brush still in hand.

As soon as I reach the empty alleyway I remember that I left my truck at Schmitty's so I head there on foot. The morning is fresh and I'm feeling particularly rested physically, but mentally it feels like a pile of ball bearings are rolling around in my head. "What is everyone doing up so early on a Saturday?" I mumble to myself as I approach the bakery.

"Hey Vinny." I wave to Vinny Cordoni, who's been running Doogle's Bakery since he married Doogle's daughter back in 1948. He motions me to come inside his shop. The succulent sweet smells of rising yeast, butter, sugar, and spices immediately stop the ball bearings in my head from rolling around and one big thought emerges as all-important: food.

"I've something *especially* for you," he says in a strong Sicilian accent. He says the same thing to everyone but his sincerity isn't diminished by that fact. He hands me a firm roll in the shape of a triangle with what looks like raisins popping from its crust, which I take eagerly. One bite and holy baseballs! My taste buds start dancing a jig and I have to keep my mouth shut while I chew to avoid drooling onto the floor. I give him my seal of approval and a ten spot after he hands me a little white bag with two more treats inside and a cup of fresh coffee. As I leave, I nod goodbye since my mouth is still full.

Once outside his shop, I dig into the bag for a second scone and quickly stuff it into my mouth, eager to get it into my stomach before my common sense reaches my head. I know I will regret having eaten two of these things, but I'm contemplating polishing off the last one too.

I hear Evie Engstrom shout my name as she bolts from the book store I just passed. I stop in my tracks as quickly as I did when she'd catch us kids up to something and my heart rate increases out of habit. I stand there with scone filling both cheeks and cease all function, hoping she doesn't tell me to spit out what I have in my mouth.

Evie sort of jogs toward me with her head down while she laboriously twists her arms from one side of her body to the other as a means of propelling her chubby legs. When she arrives at my side I look down at this bundle of woman and part my lips in a smile.

She pauses to catch her breath, then looks upward at me. Her expression immediately changes. "Close your mouth when you eat, young man," she admonishes while shaking a finger at my nose.

I obediently wrap my lips back over my scone-filled teeth.

"The book your mother ordered just came in," she says as she hands me a brown wrapped package. "Would you give her this for me," she asks, but it is more of a command.

"Yes, ma'am, I'd be happy to," I say. I juggle the coffee, the little white bag and the sticky scone, trying to free up a hand to receive what it is she is jamming toward me, but before I can do so she tucks the package into the crook of my arm. She then pats me twice on the hand holding the coffee, which causes a few drops to spurt from the little hole in the lid and splat onto the pavement.

"Tell your mother I said hello," she calls over her shoulder as she disappears into the Enchanted Isles Bookstore, which her husband left to her fifteen years ago. Since his funeral, she's intended to sell it as soon as the right buyer comes along—one that will run it like her beloved Larry. Meanwhile, she has to keep the thing 'afloat,' she says reluctantly to anyone who inquires.

"Umhum," I moan to affirm the order while my tongue struggles to pull scone from between my upper lip and back molar. I wish I had a finger available right now to dig it out of there but I don't so I keep sucking loudly until it finally dislodges while I continue on toward Schmitty's.

Schmitty's is all locked up on the front side, but I know he is in there once I go around back and see his truck parked next to mine. I put my head in the back door and holler for him. I step inside and holler again. I set my load on the end of the bar and holler once more inside before I stick my head back out the back door. Where *is* he?

Finally he comes around the side of the building, lugging a couple of empty pallets. "What's up?" he asks upon seeing me in his doorway.

"Nothin'," I reply. We look at one another while the idea sinks in that if I have nothing better to do I might want to help him. I grab one of the pallets and follow him inside to where we begin stacking empty beer cases onto them.

Afterward we stand at the end of the bar. I push the little white bag with the remaining scone from Doogle's towards him. He happily sinks his teeth into the pastry and his eyeballs roll to the back of his head. I smile as I polish off the rest of my coffee that by now has gone cold.

This Schmitty bought the place three years ago from the former Schmitty who retired and moved to Florida to live in a trailer near St. Petersburg. This Schmitty is neater than the last Schmitty, who let the peanut shells lay on the floor until enough people crushed them into a fine powder and eventually carried them away on the bottoms of their soles. This Schmitty is always wiping and sweeping between pouring and washing. I don't think I can recall seeing the guy ever stand still. Even now he chews like he has a plane to catch.

"What is your real name, anyway?" I ask out of curiosity.

He stops chewing and looks at me as though no one had ever asked him that before. Maybe no one had. "Duane," he says apologetically. Then he says his full name and spells it. "DeWayne Swenson. D-e, capital W-a-y-n-e Swenson, with an oh."

We stare at each other. We're both thinking the same thing. That name just isn't one to ever catch on here. Maybe Jack or Mack or Bud, but never DeWayne with a capital W.

"Schmitty then," I say, verbalizing that we both know he will never be called any other name around here. He nods in resignation.

"Gotta go," I tell him.

"Thanks for the scone," he hollers after me.

I jump behind the wheel of my pick-up and insert the key into the ignition. The old engine roars to life a little more loudly than it had the day before. I turn the knob of the windshield wipers to remove the dew from my windshield, but nothing happens. They've been on the blink for months, turning on intermittently without provocation. Now they won't turn on at all. I jump out of the cab and rummage around behind and under the seat for an old rag. Finding one I smear a circle large enough to see and drive over to Jake and Dude's Auto a few blocks away.

"It'll cost you a few pennies just to have me tear off that dash so I can get in there and take a look," Little Dude says about what he's explained is likely an electric malfunction common in Ford Rangers. Little Dude is the second Dude to run Jake and Dude's Auto. Jake died twenty years ago and the first Dude is in a rest home in Roseville.

"How many pennies?" I ask.

Little Dude wrinkles his nose and two black marbles twinkle from somewhere within eye sockets that seem too small for the eyeball of a mouse let alone a 250-pound grease monkey. "Haf'ta be at least a thousand just to open 'er up and close to fifteen-hun'irt to get 'er done."

I kick a piece of dirt that soon disintegrates into dust on the concrete floor.

"Prob'ly cost ya' more to fix it than the truck is worth," Little Dude offers.

My shoulders slump. I was twelve years old when I fell in love with this truck. Uncle Billy had just bought it brand new and came by to give us kids a ride in it. I'd never had anything new. I'd never even seen anything brand new, let alone a truck ... the most awesome truck on the face of the earth. A Ford Ranger half-ton with 160 horsepower, 4.0-liter V6, five-speed, manual with overdrive, red with a chrome roll bar and runners. Uncle Billy had hoisted it up on oversized tires. I still remember the smell of the leather seats. I had never felt so cool in my whole life as the day he took me for my first ride. All my friends lined up along the curb, wide-eyed and envious, watching as we paraded up and down Commons Avenue. When we parked in front of Rick's Nick's and popped open the hood, crowds gathered for hours to gawk at the shiny clean manifold and brand-new hoses.

When I turned seventeen Uncle Billy let me drive it; even let me borrow it when I took Alison Bly to our senior prom. She wore red to match the truck and I sported a red cummerbund and bow tie to match. I donned a red boutonniere and bought a wristband of red roses for Alison. Mom took our picture in front of the truck.

Uncle Billy said he'd sell it to me one day, but when I graduated from college, he gave it to me as a graduation present. Had it detailed and bought me a new key chain. The truck was eleven years old by then, but it was still the sweetest wheels in the Park, and I owned it! That was 2006—the year the universe began to spin my fate. But all I cared about back then was my red Ford Ranger and how high I could jack the tires up. That and the fact I would never have to cram for another exam ever again. That was when I still had hopes of having a job that paid enough for me to at least fix the damn truck.

"It's not raining right now," I say, half thinking that if I take it over to Mack's All Makes Used Cars up on Snelling Avenue before it does maybe I could trade it in for something with wipers that work. Little Dude seems confused, so he shrugs and jumps back into his pit.

I slump over the wheel as I head for Mack's, knowing full well there is not going to be anything there that wasn't there last week or the week before—nothing *I* can afford anyway. I hit a red light at Snelling and a Mustang convertible with the top down, carrying three lovelies, pulls up next to me. I sit a little taller and stick my elbow out the window. I look down into the car as all three hike their skirts a little higher and peer up at me innocently. I lean over the side of my truck about to suggest I buy them something to *cool* themselves off since they are so *hot*, but just then the wiper blades begin to pound back and forth like a dog wagging its tail. The girls stop smiling, look at the wipers then up at the sky, and burst out giggling. The light changes and they're gone. Damn!

It's around ten by the time I get to Mom's. I head to the refrigerator out of habit, then keep my head inside out of self-preservation while she carries on about how I should have called to tell her I'd been promoted.

"Other people know more about my own son than I do," she scolds as she plops the frying pan on top of the stove with such force it rattles the salt and pepper shakers. "Hand me the eggs."

"I'm not hungry," I mumble around the chicken drumstick poking from my mouth.

She rolls her eyes and repeats each word distinctly, "Hand ... me ... the ... eggs."

I hand her the eggs *and* the bacon and sit down at the little table next to the window to finish the drumstick that is now half gnawed. She pours me a cup of coffee and I listen to her tell me how Sylvia Menke called her at seven this morning to congratulate her on my promotion at Durkee. Sylvia heard it from her sister-in-law Marcia, who is the sister to the wife of Walter's eldest son, Richard.

Mom and I differ in our opinions about Fiddlers Park. Her version is that we live in a community of friends where everyone is interested in everyone else and we all happily share life. My version is you can't take a crap without everyone else knowing about it. She refers to the Park as arms that wrap around us like one big hug. My simile would be hands that wrap around my neck and are choking the life out of me.

"Did you get a raise?"

I grunt an affirmative. Just enough to put me into a higher tax bracket so Uncle Sam can suck it up, I think to myself, being careful not to show any signs of being disgruntled for fear she might start another one of her lectures about how Americans should be happy to pay taxes for all that taxes do to give us good citizens a good life— like freedom of speech, the right to pray anywhere we want whether it be on a public street or in any school without fear of persecution. What she doesn't realize is nobody is listening to us little people, including God, which is why I stopped praying altogether.

She smiles then turns her back on me to flip the eggs. She's still in her bathrobe and slippers. It occurs to me I've never seen her in her bathrobe and slippers past seven-thirty in the morning on any morning, workday or weekend, unless she's sick.

"What's up with the bathrobe?" I ask. "You feel alright?"

She shrugs. I sit up straight and assess her with more discernment. I glance at the clock. It's after ten. A ripple of anxiety rivets up my spine.

"Mom?"

"It's nothing, dear."

"*What's* nothing?"

She doesn't answer.

"Been in to see Kermit?" Kermit Kowalski is second generation Fiddlers Park. He studied general med at Johns Hopkins in New York and returned to the Park in the late sixties. He set up a small clinic across from Nick's and soon thereafter married Nick's youngest sister, Nicole. That was way before my time, but like I said, everyone knows everyone else's business in Fiddlers Park. We're like indigenous natives who pass along folklore from generation to generation as though it is sacred tribal knowledge.

"Of course," she replies while her back is still turned toward me. Her tone tells me to leave it alone.

I hear the pounding of footsteps coming down the stairs. Julie stumbles into the room. Julie is my kid sister who grew up overnight and is about to graduate from high school. Her hair is a mess and her nipples are showing through a worn-out shirt she's evidently slept in. Her bare legs flow to the floor and when she bends over to retrieve the cream from the middle shelf in the refrigerator, I can see her thong.

"Put some clothes on, girl," I order.

She shrugs and heads for the coffee pot. "What for? It's just you and Mom," she defends.

"It darn-well better be," I mutter.

"What's the matter with *you*?" Julie asks as she commandeers the plateful of sunny-side-up eggs and bacon from Mom and plops down across from me.

I don't know. What *is* the matter with me? All I know is these two women in my life are scaring the crap out of me for reasons I can't explain.

'Now, now, you two." Mom intervenes. Then, anticipating my usual rebellion, points the spatula at my nose and orders, "Enough."

"Of what?" I challenge.

"You know exactly what." She turns her back and cracks another egg over the frying pan. I do, but how does she always know what I know? I glare at Julie for getting me in trouble.

She squelches a self-congratulatory giggle as she takes another bite of the egg that she knows full well Mom had made for me. Then she picks up a piece of bacon with her fingers and waggles it at me. I snatch the bacon from her hand with such speed and velocity it startles her. Before she knows what is happening, I have the entire piece in my mouth and am smirking with satisfaction. Julie bursts out laughing.

Mom turns around. She has a look of total confusion on her face as she looks back and forth between Julie and me. Julie composes herself and pretends to take another bite of egg. I stop chewing and smile innocently. Mom shakes her head and smiles as she turns back to her fry pan. I wink at Julie.

"Julie sent the last of the paperwork in to Julliard yesterday," Mom says over her shoulder.

Julie was born a dancer. She tip-toed and pirouetted before she walked. After Dad left us, Mom couldn't afford to keep her in Tot Tappers, but Julie wore her tap shoes wherever she went, even to Sunday school. The little girl who lived two doors down and who was still in dance class would teach Julie the new routine on the front sidewalk which kept Julie content for a couple of weeks before she began to realize she would never be part of the dance team again. That's when she cried and didn't stop whimpering for weeks. By the time she was in junior high, she was wearing ballet tights and doing leg stretches while watching reruns of the television series *Fame*. That's when I began telling her I'd send her to Julliard School of Dance in New York when she graduated from high school. She always believed it. I'm still not sure how I'm going to swing it, but she's going. That much is for certain. If I have to sell my own body parts to get her there, she's going.

"Her references were excellent," Mom continues to tell me over her shoulder as she cracks another egg over the frying pan. The egg spatters and pops as it hits the pan. She doesn't seem to notice the grease fly up onto the backsplash. Julie and I do and we both wonder why she doesn't. Mom is obsessed with avoiding grease spatters and usually wipes them before they hit the wall.

Mom looks up at the ceiling while the eggs sizzle helplessly in the pan. "This is a dream come true for Julie," she sighs. Then something comes over her and she rushes out of the room.

Julie and I first stare at each other, then I jump up to take the spattering pan off the heat while Julie runs after Mom. I hear them mumbling in the other room but by the time I get there Mom is composed and politely rejecting Julie's gestures to console. We follow our mother back into the kitchen like little ducklings and helplessly watch her put the pan back onto the burner and resume cooking as though nothing happened. Julie and I take our seats and exchange glances. When Mom finally sets a plate of eggs and bacon in front of me, she notices Julie hasn't finished hers.

"What's the matter with your eggs?" she asks Julie. "Are they too hard? You want me to make some different ones?"

"No." Julie's voice is so abrupt it startles all of us. "I mean, no," Julie says more calmly. "The eggs are perfect." She picks up a fork and takes a huge mouthful of eggs as proof.

Mom pats the top of Julie's head and smooths the mass of auburn curls with the palm of her hand; then with her index finger she pulls the strands of hair away from Julie's eyes and tucks them behind her ear. Julie seems oblivious to this grooming ritual. "We'll just have to get used to not seeing her every day."

"Mom, you are thinking too far into the future," Julie contends.

Mom turns away abruptly and mumbles something about the future or maybe about regrets. Both Julie and I look up at Mom, then at each other with the same blatant confusion on our faces. We've never seen Mom like this—unpredictable, preoccupied. Something is wrong, but neither of us has a clue what, nor do we know what to do.

SATURDAY, MAY 5, 2007: 2:45 P.M. (CDT)

Durkee's four season ticket seats are used to stroke employees in an effort to make us happier than we should already be working for Durkee; but I'm still not happy, and today's game against the White Sox offers little hope of that changing.

After standing in line for a brat, then another line for mustard and onions, then another line for a beer, I finally make my way up the narrow steps to the seats which are just to the right of home plate. The Durkee seat numbers are twenty-five through twenty-eight, twenty-five being closest to the aisle I came up. All are near the middle of the row, which I prefer. I hate aisle seats where you are forced to pass peanuts and change back and forth and try and peer around vendors who seem to always be in your line of sight at all the wrong moments. I take seat number twenty-seven, farthest from the aisle yet leaving one empty seat between me and the non-Durkee seats to thwart any potential chatter among fans. I am in no mood for camaraderie.

The stadium is as empty as a beer bottle in a frat house, but it suits me just fine. I throw my arm over the back of the seat to the right of me and stretch my legs in front of the unoccupied seat to my left. It's unlikely the other seats will fill since the Twins have been a yawn in their pre-game season. This could be alright, I think to myself while scrutinizing the situation. I think I *am* feeling a bit happier after all.

I finish my brat and am about to start on my beer when I spot Roger Forgwerk amble up the steep steps balancing a beer and a basket of cheese nachos. Geez. Just my luck to have to put up with that lame brain for the afternoon.

Roger is the tech-head whose job is to make sure the company server is up and running and uncontaminated, or some such thing. He never looks like he's working. The only thing I ever see him do is sit in this tiny, cramped, windowless room hunched over a myriad of wires and staring at little yellow, red, and green lights all flashing in some synchronized fashion like he's awaiting orders from Oz. He's all fine and good while he's in that little room, but the lack of human interaction must ball up pretty bad for this guy because once he's out of his little box his mouth won't stop. It wouldn't be so bad if he had anything interesting to say, but all the guy wants to talk about is the gigs and bytes and, well, he loses me at gigs and bytes so I never know what he's talking about. And he talks so fast he doesn't leave an opening for you to bow out. One time he trapped me near the coffee pot in the lunchroom. I was forced to tighten my bottom lip over my top lip as I grimaced to avoid blurting out, "Shut up, asshole!"

Before Roger gets everyone to move out of his way so he can waddle down the row, I scoot down to the last seat of the four and toss my bag of garbage on the seat to the right of me, hoping to put as much distance between him and myself as possible. I'll take my chances with the guy in the Twins shirt followed by two guys wearing Yankee hats who are now ambling toward me from the other side.

"Greetings, friend," Roger says upon approach. His voice cuts through the now deafening crowd and pierces my ears even at this distance. If his hands had been free, he would have given me some finger-contorted sign he saw on *Star Trek*. Another thing I can't stand. I give him a non-committal glance and a dismissive nod, then turn toward center field where the color guard is coming to a stop. We all rise for the last bit of silence I am likely to get for the remainder of this game as we get ready to sing the national anthem. Roger is still standing, arms too full or he'd no doubt place his right hand over his heart.

A young girl in a ponytail steps to the microphone in the center of the field. Her image is displayed on both screens. There is silence among the stands. When she begins to belt out the familiar words, a sense of contentment washes over me as I stand in camaraderie with a stadium full of Twins fans, Minnesotans, Americans. If Frances Scott Key bore up well enough to write a song while being held captive in a jail cell, I suppose I can put up with Roger for the afternoon. I sit down, but I sense Roger is still standing so I turn in his direction. We both stare at the bag of garbage I had placed on the seat next to mine for a few seconds before Roger accepts the fact I am not going to remove it. He finally wiggles into the seat next to it. I turn toward centerfield purposely to ignore him.

"How about this," Roger starts.

I keep my head turned toward centerfield and my back toward him to signal rejection, but he just doesn't take the hint.

"Just you and me spending a day at the old ball game, eh?"
I can feel his annoying smiling face through the back of my head.
"Root, root, root for your home team," he starts to sing.
My bottom lip begins to creep over my top lip.
Willy Spatzer, the new starter in from Cincinnati, steps to the plate. It's a swing and a miss.
"I used to love to come to ball games as a kid," Roger says. "My dad and I used to go to every Twins home game, and even some of the away games. I got me a collection of bobble-heads for every one of the players that ever played for the Twins—even have one of Harmon Killebrew," he says. "Used to be my dad's, but he gave it to me. I love to just be here. You know what I mean?"

How the hell would I know what he means? I was the third child of four raised by a single mom who worked two jobs to keep a roof over our heads. I wished he'd just shut up about his wonderful life and let me have my belated childhood now so that I have a chance to experience what he apparently grew up with.

I wondered what it would be like to have gone to a ballgame with Dad. Somehow, I can't even imagine it. But now that I think about it, I wonder why Dad hadn't taken us kids to a ball game. It wasn't like he couldn't afford it. Mom couldn't afford to take us, I know that, but Dad should have been able to swing it. He always had a good job. He always had enough money to spend on the women he dated. He even took some pretty cool vacations over the years while all us kids got to do was camp in the backyard. Mom would get a burning permit so we could have a campfire and she'd let us pee behind the tree. I guess we still had plenty of fun, but try bragging about that to some other guy. It just doesn't fly.

"My dad has memorized the stats for every Twins game since 1959," Roger continues, his voice mercifully being drowned out by the crowd.

The Twins are down by one in the bottom of the seventh with two men on base. The problem is Nick Oberstrom is up to bat and he hasn't yet shown the world why the Twins had traded Hector Peyton for him. If it hadn't been for Hector, the Twins never would have seen even the hind end of the playoffs last year. For the life of me I don't understand why Gardenhire cut Peyton. Dumb move, if you ask me, but nobody is asking me. Oberstrom steps up to bat.

They send in the new Sox pitcher, a former Yankee player who'd been dumped by the Yanks because he hadn't impressed the people of

New York, but any sort of fresh meat on the mound is enough to scare this fan. This is the closest we'll get all day to a point against the Sox who had been knocking the snot out of everyone this season so far. But with Oberstrom holding wood we'll surely go down with a thud.

It's a fast pitch to the inside ... a swing and a miss. It's several seconds before I can breathe, but then my esophagus tightens all over again as the pitcher eyeballs his catcher while he twists the ball behind his back. He winds up again for a stretch, a glance over his right shoulder and into the pitcher's glove. Strike two.

I shake my head and look away to avoid witnessing the carnage. But my attention is soon drawn again to the pitcher whose eyes lurk in the shadow of the bill of his cap like a snake in a rock pile.

Second base runner Will Haggor leads out toward third. First base runner Gannon Riggs leads out toward second. The crowd sucks in a breath.

The pitcher winds up, every muscle in his body poised and awaiting command while he senses the developing situations on second and first bases. Once his brain sends the command there will be no turning back, no second guess—the body will respond with a deliberateness earned through relentless practice that had long since replaced conscious motion and could only be described now as instinct. But what command will he give? Batter or second baseman? A muscle flinches in his neck. His body accepts the command. Haggor retreats with all his might. The pitcher whirls around, the ball is hurled toward second. Haggor dives and slides toward second base on his belly in a cloud of dust with outstretched arms, fingers grappling for the bag. Safe!

"What are you trying to do Haggor?" I shout. Haggor is the slowest runner in the league. He's going to get himself tossed out at second if he keeps that up. What is he thinking? Who put him ahead of Gannon Riggs in the lineup anyway I want to know? Riggs is young and full of piss and vinegar and can outrun a gazelle being chased by a cheetah across a hot sand desert—and they put him behind a friggin' bus.

Two outs, two strikes, Haggor holding up the show on second and Riggs itching for a score on first. What am I hoping for? A miracle? I swallow hard and lean forward with elbows on knees. My head is just about on the shoulder of the guy in front of me, but he doesn't care. It's a windup. The ball is in the air. Outside. Ball one.

"Who is this guy?" I say aloud to the universe, seeking input about this new pitcher who is starting to make my butt twitch.

"Mean Jack Behn," the guy next to me says breathlessly without looking at me.

"Never heard of the guy before today," I say without looking at him.

"A rookie who couldn't nail a snow bank with a Mack truck in January while he was with the Yanks," says one of the guys in a Yankee's cap. None of us take our eyes off the field.

"Yanks dropped him to the Sox in oh-five and he debuted in the seventeenth game against the Cardinals in 2006," Roger butts in, having overheard the conversation. "He's got an ERA of two-point-eight this year."

Mean Jack Behn winds up again, glances over his right shoulder and releases a ball I swear reaches ninety mph before it smacks into the glove of the catcher. Ball two.

The guys in the Yankee hats sit back, re-convinced that New York had been right about Jack Behn all along. Twins fans begin standing throughout the stadium. I keep my seat, but shout out, "Bring it home" to Oberstrom. I half believe he can do it. Then under my breath I mutter once more, "Bring it home."

Two strikes. Two balls. The vendors cease vending. People stop chewing. All eyes are on the mound. Not-so-mean Jack Behn retracts every muscle as he prepares for the stretch. It's a swing ... the ball cracks against the bat and pops high above the umpire's head. Foul. The crowd exhales.

Another windup. Silence oppresses the stands. The ball speeds toward the catcher's glove. The bat slices through air. Leather meets wood—CRACK! The ball goes deep and low into right field. Oberstrom heads for first with intentions to stay put if he gets there alive. Riggs heads for second with intentions of making it to third if he doesn't find Haggor still there. Haggor heads for third with his best effort. The third-base coach sees the ball bounce to the right off the back fence while the right fielder jogs left. Fumble. While the right-fielder struggles to recover the ball the third-base coach frantically waves Haggor toward home. Score!

But before anyone can celebrate the ball is again in the air heading toward the third baseman. Riggs is slowing up at third but the coach signals for him to gas it up and head for home. Fans jump to their feet. Screams reverberate throughout the stands. Riggs kicks into gear, hell-bent for home. The catcher rips off his face guard and slings it toward the dugout. Dust lingers over home base yet from Haggor's run. Riggs is now on a dead run for home. The ball flies over the pitcher's head. Riggs dives toward home plate, melding with a cloud of red dirt. The ball thumps into the catcher's mitt. All eyes are on the ump whose arms crisscross—safe!

The crowd leaps into the air. Pandemonium breaks out in the stands. The guy to my left turns to me waving a high five. I slap him and we both hoot and whistle. Ahead two to one!

The guys in the Yankee caps just lean back in their seats, unimpressed over a half-assed ball team making a few scores against a half-assed pitcher they had been wise enough to dump.

I glace over at Roger and can tell he is looking for some male bonding. Quickly I turn back to the guy on my left hoping to engage with him before Roger gets any ideas. To get his attention, I throw my hands into the air in mock praise of the almighty and in my best Dr. Frankenstein persona I declare, "The Twins are alive!"

Roger backs off when he hears the guy laugh and tell me not to turn off the life support just yet. The Yankee fans ignore me and the rest of the stadium which has finally come to life for the first time this season.

"I was hoping the Twins wouldn't embarrass me too much in front of my friends here," the guy next to me says, pointing a thumb in the direction of his two New York pals.

I notice all three have their shirts tucked into pleated dress trousers. Who dresses like this for a ball game? I ask myself. The guy next to me is wearing loafers, but somehow they don't look like *my* loafers. These things are shiny and spotless and the stitching is better than my Uncle Billy's leather seats in his '57 Chev classic. Fingernails are as clean as my Grandma Jazz's. Hair trimmed with precision. Neat as a mannequin in JC Penney. I stand up straighter.

"Riggs got my attention in last week's game against the Cardinals," the guy says. He waits for my response.

"Yeah," I say, trying to find something intelligent enough to say that would match his image. "Yeah."

He juts a hand toward me. "Charlie Bishop," he says, introducing himself. He's about my age, my height, my weight, but he's caviar and I'm tuna. His handshake is firm, but not one of those crushing handshakes you get from guys who want to establish upper power among men. More relaxed and sure of himself but firm.

Wait a minute. "Not *the* Charlie Bishop," I say, eyes wide with the possibility that I was standing next to the former quarterback-from-heaven for Purdue. "Dave," I say eagerly. "Dave Yates," I say again as I pump his arm like an old hand water pump that hadn't been primed in a long time. I put my other hand on his shoulder to keep myself from hugging him.

He smiles and looks toward center field in a humble attempt to avoid admitting what I know in my heart. My mind flashes back to the fall of 2002, the first time I saw him play. I was still in college and Mayo and I had met at Schmitty's to watch the game. It was Purdue against Ohio State University. Ohio State was ahead twenty-one-zip in the second quarter. Purdue was so lousy Ohio put in their second-string to mop up after the half. But Purdue came out with a freshman rookie quarterback named Bishop who turned a fumble, an interception, and a blocked field goal into a twenty-eight/twenty-one lead for Purdue in the third quarter. By then Ohio State had all-hands-on-deck but couldn't hang on for dear life. The rest is history. 'The Bishop and his diocese'—as the team was soon dubbed—took the title that year and the rest of the league ate Purdue's dust until 2005 when an Illini lummox sacked Bishop and busted his knee, ending the reign of glory forever.

"Sorry, man," I drool with as much regret as I felt the instant I saw *that* happen on the big screen TV at Majors Sports Bar where the entire barroom had erupted in a simultaneous sigh-of-pain. The air in the dome is drying my eyes and I can feel them water but can't blink.

"Unfortunate things happen," he says without so much as a shrug. A shadow comes over his eyes.

I decide to drop the reminiscing as I see it is raking up too much for him to deal with right now, but his stats burst inside my head like a pyrotechnical display. He will live in the annals of college football forever as the quarterback who averaged 220 passing yards and three-point-seven-eight touchdowns per game and zero sacks for three and a half years until the final blow to his knee in the eighth game of the season in his senior year. Even with entering the season late during his freshman year and ending early due to injury, he racked up 9,244 passing yards and 129 touchdowns during his tenure and had led his team to three consecutive national titles. I was sitting right next to history.

He offers me some peanuts, which I take. I want to bronze the damn things, but instead I pop them into my mouth. Pretty soon we're leaning our elbows on our knees and sharing opinions about the Twins like we're a couple of agents in negotiations. I have forgotten all about Roger. Hell, I've forgotten all about Durkee Box Manufacturing, along with the overdue rent, student loans, and the truck repair problems. I've forgotten everything about my stinking life for the moment and am mesmerized by Charlie Bishop.

CHAPTER 2: A NEW FRIEND
MINNEAPOLIS, MINNESOTA

FRIDAY, MAY 25, 2008: 1:12 P.M. (CDT)

Charlie's father is Cowen Bishop the Third, CEO of Cyber International Systems, Inc., one of the largest corporations in the world—CIS on the New York Stock Exchange. There isn't a large-cap mutual fund anywhere that doesn't have some of CIS in it. From Buffet to the buffoons, the world is padding Mr. Bishop's pocketbook and Charlie's inheritance while we breathe.

Charlie doesn't worry about meager stuff like rent, food, student loans ... you know, survival. Charlie has always had all the perks of the upper class. While us underprivileged people hope to have food, shelter, and safety, Charlie *expects* cuisine, condos, and security guards. Charlie's allowance provides him with a $1.7 million loft overlooking the Mississippi in downtown Minneapolis and his own personal tailor on Canal Street in New York. He is welcome at any one of his parents' residences that are conveniently scattered throughout the world. A penthouse near Central Park West in New York, a beach house in the Hamptons, something he refers to as a 'little flat' on the French Riviera, a ski lodge in Switzerland, a condo in South Beach, and even a ranch in Montana where they raise Appaloosas. What more could anyone want?

I had been shocked when Charlie handed me his card before we parted at the Twins game and told me to call him ... that we should get together for drinks sometime. I called him the following Monday, half thinking he'd blow me off as just another wide-eyed fan, but he didn't and we met for drinks. Since then we've made a habit of it. I wouldn't go so far as to say we're close enough friends to where I'd ask him to help me move, but I'd cover his butt in a fist-fight and I'd let him borrow my tools.

Charlie drives a Mercedes Benz SLR Limited Edition 722 S coupe—one of only twenty-five made in 2007. Hand-built five-point-five-liter supercharged V8 that pumps out 617 horsepower and 575 pound-feet of torque. It's a two-seater convertible, black with gray and brown leather interior and tinted windows. I about crapped my pants the day he asked if I'd like to get behind the wheel.

It had been a Saturday morning and Charlie and I were north of the Twin Cities on Highway 65 just off Highway 10 where the area still remains underdeveloped. Charlie had pulled to the side of the road. I remembered hearing my blood pump in my ears as I walked around the car to exchange seats. The driver's seat was low and seemed to grab my ass like the palm of a giant hand. Just holding the wheel and feeling the engine hum about gave me an erection. The thing was like a rocket and I had my hand on the throttle. I had heard it would do zero to 60 in four-point-oh seconds, but Charlie said his little baby did zero to 60 in three-point-eight. I had revved it up to 4000 RPMs and popped it into fifth. I left rubber for fifty feet. I remember the engine purred like a fat cat and ran like a deer in November. It was capable of doing 240 mph and, though that would have been enough to outrun the Ham Lake cops, Charlie must have read my mind because he told me to keep it under 90 mph. Top down, sun at our backs ... I could have sworn I was wearing a cape and a mask.

I can still conjure up endorphins just thinking about that, but Charlie evidently needs more. Says he's ordered a Lamborghini he expects will ship from Italy in September. What am I supposed to say to that? Yeah, I have a part ordered for my manifold that's coming all the way from Michigan? For the life of me I can't figure out why Charlie and I are leap-frogging around in the same pond, but I'm glad to be sharing the log with him for now anyway.

It is May 25th and people in the Cities have begun cutting out early for the long Memorial Day weekend. Charlie and I decide to meet at the Metropolitan Club and have lunch on the veranda overlooking downtown Minneapolis. The club sits in an old posh neighborhood built in the early 1900s. It was once the home of Governor Rudolph Laziter, who had been linked with the mob in the '20s. His portrait hangs above the fireplace in the great room where lunch and dinner are served year-round. The veranda is on the second floor, off a room that had once been Laziter's bedroom. The veranda is open only during the summer months and only on non-rainy days. We sit there sipping Mojitos. I had broken down and ordered one at Charlie's insistence. They're not bad, but I gave up Kool-Aid as a kid.

After the waitress places an opened faced sandwich covered in cheese in front of me and a salad topped with smoked salmon in front of Charlie, he tells me he had gone to Harvard from which every one of his family members for three generations had graduated with a degree in law.

"Wow," I mumble with my cheeks bulging. I was the first person in three generations to even go to college in my family. "But wait a minute," I say, then gulp, "you played football for Purdue." Charlie looks sideways at me waiting for the point to sink in. "Oh. So, you went rogue," I say, respecting the balls it must have taken to go against a family with such Harvard tradition.

"Expelled," he corrects. Then he leans forward with a smirk on his face and adds, "Tossed a cherry bomb down the toilet in a girl's sorority during a panty raid."

"No way," I say jumping to attention. It's incredulous that I would know two people with such intestinal fortitude as to pull the same exact stunt. I hadn't yet matured enough to not enjoy such boyish audacity. And the higher strategy required to penetrate forbidden territory, such as a girl's sorority, pegged Charlie higher than Mayo on this one. I reach over the table and give him the ol' pretend slug on the arm in a seditious salute. "Way to go."

"Yeah, well ..." he begins to accept the congratulations, but the tone quickly changes. "If you aren't a Harvard man you aren't anything in our family," he says and then downs the rest of his drink. His eyes begin to dart around the room in an attempt to locate that internal escape mechanism we all have that avoids truths we don't yet want to deal with ... maybe never want to deal with. It takes him so long to find it I begin to feel uncomfortable myself and want to offer him some sort of bridge over his troubled water, but I can't think of a thing to say.

I glance around the room in search of the waitress to rescue us. When I spot her, I raise my index finger casually for her attention. She immediately comes to the table while balancing a tray upon the tips of her fingers. She bends slightly toward me indicating she is ready to receive my orders. Everything is so quiet in this place—so unlike Susie Milner at Schmitty's who cracks her gum before asking what you want. "Another Mojito and a Heineken," I say softly. The conversation seems to be moving toward something that might take a while, in which case I will need my standard brew.

When the waitress leaves us, Charlie seems a bit more relaxed. His breathing has steadied. We sit in companionable silence staring at the view until the waitress comes back with our drinks.

"Lawyers," he begins. "Three generations of lawyers."

Wow, I think to myself. Brains must be genetic. No wonder I'm a nobody. Charlie's family is full of lawyers, most of whom became judges, all the way back to his great, great grandfather. Cousins, Uncles, a few aunts even … all legal beagles from Harvard. I wonder what the holiday dinners are like in that family?

"There's statues of my grandfathers sprinkled throughout New England," he adds flatly.

"Wow," I think again. The only thing I can relate to is being pooped on. I realize for the first time that I never even knew what my grandparents had done for a living other than they worked hard. I was from a 'hard-working' family—I had been told that my whole life. Old people were retired by the time I could comprehend employment. Of course, I knew Dad worked construction and Mom worked in a law office. There we go! Does that count for anything?

His sister, Nancy, is an attorney at Belling, Belling and Bishop in Manhattan—yes, she's the Bishop in that title and she's married to the second Belling. She and her husband don't have any children. They live in an apartment near Central Park West during the week and have a home on Long Island where she raises dogs. More specifically, dogs are raised at the special kennels she had built on her property in Long Island by the best trainers and groomers who live on the premises behind the kennels. The only thing she does is occasionally hold a pup for photo ops and collect the ribbons and trophies her dog trainers earn, Charlie says with a notable note of sarcasm. I let that dog lie, no pun intended.

I sense a sort of bile rise up from the bowels of Charlie that isn't gas. He's about to get into some serious stuff, and I don't want to hear it. If I wanted to be in the middle of anyone's problems, I would have become a shrink. I'm a box broker who only wants to have a beer and get laid on Friday nights. My head swings in all directions in search of a way out, but I already know I'm trapped, so I decide to throw a little light on the conversation. I tell him my oldest sister, Barb, hates dogs and is afraid of anything furry, even kittens. She had been traumatized as a kid when the class mouse she'd brought home from school during Christmas break—that she was supposed to take care of—was eaten by our dog, Molly, on Christmas Day.

"Damned dog ran right by her with the tail of the frigging mouse hanging out the side of its mouth," I say, painting the picture of that day. I capture Charlie's interest and continue. "Barb shrieks and runs after Molly but the dog had already swallowed." Both Charlie and I bust out laughing. "Found a puke pile in the backyard the next day that had gray fur in it," I add, testing whether there is still another yaw left in him. There isn't. Charlie is still smiling but I can see he is traveling to his dark side again. We sit here and sip our drinks for a while.

I'm still thinking about my sister. Even though my brother Bob was the oldest, Barb had assumed the role of head of household when Mom had to go to work after Dad and Mom divorced. Barb was only a couple of years older than me, but she learned to cook and bake, and she made us do our homework, just like Mom. The funny thing is us kids listened to her sometimes better than we did Mom. I owe my sister for keeping me out of trouble as a kid. If it hadn't been for Barb, I don't know what I would have turned into because I had a real anger thing going for a while after Dad left us. But Barb taught me how to "accept the things I cannot change"—it was a poem or something she would recite to me constantly, but I've forgotten most of the words by now.

Charlie is talking before I realize it. Something about his older brother. I catch the tail end of what he is saying. "Matthew," I hear him say. Must be the name of his brother, I think to myself. "Hung Clinton with his own rope," he says.

"Bill Clinton?" I ask. How did the former president get into the conversation? What had I missed by not paying attention?

"Yeah," he says with a smirk on his face. He leans forward on his elbows like he is about to tell me a good joke. Whatever he's about to say, it has snapped him out of the dark pit. Glad to see the bright and shining Charlie Bishop back on the scene, I tune in with both ears out of curiosity.

Just then a waiter interrupts us to clear the dishes from our table. I watch him in fascination as he expertly swipes crumbs from the linen tablecloth using a little metal device, corrals them into the palm of his hand, and deposits them into his own pant pocket to avoid messing the carpet. I can't imagine any waitress at Schmitty's sacrificing their pockets to anything other than tips. When he is finished, I turn my attention back to Charlie.

Seems Charlie's own brother had masterminded a plan that hundreds of tenured corporate lawyers had been unable to achieve for over seven decades. Incredible, I think to myself. "What did he do?"

Apparently, Clinton riled up big banks by forcing them to adhere to bank regulations that former administrations had previously slacked off on. New tensions fueled old frustrations that had been brewing since the aftermath of the Crash of '29 when the government slapped regulations on banks here in the U.S. so tight that it seemed like they were written in stone ... until Matt came along. It was Matt who surmised it was an opportune time to rally the big banks into a showdown with the feds.

"No shit!" I exclaim. Beats tossing a cherry bomb down a toilet. My head spins while Charlie explains how his brother slammed the President of the United States until my intellect kicks in and shuts the party down. "No way," I say. I can't believe that any *one* person could influence the President of the United States.

Charlie smiles wide and begins to explain how things are done in the real world ... his world ... the world of big business like his daddy's. I twirl the empty water glass in front of me with the tips of my fingers and try to stay open-minded, but at one point I interrupt him to ask, "How do you know all of this?"

Charlie's eyes twinkle in response, but he can tell from the look on my face I haven't bought what he's selling just yet. In my family, this is where fists come out. But Charlie calmly continues as though he were a diligent professor shedding light on a matter for a dim-witted student. "Most people *don't*," he says in a way that implies I am one of them. Then adds, "Or *care* enough to try to understand." It's an empty compliment, but it keeps me in my seat.

What Charlie goes on to explain sounds more like a tall tale about an imaginary country, or the tangled plot of a SciFi thriller—surely not America ... not the United States of America ... the good ol' USA. This was not the government that I knew—the one I had always believed I controlled through my vote—the government I felt the right to complain about, but might be willing to die for if I ever had to actually make that choice. I'm no different than the next guy who talks smart over a kitchen table but doesn't know a damned thing about how government really works. By the time I graduated from college the patriotic attitudes that had been carefully instilled by my fifth-grade teacher, Mrs. Gamm, had long since taken a hike. All that stuff she had taught us about our forefathers being brave rebels who set out to break the laws of England and to escape to a new land to establish a new nation, under God, indivisible, with freedom and justice for all had been replaced with a mild form of apathy. To be totally honest, I am just too self-centered and lazy to pay much attention to politics. Dad fought in the Korean War. Uncle Billy fought in Nam. Bob enlisted to go to Iraq but only made it as far as Fort Langley where he drove a three-star general around in a jeep for a few years. I never had much interest in serving in the military, so there it is. I guess that makes me one of those slobs who don't pay attention to politics but just eats, sleeps, and craps in confidence.

I suspend mentally over the abyss of ignorance as though dangling over the open mouth of a tiger. As incredulous as all this sounds, there seems to be a ray of truth in what he is saying. Perhaps it is a dormant lack of faith in my own government instilled by generations of free speech, much of which is directed negatively toward the very government that prescribes such freedoms. I can hear the voice of my own father. 'The sons of bitches in Washington don't know their ass from a hole in the ground.' And Uncle Billy. 'They are taking our rights away one by one.' And Grandma Jazz. 'Our government is led by a bunch of baby-killers.' Now Charlie tells me that is exactly what the political campaign managers want the masses to say and think. It is how they get people to vote for candidates who support platforms the voters would never support otherwise.

"You know what helped win the bank deregulation battle?"

I shake my head.

"The abortion issue." He flings his hand into the air. "Turned Democrats against their own. In a matter of two elections the House and Senate were filled with sympathizers for deregulation." He chuckles at such ingenuity. "The stage was set for Matt."

I think about my Grandma Jazz who voted Republican in the last election because she believed she was saving the lives of unborn babies. She could be eating dog food so bankers can sit on bigger yachts. I feel old anger once again brewing deep within my bowels. That feeling of existing as a lesser being on the face of the earth and unable to do anything about it.

"You're talking about innocent people," I say, defending my proverbial roots.

"Ignorant people," Charlie corrects. "Everyone *old* enough to vote is held accountable *for* their vote."

"And that they will be," I sigh. Everything I've ever heard about the insanity in Washington D.C. seems to have manifested at this very moment. Confused and bewildered, I struggle to find the ground on which I stand. Am I a hard-working, tax-paying citizen of the United

States—the greatest country on Earth? Or am I just a pawn being led around by my own ignorance in some great game played by a select few wealthy players? Even if I were to believe that a band of high-rollers controlled all the wealth in this world through grain exchanges, drilling rights, and currency exchanges, and that governments—all of them—consider the rest of us puppets in a worldwide money monopoly ploy, I'd have to re-invent all the ideals I didn't even know I had until this moment. Either that, or ditch them and adapt to a whole new concept—Charlie's concept.

"It's one big game," Charlie says. "You're either in it, or you're out."

I look at Charlie. I look at the waiter with the crumbs in his pocket. I'm feeling out ... *very* out. Used. Tricked. Rooked. I want to punch something ... someone ... *everyone* who's ever denied anyone their dignity based on the size of their bank account and held power over them on account of the size of their own.

"Matt had Clinton in a headlock." Charlie tilts his head back in a laugh. "Either sign the Financial Modernization Act into law or every big bank across the nation will put a squeeze on money so tight during election time that the Democrats won't know what hit them." Charlie sits forward and leans toward me on his elbows. The blue in his irises crystallizes with delight as the small muscles around his eyes contract and pull his lips upward like the skirt of a maiden curtseying before the queen. With a wink he adds, "Clinton signed."

Matt climbed to the top of his game by muscling the President of the United States. I wonder how that looks on the résumé? I shake my head at the audacity.

Charlie raises his glass in a toast to Matt. Instinctively I reciprocate and extend my bottle of beer, then quickly catch myself and want to yank it back in refusal. But in that moment of hesitation, I contemplate what I have to gain by doing so ... and realize what I have to lose. Charlie clinks his glass against my still extended bottle and I feel my soul succumb to the gray mass between right and wrong ... the place where justification so easily spawns. We both take a swig.

Still holding the gulp of beer in my mouth, I wonder who among us hasn't failed at one time or another to stand up for their convictions? All the Christians *I* know come to mind. At that thought, my soul seems to vacillate between these two choices as though I haven't yet made up my mind, but it seems all too clear to my brain that I have, so I swallow. A shiver of guilt riddles up my spine. Gutless, I admonish myself.

Either that or polite, I think. Yeah. Polite. Minnesota nice. Avoid controversy and confrontations. Slime begins to drip off me as easily as dew in sunshine.

Charlie grabs the little book and motions for me to stop digging in my back pocket for my wallet. "I got it," he says.

We nurse the remains of our drinks after he signs and sends the waitress away. The feeling I'd been poked like a pig begins to creep back into my soul. I had never thought of myself as among the poor and deprived of the world until Charlie clearly pointed that out. I feel like crap for surviving a childhood in which I was kept warm in winter by a government fuel assistance program, full when I went to bed at night due to food stamps, and holding a college degree bought by student loans. Maybe I really was a slob who couldn't have gotten ahead on my own. But what did people like Charlie expect? That us 'little people' should all starve to death in childhood? That's bullshit, I decide. I don't know the answer to the world's problems, but I know the answer to mine. Money. I want money. As much money as Charlie has. More!

"Heading 'up-nort' like the rest of Minnesota?" he asks, mocking our prevalent Norwegian accent by pronouncing the word north 'nort.'

"Naw," I reply. "Hate the traffic. It's a lava flow on holiday weekends."

He nods like he knows what I'm talking about. "You want to fly to the Hamptons with me for the weekend?"

I gulp another mouthful of beer. "Sure." It doesn't surprise me Charlie has his own plane. He probably has his own train somewhere too. It's not easy maintaining adequacy around Charlie, but he's just too cool not to try.

He tells me it's more than a Memorial Day weekend. It's a welcome home party for his mother who has been in Australia recuperating at a health spa after breast cancer treatment she had in Switzerland. "Bring a tux," he adds.

Tux? Where am I going to get a tux?

FRIDAY, MAY 25, 2008: 9:30 P.M. (CDT)

Charlie told me to meet him at the St. Paul Downtown Airport on the West Bank. People in Minnesota don't refer to the mighty

Mississippi River by name because the river is such a given. All we need to know is which side of the river you're talking about.

I spot Charlie's Mercedes in a small parking lot and pull up next to it and follow the direction to where his plane is hangared. Earthbound objects seem to rise from the ground like goblins and appear flat against the evening sky. The last cinders of the sun burn low on the horizon. I glance upward into a deep violet starless sky that eludes oblivion and try to imagine what it will feel like to fly through it. The closest thing to a plane I've ever been in was a helicopter ride at the State Fair.

I see Charlie's head inside the lighted cockpit of a Cessna Skylark as I approach. My eyes follow the lines of the plane like I'm eye-balling a set of hooters. A ribbon of deep red swirls along the body and underscores the windows. The tail sports the same color and detail. One impressive machine, I think to myself, for all I know about planes which is little more than aerodynamics make it possible for them to stay up in the air—and I am praying to God this trip will be no exception.

Charlie jumps from the cockpit with a clipboard in his left hand and a flashlight in his right just as I get up to it. "Hey," he greets. "As soon as I complete my ground check we'll take off."

I nod and follow him around to the other side where he pokes his head under the wing and strains his neck backward and side to side, examining the underside of the appendage. He is deep in concentration, unaware his mouth is gaping or that his nose wrinkles as he squints into the thin beam of light. I stare in the same direction but see nothing of interest. Just a row of rivets. But Charlie seems fascinated by them, runs his fingers over them as though they were the spine of woman, and stares for several more minutes before he grunts affirmatively.

He gives the side of the plane a loving pat and turns to me. "Ready for blast off?" Then he opens the door to the pilot's seat and stashes the clipboard while I go around and climb in from the co-pilot's side.

Once inside, I look around the cabin. The seats are gray leather and still smell brand new. The carpet is the same deep red as the little ribbon on the outside of the plane. The instrument panel is massive. Meters and numbers, dials and buttons, tiny levers and switches, and a whole lot of things I've never seen before. I sure hope Charlie knows what he's doing.

Charlie checks the passenger door from the outside before he jumps into the pilot's seat and announces we have clearance for takeoff on runway two. The cabin lights go off and the instrument panel illuminates our faces in a greenish glow. He pushes a button with his thumb and the three-blade propeller on the nose of the plane begins to turn ... slowly at first, then all of a sudden it's like there's nothing there at all. He turns a knob from the 'OFF' position to 'STBY,' which I assume means standby. My brain can't comprehend the purpose of the other tasks he performs but we are soon taxiing toward runway two. The ride is like being on a lawnmower as the plane lists and wobbles due to a combination of ground imperfections and a five-mile-per-hour wind. Once we reach the end of the strip, it is dark but for the lights along the runway. We wait while Charlie talks to the tower.

"Clear for takeoff niner-two-niner-zero dash four-four-eight tango."

Charlie turns the knob from STBY To ALT. I feel the engines immediately rev. I look out over the Mississippi River that sparkles anxiously as it reflects the St. Paul city skyline. The sky above us has blackened to obscurity. The entire plane shakes in anticipation before being unleashed to run faster and faster down the runway, roaring before it takes a mighty leap into the air where we float. The engine immediately turns into a steady hum. I listen to the clunks and groans as Charlie wrestles with a couple of levers and buttons. I am mesmerized by the sight of the Minnesota State Capitol—the Quadriga posed upon its dome in a permanent quest toward the future.

From this perspective I watch as the layout of the roads surrounding the government district meld together while we rise further and further above them. As far as my eyes are able to see, the earth spreads like a carpet studded by rhinestones, mirroring the heavens above us.

CHAPTER 3: A WHOLE NEW WORLD
THE HAMPTONS, NEW YORK

SATURDAY, MAY 26, 2007: 2:15 AM (EDT)

We land at the South Fork Municipal Airport on Long Island around 2:15 a.m. A limousine is waiting for us. It is nearly 3:00 a.m. when we arrive at Charlie's folks' place just outside Gull Port. It's too dark to tell what the house looks like, other than the fountain in the center of the circle drive that spews water and changes color. That, and a double-door portico lit up by floodlights that illuminate from somewhere near the fountain. After brief and quiet exchanges inside the foyer I am led to my room by a house servant who is wearing a bathrobe and slippers.

It had been an uneventful trip, but I had remained wide awake the entire flight. I feel like a kid who is afraid to go to bed for fear of missing something. Once the door closes to the room to which I've been ushered, I swell with exhilaration. I am not at all ready for sleep. But the next thing I know it's morning and the sun is blasting into the room with a vengeance to rival Lizzy Borden. I roll off the bed onto the floor, still fully clothed from the night before. It takes several minutes before I comprehend where I am and why.

The room provides everything a guest could want: a private bath, fresh towels, even fresh soaps ... only I don't have to unwrap anything. I hear voices in the hallway and somewhere in the house a door slams. The view from the window stops me in my tracks. Ocean about 500 yards out. White sand beach as far as I can see ... people, beach umbrellas, dune buggies in the distance. Holy baseballs! When did the party start?

In less than twenty minutes I am showered, dressed, and bounding down the open spiral staircase as I check out the place in the daylight while my nose draws me toward the kitchen. The place is something out of the movies. I can't tell where the living room begins and the foyer stops. Everything is white and glass and green plants and open—free, unrestrained. Glass expands the entire oceanside wall of the main room. Is that a Salvador Dali above the fireplace? A cement appendage sprawls from the glass wall outward from the house and extends toward an infinity pool that seems to drip right into the ocean. From this perspective, I cannot see the beach or the people but I know they are there because I had seen them from the upstairs window of my room. From this vantage point, I am looking out over the tops of their heads as though they don't exist. I stand mesmerized by the ingenuity of people who design such things while I enjoy their accomplishments. Bliss for all who dwell here. This is pure heaven.

"There you are," I hear Charlie say.

I turn around.

"Did you sleep okay?"

"Yeah," I say. "Fine."

Charlie is in swim trunks, a terry shirt, and canvas boating shoes. I'm in jeans and a T-shirt and feeling out of place.

"Marta," Charlie calls into the thin air from which a short Hispanic woman appears. "Bring my friend a cup of coffee, please." He turns to me while she waits. "Black, is that right?"

I nod. Marta disappears.

"We're taking the boat out in about a half hour if you'd care to join us." Charlie sits on the edge of a winding sofa with no arms. He sips his coffee.

Marta returns with mine. I ease into something that looks more like a sculpture than an armchair.

"What would you like for breakfast?" Charlie asks.

"Food." I come from a family that eats what is put before them. There is no ordering. If you don't like it, you go without. I like everything.

Charlie snickers at me. "A southwestern omelet with extra cheese and a side of potatoes for my friend," he tells Marta, who had remained standing near the door for just such orders. "And Marta," he calls as she stops in her tracks. Charlie turns to me. "Do you have boating attire and proper shoes?"

I look down at my loafers and back to Charlie.

"Supply him with suitable attire for a day on the water. Same size as me and shoe size …" he turns to me again, "What size do you wear, 10?"

"11."

"Size 11 boating shoe," he continues telling Marta. "And Ms. Banks needs a visor and towel. She's in the north room, but do not disturb her until after 10 o'clock." Marta nods and leaves.

"This place is used so impromptu our guests often come unprepared. I myself keep a separate wardrobe and toiletries here," he says in an effort to make me feel more comfortable since it's obvious I'm a fish-out-of-water here in the Hamptons. It doesn't put me any more at ease, but that doesn't matter. I am too engrossed in the opportunity to hob knob with the rich and famous. 'Beat my ego to death, if you must, only don't turn me away,' seems to be my current sentiment.

"I just wear everything I own to keep life simple," I say with a smirk. Charlie laughs out loud, a little more than the joke was worth.

SATURDAY, MAY 26, 2007: 5:15 P.M. (EDT)

After an afternoon on a catamaran named *The Lobster*, I am redder than one, but the whole experience opened my mind to new possibilities. I like it here in the Hamptons. I like the ocean ... vast and untamed ... powerful! I love leaning out over the front of the bow as we glide over the waters, wind in my face, sun on my back, breathing in parts of the universe I never knew existed. I like the little sandwiches for lunch that had been prepared by the boat's steward just for our afternoon sojourn aboard. I even like the Mojitos better.

My mind is jumping. I feel alive, awakened. It is as though my spirit has been unleashed and is on a gallop toward a fate that only my soul had identified all along. The ball bearings are in place now and whatever had once gummed up my works is gone. I am flowing again, up and running ... zero to sixty in three-point-eight seconds.

I realize now I am meant for greater things than I can accomplish living above The Curl Up and Dye Hair Salon. When I get back things are going to change. I might not ever go back. Maybe I will find a job right here in Gull Port, or better yet Manhattan ... New York ... the epicenter of the world ... the place where everything happens first. Yeah.

Marta had laid out a tux for tonight's dinner at the Rolling Greens Country Club in honor of Charlie's mother. I am anxious to meet a woman who would turn her own coming home party into a fundraiser for breast cancer research. It seems like such a selfless thing to do.

When Aunt Louise got ovarian cancer and had a hysterectomy, she became the center of our family, only it wasn't generosity that caused everyone to evolve around her. If her demands weren't enough, she applied guilt and whatever else it took to get everyone waiting on her hand and foot. But instead of vying for the attention of others, Charlie's mother turns everyone's attention to the needs of others by raising money for breast cancer research. It's a whole new mentality to take in.

People are flying in from all over the world to attend. Dignitaries of foreign countries, famous artists and musicians, a few from Hollywood—the Hanks' are sure to attend. George Clooney is here according to the buzz on the docks. Of course, the business world is expected to be well represented; I heard names like Gates, Heinz, Rockefeller, and Jobs all mentioned.

A billion dollars is projected to be raised as a result of this one event. I try to fathom a billion anything. I have to work my way up to comprehend that number. Let's see ... a million days ago is about 700 years B.C. Go back a billion days and the American continent hadn't broken away from Africa yet. I stare into space letting the thought sink in. It is difficult to fathom the wealth in the world. A billion is chump change to this crowd. More than half the guests expected tonight have more wealth than half the world's smaller countries combined.

"Hmmm," I utter as the idea of owning a small country enters my imagination. I jump to a stand. "King David," I say aloud, trying on for size what it might feel like to own a country. "No, that name is already taken. They'd have to call me something different—President Yates ... no ... David, King of ..." my mind searches for a word that would describe the type of country I would want to own. It has to be a name that describes the best place on earth since this is *my* fantasy. "David, King of ... my mind searches my desires, then it comes to me: David, King of Brewland," I say into the mirror while I spread my arms wide as if addressing my subjects. Then I take a second look at my reflection. Here in the Hamptons nothing is unimaginable or unattainable.

"Mister Yates," Marta inquires softly outside the door to my room.

"Yes," I answer, a bit embarrassed at being interrupted in my fantasy, even though I know she couldn't possibly have seen or heard my drivel.

"What time would you like your limousine to pick you up?"

My limousine. I bask in the reality I have a limousine at my beck and call. I open the door to hear her tell me Charlie and his parents will be going ahead of the others. That Mr. Shapiro and Ms. Banks would be leaving together in a limousine at 8:30 p.m. There is room for me. Would I care to join them?

"Anything earlier?" I ask eagerly.

Ms. Hendicotte, Ms. Langley, Mr. Gregson, and Dr. Sunders will be leaving at 7:45 p.m., would I care to join them?

"Yeah, load me up with them," I tell her.

I lean my back against the door and assess the time I have before I need to dress. There's enough time for a quick swim in the infinity pool. I change into my own swim trunks, hoping there is no protocol for attire here at the house. I don't own flip-flops, so I pad barefoot across the marble floors of the front room and out onto the patio, which is partially shaded from the late afternoon sun.

The pool is like glass, only moving as though it were a giant scroll. When I step into the water the ripples break the image of the sky that had lain on the surface. As I slowly breaststroke toward the outside edge I swear I will swim right out into the ocean. The water is slightly cooler than bathwater, but feels softer than the ocean's water had early today. I lay back and float, staring up at the infinite sky as I try to calculate how far into space I can actually see.

"Nice pecs," I hear someone say.

I startle to a stand. The water is waist high. I rub my hand over the top of my head and squeegee the water from my face. I see legs. Slim. Tanned. Smooth. A voice inside my head beckons my eyeballs to climb the rest of the way up. Hot pink strip of material against flesh just below a tight belly with a diamond stud ... all this shadowed by a set of jugs suspended in another tiny strip of hot pink spandex. Instantly my switch flips. "Helloooo there," I say.

She ignores the greeting, turns her back and saunters toward the chaise lounge at the end of the patio. Cowabunga! Boom da ta boom. I watch her ass sway back and forth like two tiny water balloons. Pop goes my heart. I'm in love.

She bends over as she winds her long red hair into a knot and tucks it into a bathing cap. Then she turns and makes a shallow dive and without using her arms or legs propels toward me underwater until she is at my groin. When she comes up, she stands so close I can kiss her without making a move.

"Hello," she whispers. There is a sheen of water all over her body that she doesn't try to wipe away. Her breasts are heaving and so close they touch the hair on my chest. Then she stretches her arms above her head and does a shallow back dive where I get a full view of every inch of her as she glides away on the surface of the water.

For a second I hesitate out of numbness. Then I dive toward her with open eyes under water. A couple of hard pushes and I'm at her waist which I grab with both hands before I pull myself up from the water. I can feel the diamond stud with my right thumb. She smiles and lingers a bit before she hoists herself onto the side of the pool where she keeps me at her knee as she dangles her legs in the water.

Her name is Helice Hendicotte, daughter of Senator Bradley Hendicotte, Republican, South Carolina ... the same Senator Hendicotte that filibustered against the healthcare reform bill last session and destroyed its chances for another four years. She just graduated from Florida State in Communications and has her sights set on broadcasting for NBC out of New York someday. Currently, she works for a public broadcasting station in Manhattan, a short stop on the way to the big time. She's the rebel in her family since her father hates the fact she's not living and working in the south where she belongs. He wants her out of Yankee territory, as though the Civil War is about to break, she giggles.

She's placed me in the same category as Charlie and is under the illusion she's captivated my interests, and that part is true. The sins to pay for deceiving her further are well worth it if I can get her to wrap her legs around me by tonight. Game on!

SATURDAY, MAY 26, 2007: 7:40 P.M. (EDT)

Helice and I meet again as everyone gathers in the vestibule to be ushered into a waiting limo by a uniformed chauffeur. I hustle to follow right behind her and place my hand respectfully at the small of her back as we pass through the threshold as a gesture meant to lay claim to her over other males present, but I could have saved myself the trouble since Gregory Gregson and Doctor Saunders are clearly too interested in something going on between themselves to notice anything else around them. Ms. Langley is about as interesting as a toaster and must think the same about everyone else since she takes the seat farthest away from the door and begins staring out the window immediately.

Helice slides into the center back seat next to Ms. Langley and I quickly follow her in to get the seat next to her. Gregory and the doctor are so deep in discussion about world trade they can scarcely take their eyes off one another.

"Everybody in the world is looking to the American model of free enterprise and capital markets," Gregory declares as he enters the limo. He is the slightest of the two and has a nervous tremble which the proximity of Dr. Saunders seems to exacerbate. "How can you snub innovation and superior ingenuity and creativity? It is the American heritage to be the lead in everything. Why not the stock market?"

"We're in the lead, alright. We're leading the whole damned world to the slaughterhouse," Dr. Saunders says nonchalantly as he takes a seat across from Gregory. His controlled mannerisms do not hide his interest in Gregory, however. I couldn't help but stare at them, amazed to find flirting is the same even when it's between the same genders. I don't know ... somehow, I thought it would be different.

"Oh, come now, Dr. Saunders, surely you aren't a cynic when it comes to innovation," Gregory says with a defined coyness despite the seriousness of the subject matter. "CDSs make investing risk-free! What more could you want?" Gregory waves a hand confidently in synchronization with his chest and shoulders and just as gracefully coils his entire body in repose.

"Innovation," Saunders says with a firm note of disgust and surprise. "You call credit default swaps innovation?" He glances at Gregory, but his eyes turn inward to something dark and foreboding. "They think they've come up with a way for people around the world to buy little more than an insurance policy against subprime debt." He shakes his head at the thought. "There is no underlying security. Do you realize?" He looks up pleadingly to Gregory, but he is merely thinking aloud at this point. His brow furrows deeply. His eyes stare past objects. He looks down and seems to dismiss the rest of us, including Gregory. "It is idiocy, pure idiocy. The things will bring us all down."

Gregory turns his attention quickly to Dr. Saunders with a worried expression. "Oh, stocks, schmocks," he says lightly. "I'm in the mood for champagne." He leans toward the doc. "How about you? I hear she's hired Chez Daniels to do the food."

The doctor reluctantly returns to the living and slowly smiles at Gregory. The rest of us still don't count. Gregory twists triumphantly and poses for the doc as though he is looking out the tinted window, but more likely he is staring at his own reflection in the glass.

I wonder what credit default swaps are for a second before I turn my attentions to something more along my lines ... Helice, who says little with her mouth and a lot with her eyes and every inch of me begins to answer her with, "Yeah, oh yeah! Tonight's the night, baby."

The tux fits like a glove but the shoes are pinching my little toes and both feet are beginning to numb to my ankles by the time we arrive at the Rolling Greens Country Club where the PGA Tour will make a stop in another two months. I can only imagine who will be walking through these doors then ... Woods, Mickelson, Els. But *I* am walking through these doors tonight. I puff out my chest and strut upon the carpet lain just for this occasion while *my* chauffeur drives off in *my* limousine. I can't help it. Besides, I'm psyching up for the evening.

A young waiter in black trousers, white shirt, and red vest and bow tie greets us with a tray of flutes filled with tiny bubbles as soon as we are through the doors. I hand a flute to Helice. We tip the rims together in our own little personal toast to the anticipations of a great evening and take a sip to seal it. Her eyes tell me my assumptions are on solid ground. She slips her arm around mine and we begin to stroll through the sea of people that neither of us knows personally, but who she knows *all* about. I begin to nod to people I don't know. They nod back. Some smile. Some don't. But they all stare at what I have hanging on my arm. This is alright, I think to myself.

Helice's eyes dart about like a gnat on a ripe banana. She whispers names of people through lips that don't move. I can't help but gawk at her ventriloquism. Her elbow soon deters me from my open admiration and I catch on to her glide, smile, and nod technique.

"Todd Vanderbilt," she whispers. "Third richest person in the world." My eyes widen as does my smile as we pass him by.

"Celia Dole," she clues me in about a pale, skinny girl surrounded by a group of pale, skinny boys. "Daughter of William Dole," she says without further explanation.

"Dole like in Dole pineapple?" I ask her. She shushes me.

Charlie pops out of nowhere and ushers us toward his parents, Gabriella and Cowan George Bishop the Third—the guy I know more about than he'd like me to, but not enough to draw any of my own conclusions yet.

Cowen is an older version of Charlie—grayer but equally fit and trim. Posture is more erect. Eyes equally steady. Calm. Calculating.

But unlike Charlie, who empowers people with his presence, Cowen usurps awe and respect much in the same way a statue by Michelangelo does from a gawking tourist.

I watch as others move through the reception line and notice each genuflect as they come in contact with the great Cowen Bishop, including Todd Vanderbilt, Mr. Third-richest-person-in-the-world. Before I know it he is shaking my hand and I find myself bowing my head—exactly like others had done.

"Appreciate your contribution," says Cowen Bishop the Third, assuming I have contributed something—either that or implying that I should.

"My pleasure," I reply as non-sheepishly as possible.

"I'm sure it is," he says with a smile.

I quickly move on to Gabriella Bishop who is astoundingly beautiful despite a turbaned head and a high-necked gown. She accentuates her husband's strength with beauty and grace. Whether it is because I'm wearing one of her husband's old tuxes or whether she saw me with Charlie, she seems to recognize me instantly.

"David," she says with a smile. "How nice to finally meet you."

"Certainly, a pleasure to meet you, Mrs. Bishop," I reply so expertly I surprise myself.

"Oh, please," she swoons. "Call me Gabby, like everyone else."

I smile and express my gladness over her recovery and wish her good health, but before I can say anything else I am nudged out by Helice who gushes and blushes and jabbers incessantly until Charlie mercifully plucks both Helice and me by our elbows from the reception line and steers us with urgency toward the bar where the bartender greets Charlie with a fresh Mojito.

"Two more, my friend," Charlie says to the bartender as he waggles a finger over the tops of our heads.

She and I take the stools while Charlie stands between us. I see Angelina Jolie over Charlie's shoulder, but no Brad.

"There's someone I want you to meet," he tells me.

I'm hoping it is Angelina. Helice sips her Mojito indignantly for some reason.

"I want you to hear what this guy has to say about the market," Charlie tells me as he looks around the room for the person he wants me to meet.

What market is he talking about?

Charlie taps me on the shoulder in a 'wait here' gesture and darts off into the crowd.
Helice is loathing me by this time. "What?" I ask her with a shrug. She turns her back to me. I have no idea what crawled up her butt all of a sudden, but whatever it is it is now up mine. Women! And their rampant mood swings.
Charlie returns with a wreck of a person in tow. His name is Tony Byrne. He looks like's he's just out of high school, skinny with a boyish face and naturally curly red hair that blasts from his head like a fireball, but his eyes are as intense as a presidential bodyguard's. He's wearing a tuxedo, but he moves so much I can't tell it if fits him or not. One second he's stretching his neck like the shirt is too tight. The next second he's hunching his shoulders like the thing is binding him in the back. And what's with the tugging on his cuffs? He's wild-eyed and nervous, talks faster than Slick Wilson at Mack's All Makes Used Cars, and keeps looking over his shoulder like someone is after him. My first thought is he is on something like drugs or maybe he's got a disorder and he *should* be on something and *isn't*. He is not normal by Minnesota standards, but my mind has been opened since arriving on Long Island, so I hang in the conversation along with Charlie, who acts like this is everyday stuff.
Charlie quickly explains that Tony is a trader at the New York Stock Exchange.
My head snaps back to Tony. My eyes widen and before I can stop myself, I blurt out, "One of those guys on the trading floor ... *the* trading floor?" I ask like a stupid idiot.
They both give me looks that confirm my self-knowledge, then get on with their conversation of which I am to pay attention. But all I can react to is this dude. Holy baseballs! I'm standing in front of a real stock trader—New York Stock Exchange, the big time. I lean in, fascinated.
Helice expels a heavy sigh and slips into the crowd. My eyes try to follow her, but she's out of sight in seconds. Oh well. I turn back to pay closer attention to Tony.
"Tell Dave what you told me," Charlie says to Tony. Tony sizes me up. His eyes dart back to Charlie as if he were asking whether it was alright to trust me. Charlie gestures that it is.
"CDOs," he says. "Can't get enough of them. The UK, France, Germany, Iceland ... they are going faster than meth in a flophouse."
"What are CDOs?" I ask.

"Collateralized debt obligations," Tony replies. He explains they are bundles of subprime debt, such as credit card balances and mortgages, which are pooled together then sliced and diced and sold to investors. Because a guy with a bad credit rating has to pay a higher interest rate than a stellar borrower, investors get a better return on subprime debt over prime obligations. You put enough bad debts into the same bag and the percentage that doesn't default outweighs the ones that do which reduces the overall risk to zip. "Riskless investment that pays," he says, accentuating the word 'pays.'

Yeah, but you first need money to invest, I think to myself. Tony isn't aware I don't belong in this crowd, which makes the fact that I'm here all that much more fun. I turn up one corner of my mouth in a sly grin, hoping to impress him with a look that implies I know what he's talking about. All I know is you have to have money to make money and ... well ... there you are, or rather here *I* am.

"Everyone wants a piece of this action, which is why the supply can't stay ahead of demand," he adds breathlessly.

"Which means money for everyone," Charlie adds.

"What do you mean?" I ask. They both look at me dumbstruck. Evidently, I've missed some important point.

"It means until we run out of schmucks who want more than they can afford, loans will be free for the asking," Charlie's eyes dart back and forth between mine as he peers all the way to my brain to see whether I'm awake or not. "Lenders *prefer* writing subprime debt, because they can sell it for more money to investors who prefer it over prime-debt obligations. These things are right up there with growth stocks, only there's little risk."

It is obvious that his second attempt to explain didn't hit the bullseye. My underwear bunches when I notice them both staring at me, but then it finally sinks in. My eyes light up as I realize people always want more. With investors clamoring for subprime debt investments on one end and lenders writing subprime loans on the other end, the conduit is limitless. "Free money for everyone," I say.

Charlie gives me a congratulatory slap on the shoulder.

"What if the loans default?" I ask as my brain entertains the possible dark side of that bet.

"A certain percentage will. But that's figured into the plan." He pauses, then adds. "Besides, they aren't *all* going to default at the same time."

"I know," I say to pacify their reluctance to look at the obvious. "But what if they do?"

Tony shakes his head and throws his arms out wide. "It would take some astronomical world economic crisis to cause millions of people to default on their mortgages and auto loans all at the same time. What is the likelihood of that?"

The guys both focus on me, waiting to see whether I get it. The beauty of it all finally sinks in. Genius. Pure genius. My expression tells it all. I get it!

"CDOs," Charlie says as he raises his glass.

These guys really have an ear to the rail, I think to myself, raising my glass. Tony follows suit and we clink and say in unison, "CDOs."

"Swaps," says a shiny dude who interrupts us just as we are about to take a gulp of our Mojitos. The three of us look up over the top of our drinks without taking a sip.

Tony quickly sets his drink on the bar and, like a Doberman on a leash, remains at Charlie's side. The fidgeting resumes but more accelerated. He jerks his head to one side, then back again, and juts out his jaw, all without taking his eyes off the shiny dude now standing in our midst.

"Credit default swaps," the shiny dude says with the authority I'd only seen in the movie *The Godfather*. He stares at Tony as if to challenge him to say otherwise. Tony breaks their eye contact first and glances about the room as though he is searching for reinforcements—either that or a place to run.

I remember I'd heard of credit default something-or-others on the ride over ... the doc and his little buddy had been talking about them. I lean in, all ears.

Once the shiny dude is certain he has the spotlight he continues in a tone low enough to require anyone listening to listen carefully. "I have a computer-based product, gentlemen, you cannot afford to ignore. Credit Default Swaps." He smiles. "Add them to a portfolio with CDOs. Foolproof," he adds with a distinct gleam in his eye.

The guy stands erect as though he's waiting for the orchestra pit to play his entrance music. His name is Jack Garrison, an investment banker with Maugham Southerby, only I thought Charlie said 'mom' Southerby and am a bit bewildered. Maugham Southerby is the biggest investment bank in the world, I soon learn.

Charlie didn't introduce Jack to Tony, so I surmise they know one another. Tony shifts from one leg to the other and back and forth, like a kid who has to take a piss.

Jack impresses me with his power and presence. He doesn't twitch. He is in total control of every movement he makes. I'd pay a fin to see him in a poker game. He is medium height, but that's all that is minimal about this guy. He's over the top. He must have gone through some machine that scraped every inch of hair from him anywhere and buffed him to a shine before he put on a perfectly tailored tux. Is that polish on his fingernails?

Jack stands straight and says, "If you wanna catch the big kahuna … it's time to get on your ponies, gentlemen." He then pulls out his Blackberry and speed-dials someone. By the time Jack Garrison puts his cell phone back into his pocket, Charlie and I are hired by Maugham Southerby. No interview. Hired. Just like that. Jack tells us to report Tuesday morning to a guy named Dick Crosby in Minneapolis. "Seven a.m. Central Daylight Time," he tells us, then just walks away.

CHAPTER 4: OPPORTUNITY ARRIVES
MINNEAPOLIS, MINNESOTA

TUESDAY, MAY 29, 2007: 7:00 AM (CDT)

Charlie filled me in about Maugham Southerby being the largest investment bank on earth with offices in thirty-eight countries and seats on every exchange around the world. With his hand on the throttle of world commerce and trade, Charlie is at the helm of his own ship on the same sea as his father, and the race is about to begin. In the greater scheme of things Cyber International Systems, his father's claim to fame, is a mere drop in the ocean upon which Charlie is about to ride the tide.

I can't decide if this is a dream come true or the end of a nightmare for me. I never dreamt of being ultra-rich or powerful. All I've ever wanted to do was get out of Fiddlers Park. Now it looks like I might do both. Nobody has mentioned what stockbrokers rake in annually, but judging from the guys I met in the Hamptons, commissions must be in millions. I can't fathom earning a million dollars. The best year I've had so far in sales is $32,000—and I thought that was good. My mind isn't past catching up with rent and student loan payments to even consider what *that* sort of income could provide. It's incomprehensible to a guy like me.

The Maugham Southerby branch office in Minneapolis is located in the IDS building downtown. The energy pounding from within my chest is anticipation as we enter the building and cross the concourse to the elevators which will take us to the 35th floor. Still numb from all that's happened in just a few days I follow behind Charlie as he steps across the threshold to the Maugham Southerby suite.

"Good morning," greets the receptionist demurely. The words are as soft as the carpet beneath our feet. Charlie responds with comparable panache. She tells us to take a seat; that Mr. Crosby will be with us shortly, then disappears. She returns carrying a silver tray and sets it upon the glass-topped coffee table. There are two steaming mugs of coffee, two silver spoons, a sugar bowl and a small pitcher that has condensation on its sides. A stack of napkins has been fanned out to make a circle. She gives each of us a napkin first. While she hands Charlie one of the mugs, I notice the napkin in my hand is embossed with the Maugham Southerby logo.

Charlie picks up a magazine that says *Forbes* on the cover and casually begins reading. I gawk at the furnishings in the reception area and watch the inner workings of the office as it comes to life at this early hour. Men in perfectly tailored suits walk by with a sense of purpose, but without urgency. Not like Walter who nearly runs up and down the aisles at Durkee and who rarely is seen without his sleeves rolled up. These gents are polished and manicured and trimmed to a tee. Clean-shaven faces, starched shirts with white collars, silk ties tied to perfection. No sweat on their brows. The women all wear suits and closed-toed shoes. No dangling earrings or jangling bracelets. Instead they are subdued, sophisticated, confident—all business. No fartin' around here. I like it. I like it a lot.

The receptionist looks up as though she senses I need something. She's not at all like Linda, the receptionist at Durkee, who you have to practically belt to get her attention. This one's expression asks whether there is anything she can do for me. I resist sending her the message, "You bet, baby," and instead nod as soberly and as respectfully as I can. A gold and black nameplate in front of her reads Adeline Plummer, Receptionist.

Directly across from the reception counter is an empty glassed-in conference room. In the center of the room is a large glass-topped table with a mahogany base. It is surrounded by six high-backed leather swivel chairs. There are two more chairs against the opposite wall of solid windows from which I can see the tops of the Plummer Building across the street and just the tip of the Foshay Tower.

"Plummer," I shout to myself in my head. I look back to the nameplate and wonder whether Adeline is related. If she *is* related to the Plummer fortune she wouldn't be *working,* would she? But on the other hand, if a kid from the Plummer family ever did get a job, this would be a suitable place for a rich kid. Perhaps she's doing intern work for college ... probably taking economics or something like that. Tough life, I think to myself as I size her up once again. Yeah, she's a rich kid alright. There is something about rich people that reeks quality, refinement, confidence. I want it. I want what I see in this girl. I want what Charlie has. I want what everyone I met at the country club in the Hamptons had. And I want it bad.

While Charlie reads, I try to imagine what my future holds as I gaze about the office at the mahogany desks, leather chairs, oak bookcases, plush carpet, plants ... *real* plants! I walk over to a fern and finger it to make sure. Adeline Plummer looks up again. I smile and nod. Yeah, this is going to be alright, I think to myself. No more quarter raises and cake in a crappy lunchroom. It's going to be champagne and caviar from now on.

We wait nearly a half hour before a middle-aged woman in a gray suit with a white collared blouse and plain black pumps has us follow her to a corner office that is bigger than a living room. There is no interview, just introductions.

Dick Crosby is a beefy guy with a balding head of gray stubble he keeps trimmed within an eighth of an inch. He introduces himself as the Training Officer. His business card says 'Richard B. Crosby, Vice President, (CFP) (CFF) (IU) and Director of Human Resources.'

"I don't need to know anything about you because your background checks will produce the only thing I'm concerned about," he says as soon as we take a seat in the chairs opposite his desk. "First thing to learn in this business is to trust no one. No one else will go to jail for you if you fuck up." He pauses then adds, "Pardon the language."

His apology isn't meant to be sincere. He goes on to explain that in the securities industry there are consequences to making mistakes— so there will be *no* mistakes. His eyes glare with intent. If we pass the background check and drug tests, he'll take us on as a favor to Jack, but that's where it stops. We have to make the cut on our own. That means we'll have to pass all the required tests, go to New York for further training and make it through without blemish, and fulfill the quotas required of all rookies. We will have six months to prove ourselves, one month of minimal pay to keep us in gas and dry-cleaning ... eating comes after gas and dry-cleaning, he clarifies. We are given a dress code and asked to sign an agreement that says we understand that our behavior on and off the job is required to be suitable to the Maugham Southerby image or our employment could be terminated. Not so much as a parking ticket will be tolerated. We are to be presentable at all times, including backyard barbeques. There will be no downtime for us for several years. We will be on the job constantly if we plan to make it in this business. If we don't like it, we should leave now.

Adrenaline begins to pump through me. I like it.

"You get one chance to pass the security exams." He looks between the both of us. "Seven hours under surveillance." He snickers and shakes his head as though he doesn't suspect either of us will be able to pass them.

"If," he accentuates the word, "you pass, you will go to New York for further training. You'll be classified as Class 0207 (meaning the second quarter of 2007). You'll compete for rank with the other 300 rookies in that same class." He leans back in his chair. A smile of satisfaction spreads across his face. "Only the top 10 percent of any class retains positions at Maugham Southerby after twelve months. This isn't just any investment bank. We're the biggest. We stay that way by eliminating drag. You know what I mean?"

I know what he means. That we have but a tomato's chance at a vaudeville show of keeping our jobs.

"You get one go. You either make it or you are out." He pauses and looks at each of us as though he is sizing up whether we are worth his time and trouble. Judging from his expression, we are not.

"No matter how good you think you are, you have to be better than ninety percent of everyone else who hits the streets at the same time as you. Got that?" He pauses so long I feel I should reply, but don't know to what.

"Finally," he tells Charlie and me, "start lining up your targets. Don't wait until you are back from New York or you will be behind the rest of the pack."

The pack. I like the sound of that. The pack. I'll be running with the big dogs now. I'll be running with the wolves, swimming with the sharks.

"Within a month after you return from New York 50 percent of your class will be gone for one reason or another. Within twelve months there won't be enough left of you to fire anyone. Only 1 percent ever make it. Sometimes none!" His eyes narrow. The corners of his mouth curve upward in a sinister grin.

What happened to the 10 percent? How did we get down to 1 percent and none? Questions start popping up in my mind, but I don't verbalize a thing. I just nod.

"Anyone want out? Now's the time to go."

Not on your life. I'm in. I can do this. He wants focus and sacrifice. I got both. I look over at Charlie who's been pampered his whole life. He looks relaxed, like he's done it all before. This is level ground buddy, I think to myself.

Dick Crosby leans toward us over the top of his desk, and as he attempts to smile a glow from deep within him emerges through his eyes. "Gentlemen," he addresses us like human beings for the first time, "you have an opportunity to make more money than 99 percent of the rest of the world. Don't fuck it up."

With that he points to the door. Charlie leaves the office in a steady gait and heads toward the lobby. I stand in the shadow of his door listening to my heartbeat for several minutes before I can move.

Crosby's assistant sends us home with materials to crash study for the required securities exams, the Series 7, the Series 66 plus insurance licensing exams for every state in which we intend to do business. Charlie suggested I get licensed in the same states as him initially, which is 11, but to expect to be licensed in every single state soon. It's enough to scare the crap out of a college professor of economics.

We have two weeks to meet requirements or never show our faces here again. Nothing can stop me from being on that plane, I think to myself. Nothing!

Tuesday, May 29, 2007: 7:00 p.m. (CDT)

"Financial Advisor," Mayo yelps as he slams down his beer on the bar so hard it sloshes out the top. "Holy baseballs! You're now one of those money jocks on Wall Street?" He slaps me on the back and calls half a dozen fellows over and buys us all a round.

I gave Walter my termination notice this afternoon and he was nice enough to let me go immediately in support of my new endeavor. "All the best to you," Walter had said. I shook his hand in earnest and a part of me felt sad considering all he'd done for me. Walter must have sensed my sentiment because he eased it by adding, "I always knew you were meant for greater things than what we could offer you here at Durkee. You go get 'em boy," he had said as he patted my shoulder. He still calls me 'boy.' There wasn't time for a cake and a proper send-off or for sure there would have been one. But everyone lined up as I carted my box of belongings out the door and they all patted me on the back and offered congratulations

I feel like a whole new person. Like I died and came back to life, only as someone else ... not Dave Yates the nobody, but as David D. Yates, financial advisor for Maugham Southerby ... the stockbroker whose Blackberry never rests. I can't wait. I make a mental note to get myself a Blackberry.

"Met George Clooney in person," I tell the guys.

"No shit," Petie squeals.

"Why would I shit you, Petie?" I say directly into his face. "You're my favorite turd." Petie blushes. The rest of us laugh. I grab Petie around the neck with my arm and drag his head into my chest and give him a noogie.

It's hard to describe why Wall Street attracts so much attention. Money for sure is part of it. Endorphins fill our little brains as soon as the word money is mentioned. A girl I dated back in college who was a psych major once told me that. But it can't be what the guys here seem so fascinated about. Maybe it's because stockbrokers aren't toddling off to a mundane job each day like the rest of the world. The people affiliated with Wall Street are like gods ... they know something we can never understand yet can't live without. People who buy and sell stock and bonds are at the epicenter of the world. Grain commodities that feed nations, bonds that raise funds to build bridges and highway systems, stock in energy such as oil and electricity, or businesses that create everything we use from toothpaste and toilet paper to the things we desire most, like automobiles and homes. But it is still more than the humanitarian aspect that draws us to this vortex of activity. It's the frenzy, the chaos. Everything all mixed together. Fear. Greed. Risk. Power!

It isn't so much the things we can buy with money; it is the fact we can buy *anything* if we have *enough* money. What we really want is freedom from anyone else's rules. We want to make up the rules ourselves ... rules everyone else has to live by. Then, and only then, will life be worth living—when we can have everything and anything, and have it just the way we want it. Money gives us that power ... power over others, power against our own weaknesses. We don't have to be anything or do anything if we have enough money. The money does it for us. It buys us friends, servants, creature comforts, social status, respect, and even our own self-worth. We finally can stop asking ourselves why we were born. With enough money, we stop caring. We are born to enjoy life. And boy is it ever good when you have the money. That's why I'm so puzzled about Mom's reaction when I told her not more than an hour ago over the plate of Tater-Tot hot dish she had shoved under my nose.

"It's not you," she had said.

"What's not me?" I had asked her. "You mean being a box broker for Durkee is me, but being a financial advisor for Maugham Southerby isn't?"

"No. Of course not," she had replied in that 'you-know-what-I-mean' tone in her voice she uses when I don't know what she means.

"With or without your blessing, Mom, I'm going to New York and I'm going to become a financial advisor and make enough money to get you and Julie out of this dump."

She had looked around the living room with a frown. "This is no dump," she had retorted. "This is your home. Built by the bare hands of your very own grandfather."

I had to leave right then or bust. All the way to Schmitty's I shouted farewell to all the things that had held me back for so long. "Goodbye crumbling sidewalks that twine through the Park like a venomous snake. Goodbye Rick's Nick's where you can't buy a condom without everyone and your mother knowing about it." At the corner of Commons and Paine Avenues I had rolled down the window and stuck my head out and shouted, "Goodbye Fiddlers Park." Then spun my tires all the way to Schmitty's before jamming the bumper into the lilac bush and making a bolt for the back door.

"This is where it begins," I say now as I look into the eager faces of all my buddies. I lift my Heineken off the bar and raise it in another toast. "To good fortune," I say and pause to make certain everyone is paying attention. "Mine and everyone here with me tonight because I'm going to make us all rich sons-of-Fiddlers! Who's with me?" I ask. They lift their drinks high and we all shout in unison: "Ziggy, zaggy, ziggy, zaggy, Oi! Oi! Oi!"

CHAPTER 5: A FAMILY MATTER
FIDDLERS PARK, MINNESOTA

TUESDAY, JUNE 5, 2007: 5:10 P.M. (CDT)

The phone call from Bob had been unusually short. It wasn't anybody's birthday and we'd all been together for pot roast last Sunday. So why the family gathering? I'm wondering.
Barb and Julie are sitting on the sofa with Mom when I arrive. Bob is plunked in the BarcaLounger, but he doesn't have his feet up. Instead, he's sitting forward with his elbows on his knees. Barb's kids are not around; neither is her husband Barry, or Bob's wife Lori. Just the immediate family. Everyone looks up when I come into the room. They all know something I don't.
"What?" I freeze in anticipation.
"Sit down," Mom says.
Bob immediately leans back in the lounger and turns his head away. Barb scoots closer to the edge of the sofa toward me. Julie grabs Mom's hand.
"Who died?" I ask. Someone had to have died for such somber looks. Was it Dad? "Did Dad die?" Just the thought clouded my comprehension even though Mom immediately and adamantly shook her head.
"Then who?"
"Nobody died," Mom says softly. "And nobody's going to." Everyone else looks away.
Mom leans forward and Barb mimics her. I stare at the two of them who are now facing me with expressions I cannot read. Barb begins to say something, but Mom puts her hand on Barb's arm. Barb sits back. Mom leans forward and reaches for my hand. She pulls me toward her and urges Julie to move so I can sit next to Mom. While holding my hands, she tells me she has been diagnosed with cancer.
Cancer. There are cures for cancer, I think to myself. My mouth isn't working yet. Barb starts rattling about the details. A lump on the

left side of her breast. Something about a biopsy. All I want to know is the cure. "Treatment," I finally utter. "A mastectomy, chemotherapy, perhaps radiation? What?"

"We'll know better after more tests are completed," Mom says.

"Yeah, sure," I say. Charlie's mother survived breast cancer. She raised all that money for research, I ruminate to reassure myself.

Mom pops off the sofa, exuding energy, and asks if anyone wants coffee. We all nod, even though none of us do. Once she leaves the room, we all look at one another without saying a word. Julie looks as though she is about to cry. Bob is speechless. Bob is always speechless, but I can tell from his expression that this is a new reason for him to be. Barb is biting her nails, which she hasn't done since grade school.

I have to do something, say something. "Let's not panic," I begin. If it were anyone else reeling from such news, I would be inclined to tell them they were over-reacting, but since this is *my* mom and these are *my* siblings, this is a whole different perspective. One I don't like. "We need to be strong."

Julie sits up straighter and nods.

Barb shakes her head slowly, all the while maintaining eye contact with me as though she is begging me for a solution she knows neither of us has.

"Cancer is curable," I tell her. Then I look each one in the eyes to make sure they heard me. "Mom doesn't need drama right now," I say specifically to Julie. She needs our support." I look around the room at them again. Everyone returns a look of compliance.

"This is not the end of anything," I say to reassure them. I'd never acted this way before. It feels strange to talk to my family this way, like the head of it, like Mom usually does, and sometimes Barb, but I've never taken charge before. It feels strange.

By the time Mom emerges with a tray of saucers and cups and the pot of coffee, the atmosphere has relaxed a bit. We try to talk calmly, intelligently. We listen intently while Mom tells us about all the potential outcomes, the anticipated results. Likely routine surgery and a short recovery, she explains. The insurance will cover most of the cost; she has enough savings. She isn't worried about the cost or the surgery. She isn't worried about time off work—she has enough accumulated vacation and sick leave. She isn't worried about anything and neither should we be.

Right, I think to myself.

"What *does* worry me," she says to garner our attention once again, "is going bald." There is a short pause before we all burst out laughing.

It's going to be alright. Yeah, sure, I tell myself. Everything will be alright ... it'll be alright.

I stick around after Barb and Bob leave for their respective families, and I pop for pizza to be delivered from Dominos. Julie heads to her bedroom with the telephone, as usual, so Mom and I sit on the couch and watch an old movie ... something she picked out ... said it was her favorite movie. I had always thought her favorite movie was *Sound of Music* because she played it every Easter.

"It was the only show everyone liked. I wanted us to be together as a family," she explains for the first time about how *Sound of Music* had become the Easter mainstay.

"So, what are we watching tonight?" I ask since it is just the two of us.

She cocks her head and smiles at my impertinence. "*Beaches*," she says as she puts an old VCR into the old VCR player hooked up to her Magnavox television set. As she settles in next to me, she says, "Friends are most important."

My head snaps to look at her. "You're just full of surprises tonight, aren't you?"

"What?"

"I thought us kids were the most important thing to you."

"Oh," she waves a hand to dismiss my indignant remark. "Of course, you kids are the most important people in my life, but without friends I wouldn't have made it through."

Through what, I wonder? I had never thought about my mom as anything other than my mom. I stare at her—perhaps for the first time—as a person other than just my mom and realize she is a woman ... a nice-looking woman at that. Not in a sexy, glamorous sort of way. In an earthy, clean, and decent sort of way. The kind of woman you want to be the mother of your kids.

"What?" Mom asks, having noticed me staring at her.

"Nothing," I mumble and look away to divert her attention before I once again turn to stare at her, only this time sideways so she won't notice. I guess I'd always thought more about myself as a kid growing up without a dad around. I had never thought anything about what it had been like for a woman to raise children all by herself. She was my mom. She was supposed to be there. There had even been times when

I blamed her for Dad not being there. But it had never crossed my mind that *she* wouldn't be here.

She went to work, did everything around the house, sat on the bleachers by herself, went alone to our recitals. She was always there, but she was always alone.

She didn't date until a couple of months ago. Our neighbor, Lucy, fixed her up for a blind date with Lucy's nephew. Some guy named Stuart, or Stanley. I haven't met him yet and don't care to, but apparently they hit it off and have been seeing each other regularly.

"Did you ever miss not being married?" The question grabs her attention and she turns to look at me. I expect her to say something like, 'No, of course not. You kids were all I needed,' but instead she says, "I *always* missed not being married." She turned back to the movie. "I miss not being married to your father."

"To my *father*," I reiterate with surprise. I thought she hated my father. Although I never heard her actually say that.

"Not because I still love him. But because parents can't be replaced. I never had anyone with whom to share the joys of parenting." She sighs. "I missed that. I still miss that." She pauses in thought, then adds, "And then there are grandchildren."

"So, it wasn't you who wanted the divorce? Because I always thought it was you who wanted the divorce."

She looks at me in contemplation.

"I'm old enough to understand," I assure her.

She pierces her lips in indecision.

"I'm twenty-four years old, Ma. I'm all grown up. Believe me. I can handle the truth."

"I never wanted a divorce. I loved your father. "

"Then why did he leave?"

She doesn't answer. She just turns back to the movie and grabs a tissue.

I can't take my eyes off her. She looks so frail and vulnerable all of a sudden. This woman who had taught me to stand up against a school bully and how to punch in case I had to defend myself when I was in third-grade; who had sawed off the end of our Christmas trees herself every year; and who showed up to every parent-teacher conference despite our best efforts to get her to avoid them. She is really just one ordinary woman. Not half of a parent-team like other moms. Just one parent who had to play the roles of two. One woman who did the best she could even though it was never enough. No matter how much she did for us, I had always felt deprived of something other kids seemed to have. I wonder if she ever felt the same way. She never complained. She went all those years alone without anyone to talk to … except her friends. Ah, I think to myself. Now I get why she thinks her friends are so important.

"You're not alone," I tell her softly.

"I know," she whispers and shushes me.

We watch the movie. Both of us wind up crying.

MONDAY, JUNE 11, 2007: 9:30 A.M. (CDT)

By the next week, the whole Park knows Mom has cancer. I can't go anywhere without someone stopping me to tell me how sorry they are to hear she is ill, that they will be praying for her, that if there is anything she needs, to just give them a call. It's like nothing is sacred or private. Everybody knows everything.

"Oh stop," Mom admonishes when I whine to her about the gossip going around. "They are good people showing their concern." She takes the banana bread Maggie had given me to bring over and places it next to a tin of something else someone else has previously dropped off. Her kitchen counters are crowded with baked stuff.

"Well if they are such good people why don't they keep their noses out of our business?"

She looks at me sternly. "I *am* their business. We live in this community. They are our neighbors and friends. We are part of their lives as much as they are part of ours."

"Yeah, yeah … one great fabric and all." I've heard it all before. I will never understand how Mom loves everybody knowing her business. She's never tried to keep anything from anyone. I wouldn't be surprised if someone asked me what color underwear she has on, and expected me to know. How can she not want more privacy than what living in the Park allows? "I'm going to get you out of here one of these days," I tell her.

She shakes her head.

"I'm going to buy you a condo overlooking the mighty Mississippi where a doorman will thwart any unwanted visitors."

"Just get me to the doctor's office," she tells me with a noticeable sigh of exasperation.

The cancer clinic is across town in the Edina Medical Center, a revamped former hospital with ample parking and skyways over France Avenue just off the Crosstown, Highway 62. The area has become a cluster of medical specialists, prosthetics, orthodontists, cosmetic surgeons, psychiatrists, and a litany of boutique shopping malls and restaurants over the years.

"We can go to Ruby Tuesday's for lunch," Mom suggests, attempting to calm the nerves I seem to be wearing on my sleeve as we drive over.

How can she sit there so calmly? The bullet is still in the air. As a family we had decided someone should always go with mom to all her appointments. We didn't verbalize why that would be necessary because by doing so the fear would somehow be real. Moral support we called it. Mom would have our moral support we had told each other. What I wasn't anticipating was needing some of that myself.

The skyway from the parking ramp to the hospital is quiet as a library. The carpet is soft. A flock of geese in v-formation fly overhead. I look up and watch their bellies pass over us as we continue to move silently through the glass tube that arches over six lanes of traffic below.

Doctor Wesowaska's office is on the third floor. Doctor Sundihar's office is on the fifth floor. The lab is on the first floor. Radiology is on the lower level. There are waiting rooms at each stop but none have reading material. After the second stop, I ask where I can find something to read and am referred to a newsstand on ground-level. Apparently, periodicals host germs. Evidently it is okay to own your own germs, just not borrow them.

While Mom is in seeing Dr. Sundihar I run down to the newsstand. I buy a *USA Today* and delve into world affairs and financial matters like a toddler into its blankie. Now that I am an official financial professional, I have to have my eye on the ball. There is growing concern about subprime debt obligations—the fun and games that got me into this business in the first place. Only now I need answers and no one at Maugham Southerby is providing any. While hot air has been flying among the FAs, there's been nothing from the analysts in New York. I am desperate for any information.

I'm drawn to an article that insinuates banks might tighten international markets later this year, which could limit growth, but it doesn't explain why. I shrug. In another small article is says firms relying too heavily on short-term overnight and term repo funding will have problems. I have to wonder who isn't over-exposed to such these days. Much larger headlines convey that U.S. equities outperformed international equities and international equities outperformed emerging markets. Investors still consider U.S. equities least risky. There's an article about how small-cap and mid-cap equities outperformed large-cap in 2006, when the country was still recovering from the bursting tech bubble back in 2001, but large-cap has outperformed small-cap the first half of *this* year, which implies we are well away from harm. Large-cap and small-cap equities can expect to see a 6-7 percent return, and emerging markets as high as 13 percent. Nice. If subprime mortgages were any real threat it would be all over the papers, I assure myself.

I find one last article on the bottom of page four issued by the associated press that says Morton Salzman, a firm which had been a forerunner in selling CDOs, had reported it held $27.2 billion in collateralized debt obligations and subprime mortgages. While there was a discernible worrisome tone to the article, it did not draw any conclusions. I recall Bernanke addressed the same topic last week on CNBC and assured the listening world that the only threat subprime mortgages could cause would be to a few mortgage lenders.

Old Crosby must be right. "It's nothing more than what high yield bonds have always been," he had explained at yesterday's meeting. "Just because someone finds a little subprime debt inside a fund that was sold as investment grade is nothing to get your underwear in a bunch over. That stuff happens. It's Wall Street. You want perfection—join a seminary. When people come to you, your job is to fasten them to the bungee cord and tell them to tuck in their arms and legs. Investors are like every other thrill seeker. They demand the biggest thrill, but they don't really want to plummet to their death. But don't think they don't know death is a possibility. It is part of the thrill."

By the time Mom emerges from the lab with her reports in hand, I draw the only conclusion I am able to draw about the stability of the markets relative to subprime debt: business as usual.

"Are you hungry?"

"Starving," I answer as we head toward Ruby Tuesday's in the Southdale Shopping Mall. I'm ordering a steak sandwich and a plate of fries, I tell myself.

"How'd your tests come out?"

"Fine. I'm scheduled for surgery on Thursday."

"Thursday," I say in astonishment. I stop dead in my tracks. She nods and keeps on walking, waving her hand for me to catch up. I catch up and say again, "Thursday? Why so soon?"

She smiles. "Cancer doesn't wait. It'll be good to get it over with quickly."

"Yeah, but Thursday?" I lost my appetite. I need more time to process this. I don't know what I had thought, but I didn't think it would happen so fast. One day you're a whole person and two days later parts of you are being hacked off. I need to mentally prepare for my mother to undergo a mastectomy within two days. Me? I can't believe I am worried about myself. I should be thinking about her. I'm not used to thinking about her. I'm used to her thinking about me.

"Are you ready for all of this?" I ask her.

She doesn't look at me. She just keeps walking.

THURSDAY, JUNE 14, 2007: 2:30 P.M. (CDT)

The fifth floor of the Upper Edina Hospital is carpeted and quiet. Still musing about the word 'upper' in the title, I walk down the hallway and look for signage that will lead me to room 509. The room is a double but there is no one in the first bed. The curtain between the two beds had been pulled back. There is a large box that displays quartz numbers in red: 129, then 131, then 128 … A tall chrome bar holds a bag of something that drips into a hose that was stuck into the arm of my mother.

Geez. I recoil from the sight of it all, but I force myself to stay. There are no words to describe how this makes me feel. Powerless against an angry force as dark as the devil. Barb rushes to greet me, then without a word pushes me in front of her as we near the bed. Mom's head turns on her pillow. The rest of her body remains dead still, but as we approach, she stirs ever so slightly. Her eyes open.

Bob is slumped in the chair in the corner. Julie, having just graduated last week from high school, stands erect as a ballerina at the foot of the bed. Barb is still clinging to my arm while I hold Mom's hand in both of mine.

"You okay?" I ask. Mom closes her eyes and nods slightly. Still groggy from the anesthesia she fades in and out of consciousness while we stand about gawking with worried expressions. The nurse informed us this was natural, that she was doing well, that we have nothing to worry about—but we worry anyway. Talk begins to fill the void; disjointed conversations meant for nothing more than to avoid the subject on everyone's mind.

"Julie, you have to remember to water the plants," Barb says.

"Yeah, sure," Julie replies.

"They will need the first half of my tuition by the end of next week," Julie tells me absently.

"Yeah, sure," I tell Julie. The fact that it will drain my savings account doesn't register. It doesn't matter at the moment.

We hang around the hospital until 10 p.m. They bend visitation hours for family members on the day of surgery, but we were given a brochure with the visitation times clearly printed for future use.

The room is filled with flowers and balloons. A basket of daisies from neighbors Lucy, Rosie, and Judith: "Get Well Quick." A bouquet of a dozen roses from—I have to lean closer to read the name—Stuart. Ah! The man-friend. Still haven't met him. Still don't want to. Three carnations in a skinny-necked vase from Barb and Barry's kids, Nicholas, Nathan and Natalie: "Love you Grammy." A tidy centerpiece: "Cooper, Cooper and Zarembinski, Attorneys at Law." A bowl of begonias: "Rick's Nick's and everyone in the Park wish you well." A bouquet of balloons from Grandma Jazz: "You Go Girl!" A potted philodendron with a purple bow: "Get Well, Bob." I look at Bob. He looks back blankly. Then I realize the bouquet must be from Bob Senior—Dad. Imagine that.

A stack of cards fills a basket but I avoid riffling through them. I'm feeling anxious and want to leave, get out of this hospital, away from death. But I don't want to leave Mom here by herself. I want to scoop her up and take her with me.

"Go home," Barb tells us. "Mom needs her rest. We all look toward the bed where our mother lays sound asleep. The monitor beeps softly and rhythmically next to her. "I'll tell Mom you said goodbye. Don't wake her now. Let her sleep," she tells us.

Bob, Julie and I walk three abreast down the hallway without saying a word to one another. I press the down button to call the elevator to the fifth floor. We remain at attention facing the doors until they open. When they do, we all step inside, turn around and face the doors like well-practiced soldiers. Our descent begins with a jolt. The floor of the elevator seems to pull away from the soles of my feet a little faster than my brain says it ought to and causes butterflies to swarm in my stomach. We ride in silence as though we each are

73

descending in our own private chambers. When the doors finally open, we are mercifully at the lobby level. We pile out and nearly bolt for the door. Outside the air is so thick and humid it's as though we are engulfed by great arms and clutched to a generous bosom, but it is a relief from the cold, air-conditioned atmosphere from which we had just come. The three of us form a tight circle to where our shoulders nearly touch as we struggle to regain our individual momentum while we each look to one another for reassurance.

"Do you want to stay the night at the house?" Julie asks me.

"No," I begin to say, then realize it was a request rather than a question. "I mean, yeah. I think I'd like that. My old room available?"

Her face brightens. "Who else would take it?"

Bob bugs out for his place while I follow Julie back to Mom's. Once away from the hospital my emotions level out and my confidence in modern medicine returns. Mom will be fine in a few days, I think to myself while staring at all the bumper stickers on the old family van as I follow Julie home.

There are about fifteen or so plastered all over the backside of the van in no apparent sequence. Several read "The Fiddlers Park Fantasticks." Julie got a little carried away with the stickers her first year on the dance squad. The appearance of only one each of all the others stuck there was more civilized, such as the "Fighting Piranhas"—the school football team on which I had played—and the maroon and gold insignia for the University of Minnesota.

As we turn into the driveway our headlights flash against the privacy fence. I purposefully look around the back yard with more observation than I usually exercise. The old swing set continues to rust in the far corner. Grass grows over where the garden used to be. Clothespins dangle from the clothesline strung between the two posts. The garage needs painting, I think to myself as I mount the back steps behind Julie.

Once inside I head to the counter where there is a line of pans with food.

"What a pig," Julie says as I grab a clump of cake with my fingers and stuff it into my mouth, then lick chocolate frosting from between my fingers.

"Mmmmm," I moan, much to her disgust.

She puts on the teapot and pulls a couple cups from the cupboard. We don't use saucers if Mom isn't around, but Julie thinks twice and pulls two saucers from the cupboard as well.

While I wait at the table, I open my briefcase and pull out my checkbook. "How much should I write it for?" I ask, eager to change the focus toward the future and give us both some relief from the past few hours.

"Thirteen-thousand-two-hundred," she replies. There is a note of reluctance in her voice as her childhood dreams materialize into adult-like appreciation for the sacrifice others are willing to make on her behalf.

"I'll make it out for $15,000. Let me know when you need more." It leaves me exactly $302 in my savings account, but I keep that fact to myself.

She walks over and puts her arms around my neck and kisses me on top of my head while the teapot screams.

CHAPTER 6: INTO THE STARTING STALLS
NEW YORK, NEW YORK

SUNDAY, JUNE 17, 2007: 2:49 P.M. (EDT)

My first glimpse of New York City is from a porthole on a Boeing747. It is from this tiny window that I first witness more concrete than I am able to comprehend. Manmade everything spreads over the entire island of Manhattan and what I can see of New Jersey. The magnitude of artificial material to the exclusion of anything natural overwhelms me. The lack of tree-shaded streets and grassy boulevards seemed unnervingly odd, yet terribly exciting and different. New York City! To Charlie, who seems to doze with his seat in its upright position while landing, this is nothing unusual.

While I continue to stare out the window the plane banks sharply to the left, over rows of cubicle-like fencing that surround tiny little houses with yards so small a dog would have trouble finding a place to crap. It looks like the federal housing projects we have back in north Minneapolis.

"The Bronx," Charlie says over my shoulder.

Looking down I feel stifled by what I see. I've always thought of New York as being the place where dreams come true. Not too many dreams came true for these folks, I think to myself.

Once we disembark, we are pushed along in a stream of people down an escalator and past rows of baggage carousels. Charlie and I walk past it all and out the doors with our bags slung over our shoulders. A sense of possibility overtakes me as soon as we step from the terminal. Thoughts of everything that has gone on before and everything yet to come culminate in an instant and seem to rumble up my spine as though they will blow out the top of my head. New York. It is no longer a vision. It is a reality. My head snaps in all directions, taking everything in. I promise myself I'll stop acting like a jerk-tourist once I get to the hotel, but right now I want to absorb everything ... I want to become one with New York. Charlie just wants me to get into the damned cab.

"C'*mon*," he hollers from the backseat of a yellow taxi.

I get in and immediately sink to the floorboards for lack of any life left in the seat cushions, or perhaps due to too much life that had occurred upon them. Mohammad Karim, #44234 is the driver. The four or five pine-scented air fresheners dangling from Mohammad's rearview mirror don't begin to cut through the smells of curry and gym shorts. I am forced to grab the armrest to avoid sliding over to Charlie every time Mohammad takes a corner. Charlie slams up against his side of the vehicle and yawns.

Maugham Southerby had acquired the respect of the financial world not only by being the largest investment bank in the world but also by being known as the best trainers of financial advisors in the industry. At least that's what old Crosby told us. We hadn't seen him during the past two weeks while we crammed for our securities licensing exams, but just before we left the office Friday, he was right there giving us orders in no uncertain terms.

"You are a couple of lucky sons-of-bitches," he had said, pointing his index finger toward our noses to accentuate what a golden opportunity it was for a couple of piss-heads like us to be with Maugham Southerby.

"Should I get on my knees?" I said before I could stop the words from leaving my mouth.

Crosby just stared into the pupils of my eyes for several minutes before he continued. "About ten in every training group gets sent home because of something they did or didn't do. If you didn't complete an assignment, if you were tardy more than three times, if you didn't conduct yourself appropriately at all times … if you fart, for Christ's sake," he added. "No funny stuff like going out on the town all night and crawling into training thinking you can sleep your way through class because you can't," he told us. "No acting cocky either," he went on. "You are just a couple of bums off the street and believe me when I tell you neither of you know anything about anything in this business … do you understand me?"

He looked at Charlie first and when he turned to me I had quickly nodded.

"You got one go-round to make it at Maugham Southerby. One." He emphasized the number one by holding up his index finger so close to my face I went cross-eyed looking at. "Learn it in New York because I ain't teaching it to you when you get back. Understand?" We said we did, but neither of us could have understood what we were really getting into.

"The party is about to start, gentlemen." He left the room and it was minutes before either one of us spoke.

Now, as I stare at the back of Mohammed's head, I recall Crosby's final words. Our training would culminate with a graduation ceremony if we were one of the lucky ones. His snort was clear indication he didn't think we would be among that group. He blew us off with a wave of his hand, as though it would be the last time he'd have to deal with us. Wrong, I now think to myself as I recall that look in his eye. I want it. I want it all! "I'll be back," I say aloud, as though I'm telling Crosby to his face. Charlie looks over at me. Mohammed looks at me in his rearview mirror. I don't notice either of them. I am too engrossed in my own intention of making it to the top at Maugham Southerby. My eyes wander upward toward the tops of the skyscrapers though I cannot see them from inside this cab. Brick walls surround us in every direction, yet we keep moving.

A uniformed doorman of the Manhattan Grand Hotel opens our cab door with a white-gloved hand the second it comes to a stop. He gives us a quick nod and with the flick of his finger has two white-gloved bellhops reaching for our bags. A tall man rushes toward us as we enter the lobby. He wears a blazer of the same royal blue only without a gold braid around the cuffs like the doorman and bellhop uniforms. On his lapel is a red rose and just below it is a gold nametag that says Sherman Scholze, Manager. As soon as he learns we are with Maugham Southerby he motions for one of the busy clerks behind the desk to drop everything and attend to getting our room assignment, which the clerk promptly does.

Without losing a step the manager hands us off to the two bellhops whom we follow into an elevator being held open for us by a white-gloved elevator operator. The panel buttons are numbered 2 to 42. Button 38 is pressed by a gloved hand. The copper panels inside the elevator are polished so well I can see the sweat beads on my temples.

Classical music accompanies us upward. The doors open to a posh ancillary foyer carpeted in a busy print of royal blue and gold. Opposite the elevator is a gold-framed mirror the size of a picture window flanked by tall thin lamps with black shades trimmed in gold on a gold-filigreed table between two wingback chairs upholstered in royal blue velvet. Similar tables and lamps line the hallway in both directions. Next to each door is a frosted glass wall lamp in the shape of a tulip. Each door is painted a glossy black and embellished by gold numbers. I swear if you yelled down the hallway the fibers of the floors and walls would absorb the sound entirely. It feels like a womb. Quiet. Protected from the outside world. Safe.

We follow the silent bellhops down a long corridor to the end of the hall, turn right and continue down another long hallway to the very last door. The lead bellhop seems to open the door by magic as we are led efficiently inside. Our suitcases are quickly set upon mahogany benches at the foot of each queen size bed. Draperies are flung open by experienced hands. Charlie stuffs money into the palms of both hops and heads for the bathroom with a groan about how he's had to pee since we left the airport.

I walk from window to window, looking first out over Madison Square Garden. Moving to the south window I am transfixed as I gaze down Seventh Street toward Times Square. Times Square! I'd seen it every New Year's Eve on television since the time I could stay up late enough to watch. Two years ago, I had gone home alone from a New Year's Eve party because my date was mad I wouldn't kiss her until after the ball finished dropping. It's bad luck if you don't watch the ball drop. And I was right, because I am one lucky guy right now, man. One lucky guy.

I look over to Charlie who is coming out of the bathroom still zipping up his fly. "I know why I'm here," I begin. "But why are you here?" I ask. Charlie had been stroking prospects since the day we met. He was a whole-life insurance agent with Tri-Star. Until this very moment, it hadn't occurred to me to ask why he worked in the first place. Why isn't he soaking up big daddy's bucks? My brow scrunches in confusion.

Charlie shrugs and opens the minibar. As he uncaps a tiny bottle of scotch and pours it into a lead crystal glass sitting on a silver tray he mumbles a few incoherent words and gestures, like he doesn't have an answer.

In my world, everyone *has* to work. In Charlie's world, there are options. Why not open a bait shop on some sandy beach? Why not travel to Antarctica and explore new species of fish? There must be something in the world for a rich kid to do besides sell insurance—or securities. Charlie takes a swig of his drink and winks at me over the rim of his glass. What is he up to, I wonder? But that's all he's going to say right now.

I turn to look out the window again. Four lanes of yellow cabs stream up Seventh Avenue like those rabbit races at the carnivals. The traffic drone is faint from up this high, but I can still discern the horns honking. People are everywhere. They pour from buildings, from around corners, they eke from subway portals like some great lava flow that bubbles up from the bowels of the earth. Everyone wears black or shades of gray. One giant stream of humanity. I suck in the chronic energy of this great and grand city through my eyeballs. To a Minnesota boy who grew up listening to loon calls across a quiet lake while watching a bobber every summer and hearing squirrels scurry among dry leaves while sitting in a deer blind for hours every fall, it is hard to comprehend this magnitude of manmade energy. An energy so great it drowns out the very existence of nature and replaces it with brick and mortar, steel and iron, tar and rocks; then tops it off with bronze icons—statues that remain transfixed in their epitaph on humanity and that symbolize defiance against all powers of nature now and forever.

I wonder what this very spot on the face of this earth had been like before endless motion overtook it, when wild game wandered and prowled here, when birds perched upon branches and listened for the sound of worms burrowing through the earth, when thunder was the only noise that could drown out the sound of the wind? It was upon this very spot that all those things had happened for millions of years ... until man covered it in concrete and began to trod upon it one generation after the other, a passing of the baton ... one continuous motion that now throbs like an immortal heartbeat. This is a place of human energy that is churned by its own perpetual motion—a motion that cannot stop—will not stop until the last heart ceases to beat on this planet. New York City.

MONDAY, JUNE 18, 2007: 6:10 A.M. (EDT)

Charlie's snoring isn't what kept me awake last night. It was the voice in my head that kept reminding me I am in New York City ... the place where everything happens ... where everything is starting to happen for *me*.

We were told a chartered bus would pick us up across the street from the hotel at exactly 6:25 a.m. every morning. We had been given orders to board the bus between 6:25 and 6:30 a.m., no sooner, no later. If anyone missed the bus it would be one demerit. Precision is paramount in this business, we had been told. It had all sounded good to me—even made me feel proud to be among those who had been chosen for this mission. But in light of a missed wake-up call, it all seems a little stringent when Charlie and I bump butts in front of the mirror as we try to get our asses in gear to meet the damned bus in time.

We are forced to sprint across the street, dodging cabs. By the time I place my foot on the first step of the chartered Greyhound, the driver has his hand on the door handle. He rolls his eyes like we just stole his only joy in life and tells us, "It is 6:29 a.m. and twenty-nine seconds. Thirty-one seconds more and you would have been left behind, gentlemen," he says, tapping his finger to the face of his wristwatch.

I marvel at the magnitude of skyscrapers as we drive through lower Manhattan and wonder if an island can sink under the weight of such things. We arrive at the east entrance to the Broadmoor Building at exactly 6:43 a.m. The Broadmoor Building is where the headquarters for Maugham Southerby repositioned after the World Trade Center was attacked on 9-11. It is nearly as big as the North Tower once had been and, in many ways, equally impressive but not as tall—only seventy-five stories high. Its exterior is glass and reflects the images of all the other buildings around it. The sidewalk surrounding the building is wider than the street and there are benches and marble urns of flowers and a statue of some guy ... must be Hamilton Broadmoor, financial tycoon and father of Broadmoor Mutual Funds, now the second largest family of funds in the world and also headquartered in this building.

We are eager to disembark the bus, but the driver refuses to open the doors until 6:45 a.m. His orders, he says. When he opens the doors, succulent smells waft in from the street carts that circle the exit of the bus hosting coffee, Danish rolls, bagels, and muffins. My stomach growls so hard my whole body vibrates. Charlie pulls me away and pushes me toward the entrance of the building with one thing on his mind. We still have to cross the concourse, pass through security checkpoints and reach the training center by 7 a.m. I am hot on Charlie's tail, but when I glance at the guys behind us lining up at the coffee cart my anxiety rises, although I don't know whether for them or myself.

The concourse to the Broadmoor Building is nearly empty this time of morning considering the 150-thousand or so who will fill its seven-million square feet of office space by nine—plus the thousands of mall shoppers and tourists who infiltrate like an Alaskan salmon run. I can distinguish my own footsteps as they clash against the polished granite in my effort to keep pace beside Charlie.

A few men emerge from the massive stairwell that leads to one of the seven levels below ground, and access to the IRT Broadway-Seventh Avenue line of the New York City subway. They begin to stroll in the same direction as us, each impeccably dressed—starched white shirts, well-polished shoes. Some carry thin briefcases, but all have *The Wall Street Journal* under their arm. My neck strains as I watch one guy walk with a calm sense of direction toward the same set of elevators for which Charlie and I are now breaking into a sprint. He looks me in the eye and smiles slightly. It must be obvious I am part of a pack of rookies. Someday I'll be like him, moving by my own volition through the corridors of this financial district, intent upon my goals and sure of myself. But today, I just better get my cheeks in a seat in the training room on time.

What did they do, hire an Olympic runner to determine the minimum amount of time it takes to get from the bus to the training room? What was the point of timing every move we make? I pick up the pace to get ahead of the pack, which has grown now that we are closer to the checkpoint. Charlie and I are the first ones through the gates. We pull out our Maugham Southerby badges and identification and sign a sheet fastened to a clipboard. A fat little guy in a maroon uniform with a patch of the Broadmoor Building on his left sleeve is ready to give us instructions. We are to take this elevator to the forty-fourth floor, get off, turn to our right, and go to another elevator that will take us to the sixty-first floor. "Are there any questions?"

"Would that be to our right facing the elevator as we now stand, or from inside the elevator?" someone asks.

I'm glad it wasn't me who asked the question as the fat little guy in the maroon uniform glares at the woman who did and explains that it was from "inside" the elevator from which she would take a right. That now being crystal clear we are all herded into the elevator. Charlie checks his watch.

As soon as the doors of the elevator close there are grumbles about the early hour, comments about the stringent time limits that had been imposed on us, and a few insinuations of having our civil rights denied. But it doesn't mean much in light of the fact we are all still high from being courted by one of the biggest investment banks in the world and being catered to in styles which few of us have ever been exposed to our entire lives.

The elevator lobby opens to the sixty-first floor, which is full of rookies all trying to squeeze through the doors to suite #6101, Maugham Southerby Training Center for Financial Advisors. A big black man with a gold name tag that reads "George" and a smile that says "Don't make me have to kill you" forces us all to succumb to his personal requirements before anyone is allowed to enter. Soon the mob forms a line that passes civilly through the threshold. It is now 6:51 a.m. We will be told fifteen minutes from now that five people didn't make it on time and got their first demerit. Two more demerits and they are out. It will serve as a reminder to the rest of us to always be on time.

To our left is a cove in which there are four giant coffee dispensers that are polished to a shine I haven't seen since Uncle Billy's bumper on his '57 Chev classic. Next to that is a marble counter that looks like the check-in counter at the hotel, only there is a small gold plaque to one end that reads "Maugham Southerby Trainee Assistance and Service Center." Three gray-suited young men line the back wall as though ordered to stand at ease by a military commanding officer. One similarly dressed young woman behind the same counter listens intently to a man in a brown tweed sports jacket and tan Dockers asking where he can plug in his cell phone while he's in class.

Charlie walks past it all like he's been here before. We step through an arch held up by two columns that would rival classical Rome and onto carpet that seems to embrace every footstep in luxury. The entire opposite wall is glass from floor to ceiling and wraps around the room capturing a view of all Manhattan and most of New Jersey. My mouth opens in awe, but before I can say a thing, Charlie lowers his lips to my ear and tells me to stop looking like I am just off the farm. I close my mouth and look around the room. When I turn back toward Charlie he is gone.

I shove my hands into my pants pockets and find a couple of quarters to twirl in the right one. The sun is just on the horizon, or perhaps I am up so high I can see *over* the horizon. This must be what God sees ... the world at his feet. For the first time, I feel like the title on the business cards—the ones I had tucked neatly into a new leather holder and placed in my right suit pocket—the ones that read: David D. Yates, Financial Advisor. This is the turning point for me, the new persona that I will assume, the one that dismisses my authentic self and transforms me into someone I long to become. I have already begun to live and breathe my own delusion as we all must do to survive in this business.

I walk over to a small group of people gathered near the windows and listen to their chatter. It's all about how the money is made, where the money is found, what you have to do to get at the money. They tell each other because nobody else in their life is listening ... just yet. So they use each other as practice, I guess. It all sounds good to me. It is the external noise we all must learn to make if we are ever to gain a client. I stand here smiling and nodding like I agree with what the guy on the couch is saying. Then he turns directly toward me and says to the few people standing around him, "You can't be afraid to get into futures and commodities, even during the good times, am I right?" He looks to me for the answer.

I nod as though I am on cue, but I don't have handle enough on any of this yet to offer a viable opinion. Since I don't want to appear like the dummy I really am, I side with the guy who seems to know it all.

An indiscreet bell goes off and everyone stands up straight away and begins to migrate toward the top of a slight ramp where double doors are now open to the training room. One large garbage can is receiving the Styrofoam cups with leftover coffee that some had just poured themselves in the lobby, and plastic bottles of Diet Coke, Mountain Dew, and Fiji water that had been brought in by a few rookies who didn't read their briefing notes: "Do not bring food or drink to the training center." Two men in business suits stand guard at the door to enforce that rule, much to the groans of many who still can't see the point.

"They use this same tactic in boot camp," says a guy to my left sporting a heinie. "It's how they remove a person's self-reliance. Control their food, drink, and freedom for twenty-one days and you can break a person's independence," he tells me. He looks me in the eye to see whether I am swallowing this.

I'm not. Why would Maugham Southerby want to control its financial advisors? We're not here to learn to take orders. This isn't the military. We're here to learn how to make people a lot of money. I brush the guy off like a bum on the street. Besides, training is twenty-six days, not twenty-one.

By 7:00 a.m. sharp the doors to the training room are closed. The guy up front orders everyone to quickly find a seat.

Three hundred desks complete with computer monitors and materials fill the main floor in rows of sixteen, divided by two aisles. There is an elevated area that is separated from the main floor by three steps. Screens are placed at each side at the midsection of the room for those who sit farther back from the front. I choose a desk in the middle of the left row on the main floor. Charlie comes out of nowhere and sits at the desk next to me on the inside isle.

About twenty men, all wearing suits, line the far wall. They stand erect with arms across their chests like thugs at a mafia meeting. Another clone steps in front of the room and stands in a similar position only his arms hang loose at his sides. His eyes rove about the room, and for some strange reason his posture commands everyone's attention. The shuffling and talking die down quickly. Charlie and I look at one another and shrug.

The guy at the front of the room does not introduce himself. He reminds us that no food or drinks are allowed in the training room. We are to refrain from using the restrooms except for scheduled breaks. Should we not return from break before the doors close, we will receive one demerit. Three demerits and we will be immediately terminated from Maugham Southerby forever. I audibly groan at having heard all this before. The guy in front pauses to stare at me before he goes on to tell us there is a key in the top drawer of each desk that fits a lock on the top drawer, which locks the entire desk. We all open our drawers and locate our keys.

We are responsible for the safety of our own belongings and for returning the key on the last day of training. Someone cries out they are missing their key. That person is ignored, but the man up front raises his voice. "Please address all your needs to a person at the Trainee Assistance and Service Center." Then he continues in his monotone. The room will be locked each night and during breaks. The bottom right-hand drawer of the desk is a file drawer. Inside we are to find our training manuals and an adequate supply of paper and folders.

I inventory my drawer. Three legal pads, five hanging file folders with tabs that read: Compliance and Penalties, FinRA, Continuing Education Requirements, State Regulation, Due Diligence; and one three-ring binder that is thicker than a can of coke is high.

The nameless guy at the front of the room gives us a few seconds to survey our materials before he commands our attention once again. "You're here to learn how to become a financial advisor for Maugham Southerby," he says as he holds his hands behind his back and stands feet slightly apart, back straight. "Time is money. If you're not making money, you are wasting time." He pauses and looks about the room. "Anyone here interested in money?" he asks. The room erupts in cheers and whistles. I feel a surge of adrenaline so strong I have to mentally restrain myself from jumping out of my seat. I feel like a racehorse in the gates.

THURSDAY, JUNE 21, 2007: 8:22 A.M. (EDT)

The training center is three blocks away from the New York Stock Exchange—the heart of world trade. By the end of the first day, I swear I felt the world's pulse beating in my very own veins, but each day a small group of rookies is taken to the exchange for a *real* glimpse of Wall Street. Charlie and I are the lucky ones on day four.

At exactly 8:22 a.m. a husky fellow enters the room and points a finger at the next rows of trainees destined to tour the trading floor. We know the routine by now and rise and follow him out of the room. Husky ushers us down the elevators, across the mezzanine, out the doors and over the two blocks to the stock exchange. A line of tourists huddle near the front steps but Husky leads us right past and into the building ahead of them all in spite of their protests.

Once inside the exchange, we are passed off to a gawky guy wearing an usher's uniform with a patch that bears the emblem of the New York Stock Exchange. He leads us down a hallway filled with history panels that can't be read at the pace we are walking. We are to come back on our own time, he tells us over his shoulder. Gawky lines us up in front of the observation window from which we look out over the entire trading floor from the second story. I see the clock above the small balcony to our right. On the opposite wall and above the heads of all is a row of huge clocks that bear the world's time zones: New York, London, Frankfurt, Hong Kong, Tokyo.

The observatory room begins to fill with grumbling tourists who are still annoyed we were led in before them and had nailed the best spots for viewing. The floor below is just coming to life with people strolling to their stations, some with coffee cup in hand or a donut in their mouth. The floor is dotted with several kiosks with monitors that are lifeless. Two men huddle in urgent conversation near one, then one of them leaves on a dead run. Another person looks toward the observatory window and yawns, triggering one from me. I try to resist, but before I know it my mouth is gaping at the ceiling and my eyes shut involuntarily as my brain shudders between my ears. By the time I re-open my eyes the floor seems to have come alive with bobbing heads. The paper coffee cups are now being tossed into wastebaskets. I glance at the clock above the balcony where the infamous bell is waiting to be rung by some honored member of society and wonder who it will be this morning. It is three minutes to nine.

Our attention is drawn to the rush of someone coming toward us. It is a wild-eyed woman in a white blouse buttoned to the neck and hair pulled back into a bun wearing thick black-rimmed glasses and a Blue Tooth stuck to her ear. She is clutching a clipboard like it is a child whom she had just snatched from the path of a speeding bus. Breathlessly she points to five of us, me being one, and tells us to follow her. I glance over my shoulder at Charlie who is left behind. He nods. I shrug.

As the five of us scurry after the woman, she confirms we are members of the Maugham Southerby training class, which are regulars at the NYSE. We confirm we are. She cups her hand over her earplug and says something to someone listening on the other end.

Mayor Booker from Newark was supposed to ring the opening bell this morning, but had an emergency and the backup they'd lined up just fainted, she tells us. We are to fill in. She points us through a small door that leads to the balcony over the trading floor of the New York Stock Exchange. The mumbling and scuffling from the floor below remarkably fall silent at the same time someone else pushes against the back of my elbow, forcing my arm to thrust forward in an awkward position. I freeze out of fear and anxiety, my arm still suspended in mid-air. Then someone says between their teeth, "Press the bell, stupid."

I swing my arm downward and feel the vibration of the bell ring through my body. The frenzy that erupts on the floor of the NYSE below me is indwelled in my mind indefinitely.

The next two weeks are a blur of terminology and strategies I'd never heard of before. Growth potential, earnings, price-to-value ratios, price-to-earnings comparisons, liquidity ratios, price-to-book value—it's all Greek to me, but I write things down furiously hoping to capture enough that it might make sense in the future. But some don't take any notes. I wonder why they feel so confident, or if they know so much.

A string of highly paid financial advisors within Maugham Southerby parade before us in tailored suits and white collars—gold cufflinks and Rolex watches living testimony that success in this business is attainable. They reveal that their annual commission checks surpass the multi-million dollar mark. Then they tell us how we can do it, too. We drool with abandon.

On the second to the last day of training, Mike Valento, Maugham Southerby CEO, takes the podium in the grand hall. The room falls silent as though the trumpets just sounded and the king had emerged. He reeks of power. He's calm with confidence. He smiles politely, somewhat humbly. His eyes look with intent throughout the room as though he is taking in every single face here. Every eye is upon him while everyone in the room waits for him to complete his survey. Then, he speaks. "Ladies and gentlemen." His voice is almost a whisper. Everyone in the room leans forward in their chairs. "You are the most qualified security agents in the entire world." He says the words 'entire' and 'world' distinctly and raises his voice with every word he utters. "This is *your* time," he belts out, then pauses and again looks about the room. This time our eyes meet dead on. I feel a surge of adrenaline.

He continues. "The bar is set high on purpose. Only the best of you will survive the first year at Maugham Southerby. We can afford to do no less if we intend to remain the most powerful investment bank in the world." Charlie's neck stretches to those words.

"Twenty-nine people have been cut and sent home."

That little announcement ramps up the stakes. However, the more they poke at my insecurity the more it builds my resolve.

"Ladies and gentlemen," he says again. "Welcome to your destiny. This is where it all begins or ends. The choice is up to you." He looks about the room one more time, then raises his hand in the air in a wave as he leaves. "Best of luck to you all." Cheers erupt as everyone jumps to their feet and all begin clapping in a standing ovation to which there is no encore. Charlie heads for the door and tells me he'll catch me later back at our room, that he has to meet someone for dinner.

It's nearly 8 p.m. by the time the last of us leave the training floor. Someone suggests we get something to eat. We wind up at the lobby bar of our hotel. For the first few minutes we all stare at the TV screens, giving respite to our weary brains, but pretty soon someone starts talking about how they are going to make it big in this business. Then some wise ass decides to run the numbers on our little group. He counts heads. "Out of the ten of us standing here right now," he says, "only one of us will be left standing in less than twelve months." We all fall silent as that little tidbit sinks into our meager brains. Eyes glance around the group as each of us try to figure out who that one person will be.

"What happens to the 90 percent?" I ask of the greater magnitude of trainees who are anticipated to fall off the vine. They all look at me like I've asked them if I can stick my finger up their butt.

"Who cares?" someone replies. "They're the losers." They all laugh and close their shoulders toward me as they huddle closer to the bar.

I wasn't asking out of compassion. I was asking because it should be a question we should *all* be asking. We had been geared up to think the game was high stakes and competitive, which is fine. But nothing was said about the cards being stacked against us. The sudden reality shoots through me like a bolt of electricity.

My mind starts calculating the odds. If 90 percent actually fail in the first year, then the standards *must* be set too high—or set high on purpose. Let's see, I think to myself as the numbers come to mind ... I grab a napkin and take a seat at one of the little tables to figure it out. After making a few scratches I sit back, take a pull on my beer, and stare at the numbers on the napkin in the palm of my hand—a low estimate of the assets left on the table when a rookie gets the boot. Not a bad way to grow business, I think to myself. Ingenious. They make us believe we are behind the wheel of an SCC Ultimate Aero that will take us to our fortune in record time when, in fact, we're driving nothing but a dump truck and hauling in assets for them!

"Fuck," I say loud enough that a few from the group hear me and turn their heads. All that talk from Valento about being the best was nothing but hype to get all us rookies to pony up. I tip my Heineken to them. "We're on the list to be fucked over," I say to them.

They turn their backs to me, certain I am one of the future losers. What they don't know yet is so are they. This sucks, I think to myself. I've been screwed over like an idiot. Then I realize Charlie must have known this all along. I pelt from the bar area and head to the elevators.

I stomp down the hallway, blast into the room, and grab Charlie by the shirt collar. Our eyes meet as I pull his face toward mine. He doesn't blink. "What am I doing here?" I ask half growling, half sneering and fully ready to bury my fist into his pretty little face.

"Training," he replies, casually ignoring the fact that I am choking the life out of him with his own tie.

"Training for what?" I tighten my grip and give him a shake. "For you to offer me up as some sacrifice to the Wall Street gods?"

"I probably should have told you."

I shove him back down into his chair with such force the chair nearly tips over. "Told me what?"

It had been Jack Garrison who first revealed to Charlie how Maugham Southerby pads its pockets by continually rolling heads of rookies. It was no wonder it had gained a reputation of offering the best securities training in the industry. The more people it hired and trained, the more money rolled into its coffers. The very sales pitches they are teaching us in training class are the very blades they use to stick into our backs. It is pretty difficult to un-sell something you've just sold, especially when it is sold to family and friends—which is the first sales list they tell us to make and work from.

"When Jack told me what Maugham is doing I initially felt the same righteous indignation as you." Charlie gets up and grabs another little bottle from the mini bar and pours himself another scotch on the rocks. He takes the glass in his hands, leans against the edge of the dresser, and crosses his ankles. He takes a sip and smirks, then continues. "But two can play the same game." Charlie sits back down across from me and explains an elaborate plan to use Maugham for all its worth before absconding with what he will need to build his own empire—a boutique international investment bank.

As I listen, my eyes roll a few times and I whistle softly as though I fully comprehend what he is saying, which I don't. But I get the drift. He anticipated my being part of the plan all along, but wanted to verify everything before he pulled me in on it. "You had nothing to lose, and everything to gain," he adds, using my maxim to assure me he'd thought things through on my behalf.

"And if you were wrong?"

"You'd be working for my father someplace."

I let that gel before I ask whether Charlie's plan is better.

He nods with a wry grin.

"What do you want me to do?"

"*You* keep your job at Maugham. Make stats," he orders, pointing a finger at me. His eyes narrow.

So do mine.

FRIDAY, JULY 13, 2007: 12:11 P.M. (EDT)

It is the final day of training. By the time they let us out for lunch, I'm a bundle of testosterone and feeling like a bull in the chute; but instead of busting into the arena all I can do is follow Charlie through the crowd in the cafeteria to find an empty table. He leaves me holding the table while he goes for food. By the time Charlie returns with a couple of hot dogs for each of us, I am absorbed by a small article on page two in *The Wall Street Journal*.

"Says here CDOs are about to explode," I convey to Charlie with a note of sincere concern.

He nods while a sliver of tomato-based sauerkraut and frankfurter juice escapes his lips.

Evidently, he didn't hear me. I read on. "It says here they are a house of cards ... that since there are no underlying securities these things are little more than bets, and that the whole thing could cave in, causing a world economic crisis." In all seriousness, I search Charlie's eyes. If Charlie plans to stake his future dreams—our future dreams—on these things, does he realize how fragile they are?

His eyelids close as though he is blocking out the ridiculous thing I just said. He pushes the last of his hot dog into his mouth and slowly chews, then swallows. He wipes his fingers thoroughly on the paper napkin unhurriedly while he sucks on his teeth and probes his mouth with his tongue for lagging bits of hot dog. He's fully aware I am waiting. It's his ritual to pause at length whenever he thinks I've asked a dumb question. I never know if he is contemplating an answer or merely counting to ten. Despite Crosby's warning to not trust anyone in this business, I evaluate my alternatives. None. So, I wait.

"First of all," he begins with a note of authority, "you can't believe everything you read. Journalists look for the sizzle in everything just to sell newspapers."

"What's second?"

His expression questions whether I am serious or not.

I am.

He leans across the table on his elbows and with sarcasm repeats himself. "Secondly," he pauses for added effect, then finishes, "risk is the *name* of the game. Everything eventually goes boom!" His eyes widen and he waggles his fingers into my face to accentuate the word 'boom.' Then he gets up off his chair so abruptly it tips and clanks loudly to the floor. Charlie walks away, oblivious.

People turn in my direction while I contemplate the ignorance it takes to ignore such indicators, but then what do I really know? I'm just a rookie fresh out of the chutes. If there was something to be concerned about wouldn't you think they would tell us in class, or a memo, or something? I sit there a few seconds longer, wallowing in reluctance before I take off after Charlie.

CHAPTER 7: RUNNING WITH BULLS
MINNEAPOLIS, MINNESOTA

FRIDAY, JULY 20, 2007: 7:35 A.M. (CDT)

Since returning from New York there's been an extra spring in my step. Nothing seems to irritate me these days except Manny Vulpine, a rookie who started nine months before Charlie and I.

I see the top of Manny's head from where I sit in the bullpen. The bullpen is eight cubicles of mahogany walls just high enough for our eyes to peer over if we are sitting down. It's where everyone starts at Maugham Southerby. It's meant to distinguish the big dogs from the pups and to remind the pups they are nothing but pups.

It also keeps office expense to a minimum. With the average length of stay for a rookie being less than six months, it makes no sense to give them an office and their own waste-basket. Instead, rookies get a tabletop, a not-so-ergonomically-correct secretary's chair, and a set of headphones. There is one waste-basket for all eight cubicles. I'm on the opposite side of the waste-basket that sets right next to Manny. We do, however, get our own terminals from which we can watch every trade made from the floor of the New York Stock Exchange. That's all that really matters in this business.

Most of the other brokers in the office by-pass us without so much as a glance. The few who talk to us have one of two reasons for doing so. They either are sniffing around our accounts so they can vie for them once we get the boot, or they are in need of a cheap ego boost. Either way, they make me sick; but not as sick as I get just looking at Manny.

Manny has exceeded his six-month expectation here at Maugham, which is surprising since the assets he has under his management are less than eight million. It can only mean he churns accounts to make his numbers and hasn't gotten caught yet, or he's into something more clandestine.

Manny is a slimeball. Brags that he has the corner on little old ladies here in the midwest, that they are so much more gullible than the old bats in Newark where he's from. Says he gets them wishing he was the son they never had. Takes them to lunch, buys them flowers, and never forgets their birthdays. Then bilks them for fee-based services he never performs. His lack of decency makes my skin crawl.

"Hey, Manny," I holler softly. He looks up over the top of the half-wall. "You're up today," I remind him of his duty to pull rotation. It means he has to stay in the branch until five o'clock to be available to potential walk-ins. They make rookies take turns doing this because everyone else cuts out early most days and especially on Fridays. He ignores me but I know he feels the proverbial dust I just kicked in his face. I smile. My eyes narrow. My nostrils flare.

Monday, July 23, 2007: 6:30 a.m. (CDT)

New York training had introduced me to powerful things: derivatives, options, futures, IPOs, convertible bonds, investment-grade bonds, hedge funds, exchange-traded funds—tools of our trade. I learned investment portfolio management theories that make money on investments during any type of market or economic upturn or downturn. Maugham Southerby is the largest brokerage firm in the world, holds seats on every exchange, and has a legion of people who pump out the best stock analysis and research in the world. I have access to any publicly traded stock, bond, fund, trust, or certificate of deposit out there. I feel light-headed just thinking about such power.

I grab a cup of coffee and check my email before I head to the conference room for Morning Call, note pad and pencil in hand. The room is large enough to hold all fifty-or-so advisors assigned to this branch, but only the rookies and a couple senior advisors ever show, and it is only the rookies who ever take a seat. Senior advisors stand at the open door with Blackberries in hand, fully prepared to dash to their offices for important calls. It is where the pack draws the line. I take a seat closest to the door. The light from the hallway is all that illuminates the room. A blue glow falls on our upturned faces as we wait for the first report. I can smell the starch in the shirt of the guy sitting next to me … or maybe it's my own.

They are having some difficulty with the closed-circuit connection, as usual, but nobody shows any sign of annoyance nor makes any comment. We have more things to worry about than minor technical glitches. It is our job to be focused on bigger matters ... worldly matters ... trends ... even political and military movements. We are the keepers of dreams. It is our main mission to find money and bring it back to Maugham Southerby as fast as we can. Our eyes meet, but we keep to ourselves. No one speaks or even nods. We sit poised in our chairs, waiting for intelligence from headquarters.

Adrenalin surges through my veins. My jaw clenches. My eyes narrow. I snort pompously. This is the cusp of the entire planet's core ... the source of everything ... the power of the universe. This is where everything in the world revolves. Every baby born becomes a statistic that some economist uses to calculate the number of diapers it will need, how many people that will be needed to make the diapers, the number of gallons of gas needed to ship the diapers, which stores will sell the diapers and whether they will make a profit or not. Every aspect of life is examined in order to anticipate a market's movement. What does the consumer want? Who will provide it? Who will sell it? How much money will be made on it? Place your bets, ladies and gentlemen. The race is about to begin. Nostrils flare. Someone clears their throat. This is how we get ready for the hunt. You can see the testosterone swirling in the air.

Morning Call is a parade of panelists out of New York who report on the various markets and provide us brokers with up-to-the-second economic and political movements. It is supposed to help us talk smart to clients about things we have no time to pay attention to since all our time is spent on finding prospects with money and talking them into writing us a check. I wonder how the smaller companies support their agents in the field with information when they don't have a legion of analysts who study the markets round the clock. I shudder to think about anyone having to be on their own to determine market trends and anticipate market swings. I learned enough in New York to know it is impossible for a layperson to know anything more than just enough to hang themselves. But that's not my problem. My problem is trying to convince a prospect that our company, with its legion of analysts, is a better bet than the firms without any. You'd think it'd be an easy sell, but we all look alike to the ordinary prospect and one pitch sounds the same as another to them.

The training room is dark, all but for the glow of the screen at the front of the room bearing the Maugham Southerby logo. I look for Charlie, who isn't here yet. Manny is slouched in the back row. I see a bald head in the second row and know it is Rolly Anderson. Rolly is part of the Bascomb Group—a group of financial advisors within Maugham Southerby who manage a book of business as a team and share in the commissions. Rolly is low man on that team, which is why he's here every morning to scout information to bring back to the Bascomb lair.

Vincent Dombrowski from the New York research office opens the panel with an economic summary. Equities are up. There is pressure on bonds due to rising interest rates.

Sometime shortly after the broadcast began, I noticed Charlie standing at the doorway. He never takes a seat or brings a notepad. I scribble a few points of interest. TED spreads are closing. The Yen is up against the dollar. Standard and Poor lowered their rating on Blight Pharmaceuticals to AA+. CIS is down two basis points due to a rumble in Silicon Valley over product registrations that is shaking up several tech companies. Some lawsuit filed yesterday names every known tech company and accuses them all of stealing a product registration for a part found in virtually every electronic device. I glance at Charlie and wonder if the conversation at the family dinner table has changed since he became a securities agent. It better have, or he and his father could wind up in prison for insider information. But the real question is whether or not Charlie knew something before he came under regulation. My mind turns back to the monitor to learn what is permissible for me to say during a sales pitch. I soon determine I have enough fodder for conversations with prospects and rise to leave.

"Got a moment?" Charlie says as I am about to pass him in the doorway. He follows me as we walk without conversation back toward the bullpen. He takes a seat on top of my desk as I slap on my headset, intent upon reaching people at their offices before their work obligations take them off track of their real aspirations—the ones I remind them about. He doesn't take the hint.

"Did you call Squally like I told you?" he asks. To stay low on the radar Charlie elicited my help in pumping the internal hedgies for information. Wall Street has grown lousy with hedge funds developed on bar napkins by small-time bandits. The larger investment banks were slow on the draw, but have since loaded their guns by hiring mathematicians and physicists to develop their hedge fund strategies, which is what Charlie is after. Derivatives are the not-so-secret ingredient; but like any good brew, it's all in how you handle the hops.

Dorian Squally is the newest hedge fund manager at Maugham. While he brags about the strategy behind his fund, I take notes. Consumers around the globe are easy targets for the latest obsession on Wall Street: subprime debt. When gathered in bulk and sliced thin enough to see through, investment banks turn poor-quality loans made by lending banks into high return securities with virtually no risk to the investor. Never mind the poor slob who gets in over his head in credit card debt, student loans, and the mortgages that make up these securities. The poor slob is the pawn in this game—and expendable. Since deregulation, lending banks can become investment banks and vice versa. Now one hand can grease the other. It is virtually a perpetual money tree. The biggest glut in the process is loan officers who still think they have to perform due diligence. They can't get it through their thick skulls that the game has changed—that all their employers want them to do is just give people the money! Who says 'no' to free money? Zero down mortgages, credit card offers of zero-percent interest rates, low interest loans. You want it, you can have it. Madam Desire now dances around the globe and kisses the lips of all who pucker up.

"Yeah." I reply, withholding what Squally told me to savor the moment in which I know something Charlie doesn't. I've been reduced to such pettiness as a result of having to crawl to everyone else around here lately. He indulges me amicably with a little smirk— a luxury he can afford since he has nothing to envy about me. Once I usurp enough power to quench my floundering soul, I divulge what Dorian Squally never realized he told me—an ingenious twist on convertible arbitrage by buying the convertible debt of mortgage lenders, then turning around and short-selling their stock, thereby isolating the interest coupon, and then doing a little distressed investing to hedge the hedge.

Charlie smiles. Time passes between us while we each envision how this little tidbit of information will play out for the benefit of us both. "Heard his fund has a positive carry," Charlie adds with indifference. My ego is so bruised these days I can't help resent Charlie's simple compliment to Squally.

I am filled with emotion. Envy. Anger. Lacking logical reason, I am pissed, as though Squally is somehow better than me; and I'm angry at Charlie for noticing. I shrug. "Monty's at the bell," I order with more vehemence in my voice than I intend. Monty's is where local FAs level out their testosterone after a day of trading. Charlie puts a hand on my shoulder as a way of telling me everything is going to work out.

It better work out soon, I think to myself, because I'm running out of viable leads. I don't have the contacts Charlie does. The people I know barely have enough money to qualify opening an account at Maugham let alone invest in derivatives. While Charlie is already on the bandwagon with CDOs and swaps, I'm clamping onto anything I can get these days just to keep my stats up long enough to still have a job by the time Charlie's plan comes together.

"Monty's," he replies as his hand slips from my shoulder.

TUESDAY, JULY 24, 2007: 5:25 A.M. (CDT)

I had hit Durkee as soon as I got back from New York, having previously primed Walter who was eager to help the little lad he's felt all along he's helped raise. He handed over everything both he and his wife had in IRAs and joint accounts. In addition, I got him to change the company's retirement plan provider to Maugham Southerby just so I can oversee every employee's retirement plans personally, which is what I immediately proceeded to do with devout due diligence. Walter said he's never been more proud of me.

"It's comforting to know we have a good honest man to help everyone here at Durkee plan for the future," he had said as he slapped me on the back. "I know I can trust you to not let us down."

Raked in nearly $3 million in assets. It boosted my stats so high last week even Crosby smiled, I think. But that was last week. History. I have to do it all again this week to keep my ass out of the wringer.

I remind myself of all this as I head toward Starbucks and take my usual place in line. It's 5:25 a.m. and my job begins like this each day. Everyone is focused on a laptop or newspaper. I size up the room for any potential worthwhile prospects: Armani suits, Prada heels, Coach purses, Samsonite briefcases ... anything that indicates money or position. I'm ready for game, wearing my Brooks Brothers suit I still owe $938.00 on. You do what you gotta do to make it in this business. Looking credible is number one. Packaged for sale this morning, I tell myself as I glance around the room for a potential buyer.

"Next," the skinny, gaunt boy with dark circles under his eyes says from across the counter.

"Grande Irish Cream latte with a heavy sprinkle of cinnamon," I say. Someone told me cinnamon increased your metabolism. After a few sips you barely notice it. "I'll take one of those, too," I add casually referring to a stack of this morning's *Wall Street Journals* next to the till.

With *The Journal* under my arm and my latte in hand I weave my way through the crowded room toward a tan Coach handbag that is hanging on the back of a chair. I size up my prey as I close in. Gray suit, high white collar buttoned to her chin, natural brunette hair tightly wound into a bun at the nape of her neck, gold cufflinks, short manicured nails, no polish ... all business. It usually means nice wages, and money.

"Excuse me, but is this chair taken?"

She looks up from her Blackberry momentarily and shakes her head, almost oblivious to me. I sit down and immediately absorb myself in *The Journal*, noisily flipping through the pages to draw her attention, but before I capture hers a small headline on page three captures mine: 'Paris Bank Suspends Withdrawals.' The article says an inability to properly price a book of subprime related bonds led France's largest bank to suspend customer withdrawals. Good God! That's just another way of saying they couldn't find a buyer at *any* reasonable price. My suspicions about CDOs just escalated all over again. If a value can't be established for these things in a declining market there would be no access to capital. Wall Street could paralyze. "Jesus, God Almighty," I sigh in earnest.

I gasp, and unwittingly attract her attention. But I no longer have the resolve to pursue her as a prospect; I'm distracted by the article. I pull out my cell phone and speed-dial Charlie, but before he answers I think twice and hang up. This is exactly the sort of thing I have to stop doing. Charlie will only point out that it is a story on page three. If it were important it would be on the front page, wouldn't it? Let it go, I tell myself—a result of hearing it from Charlie countless times. I suck in a deep breath, doing my best to squelch my fears about whatever is happening in the markets.

The woman sitting opposite me stares hesitantly, as though I might be having a heart attack or choking on something. I smile to assure her I am okay. Then I realize my emotional display can be used legitimately.

"Troubling," I utter, then smile reassuringly. "But for every problem in the market, there is a solution." I smile and offer my hand across the table. "David Yates. Maugham Southerby."

Tuesday, July 24, 2007: 7:30 a.m. (CDT)

"It's nothing 'til you see the commission," Crosby says, bursting my bubble for the umpteenth time after I share my fish story back at the office.

"She's the director of human resources for Midwest Medical Devices," I somewhat lie as proof the girl I met at Starbucks is the real deal ... that she's a big fish that can lead me to a whole school of fish ... maybe even bigger fish.

The pot of gold in his business is finding a contact person who can open doors for you. Big targets are human resource directors. Since they have their finger on all the employees of any particular company, they know which ones to tap, and that makes *them* a great contact for someone like *me*. They also know when the company is about to lay people off and one whiff of that and a good financial advisor will be waiting at the gates offering help to move everyone and their mother's uncle's 401(k)s. Stuff like that is what every rookie is hoping to sniff out.

Crosby isn't impressed. He leans into my face and rubs his thumb and index finger together in the space between his nose and mine before he walks away.

I give the cubicle wall a kick to spin my chair around. I reach over my desk, grab my headset, and peer over my shoulder at Crosby as he trudges down the hallway and into his office. I slap the headset on and immediately feel the blood begin to drain from my head as I begin another day in the bullpen, dialing and smiling.

I leave a message for Mary Willis on her answering machine, knowing it's unlikely she'll call me back. I jot down her name, phone number and everything I can recall from our conversation in Starbucks to my preferred prospect list. Crosby is right. That's why I hate him.

After a few weeks on the dial-and-smile routine—getting whacked in the ego for eight to ten hours a day—I've hardened up to just about anything anyone says to bring me down. I've now taken on a demeanor of come-on-toss-me-another-one-right-here-asshole attitude. I can take any abuse with a smile so long as it gets me a sale. He who laughs last laughs best.

Using the yellow pages to target small attorney offices, I leave four voicemail messages before I get a live voice. "Crocker and Gamble PA," says the voice. I reached a receptionist—or worse, a private secretary. They are the front lines, the barricades to glory, as I refer to them.

"Is Sam in the office yet?" The directory lists a Bernard Crocker and a Samuel Gamble as Attorneys at Law. I've never talked to either.

"Who's calling, please?"

"Dave Yates with Maugham Southerby."

There's a pause. "Is he expecting you?"

"Yes," I reply.

There's another pause. "Mr. Gamble is deceased," she says.

I take my feet off the top of the counter and sit up. "Really," I say. Then with as much sincerity as I can muster add, "I am so sorry to hear that. When did that happen?"

"Fourteen years ago."

Busted. There is something sinister about pushing securities. Money is personal. It is connected to everyone's dirtiest little secret. People feel vulnerable when the subject comes up and they revert to their core instincts of either fight or flight. It is natural to be leery about anyone prying into the very thing we hold most near and dear: our secret desire and the money we need to either feed it or protect it. Women particularly shut us brokers down quickly over the phone. Men with egos like to yank our chains for a while before they slam dunk us. Gives them their jolly for the day. It is not fun being the brunt of everyone else's joke, but it is what you have to do to find prospects in this glorious business. I am about to press the disconnect button when she asks, "What do you know about the Silicon Valley shakeup?"

Bingo! I'm in business. I share my notes from Morning Call and tell her a few things she was eager to know. She's ripe, just waiting to be picked. She wants equal Put contracts against DynoCom and i-Fest. She couriers a check for fifty grand along with the signed paperwork I couriered to her right after our call. I drop the trade at Opening Bell and am up $750 bucks in commissions before 9:05 a.m. Not the mother lode, but it could be a good day.

Friday, July 27, 2007: 6 p.m. (CDT)

Helice called two nights ago to say she'd be in Minneapolis for a few days to cover an event at the Guthrie. She said she wanted to get together for dinner the first night, but wouldn't commit to anything further. Said, "We'll see what transpires." In other words, she's wondering if I'm worth her time. Calculating bitch. I love it. You're gettin' it tonight, girl, I think to myself as I head toward the airport to pick her up. You'll be begging for more of what I intend to give you.

I park in short-term parking at the Minneapolis-St. Paul International Airport terminal and walk to baggage claim. She's arriving on flight 2243 from LaGuardia at 6:15 p.m. I check the monitors and discover her flight is delayed twenty minutes. I grab a Starbucks and take a seat on the concourse near the baggage kiosks to wait.

I haven't seen Helice since the Hamptons nearly two months ago, but those two nights register as the all-time best sex I've ever had. It's why I've since suffered through countless phone conversations with her talking about absolutely nothing. It's all for the hope of a repeat performance like the one we had in the Hamptons. I swear she has more than two legs because I felt those babies simultaneously wrap around me in places one couldn't be without the other. I'm getting a hard-on just thinking how close I am to encountering it all over again. Where the devil is her plane?

The baggage conveyor belt starts up. The monitor flashes flight 2243 from LaGuardia. People begin to slowly gather around the empty conveyor belt. Soon a few bags drop from the shoot and make a few rounds in a lowly attempt to garner interest from those standing around it with blank stares. I lean against a pole near the kiosk to wait.

Once Helice shows up, I grab her around the waist and pull her into me dramatically. She swings herself to one side and I am forced to put my hand at the small of her back to keep her from falling to the floor. I play along as she bends backward and I plant one on her right there in front of God and everybody. The crowd roars. Claps and whistles break out all around the baggage kiosk. Someone shouts out, "Get a room."

We are not long-lost lovers. We're toying with one another for a second round. She pulls away and begins jabbering about the meetings she has to attend while she's here, the important things she has to do … yeah, a few things come to *my* mind.

How much stuff does one woman need for two days? I wonder as I haul three suitcases through the terminal while she carries a leather carry-on over her shoulder. Her red hair is bouncing more than her boobs. Her lips won't shut up. Her legs are distracting me so much that I forget where I parked the truck.

The rest of the evening becomes a blur while we roll around her hotel room at the Downtown Radisson. Her wild mane, illuminated only by the city lights, looks black against the pillow. "More," she yells. She arches her back. "Tell me more," she moans. Tell her what? I wonder. "You're beautiful, baby," I groan. "No," she shouts back angrily. Then murmurs like a kitten, "Tell me about the market ... tell me how the market goes up and down."
"The market goes up and down, up and down, up and down ..."
"Tell me about the money—I want to hear about the money."
"There's lots of money, baby ... lots of money."
"I want it," she moans. "I want all the money ... I want it all ... I want it alright ... right ... now!" The pitch in her voice escalates to a piercing whine.

"I want it all, too, baby," I expel, giving her one last thrust before I flop on top of her and we lay in a sweaty mess for a long while until one of us comes back to life, and then we do it all again.

When I wake the next morning she's gone, but there is a note on the pillow next to me: "Tonight. More. 9 p.m." I roll onto my back and smile wide. My dick is straight up in the air. "Round three coming up," I mutter as I stretch and yawn.

SATURDAY, JULY 28, 2007: 10:30 A.M. (CDT)

I stumble on a crack in the sidewalk and catch myself from taking a nosedive. Embarrassed, I look around to try and locate the reason I tripped. A corner of the slab is missing and I had stepped right into the sucker. I could have broken my neck. I scuffed the toe of my Gucci loafers. I spit on my thumb and try to rub the scuff out. It doesn't rub out.

Everything in Fiddlers Park is deteriorating. Mom's gotta get out of here, I think angrily to myself. I'm going to get her out of this decrepit neighborhood. I kick at the piece of cement that had dislodged from the sidewalk slab and watch the tassels on my loafers flip every time I kick it down the sidewalk toward Rick's Nick's where I am headed with high hopes of doing a little prospecting. Might as well get something out of the Park before I leave it for good.

Fish in your own pond, they told us in training. Work off the reputation you've established. I'm not so sure that's the best idea where I'm concerned. There are a few things people around here know about me that could do more harm than good for my prospecting efforts, but it's all I've got.

It still irritates me that I hadn't yet gotten Mom's approval for becoming a financial advisor with Maugham Southerby. She says she's proud of me, but I see the same old thing in her eyes as I've seen all my life: "I expect something better of you." The only glimmer of pride I witnessed was when I mentioned I'd said a prayer at Ground Zero. She had come over and hugged me as though she was trying to comfort me. She must have thought the experience of seeing where so many people had died had emotionally upset me, or something. It hadn't. It just made me mad all over again at the terrorists, and more determined than ever to defy their intentions of destroying the economic base of this country.

I told her all about ringing the bell at the New York Stock Exchange, seeing the Statue of Liberty and the Empire State Building, and bumping into Regis at Tavern on the Green. That's enough fodder to keep any mother in the Park popular on the grapevine for a long time. What more does she want?

In my head, I practice my pitch but I remind myself more of a barker at a carnival than the financial advisor I am. "Step right up and let me put your money in the market for you, ladies and gentlemen ... one chance to win big, little lady. Take the risk and get the reward." I smile at the truism of my thoughts.

I hear my name called and turn around. It's Alison Bly. "Dave," she says again. "I barely recognized you in that suit, all dressed up." Her smile changes into a serious look. "Did someone pass away?"

"Hey, Alison," I respond. "Yeah ... I mean no ... no one died. I'm just on my way ..." I let that trail off. "So what have you been doing with yourself these past—what has it been two years?"

"Five," she corrects.

"Five," I repeat with a note of surprise in my voice. Five years since I'd last seen her. I scarcely remember why, how, or when we drifted apart, but I do recall us sharing a lot of good times all through high school. Alison could toss a basketball like a guy and I only had a 50-50 chance in a game of one-on-one with her. I remembered that much. Plus, she could always outrun me, which I hated. It's all coming back to me. It's great to see her. I can't stop smiling.

"What?" she asked referring, no doubt, to the stupid grin on my face.

"Nothin'," I reply and bop her with my elbow like I had done when we were kids. She smiles back but doesn't reciprocate the bop as I remembered she had done in the past.

"So," I urge, "what have you been up to?"

She shrugs. "Work. Research. Writing. That's about it."

"What work? What research? What writing?" I prod.

She stops and looks up at me. She hasn't changed a bit. That same fresh look, inquisitive eyes, gentle lips that always seem on the brink of a smile, a hint of a dimple in her chin, thick brown eyelashes. Her ashen hair naturally streaked with sunlight is pulled into a ponytail. Lose strands wisp about her shoulders. Her fingernails are short and unpolished. No make-up, unadorned but for a thin leather strand around her neck that bears one very small turquoise stone. Lovely in a plain, earthy sort of way.

Her eyes search mine before she turns and begins to walk again. "You don't want to hear about me. Tell me about *you* instead," she says, expecting me to follow her, which I do.

"I'm with Maugham Southerby," I say, as I stand up a little straighter.

"Who is Mom Southerby?" she asks as though she thinks it is a little old lady.

I stare at her incredulously. "Well," I say, trying to keep the irritation from my voice, "Maugham Southerby is the largest brokerage firm in the world and headquartered out of New York," I explain. "They have offices all over the world," I add, hoping to expand her awareness. "I work out of the downtown Minneapolis office in the IDS Center."

Nothing. She says nothing to all of this. We take a few steps before she asks, "So what do you do there?"

I stare down at the top of her head for a second before I reply, "I am a financial advisor," in a futile attempt to impress her.

"I don't know much about that and I'm not rich enough to care," she says, looking up at me.

As irritated with her as I am at the moment, I can't help notice her eyes. They are aqua blue with specks of lime green and so clear they make you feel like you could just step right into them and paddle away to Never-Never Land. With her hair soft and blowing in the breeze it seems just like old times and I'm tempted to grab a basketball and drag her to the court behind Fiddlers Park Middle School.

"Listen," she starts. "It's been fun running into you and I'd love to stay longer and catch up, but I *really* have to run." She puts a hand on my arm and smiles. Before I know it I'm watching the way her ass sways as she walks quickly up the block and across the street without looking back. I can just see the top of her head as she moves through the parking lot at Dorsette's Grocery Store and it reminds me of a fawn in springtime bounding gently through the woods. Nice girl. It was great to see her again. She looks great. Not like I remembered her. More grownup. More ... I don't know. Just different.

I spent the day wandering through the Park, talking with shop owners, catching up on local gossip, passing out business cards, basically hustling anyone I could. I was starving by the time I headed back to Mom's around suppertime. The aroma of pot roast and carrots pours out of the house as soon as I open the back door.

"Ma," I yell. The smell is so thick and juicy I swear I can stand right there in the mudroom and eat the air and still get full. My stomach growls like a Doberman pinscher with a mailman in its sights. I kick off my shoes and toss my sport coat on top of the dryer instead of hanging it on the hook that used to be mine when I lived here. With Julie soon off to college, I realize the place is no longer *our* home. It is just our mother's. "Ma," I yell again.

I hear a faint "What!" from upstairs as I enter the kitchen. I stick my head in the refrigerator and hang there on the door staring into a row of plastic tubs with little blue lids. Judging from the leftovers in mom's refrigerator I'd say Dr. Sandihar was right about Mom getting back to her old self quickly after her surgery.

"Get your head out of the refrigerator," I hear her holler down the stairs. How does she know what I'm doing all the time? I grab a diet Coke from the door compartment and sit down at the table to wait for her to come downstairs and feed me like always. "You'll need to go through some of those boxes up there one of these days," she begins for the umpteenth time as she comes down the stairs.

"Yes. I had a lovely day. And you?" I say sarcastically, ignoring her comments.

"Don't get smart with me, mister," she says as she taps me on the back of the head on her way to the oven. She wants me to pack up the stuff in my old room and take it home, but I don't want the stuff. It's just a bunch of old model airplanes, train sets, army men, books, some old yearbooks and other junk I don't need or want. I keep offering to throw it out, but she won't let me. She just keeps harping about me going through it. Ever since her surgery she's been in a major purge mood. Either that or she is adjusting to her life without kids in it. Maybe she's getting ready to rent our rooms out or something.

"Is that a new wig?" I ask her. She's started losing her hair as a result of the chemo treatments that followed her surgery—and in anticipation of losing it all, she's bought several wigs.

"You like it?" she asks as she pats the back of it.

It isn't that I don't like it; it's more that it just doesn't look like Mom. But it must be the look she's after since it is a flaming red short bob, vastly different than the mousy brown short cropped hairdo I've seen her in my whole life. The first wig she got was at least similar to her normal hair in color, but the healthier she gets the more flamboyant she becomes.

"Pretty hot stuff there, little lady." We laugh out loud together, each knowing full well she is anything but.

"Where were you all day?" she asks.

I didn't want to tell her I had been prospecting in the Park, that I'd hung around Rick's Nick's and Schmitty's hoping to nail a few clients. It would sound to her as though I was goofing off all day. Then I realize it probably seemed the same to everyone I met today. They don't understand it is part of my job to find and pursue prospects—anybody with money. Which brings to mind why I thought I'd find anything in the Park. I shrug over that thought, but Mom doesn't notice.

"I ran into Alison." I say it more to change the subject than to make conversation. Mom stops everything she's doing and turns around to face me. Her eyebrows lift. Surprised at her reaction I try to answer the question on her face by adding, "We had a nice chat," but evidently that isn't what she wanted to hear. Her eyebrows remain raised. "She said to say hello," I include, but she just stands there with her spatula suspended and lips pursed.

"Humph," she finally grunts as she shakes her head at me.

"What?" I ask, throwing my palms upward.

"Did you invite her over?" she asks as she bends over the oven and lifts the cover off the roasting pan. A waif of succulent aroma is released. My nostrils flare with anticipation.

"No," I reply, wondering why she expected me to. "When are we eating?"

"Why not?" she questions as her brow furrows further into her forehead. The question of why I didn't invite Alison to dinner hangs in the air.

"Why should I?"

She puts her hand firmly on her hip.

I scrunch my shoulders and shake my head from side to side. I don't know what to do or say.

"You are such a guy," she mumbles as she turns back to her roast.

"That's a good thing, right?"

She peeks around her shoulder at me but doesn't confirm it.

What did she mean by that? Did she mean it was good that I was a guy, because it didn't seem like she meant anything good? But I don't think she wants me to be anything other than a guy. I swear women live in another dimension. They say things that don't make sense sometimes. We are the only two in the room and have spoken less than twenty words to one another and all I know is the conversation has something to do with me being a man—or a guy—maybe there is a difference in which one I am. See, this is the stuff I just don't get. "When are we going to eat?" I ask, attempting to steer the conversation toward something I *am* more certain about.

"Did she tell you she's about to become a doctor?"

My wide eyes revealed the answer to that question. A doctor? Alison? The perky little boobs under a tee-shirt and nice little ass I ran into today? She's got brains, too?

"I thought you said you had a chat with her."

"I did."

She looks at me and shakes her head, then tells me Alison is doing graduate work in environmental science through the University of WA in Seattle. She had given a free public mini-lecture at the Enchanted Isle Bookstore about how Americans are literally throwing Mother Nature out with the trash.

She should see the waste in New York, I think to myself, recalling the Styrofoam-bloated garbage trucks I saw daily while I was there for training. That's where she should be giving her little talks.

"That girl is smarter than a whip," Mom assures. "I always knew she'd amount to something someday. While you're both here in town you two should get together and go out to dinner or something," she suggests. She kept her back to me to avoid giving me the opportunity to frown down her idea.

Mom doesn't know about Helice, but she soon will if episodes like last night keep up. My tastes in women have matured far beyond Alison Bly. I like my women hot and ambitious—like Helice. She's going to the top, and that's where I'm going, too. *That's* my type.

Besides, Alison is a tree-hugger. I still toss gum wrappers out the window. We have nothing in common. Although I must admit I *am* a bit impressed. And I am sincerely glad for her. Knowing Alison, it must mean a lot to her, doing what she does for mankind and all. But for me ... I mean ... c'mon. I have much bigger plans for my life than hugging trees.

I shake my head. God knows I love my mother, but will she ever see me for who I am and what I'm capable of accomplishing? I reach out and slap her on the ass. "I love ya, Ma," I say.

She swats my hand away and raps me a good one on the top my head in a loving gesture meant for a difficult child. We sit in the kitchen eating our supper where I can be closer to the stove and the gravy pot. When my stomach bulges like Uncle Billy's I know it is time to sit back, but Ma has no intention of letting a good cake go to waste.

"I can't," I plead, thinking about my little rendezvous with Helice later this evening. A bloated belly takes me off my game.

"Can't isn't a word we permit in this house," she instinctively replies. Then, arching her back she looks me in the eyes and asks, "Remember?" She was pointing the spatula at my nose. She stands motionless except for her eyes that dart back and forth between mine in search mode. She's using her parent torture tactics.

Of course I remember. 'Choices are allowed. Excuses are not.' But we're only talking cake here, I want to say; but I don't. I know what she's doing. She's driving one more nail in the project she's been working on my whole life—the good son. She drives me nuts, but I love her. "One small piece," I tell her. She flops a piece of cake the size of a city block onto my plate. "Thanks, Mom."

Wednesday, August 1, 2007: 6:45 a.m. (CDT)

Crosby walks by a little too close to my side of the bullpen. It's the first day of the new month and I know he's looked at last month's stats.

"I want to see you in my office," he says.

"Dang," I think to myself without moving a muscle.

"Now," he retorts.

I hop to it, nearly run down the aisle after him, and slide into the chair in front of his desk just as he plunks himself down in the big leather one opposite me.

111

He doesn't bother to look at me before he begins. "Your stats are dangerously low," he grunts.

I don't respond, so he looks up to make sure I'm sitting in the chair. His expression begs to know why I am not offering an explanation.

I'm all out of explanations. I'm smiling. I'm dialing. I've called every friend and relative. What little money they have, I already pulled over. I'm holding seminars each week through community education in Fiddlers Park. So far the only thing I've acquired is a reputation as being a well-informed young man who the Park is proud of, according to Mom. I'm trolling Starbucks regularly. I wander the skyway around lunchtime looking for potential prospects on their lunch breaks. I once ate the same sandwich for two and a half hours moving from table to table while introducing myself outside a bistro in Gravidae Commons. I got one lead that never materialized into an appointment. I joined two athletic clubs and have been in both daily trying to establish relationships. The only country club that will let me join is Midland Hills, which by its name declares the sort of leads I find there. Cold calling seems my best shot with a 50-to-1 chance of reaching a person who would be willing to place a trade. I'm out of other ideas. I shrug.

Crosby snorts and one corner of his mouth goes up at the thought he won't have to look at my mug much longer. I feel a twitch start at the corner of my eye just thinking about the car I have on order. Not just any car. A BMW M6, due to arrive direct from Bavaria the first part of October. Perhaps it is a little premature to think I can afford a $65,000 car while still living above Maggie's but I have my priorities. Besides, Charlie is about to play his cards.

"About this mortgage you put through on a …" he pauses to look at a paper in front of him, "… Maynard and Ruth Gorski. I want to know whether you think they will make good on their obligation because their debt-to-income ratio is a little high." Crosby is still tied to old-school thinking—that before a lender lends they should be pretty sure the borrower can pay back the loan. But that isn't the way things are done these days. There is a race against time to make as much subprime debt as investors are willing to buy, and so far there is no let-up in demand for CDOs around the world. Lending institutions can't hand out the money fast enough to keep up with demand. This isn't just American dreams coming true. People can upgrade their huts in the Amazon with zero-down financing. That's how bad investors want this stuff, and here Crosby is holding up the show.

Wall Street is a literal manufacturing ground for debt these days. Various enticements rival traditional lenders. The Financial Modernization Act—the very same that Charlie's brother pushed through—allows investment banks to now offer mortgages on margin. Unbelievable. As a result, I was able to get Mayo—who didn't have a dime for a down payment on a house—a mortgage by getting his dad to withdraw his life's savings from the Fiddlers Park Community Bank and put it into a nice little conservative mutual fund I sold him. Then I had him put it all on margin as collateral for Mayo's loan. Zero down, interest only payments on an adjustable rate mortgage which is two points lower than a conventional mortgage rate, and Mayo will soon be living in a 2,500 square-foot home with a 150 by 100-foot wooded lot with a creek running through it for less a month than I pay for rent living above the Curl Up and Dye.

That's the way we play the game on Wall Street. Not a dime leaves anyone's palm, yet hundreds of thousands of dollars move around the board. Crosby's reluctance is nothing more than proof the Street is moving so fast these days it can't keep up with itself.

"Yeah, I know," I say, trying to appease his antiquated rationale. "Mr. Gorski is in line for a promotion in January of next year. It's just that his wife is pregnant with their second kid and they want to get into a house before the baby comes. It's just a few months before his pay will be bumped."

He writes a note of approval across the application and shoves it back at me.

I call Mayo on my cell phone before I get back to my desk. "You're in, buddy. It's a go."

TUESDAY, AUGUST 7, 2007: 3:30 P.M. (CDT)

I am up $120,000 in assets under management and feeling the jingle in my pocket by Closing Bell, so I decide to stretch my legs by taking a jaunt through the skyway. The elevator is packed with securities agents by the time the elevator comes to a stop at the skyway level. The skyway is nearly empty compared to its usual bustle. Food stands are winding down as the downtown crowd begins to head home for the day. I stroll toward Caribou while I calculate today's commissions. I feel like I'm pitching a no-hitter in the ninth when I bump into Lester Beasley, the kid I pasted behind the lockers in eighth grade.

I met Lester in third grade when his family moved to town from Arkansas. He had a funny accent and dressed like what we'd wear on Halloween when we tried to look like hobos. He had an older brother in the fourth grade who should have been in the sixth grade. He had a younger sister in kindergarten who should have been in second grade. That made Lester the brightest one in the bunch since he was in the grade in which he belonged. But he didn't belong anywhere, especially not in Mrs. Hanson's third-grade class. I was as much a part of the ostracizing as anyone until one day Lester cried. While the other kids continued to taunt him and call him a "baby," something inside me snapped and suddenly I overflowed with compassion for the poor little urchin who by no fault of his own was born into a measly family that couldn't afford clothes ... or soap, apparently. I stepped forward and shielded Lester from the rest of the class and ordered them all to stop—which to my surprise they did.

"This isn't fun when people get hurt," I had shouted. This is just plain mean." Then pointing a finger at a few fellows, I asked, "Are you a mean person, Petie? Are you one of those mean guys, Maynard? How about you, Carlson, are you a mean person?" They all shook their heads as the rest of the class backed away. "Nobody here is mean, Lester," I had told him while still scanning the faces of every class member, daring them to disagree. I put my arm around the pathetic little guy and walked him through the crowd. "Nobody here is going to hurt you, Lester, because you are our friend and while we may poke fun at each other now and again, we never mean to hurt or harm anyone—isn't that right, guys," I asked raising my voice. The class all chimed in agreement.

No one bothered Lester all the rest of that year, that I knew about. Lester hung on me like peanut butter on fresh bread for the next three years. I taught him how to tackle a running back, to dribble a basketball, to pin a wrestler, and to hit a home run, although he couldn't have done any one of those things without me sandbagging the situation. I witnessed him puff up with hope every time. Everyone ought to have hope. Maybe it was that I identified with Lester in not having a dad around to teach him anything. I, at least, had Bob, my big brother who was always and forever there for me. And when Dad did show up, he was cool and did what all good dads ought to do: play ball with his boys and take them fishing. But Lester's dad was a drunk and his mom was really ugly. I had it a little better than Lester, but we were the same in not having a dad full time, which made us both different from most of the kids in class.

I lost track of Lester in junior high. I remember something about him being in a special class, but never knew much more about it. It wasn't until eighth grade when all the phys ed classes, boys and girls, were joined together for a final group sex education session that Lester emerged from the shadows. After class, Lester and few of his new-found friends had cornered Sally Weatherstrom and were taunting her with lewd comments about her reproductive parts. Before I knew it, I'd elbowed past his friends and pasted old Lester squarely on the nose and grabbed Sally by the wrist while muttering loud enough for the thugs to hear me call them all a bunch of hyenas.

I don't remember ever seeing Lester's face the rest of my high school years, but here he is … full-grown and wearing a suit.

"What the hell?" I comment shaking my head in disbelief over seeing this monkey in socially acceptable attire. He still looks like the same Lester and I still want to paste him one without legitimate provocation. "What are you?" I ask craving an explanation for this outrageous sight before my eyes.

"I'm a financial advisor," he says as he pumps up his chest.

Suddenly I want to take him down and make him take it back. There is no way this goon could be anyone's financial advisor. He's 40 watts short of a 40-watt bulb. The guy flunked out of math and had to be put into the 'special' class. Now he's a financial advisor! "You don't say," I reply as casually as my now constricting throat will allow.

"Yeah—makin' the big bucks, now. Got me a BMW and a couple of snowmobiles," he says, like that would impress me, which it partly does.

"And I suppose a brand new bowling ball, too," I add sarcastically, but the dope takes it seriously.

"Yeah, how'd ya know? Got my initials engraved in gold, too," he adds, raising his eyebrows.

Curious to know more about how this pinhead managed to get where he is, I suggest we go have a drink together. We wander over to McCormick's and grab a couple of stools at the bar. Leaning on elbows we swing our Heinekens around as we catch up on each other's lives. His older brother is doing time over in Stillwater for breaking and entering. His younger sister has four kids, all with different fathers.

He'd been married and divorced—no kids thankfully, but has a hot girlfriend who is the only daughter of a *very* rich man.

"I'm going to marry her and get in good with old daddy," he says with a wink.

He hadn't seen his father since the guy went out to buy a pack of cigarettes and never came home. His mother, who never issued a missing person's report, immediately packed up him and his siblings and moved back to Arkansas—in case the old man returned, is my guess—either that or she buried the juicer in the back yard and had to blow town before his corpse started stinking up the place. It explained why I hadn't seen Lester during high school.

He moved back to the Twin Cities to get a job when he graduated from high school—the only one of his family to do so—which I had to hand it to him was a feat to be proud of under those circumstances. He got a job as a grease monkey at Abra-Ka-Dabra Auto Works on University Avenue in St. Paul and eventually picked up part-time work as a limo driver. That's where he met Darcy Campbell, Branch Manager of Surety Securities, a small broker-dealer on the east side of St. Paul. Darcy hired him and tutored him through his securities exam and insurance licenses.

"How about that … both of us meeting up again after all these years, and both of us in the same business," Lester says, clarifying the growing discomfort I've been experiencing since I laid eyes on the goon, but, there it is. I am no better than Lester.

I eyeball his threads from his cufflinks to his wing-tipped shoes and while they aren't 24 karat gold or Ferragamo's, they are pretty good knockoffs. The dude looks authentic.

"How long you been selling securities?" I ask.

Lester stops in his tracks as though on cue and begins to recite his elevator speech. "Experience isn't as important as expertise …" He sees me shake my head and roll my eyes, then realizes we've both had similar monkey-trainers. He turns away from me and gives his beer a good chug. "About six months," he finally says.

Six months. That makes me more of a novice than him. I adjust myself on the stool in anticipation of hearing more about how this worm turned into a butterfly so quickly.

"Trailer parks are full of new parents. They are easy targets for term insurance. Once in the door, I sell them on securing the future for little Johnny or Susie for only a couple bucks a month." His eyes begin to sparkle like a kid who just got handed a brand-new Wii. "Then I get them to call the grandparents to explain how they might help send little Johnny or Susie to college." He winks. "What new grandparent is going to tell their kid they aren't interested in their kid's new baby ... their own grandchild?" He shakes his head at his own genius.

I get the rest. He's after the grandparents—where there is likely more money and not any better brains. Trailer parks usually don't flow with academics. When he calls on the grandparents, he sells them variable annuities for their retirement—nice little vehicles with upfront commission and five to seven-year trailers. I have to hand it to him. It *is* ingenious ... for a pinhead. He'll never make the big bucks, but he should be able to knock off a hefty enough paycheck. A nice cushy little racket that requires hardly any brains. I wonder how many other goons like him are running around trailer parks pushing themselves off as financial advisors. The thought of vulnerable people being preyed upon by weasels like Lester makes me want to take a swing at him.

"I make people's dreams come true," he says as he shakes his head again.

"Whose dreams are you making come true selling variable annuities?" I guffaw. Variable annuities are a fool's paradise, little more than gimmicks sold by slackers.

He turns to me initially dumbfound, but quickly erects himself, cocks his head, smiles wide, throws out his arms like he was walking onto a stage, and replies, "Mine." To drive his point home, he leans so close to my face that I know he had onions for lunch. He repeats himself, this time in a sinister whisper, "Mine." I see my own reflection in the glassy pupils of his eyes.

WEDNESDAY, AUGUST 22, 2007: 7:45 P.M. (CDT)

Listening to Mom prattle on about the Park has become a weekly ritual that pays off in more ways than one. Not only do I get a home cooked meal, but I also pick up valuable prospecting information. When old man Skinner received the settlement from his lawsuit against the library after he fell down the steps, I was the first financial advisor at his door. And when Mom told me Martha Johnson caught her husband cheating, I invited her to a seminar just for women. I was the first person she called after she drained their joint accounts.

Tonight, Mom made Tater Tot Hot Dish that I choked down, all the while letting her think it is still my favorite meal. I am now in a prone position on the sofa rubbing my belly for reasons yet unknown while we both watch a documentary on the great money barons of the Roaring 20s on PBS.

Everyone was getting into the stock market back then. A new era had been created in which men no longer had to do hard labor to make money. They invested instead. Millions of dollars were being made. Poor men became rich overnight. Rich men became richer. The middle class was born. Now everyone could afford nannies, cooks and housekeepers—even the nannies, cooks and housekeepers had nannies, cooks and housekeepers.

Instead of scrubbing floors, women strolled around wearing fur coats and smoked from long cigarette holders. Men wore top hats and tails to dinner. The economy soared. The average home was 4,000 square feet. The Dodge brothers pumped out more cars than Henry Ford. Everyone wanted more stuff. Industry boomed. The stock market rose with the demand.

I roll onto my side and grab a handful of mints from the little dish on the coffee table and try to imagine what it must have been like back in those days. Just imagining being rich felt like lemonade flowing through a straw on a hot summer day. Having everything you need or want. All your dreams within reach. Yeah, I think to myself. Heaven. Pure heaven.

I toss another mint into the air and catch it in my mouth, which has four or five mints soaking up saliva. While I play trained seal with myself and the mints, Mom grabs her darning basket. Neither of us look at the sixty-four-inch flat-screen television us kids gave her for Christmas, but we listen to the narrator name off icons of the American dream such as Rockefeller, Vanderbilt, Heinz, Carnegie.

"You're a Carnegie," Mom says.

My head pops up from the armrest and the mint I'd tossed into the air hits me in the forehead. I stare at her. I stop sucking. I stop breathing. She doesn't look up from her mending. "What do you mean?" I ask, mumbling over the pile of mints in my mouth. All of a sudden I am confused. Had I ever been told this before? I sit up to avoid gagging. "A Carnegie? Like *the* Carnegie? Like the library Carnegie? *That* Carnegie?"

"Yeah," she says and shrugs, like I should already know this.

Do I already know this? I search my memory. I don't remember a thing about being a Carnegie. Nobody's ever said anything about being a Carnegie. All I know is we're a bunch of nobodies. I jump to a stand and hold my arms out wide in front of Mom to beg for an explanation. My head begins to waggle back and forth while my brain struggles to understand why I never knew this. Then a few things come to mind. Maybe I am the illegitimate son of an illicit affair. Maybe Mom is confessing. Maybe that's why she continues to darn that sock instead of look at me. She's too embarrassed to tell me I'm a love child. I frown. Then I smile. I *knew* it. I always knew there was something about me that didn't belong in this family ... in Fiddlers Park ... in Minnesota, for that matter. I belong in New York. I belong in the Hamptons. I'm a Carnegie! I feel giddy. "Who is he?" I inquire as to who my real father might be.

"It's not a he. It's a she. Your father's great great grandfather ... or is it great grandfather? I get that confused. Anyway, he married a Carnegie. They'd grown up together."

My eyes dart to the floor searching for my heart, which I swear just fell out of my chest. My *father's* family? Hard to comprehend anyone on my father's side being anything but a loser. I flop back down onto the sofa and grab another handful of mints and listen while Mom conveys how I have Carnegie blood in me.

Beauregard Bronson Yates had been my great great grandfather on my father's side. I remember hearing lots of stories about this dude throughout my childhood, none of which anyone took very seriously. My favorite story was how he had opened a mercantile in Pig's Eye. That's what our state capital was called before they changed the name to St. Paul. I still get a chuckle out of that. Anyway, old Beauregard decided to expand his business west of the Twin Cities into a little town called Hopkins. To entice the local farmers to come to his grand opening he gave out free raspberry bushes. Before long the entire town was growing raspberries in their back yard and a few farmers had given up growing corn in favor of growing raspberries. Eventually, the town itself became the epicenter of raspberry festivals and parades. I used to love to hear that story when I was a kid, back when I loved to imagine a field of raspberries where I could eat to my heart's content. It began to irritate me as I grew older, however, that nobody ever gave my great great grandfather any credit for bringing the raspberries to Hopkins. It's just like one of my family members to give all the credit to someone else. I hate that about us. I wish I came from a family that I could be proud of. But the best story this family has is some guy handing out raspberries—only to be forgotten by the very people who took them from him. What a sap. And that's my lineage.

But now Mom's telling me he was married to a Carnegie, a member of *the* Carnegie family ... Andrew Carnegie, according to her. I ask, "So what was she ... Andrew Carnegie's sister or something?" She shrugs. "Ask your father. It's his relative. I can't remember exactly."

"What *do* you remember, exactly?"

She scowls at my sarcasm but understands why I might be curious, so explains everything she could remember. To her it was ancient history about a time that was so devastating to everyone that people wanted to forget. Josephine Carnegie was a rich man's daughter. Beauregard was a dashing young man from an upper-class family. They met at a cotillion. Mom always thought that was quaint ... to have met at a cotillion. I don't know what a cotillion is, or care. All I want to know is how much money did we once have? Lots, according to Mom. Lots. But lost it all in the stock market crash. Beauregard was one of the resilient ones, she offers. Others from both sides of that family fell by the wayside, ruined forever financially and mentally. Only a few survived.

"Your father's side of the family survived," she says, as though being able to put a roof over our heads and eat was a feather in the caps of those who had made it. We differ vastly in our definition.

"What about your side of the family?"

The look of bewilderment on her face told me I'd stepped in the wrong puddle. "Your great grandfather Munson was ahead of his time. He opened up the housing development here in the Twin Cities long before Vern Donnay and Orrin Thompson. He built this house."

"Why wasn't there a Maynard Munson brand of housing then?" I asked.

"*Well*," she huffed indignantly. "I am not going to honor that question with an answer."

I get up from the sofa and walk to the window. The house across the street has all its curtains and blinds closed against the stifling August heat and the glow of the setting sun. Other than a couple of kids running through the sprinkler, there is no sign of life. Not even a car passes. Not that I'd notice. My mind is seeing only the inside of my skull as I enumerate the things I know about my father's side of the family. I never thought anyone from his family amounted to much more than what I saw in him—which wasn't much more than a person who could operate a crane ten hours a day in 9-degree heat and humidity, and throw a horseshoe with such aim and accuracy as to lay claim to the title of best horseshoe tosser for Schmitty's Bar. His record of wins remains unbeaten. So, that's pretty much it—a horseshoe champion and a raspberry nobody. But all of a sudden out of the blue a Carnegie pops up in my ancestral footprint. "How come you never told me this before?"

She looks up from her mending. "Why is it so important?"

"*Because*," I whine.

She stares at me while she suspends her needle above the sock she is mending. Her eyes are doing that question thing again and I know I have to explain myself or else. I never learned what the 'or else' was, but now isn't the time to find out. "A person ought to know if they come from important people," I say.

Her eyebrows shoot upward, then furrow deeply. "So the people you *do* know aren't important enough for you? Is that it? Your parents aren't important enough? Your grandfather who built the very floor you are standing upon–he wasn't good enough for you? Only the Carnegie's are good enough for you? Is that what you are saying?"

I had to think, but only for a second. "Yeah, I guess," I reply.

Her lips pierce. I hate when her lips pierce. She looks back down at her mending and begins to jab the needle into the sock she has wrapped around a light bulb.

"Why do you do that?" I ask, irritated at her incessant mending efforts. But I don't wait for a reply. I reach into my wallet and pull out a ten spot and put it in her lap. "Go buy some new socks."

She flicks the money onto the floor. "I don't need your money and I don't need new socks. Why should I pay four dollars for a new pair of socks when twenty inches of thread will do?" She glares at me.

"Because it's … it's …" I search for the words to describe what I am feeling, but she beats me to the punch.

"Too low-class?"

I stare at her. Somehow that doesn't sound very good when verbalized. Was that what I was thinking? I guess it was. Maybe that's what's been eating me. Ever since I met Charlie, I have become acutely aware that we are not of the same class. I just never thought of myself as being in *any* class, let alone *low* class. And now that I think about it, it seems unfair to categorize anyone into *any* social class. How and when did we become a society that judges the merits of a human being according to his or her social class? Isn't a person's character more important than their income bracket? Or is that my way of justifying my own social level? I don't know what I mean anymore. All I know is right now I want to know more about why I was never told we came from money.

Mom looks down again at her mending. The ten-dollar bill still lies at her feet. It doesn't look like I'll get any more answers tonight.

I sit on the edge of the sofa with my elbows on my knees and try to let the television devour my attention, but all I manage to do is vacillate between awe and anger. While the documentary continues about the Roaring Twenties, I can't help but wonder where all our family money went and why there wasn't any left for me. Charlie and I could have been equals. That thought shocks me. I pause to consider why I don't believe we *are* equals. Perhaps I *have* been influenced by social class distinction all along.

"Shit," I mumble.

"Don't swear," Mom scolds.

I jump up from the sofa. "I gotta get going." I kiss Mom on the top of her head. She doesn't look up.

I turn north out of the driveway and head toward Commons Avenue, but instead of turning right toward the Curl Up and Dye, I hang a left toward Minneapolis. I don't yet know if I am heading to the office or Charlie's loft yet. All I know is I don't want to go home and I'm not in the mood for Schmitty's.

The ramp onto Highway 280 off Commons is congested even at this late hour. It has become the alternative route into downtown Minneapolis since the collapse of the I-35 bridge. The thought of the gaping hole left in the middle of the Twin Cities as a result makes me realize how one event can affect so many lives, some permanently. Nine people had lost their lives two weeks ago in that disaster. Meanwhile, the rest of us take detours and praise God it didn't affect us personally. But, it did. What isn't and what will never be, as a result, plagues all of us in one way or another indefinitely.

Just like we are all still reeling from the Crash of '29. The average American family doesn't have a nanny, cook or housekeeper—and if they do their nannies, cooks and housekeepers don't. Our society has not gotten back to where it was in 1928. We changed our values and our standards to survive, and perhaps for the betterment of society in many ways. But if you were to add up all the pluses and minuses, we are still in the hole.

I wonder again what it might have been like had my family not lost its fortune. Grief mixed with rage overwhelms me. I slam my palm into the steering wheel.

A guy in a rusted-out Ford pick-up cuts in front of me. I wonder what he would be driving if it were 1928 instead of 2007. I wonder if he realizes how the Crash of '29 affected *his* life. I pull up alongside him to get a better look. He stares back at me. I can almost smell the mustard stain on his t-shirt. He must be reading my mind because he flips me off. I gun it and take the next exit onto Fifth Street. It's not true that what a person doesn't know doesn't hurt them. People still hurt. They just don't know why.

I feel motion but no emotion. I ride along for a few blocks without a thought or a feeling. Then, without warning, thoughts burst into my head with a vengeance and scream from my lips. "I want it back. I want what was supposed to be mine. I want what the universe stole from me. I want it *all* back!" My fists pound the steering in such vehement succession that I feel the whole car vibrate under me.

TUESDAY, SEPTEMBER 11, 2007: 6:26 A.M. (CDT)

"Eet ees goink to be a goot day on the Street, eh Mr. Yates," says Benny, the periodical stand vendor on the concourse of the IDS Center. He hands me a copy of *The Wall Street Journal* along with two rolls of peppermint flavored breath mints. The headline reads: "Ground Zero Pays Tribute" and is followed by an article on the ceremonies planned to take place to commemorate the sixth anniversary of the worst attack on our nation within the confines of our borders. I pause, recalling the moment when our nation came together in agony and simultaneously erupted in screams and wails over an unthinkable act that defied humanity. Still in college, I had been in the university canteen that morning between classes. I had just crashed a birthday party where a bunch of girls I didn't know gave me a chocolate-covered donut to get rid of me, but within seconds we were clutching each other like long lost kin in shared horror while we stared at the television monitor.

It occurs to me now that Maugham Southerby had been one of the largest tenants of the World Trade Center Towers, and both a renewed and new sense of loss overwhelms me. There surely would have been a training class of 300 or so rookies in those towers on that fateful day. "Jesus, save us all," I mutter at that realization.

"Eh, Mr. Yates?"

"Nothin' Benny. You have a nice day," I say as I tuck *The Journal* under my arm, deposit the two rolls of mints into my pocket, drop a fin and walk away.

The building is quiet at this hour, apart from the almost silent migration of workers lining up at Starbucks and the belching of the cappuccino machines. I listen to my footsteps against the marble concourse on my way to the elevators while a growing sense of vulnerability crawls up my leg and claws its way into my chest cavity. By the time I step into the elevator my heart is pounding with empathy for those trainees who had been caught at the wrong place at the wrong time. The doors close and I am alone, feeling more vulnerable than I'd ever felt. The subtle vibrations of the cable straining from the weight of the elevator resonate through the soles of my shoes. My thoughts loom. People must have been in elevators ... on the stairs ... heading to their offices ... just as I am doing right now. Anger fills me. I want to break someone's neck. I want to make someone pay for what they did. I want to do onto others like they did onto us!

This is the epicenter of international trade and business, and the very thing that was attacked on 9-11. Commerce. Capitalism. I am a living testament that our nation has overcome.

By the time the elevator doors open onto the thirty-fifth floor, I am possessed with renewed resolve. With a sense of purpose, I step from the elevator shaft and *march* toward the Maugham Southerby office suites. I cross the threshold, aware of who I am, what I am, and what I have to do. Sell securities. Sell a *shitload* of securities. We'll show those scumbags. If they think they can take us down by destroying the Towers, we'll show them that nothing can take us down. We're Wall Street. We're America! We're invincible!

Without missing a step, I grab my messages and trade confirmations from my mail slot just outside the cage. The cage is a literal cage—locked and forbidden to agents to avoid any tampering with trade orders once they've been placed. With my heart still pounding and nostrils flaring from thoughts about 9-11, I head to the bullpen. My thoughts dissipate quickly however, as soon as I open my top drawer and see the pile of breath mints that have accumulated.

Benny knows nothing about investments, but he sure knows how to push his products. The first time I bought *The Wall Street Journal* from him and asked for a roll of peppermint breath mints— *one* roll of mints—Benny put two rolls on top of the *Journal* and smiled. 'Better to be prepared,' he had said. It had sounded like good advice. 'You're a wise man, Benny,' I had told him. Now every time he sees me coming, he puts up one *WSJ* and two rolls of peppermint breath mints and I pay him for all of it every time, without protest. I toss one more roll of breath mints onto the pile. "Kudos Benny," I mumble to myself, "I should be taking lessons from you.' I pop another mint into my mouth and begin sorting through the stuff from my mail slot.

The three trades I made last Friday settled. I make a mental note to call Willard Rybach. I continue to thumb through the pile, eager to move onto the emails and get to Morning Call. A couple more trade confirmations, a phone message from Mary Willis, a second phone message from Mary Willis. Sweet, I think to myself. She's ripe. A memo from the cage admonishing my handwriting—"errors can be avoided if we write clearly and legibly." Kiss my ass, I think as I crumple it up and lob it into the communal wastebasket. Four points!

I continue to flip through the stack. There's a sealed envelope from the office supply cabinet bearing the Maugham Southerby logo. It is hand addressed to Manny. I look over at the still darkened cage from which this error has perpetrated. Maybe I should send them a memo and tell them to open their *own* eyes, like there isn't enough difference between our names. It isn't the first time Manny's mail was put into my mail slot. Wonder how many times *my* mail winds up in *his*? I'm about to flip it into the wastebasket when I realize it is Charlie's handwriting on the envelope. "What the ...?"

CHAPTER 8: SWEET SUCCESS
MINNEAPOLIS, MINNESOTA

FRIDAY, SEPTEMBER 21, 2007: 3:10 P.M. (CDT)

Mary Willis, the woman I had met at Starbucks a couple of months ago, turns out to be the gateway to a goldmine. Human resource directors of large companies are harried and overwhelmed and she was no different. Her job depends on her ability to woo the 2 percent at the top while still addressing the needs of the other 98 percent of the employees in the company, all the while trying to keep up with overwhelming state and federal mandates without sufficient human resources in her own department. It's a paradox made in heaven for a financial advisor who knows how to give her assistance without costing her or her company a penny. That's where I come in.

Maugham Southerby has resources unparalleled by any other securities firm doing business in the Midwest. It is one of the reasons Charlie decided to initiate his plan from Minnesota and not New York—minimal competition. "Maximize potential by using optimal effort among the least competition," is what he had said.

Eventually our combined books of business will be able to afford our own professional counsel—albeit a narrow scope to provide boutique services—at which time we will go independent and expand to both coasts. Right now we wrap up the central region using the resources of Maugham Southerby under presumed normal business practices. Plan A.

I had a few guys in the internal tax department back at headquarters take a look at the benefits package offered by Midwest Med. They can now advise optimal times for any one employee to exercise stock options relative to their personal financial situation. I'm Mary's connection to big fat happy employees. She's my connection to big fat investment portfolios.

Things got very nice for me very quickly. Just a few weeks ago I was worried about keeping my job long enough for Charlie's plan to materialize, and now I live in the condo next to him overlooking the Mississippi River.

It had become impossible for me to go back to that stinking efficiency after moving Mayo into his mini-mansion. I looked into my own possibilities and discovered zero-down, interest-only payments on a five-year adjustable-rate mortgage could put me in a $1.5 million dollar condo. Closed in less than ten days. Took me less than an hour to move everything I own and I was out of Fiddlers Park—for good!

Julie's attending the Julliard School of Dance in New York. I acquired a home equity line of credit on the condo in anticipation of paying her next tuition payment and give her what she needs for room and board. Now if I can just get Mom to sell the house. Says she wants to die there, but that's exactly what I'm trying to avoid. Her health setback last month has me concerned. Getting her out of there will do her good.

Trade confirmations fill my box. I flip through them and mentally add up the commission. "Yahoo," I shout as I rap out a drum roll with my fingers on the counter surrounding the cage. The young assistant in the cage looks up, startled. I snap my fingers and give her a wink.

The duds in my closet these days are tailored and coordinated. I still have to get some furniture, but I think I'll give Helice my credit card and tell her to go crazy the next time she's in town. She's been making a point of being in town more often. Could be an indication she is thinking about signing up for the long haul. Just could happen if she plays her cards right, too. So far, she's played a Royal Flush every time we've gotten together. I get hot just thinking about her.

I plunk the whole pile of trade orders into my top drawer before I lock up the desk for the weekend. Now that I have a few qualified investors in my book I've been able to push CDOs, and have even wrapped some in Swaps just like Garrison was telling us to do back in the Hamptons. I pat the top of my desk in appreciation of what lies confirmed in my top drawer—commissions. Big commissions.

"Hey Manny. It's your turn to pull rotation tonight," I shout over the wall between us, intending to push his buttons. He ignores me, as usual, but I see his back stiffen. It gripes me that Manny is part of Charlie's plan. Something still doesn't sit right with me about the whole thing. After confronting Charlie about the envelope, he explained his reasons for wanting Manny in the plan. While Manny will be rewarded sufficiently for his contribution, it will be a lot less than Manny assumes. What irritates me most is Manny thinks he's been selected on account of the size of his balls. Maybe I'm thinking the same thing. Normally I would never put up with this, but since I have nothing better going, I have to stick around for the curtain call.

I shut my station down and grab my briefcase. I purposely kick Manny's chair as I pass him, then look over my shoulder as I pass to I give him a toothy sneer and tell him, "I'll *try* to save you a stool at Monty's." I know he's flipping me the finger, but I refuse to give him the satisfaction of noticing. By now we both know the rules of our game. I convey *my* sentiments by not turning around. "Gotcha!"

SATURDAY, SEPTEMBER 22, 2007: 1:30 P.M. (CDT)

Helice is on her way from New York. It's become routine for her to fly into Minneapolis on weekends. I combine business with pleasure these days. Opening nights at the Guthrie, backstage parties at the Orpheum, cast parties at Hey City Stages, political teas at the Metropolitan Club, and a few private yacht parties on Lake Minnetonka. Always in the right spots, with business cards at the tips of my fingers.

Having Helice on my arm steps up the process. Men are drawn to her like flies to a horse's hind end. While they gawk, I talk money. Once I referred to us as Bonnie and Clyde, only nobody shoots at us. She since has named our private parts thusly. Now whenever she calls, she asks how Clyde is and I tell her Clyde is missing Bonnie terribly. I don't understand why women name genitals, but it doesn't matter so long as she plays *my* favorite game.

I'm bringing Helice by the house Sunday to meet everyone. Mom has started another round of chemotherapy treatments. I figure since Helice is working out she might as well meet Mom while Mom still has hair. Should be fun to see the look on their faces when I walk in the door at Mom's house with Helice on my arm, I think to myself as I park the car in short-term parking at the airport.

It is shortly after three by the time I corral Helice and all her luggage. We go back to my loft where we do our little romp about four times before we hit the shower for one last go-round wet and wild before we dry each other off and dress for the evening. Tonight we're taking in a play at the Prairie Stage Theatre, a folksy evening I've arranged for a couple of clients from rural Minnesota, the Metzger's, John and Dorothy. It's going to be several levels lower than what

Helice is used to. When she emerges from the bedroom wearing a floor-length gown with a slit up the side, I have to tell her that most people just wear jeans to where we're going.

"Then let's go slumming," she says with a wink.

I brief her about the Metzger's on the way there. They look like a harmless little old couple, I tell her, but they are worth around $20 million in my estimation. Both their daddies had big farms in the right spots. As sudden millionaires, they haven't as yet developed a taste for lavish living.

She can't even entertain such a ridiculous notion. The only time a person doesn't spend a lot of money is when they don't have it.

I have $5 million of their assets under management in a municipal bond strategy. His other three brothers have the rest and I want it ... all of it.

"Be careful when you work old man Metzger," I tell her. "His wife won't go for any funny stuff. Helice cocks her head and gives me a sideways glance that denotes confusion.

"Exactly," I confirm. "Minnesota women have rules. If a man wants to stay married, he doesn't break them. If you cross the line with a husband, you're history ... and so is he. So bond," I tell her. "Do whatever women do to become the best of friends, but don't flirt with her husband."

Helice slumps back in her seat. She was all geared up for a night of vamping. Now what? I reach over and give her a pat on the inside of her leg. "Just be subtle and you can still have your fun." She blows me an air kiss.

The Prairie Stage Theater is one of the oldest continuously operating professional theaters in the United States, but if more Minnesotan's had been to Broadway it never would have lasted this long, I think to myself. We follow the lighted path toward a barn-like structure amidst a farm-like setting. Quaint, I'll give it that, but nothing like the theater district in the Big Apple.

The Metzger's are avid patrons and are now esteemed charitable donors of the theater since they came into money. According to them, the theater had begun on a dirt floor in a shed near the farms where each had grown up. Every time we meet, they inundate me with stories about how when they were young they had met so many actors, had worked as stagehands, and even played a few bit parts in summer stock.

The Prairie Stage Theater seemed the perfect place to bring them for a night of schmoozing. As soon as we are through the doors, I have an overwhelming sense I've been here before, although I don't recall when or with whom.

The Metzger's rush to meet us as we enter. Handshakes and smiles, short introductions, small talk about the weather and the drive over—which way had we taken they want to know—how the theater is so quaint they tell us, how we all love plays we say to one another. I can't help notice how both John and Dorothy keep looking at Helice from the corners of their eyes. They haven't seen anything like her here in Minnesota—or anywhere, for that matter.

"Helice is from South Carolina," I say to answer the questions on their faces. Their eyebrows rise in unison.

"Her father is the Senator from South Carolina, Brandley Hendicotte." Their eyebrows rise even further. Dorothy lets out an "Oh, my."

"Didn't he filibuster the healthcare bill?" John asks, his brow beginning to furrow.

Helice proudly nods. I forgot to tell her they were Democrats. Helice's sentiment is anybody with any real amount of money should be Republican. Why would they be anything else? Who in their right mind wants to pay taxes that go toward helping lesser beings? To her way of thinking, it is a natural form of social weeding.

Until both John and Dorothy had received the proceeds from the sale of the land from their parents' farms as an inheritance two years ago, neither had ever known wealth. Their children had gone to public schools and gotten through college on student loans. Five years ago, when Dorothy had a stroke, however, they became devout advocates of Medicaid—part of the Democratic platform they explain to everyone, as though it is their testament as to how they found God. It had been a bad crop year and they would either have lost Dorothy, the farm, or both, had it not been for Medicaid. Since getting back on their feet financially they have become strong advocates for affordable healthcare for all.

"Why are people so against national health care?" John begins. "Don't they know we already have it?" His head cocks in disbelief, but it is not a challenge for anyone to comment. "It works brilliantly," he goes on. "It's called Medicare."

He was about to say more, but I jump in with a diversion. "Helice lives in Manhattan," I say.

John is slow to react. His mind is still on healthcare reform and all, but Dorothy is immediately on board. I enjoy watching the wrinkles in their faces disappear as their heads tighten in astonishment.

They look at Helice as if for the first time. "My, my, dear," Dorothy utters. "You've come such a long way to see the play."

Helice is about to roll her eyes, but catches the look in mine. Correctly interpreting my expression, she quickly smiles and says, "What's a few miles to us play-buffs, right?" She gives Dorothy a little bonding nudge and winks at me.

Dorothy, seeking to equally impress, grabs the arm of Rory Standish, the owner and director of the theater. She pulls him from the milling crowd and introduces him specifically to Helice as though she is offering him up for sacrifice. "Rory has been with the theater for over sixty years," she says.

"And you were my first leading lady," Rory says with exaggerated theatrics.

Dorothy dismisses his flattery but admits she had played Ned Cobb's daughter in the first play Rory ever directed at the Prairie Stage Theatre.

Helice looks over the top of Dorothy's head. Her eyes plead for help. Rory notices the exchange between Helice and myself and pulls the back of Helice's hand to his lips. "All the world is a stage, my love," he says with a smile, then begs our pardon, explaining he must see to things backstage.

At dinner, we sit opposite John and Dorothy at a table set for twelve. It feels sort of like a mess hall only the tables are draped in linen and are preset with salads and breadbaskets. Plates of bland food are passed from one patron to the other until it reaches its rightful destination. This particularly jogs my memory. Alison! That's who I had been with. It had been her birthday or something. I chuckle at the thought of us thinking how special all this was back then.

"What?" Helice asks, curious as to what is making me smile.

"Nothing important," I say as I pat her leg under the table. But I still have to stifle a laugh just thinking about how small my world had once been.

By the end of dinner, the demeanor of the Metzger's becomes almost nurturing, as though they are our elders to whom we should listen.

"You need to meet my brothers," John advises me. I half suspect it is as much to show his brothers that he has a financial advisor as it is to help me network, but I let him feel his oats. He's the old buck teaching the little buck what to do now. He acts as if marrying the right girl and outliving your rich father is something he attained by wits instead of luck.

"Absolutely," I tell him. "I'd love to meet them." Not to mention get my hands on more of that family money, I think to myself. But we both know what I mean. After all, we are men—men who have to earn good money to take care of our little women. By now old John thinks Dorothy is in the same league as Helice, his memories of his wife on stage no doubt being conjured.

We all take our seats. The play is an off-Broadway rendition of *Peter and the Starcatcher*, which I know nothing about. I flip through the playbill, but between the conversations among us and of those around us it is impossible to read. The lights flicker. The house lights lower. Dreams of being able to fly and desires for magic dust captivate my interest for the next two hours, only to find that nothing stays the same and that we all eventually must grow up.

Still enchanted by the performance I follow Helice and Dorothy, who walk arm-in-arm up the aisle as we file out of the theater. John is bringing up the rear and gives me a little sock on the arm with his fist along with a smile as though to say he is proud of me. For what? I wonder. He points to the two women and smiles. He equates my ability to get Helice with my ability to make him money. Whether he's right or not doesn't matter. The only important thing here is that *he* thinks that's so. Paint them a picture of their own delusion and they become puppets on a string. I point to Dorothy and give him a wink and a nod. He smiles ear-to-ear.

Dorothy, however, is another matter. While she might be a bit overwhelmed by a New York woman in a designer gown, she knows who she is and she knows she's married to a curmudgeon. She doesn't see herself as John's babe at all. She's just an old mom. Just about cut up my steak for me at dinner. "Better get home and get some sleep now," Dorothy tells us. "Tomorrow is church."

"That's right," I assure her, as though I were answering my own mother.

"Come along, John," she commands gently.

We wave good-bye and head for our respective vehicles. The temperature has dropped and there's a hint of winter in the air, but the skies are clear and sparkling.

"I need a drink," Helice sighs as soon as we are out of earshot. We both laugh and head for The Sheiks Club. The night is young and I have to explain how big the pile of money is that we just moved a little closer to. There's lots to do yet tonight. Lots!

Sunday, September 23, 2007: 12:12 p.m. (CDT)

It's after noon by the time Helice and I arrive at Mom's. I'd never brought anyone home before, except Alison, but that didn't mean anything. Not that this means anything. Alright, I admit it. I just want to show off Helice, make my family see how far I'd grown from the boy I used to be.

I wave my hand at them behind Helice's back for them to stop gawking as soon as we enter the front door, but Grandma Jazz doesn't notice. Her mouth just keeps getting wider the longer she stares at Helice. She has never seen anyone like her. The girls around here still wear blue jeans and canvas sneakers and pull their hair into ponytails. Helice has so much hair you can't see her face unless she turns in your direction. She is wearing leopard print tights under a sheer black blouse that reveals a black teddy. She's carrying a bright yellow purse, either that or one of her small suitcases, and her toes are at a 45-degree angle from her arches in the heels she is wearing.

Bob jumps to a stand. The lounger rocks rapidly from his quick abandonment, while his wife Lori slumps back in her chair, eyes widening as though she were backing away from a rattlesnake. Her fingers entwine and tighten into a white-knuckle clench while she contemplates taking a swing at her husband for his obvious infatuation.

There is a long awkward pause while everyone looks at Helice and she back at them. Finally Barb rushes over and introduces herself and asks if there is anything she can get her to drink. When Helice tells her a Perrier, Barb stares back blankly.

"Water," I translate for Barb.

She rushes off to pour a glass from the tap.

Barry seems oddly busy with the kids. While Nicholas and Natalie stand next to him, speechless for a change, Barry is wiping Nathan's nose, tucking in the little tyke's shirt, and pulling up his socks. He glances at us in between all the fussing, acts as though he's nervous or something.

Helice looks around the living room as though she's sizing up a homeless shelter and looking for a clean place to sit. Maybe I shouldn't have brought her here, I think to myself. Maybe she isn't ready to see this side of me yet. It's got to be a shock from what she had originally thought. I told her about my meager beginnings, but also about our link to the Carnegies, the Roosevelts, and the Hudsons. *That* had impressed her. This clearly doesn't.

"Tell us about yourself," Grandma Jazz says as soon as we are seated. "Where do you come from?"

Nicholas snickers and Barry shoos him from the room.

"South Carolina," I answer on Helice's behalf. I don't know why I answered for her, but I feel compelled to protect her from ... from ... well, I guess from my Grandma Jazz.

"Can't she talk?" Grandma Jazz asks, but she clearly doesn't expect me to answer. What she expects is for Helice to answer her ... now.

Helice tosses her hair back and smiles. "All my people are from Charleston. Seven generations."

"Are you part Mohican?" Grandma asks in all sincerity. She believes anyone with family that goes back farther than three generations in this country must be part Native American. She's been on the refugee committee at church and learning about social diversification for the first time in her life—something much more difficult for a person who grew up hearing racial slurs for every nationality and told that was proper English. But she's trying hard to learn new ways of thinking.

Helice isn't impressed with my grandmother's capacity for understanding social norms of the south and takes offense at not being recognized for who she is: the daughter of Senator Bradley Hendicotte of the Charleston family of Hendicottes, noted for their efforts in making the south into one of the greatest cotton resources in the world, and for their service and bravery during the Civil War, in spite of the despicable outcome. She ignores the question altogether, which doesn't sit well with Grandma Jazz.

"David tells us that you are a junior reporter for NBC," Mom says quickly. "We watch NBC all the time, don't we?" she says to Barb who hands Helice a glass of water. Mom nods her head up and down profusely and Barb nods in reciprocation just as eagerly while Helice examines the glass of water for floating debris.

By now Barry looks like he's squeezing off a fart. Lori sighs and tosses her head to one side as if to ignore what she can't believe is going on before her very eyes. Bob remains standing at attention in front of the empty lounger.

"Sit down," Grandma Jazz tells him. "You make a better door than a window." Bob sits as straight as I've ever seen anyone sit in a lounge chair.

By the time the pizzas come and the boxes are opened, it looks as though Helice is about to puke as she struggles to avoid even smelling anything.

Nobody appears to notice except Mom, who holds yet another bowl of Jell-O in her lap, her primary source of sustenance since her treatments began again. Our eyes meet for a second, but I turn away. I realize this was a bad move. Helice does not fit into this family. *I* don't fit into this family anymore. Helice doesn't need this. I lean toward her and whisper in her ear, "I will save you, damsel." Then, using a technique I mastered for such occasions, I discreetly reach into my pant pocket for my cell phone and speed-dial my blackberry, which is in my breast pocket. Urgently I answer while I run into the other room, my line of business being confidential and all. When I come back into the room all eyes are on me, expecting an emergency. After making all the typical gestures of regret, Helice and I bug out.

"I'll come by later tonight," I promise Mom as I kiss the top of her head. "See you guys later," I say to the others.

We drive for several minutes before Helice says, "David …"

I don't like the way that sounds.

"When you said you were related to the Carnegies and Roosevelts and Hudsons, did you mean the same families as from the coast?"

"Yeah," I reply anxiously. "The very same." She looks at me doubtfully. "The Crash of '29 wiped out all my family's fortunes, or I'd be as wealthy as Charlie right now." Now didn't seem like a good time to explain that only one of my ancestors avoided losing everything in the Crash of 1929 because he had the foresight to pull everything out before it crashed. Now was the time to convince her that I came from wealth. "Every one of my ancestors who came to America either came with wealth from the homeland or made it in the new world. They lived all up and down the east coast in some of the biggest mansions and penthouses ever built—Long Island, Nantucket, Central Park West. They were businessmen, some even politicians. They had upstairs maids and downstairs maids and chauffeurs and nannies. But they had their money in the very same investments that broke the banks. When the banks stopped lending money, my ancestors could no longer operate their businesses. Having lost all their savings and investments due to the Crash there was little any of them could do." I waited for her reply.

Her expression didn't change. "I didn't realize you don't have any money," she says, like she didn't hear a word I said.

"I'm makin' it, baby," I plead with her. "I'm in the money, honey. In no time at all, I'll be pulling in more than a million a year."

She just looks at me. I can tell that wasn't what she wanted to hear. A million isn't going to be enough for her.

"Look," I tell her. "I'm not supposed to tell anyone about this yet, but Charlie and I have a plan that will make both of us the two richest people in the world."

She looks deep into my eyes, searching for truth. It takes her a little longer than is comfortable before she asks, "How?"

"Never you mind. Just trust me." I sit back and straighten as tall as I can behind the steering wheel of my old Ford Ranger and tell her, "You're looking at the next Warren Buffet, baby." It's the best I can do under the circumstances. I'm not placing any bets on Charlie's idea myself, but it's all I got. Besides, Charlie's plan *could* work. He certainly has the contacts and the smarts to pull it off. But it is sort of like heading to Hollywood to become a star. Just because a person can sing and dance doesn't mean they get discovered.

I don't know whether she believes me, or whether she's just lacking better options, but she smiles and thankfully we're back on track.

WEDNESDAY, OCTOBER 31, 2007: 3:02 P.M. (CST)

I'm up fifteen grand by Closing Bell and hear my brand new BMW M6 calling from the underground garage. Since I picked it up last Tuesday, I've put nearly a thousand miles on it just driving around town. I shut down my computer, grab my coat, and bolt from the windowless room they gave me once Crosby could no longer deny that my status deserved an office.

I walk toward the bullpen where three new rookies now sit, one of which is in Beef's old spot. A moment of regret washes over me. Darrel Beefknack fell for his own disguise—the one they give us when we're hired and hand us a business card that says 'financial adviser.' The vultures have picked over the spoils he left behind and tossed Charlie and me a few bones as a way of admitting us to the pack. A constant flow of fired up rookies is what keeps this firm afloat—never mind their short duration. It is what they leave on the table that counts.

I feel eyes on my back as I walk past, but I refuse to make eye contact. I've learned not to get too chummy with the newbies. It only makes matters worse for them when they get the boot.

Barb had called earlier and told me she needed me at her house by five. I had been too busy when she called to ask why. Guess I'll find out when I get there. I glance at my watch. I have just enough time to stop at Monty's for a wind down.

It's like I'm on fire lately. Crosby smiles when he sees me. I spend less time in the office and more time in front of prospects—usually over drinks, on the golf course, or at one of the many upscale restaurants here in the Twin Cities, where the maître d's quickly learned my name once I started dropping them hundred-dollar bills for tips.

Stan at the Dakota Room says, 'Right this way, Mr. Yates.' Basu at the Indian Garden says, 'Mr. Yates, Mr. Yates ... the best table I saved just for you.' And Jason at Kincaid's always snaps his fingers at a couple of waiters and makes sure my table is hovered over like royalty.

I stepped up the image another notch with a close-cut haircut, no facial hair—even wax the brows. Nails manicured weekly, with polish. When I step out the door each morning, I shine brighter than the sun, if it were up; but that's another thing—I'm up by five and out the door before there's even a glow on the horizon. I could just as easily have wound up on the scrapheap like Beef. I learned you don't waste time explaining the finer points of money management to people. They don't want to hear it anyway. All anyone wants is for me to make them money ... *more* money ... *lots* of money. Nobody wants to hear about political changes, tax laws that might affect their financial situation, not to mention moral obligations to themselves. All they want is for me to tell them I can get them a better rate of return on their money than anyone else. The mutual understanding being they will go elsewhere if I can't.

It's a Tai Chi concept. Use your opponent's momentum against them. Greed. That's the momentum I use. And now that I understand the rule of this game my winnings have increased ten-fold. By the time

I disclose all the risks of investing they aren't listening to a word I am saying. That's when I really cinch it. I turn the tables and tell them the deal is off. 'Can't let you do it,' I tell them. 'If something happens, you'll come back and blame me.' That's when they panic. They are right there at the trough looking down at the reflection of their own dreams in the water. All they have to do is reach out with their tongue and take a lick, but I hold them back until they drool. Then I say something like, 'What if I lose all your money and you have to move into a homeless shelter?'

They think I'm joking.

I'm dead serious.

As soon as they sign the papers and leave my office, I record everything I just asked them and jot down word-for-word their response. Then I record the date and time for our corporate defense lawyers in the event a client comes back and tries to say I didn't tell them about the risks. You bring your balls to this playground, expect to play with the big boys. We play to win.

I slam my Daytimer closed and head for the elevator. On my way out I notice the door to the Bascomb Group suite of offices is closed. Usually everyone there is long gone by this time; yet through the window I see the entire group huddled around the conference table, Martin Bascomb in the middle looking seriously grim.

My prolonged stare attracts the attention of his assistant. She looks up. Our eyes meet. I smile. She pulls the drapes closed. I shrug.

Outside the Maugham Southerby suites, a crowd of brokers gathers near the elevator. This occurs every day like clockwork at the close of the New York Stock Exchange. It is dubbed throughout the building as 'The Running of the Bulls.' I step into the herd and smile. Life is Heaven. Pure Heaven.

CHAPTER 9: NIGHTMARES AND NOOSES
MINNEAPOLIS, MINNESOTA

WEDNESDAY, OCTOBER 31, 2007: 5:00 P.M. (CST)

"**H**ey, pard'ner," I say to my five-year-old nephew Nathan, who is dressed in some sort of getup when he meets me at the front door of my sister's house.

"I'm not a pard'ner," he says defiantly. "I'm the Paw-es-a-dent!"

"I guess you are," I relent, not knowing what a paw-somethingdent is. He runs off with an urgency all children seemed to possess that makes them run everywhere. Barb is ripping open bags of little Snickers bars and dumping them into a huge plastic bowl in the hallway. I grab a couple as I pass as a way of saying hello and head to the couch. With one Snickers bar in my mouth and the other half opened I ask her what she's doing.

She stops opening candy bar bags and puts her hands on her hips and stares at me.

"What?" I say around a mouthful of caramel, nuts, and chocolate.

"Are you even among the living anymore?" She shakes her head.

"What?" I ask again, arms flung out wide.

She walks over to where I am now sprawled on the couch and looks down at me. "It's Halloween. You remember what that is, don't you? Goblins, ghosts ... bluhhh la bluhhla blu," she wiggles her fingers at me in a ghostly way, then tickles me in the ribs.

My abs spasm and pull me into a sitting position. Chocolate drools from my mouth onto my white shirt. "Aw, man," I say, "You made me spit on myself."

She laughs and walks back to her bowl of candy bars. "Good. You can go as the slob you used to be."

I frown at her.

She ignores me. "Might be nice to see that guy again," she mutters.

Just then, Natalie comes around the corner crying. She clings to Barb's pant leg and buries herself between her mother's thighs. "Mommy ... mommy ... Nick-o-las said I am the ba-wide of Fa-wank-en-stein. I don't wanna be the ba-wide of Fa-wank-en-stein. I wanna be the ba-wide of the han-some paw-wince."

Nicholas screeches to a halt in front of his mother, then teases Natalie one more time with a ghoulish groan and says, "Bride of Franken-stein ... hee, hee, hee."

Natalie wails. I cover my ears. Barb tries to peel Natalie from her leg. The dog starts barking. The doorbell rings. All three kids, the dog, and Barb rush to the door. "Trick or treat," I hear a mob of kids say from the front porch.

I lie on the couch for a good half-hour and listen to a relentless parade of feet upon the porch-boards and the screams of little voices begging for candy and I can't help smile. I remember when we were kids and couldn't wait for Halloween. I mean, what could be better than free candy at as many doors as you could make it to before your mom called you in to go to bed? Bob and I used to run as fast as we could, pelting up steps two at a time and jumping off porches to shave time off the mission. It was better than Christmas and Easter put together. We were in charge of our own fate and didn't have to be good to get anything. In fact, the nastier we were, the more people liked it. We'd dress as bums because we couldn't afford costumes, but always had enough old ripped clothes. We'd smudge our faces with mascara and draw streaks with red lipstick to look like blood ... there always had to be blood on us somewhere. Sometimes we'd paint on tattoos of snakes and daggers. Sometimes we'd put pantyhose on our heads thinking it did something to make us look more like bums but the only thing it did was make us look like bank robbers. We ran with complete abandon through the streets of the Park and begged at every door. We'd come home with sacks full of candy that would last us the entire year if we didn't lose it down the heat ducks.

Barb must not have been able to keep up, or maybe she didn't go. I can't remember. Julie was too little to go alone, I remember that. Mom walked with her. I guess Barb stayed home to pass out candy. And here she is, still passing out candy.

"We're ready," shout the three rug rats.

I look at them. "So?"

"That's why you're here, buddy boy," Barb says. "Either you take them trick-or-treating or hand out candy here at home. Your choice, but it is the only two choices you get."

"Where's Barry?"

"Had to work late."

I jump up and put on my coat. "There's no slackers on my tour of duty," I warn as the four of us pelt for the door. The night is chilly but perfect for a rigorous romp through the neighborhood. I lead my little band along the same route Bob and I once used, which we had strategized as the shortest distance between all the doors in the Park.

Barb starts texting my cell phone at eight o'clock and every two minutes thereafter. "They have school tomorrow."

I plead on their behalf that we're almost done.

By the time I bring them back, I am carrying Natalie and Nate the last two blocks, but Nick hangs right in there until we hit the steps to his house, then he bursts out crying about something that didn't make any sense and runs to Barb.

"They're exhausted," Barb scolds as she rushes them upstairs to the bathroom. I stick around and listen to the protests of having to wash off all the fun and brush all the candy from their teeth. By the time Barb comes down the stairs she looks like she could use a drink, but she begins cleaning up the kitchen from the supper that never got put away.

I hang at the kitchen table and watch her, just like I used to do as a kid. She sticks a few pieces of cold pizza in front of me. Just like old times, I think to myself, since it was usually Barb who put most meals on at our house while we were growing up—Mom wouldn't get home from work until after six.

"You and Barry decide anything?" I ask. I'd talked to them about buying a bigger house. Told them they could buy anything they want and I would get them a mortgage. There was no need for Barb to live two doors down from Mom any longer with me and Julie gone. She and Barry had bought old lady Jensen's house on Contract for Deed when they were first married. It had been convenient for Barb to still keep an eye on Julie and me, but that was before they had any kids of their own. This place is way too small for them now.

Barb shrugs. "We sort of like it here."

"What? All I ever heard you talk about was getting out of Fiddlers Park. Now's your chance."

She shrugs again.

I slump in my chair. What is wrong with her and Mom? Don't they know there is another world outside the Park? One worth living? Neither of us says anything for a long while. "What do you think of Helice?" I ask, ready to move on to another subject. Nobody has said anything to me since I brought her to the house nearly a month ago.

Barb turns around and gives me a cautious look. "The only thing important is what *you* think of her," she says. Her eyes freeze on mine.

I turn up my bottom lip and raise my eyebrows in disbelief. "What's not to like about Helice?"

She smiles. I can't read her, but I think *she* thinks Helice is alright. I think. "She'd not like the girls around here," I suggest.

"No, she's not," Barb agrees.

"She's hot, ain't she?"

Barb looks over her shoulder at me and smiles like we know a secret. "*That* she is."

Barry walks in the back door and plunks his computer bag on the floor as he reaches down and scratches the dog's ear. Barb puts a piece of warmed up pizza in front of him and a beer. "Want one?" she asks pointing to the beer.

"No, I gotta go … early day tomorrow."

Barb raises her eyebrows. Since when has she ever seen me pass up a beer? But this is the new me. I have to be disciplined now.

"We were just talking about Helice," I say, hoping to get Barry's reaction. Nothing. He just eats his pizza.

Barb joins us at the table with a beer of her own. "You serious about her?" Barb asks.

"No. We're just getting to know each other."

"And there's a lot of her to get to know," Barry says with a mouthful of pizza. Barb slaps him on the head. We all laugh.

My family will never understand someone like Helice. She's too sophisticated for them, too worldly … too everything. I can see that now. But that's alright. I want nothing but the best. I want the best car, the best girl, eventually the best house … I want it all, and so does she. We're right for one another. I see that more and more. But I love my family. It's okay they might never understand this part of me. It's okay.

"I gotta go home," I say, but the truth is my new condo doesn't feel much like home. There are times I miss not having Maggie trail me out the door asking for her rent and—I never thought I'd say this—I seem to be suffering from the lack of perm stink. Can a person become addicted to that stuff? Maybe I developed an addiction living there all those years.

I walk around my car to make sure nobody egged it or soaped the windows before I climb in and feel the power. I love driving this thing, the way it makes me feel ... like I could drive right into outer space. I step on the gas and burn rubber as I leave Fiddlers Park.

My place is near the old Pillsbury flourmill along the river. It's an old warehouse that was converted into million-dollar condos they call lofts—because it's easier to market a 'river loft' than a condo. It isn't a place for kids.

The only ghouls I see tonight are a few drunk adults in costume near the bars on Washington Avenue. The street where I live is barren of traffic. I pull into the secured underground parking. Automatic lights go on and off as I pass the stalls until I get to my own, then the light above my stall illuminates. Once I leave the stall, that light will turn off, too. The garage is quiet. I take the elevator to the seventh floor. The hall is empty. The only sound is my key unlocking the deadbolt in the door. When I close the door behind me, the place echoes with every movement I make. I head for the refrigerator and grab a beer, but I don't bother to turn on any lights. The place is illuminated enough by the city's lights for me to see everything in my near-empty living room. I really do have to get some furniture one of these days. A bed anyway.

I stand at the patio door where I am able to overlook both the city and the river. There is much drinking and partying going on seven stories below and up a few blocks where the taverns are filled with adults taking full advantage of the spirits of this evening. Meanwhile, the mighty Mississippi with all its beauty and treachery crawls through the chaos, carving out its own path without regard to anything but itself.

That was fun, I think to myself, recalling how excited the kids were to go trick-or-treating tonight. Nick in his Spiderman cape, Natalie as the "ba-wide of the handsome paw-ince" ... and Nathan as ... what was he again? Oh, yeah, he was the Paw-es-a-dent ... President Clinton. That's right. Former President Bill Clinton. Nobody guessed who he was, which made him tear off his mask by the second block. After which, he made funny faces and growled at the sound of a doorbell.

I muse awhile longer while I sip my beer. Funny how as a kid I used to think time dragged, to the point I thought the weekend would never come, when in reality it was flying by so quickly my entire childhood is now so far into the past I can scarcely recall it.

By the time I crawl into the sleeping bag I have rolled out on the floor of my living room, I'm recalling the days Bob and I would camp in our backyard. I fall asleep feeling like I'm lying under that old oak tree as a kid, listening to the hoot owl.

MONDAY, NOVEMBER 5, 2007: 3:05 A.M. (CST)

I wake up in a sweat. It takes me a second to realize I am not in my efficiency over The Curl Up and Dye ... that I am lying on the floor of my loft tangled in a sweaty sleeping bag. Shards of the dream I had been having dissipate in spite of my attempt to hold them. Clinton. President Clinton. Something about a rope. He was hanging from a rope. Then, the rope was around me ... it was around my neck ... *I* was hanging by the rope!

It's 3:03 a.m. I toss. I turn. I can't go back to sleep. I get up and take a shower, dress and head into the office. Arriving too early for Benny's or Starbucks to be open, I make a pot of coffee in the lunchroom and take it to my private office and close the door. It isn't until I take the first sip of plain old black coffee that my brain stops swirling from the nightmare I had. I flip on CNBC and sit back in the deep leather chair and allow the announcers to carry my mind to places elsewhere around the world. I'm back in the saddle by the time Morning Call comes around at 7 a.m.

Charlie isn't at Morning Call, as usual, so immediately upon hearing that the CEO of the largest retail bank in the world announced he is stepping down and that the second-largest bank in France just froze funds amid a subprime concern, I bolt from the room and go looking for him. I blast in without knocking and find him behind his closed office door talking to Manny. Charlie looks up. Manny swings his head in my direction.

Before I even wonder why I haven't been invited to this meeting—and why Manny has—I blurt out, "You guys hear that Jonathan Baldwin is stepping down from Citizens?" This means the ground is shaking and stemware is falling off shelves. The whole world should be stopping in its tracks.

Their blank stares tell me they hadn't heard.

"Pressured by the board due to $11 billion in additional subprime write-downs," I add, to clarify the reason for concern. Their expressions still don't change.

"We'll be done in just a few minutes. I'll come by your office and talk to you then," Charlie says calmly, in a gesture meant to politely dismiss me.

What the hell is going on? I wonder as I head back to my own office. Pillars among the investment world are tumbling from mountaintops and no one notices, or seems to care.

I run downstairs for a copy of *The Wall Street Journal*. Benny slaps it on the counter along with two rolls of peppermint flavored breath mints, takes my money, and avoids idle chit chat this morning having judged correctly that my mind is on other things. Back in my office, I pop a mint in my mouth, then another while I scan the headlines. At the bottom of page three a twenty-point type headline above a two-inch article reads: 'Citizens CEO Resigns.' Is that it? Is that all the publicity a story like this gets from *The Journal*?

I find an article about a world bank in France freezing funds on the next page, but before my head can grasp the severity of *that* I find another small headline that causes a major surge of adrenaline. It reads: 'Salzman Overexposed.'

Morton Salzman is the fourth largest investment bank on the Street and just reported $27.2 billion in subprime debt. Geez. That sounds like a lot to me. Isn't that a lot? I review what I know. Morton had recently taken a hefty credit hit, which is why it didn't make sense to me earlier why Citizens World Bank had recently bid to merge with Morton. Why would a company want to purposely take on trouble? What is going on? And why isn't anyone in this office interested?

The irony over the fact the very investment banks who had put the proverbial gun to Clinton's head in 1999 forcing bank deregulation was that those same banks were now hanging themselves with that same rope. "Ah," I groan. My head begins to nod rapidly as I realize the reason for my restless sleep. It is all making sense to me. In less than eight years of freedom from the Glass Steagall Act—the meat of the Banking Act of 1933 which had kept the world from the same disaster that caused the Crash of 1929—Wall Street had created derivatives which currently are unable to quench the thirst of investors worldwide. Citizens World Bank—the very bank that pulled the trigger on Clinton—was the first to fall. I'd laugh if it weren't so serious. My head spins as things begin to coalesce.

A few minutes later, Charlie is in my office trying to calm my nerves by explaining acquisitions and market capture as though we both didn't attend the same securities training.

"Listen to yourself. You're starting to believe your own bullshit," I tell him. Charlie gives me the same exasperated look everyone else around here does whenever I raise similar questions. "I can explain this shit just as good as you if only I knew what sort of shit I was explaining, but that's the problem." My arms spread wide while I wait for his full comprehension. "I don't know what is going on and neither do you."

Charlie bites his lower lip.

"I admit I'm a novice, but it doesn't take a genius to see *something* is happening," I continue. "There's someone out there with a loaded gun pointed at us, Charlie. But who? And why?"

"The little knowledge you have is gone to your head," he says. "If there is something to worry about don't you think the economists, researchers and analysts at headquarters—you know, the people working full time to know such things," he adds satirically, "don't you think *they* would be the ones worried and not you? Geez, Dave. If you get any more paranoid, I'm going to have to cut you out of the plan."

I bolt out of my chair, but before I reach his throat with my bare hands my phone rings. I reach for it at the same time Charlie escapes my grasp.

"Fannie Mae," the voice begins. "Buy six hundred round lots of Fannie Mae." It's Willard Rybach, a retired former CEO of Data Processors out of Arden Hills, the same guy who's been trying to get me to buy real estate in Miami. He holds two million in Fannie Mae, Ginnie Mae and REITs but it's not enough of a hedge against the $16.5 million in real estate he owns throughout the nation.

"Why, Willard," I plead, "why do you want to buy more Fannie Mae? How about some nice little U.S. Treasuries?"

"No, no," he protests. "I don't trust the government."

"But you trust homeowners?"

"Homeowners will eat dog food—they'll eat the damned dog—before they'll lose their house! Buy me more Fannie Mae!"

As soon as I hang up, I make notes of our conversation to help the lawyers who will no doubt have to defend my ass when this guy loses his. I can hear the judge now: 'It says here on your business card that you are a financial advisor; is that true Mr. Yates? As a financial advisor is it not your obligation to advise people on financial matters, Mr. Yates? And you say your client wanted to buy Fannie Mae on the morning of November fifth after it lost forty basis points the week prior and its share price dropped to its lowest in over a decade? And that against your own better judgment you placed trades that amounted to nearly one and a quarter million dollars for Mr. Rybach, a retired eighty-four-year-old. Is this correct, Mr. Yates? Now, I notice, Mr. Yates, that you made nearly a million dollars in commission last year selling your—ahem—advice. So, forgive me if I have to ask just how good an adviser *are* you, Mr. Yates if your own clients refuse to listen to you?' Oh, yeah. Everything is fine. Just ducky.

Charlie swings back into my office and closes the door. He takes a seat in one of the two chairs opposite me. He puts the tips of his fingers together and rests his chin on the pyramid he's made with his hands. My blood pressure rises. They say blood pressure is silent but I can hear mine ring in my ears. Before he takes charge of this conversation, like he always does, I confront him with, "What was that little meeting all about?"

"What meeting?"

"You *know* what meeting."

"You mean the meeting with Manny?"

My glare tells him he's pinned the tail on the donkey.

"You need to trust me."

There's a long pause while the chasm between us grows wider.

"Why did Baldwin so abruptly resign?" I ask pointedly, returning to the former topic.

"Who knows? People resign."

"Who cares?" I say sarcastically.

He looks at me with an expression of hope. "Exactly," he says as he leans forward. "It is not our job to care. Our job is to sell securities. Just … do your job." With that, he gets up and leaves my office.

I get ready to place the trades for Rybach and have my finger on the button, but I feel like a freshman caught without a condom at a frat party. I drop the trades at the opening bell and immediately call the BMW dealership as a mental and emotional diversion.

"Ready to trade up already?" Cramer asks, just to make me chuckle. I picked up Darrel Cramer as a client while prospecting my way through imported car dealerships in Edina. Now we're scratching each other's backs.

"How's my money?" he asks.

I pull up his accounts and tell him his portfolio is up four basis points as of the close of trading Friday.

"All is well," he says.

"Yeah," I reply. "Everything is just the shits."

Cramer takes that to mean something positive. He's one of those guys who twists everything anyone says into what he wants it to mean. He accepts life on his terms. Whether he buys you a drink or punches you in the nose depends on his mood.

I contemplate our differences and wonder if he's ever felt like his balls were about to be squeezed without knowing who might do the squeezing. I scratch the top of my head profusely. If a person suspects they are paranoid, does it mean they actually *are* or *aren't*?

CHAPTER 10: PREPARE TO STUFF IT
FIDDLERS PARK, MINNESOTA

THURSDAY, NOVEMBER 22, 2007: 10:45 A.M. (CST)

"How can you say that?"

It isn't really a question. It's Mom's way of making a statement. I hadn't heard her 'ask' in such a way since I was a kid, when she'd say things like: 'How can you wear that?' or 'What makes you think you know everything?" She never wanted to legitimately know. It only meant I should already know something that I obviously didn't. All I'm trying to do is find out why I have to share a Thanksgiving dinner with a person named Bobo, who happens to be the friend of the little-bit-weird son of the guy my mom is dating. It is all just a little too much for me to handle in the wake of things. I had been hoping for a bit of respite with family. Just us. No outsiders.

I'd imagined we'd eat a big noon dinner, rub our bellies, gape at the ceiling, maybe play a game of touch football before settling down to watch the Vikes vs. Packers. That's all I want. That's all I need. That's all I expect. There is nothing in my plans that includes strangers—least of all one who is sleeping with my mom—and none of whom have anything to do with some gay guy named Bobo.

"What kind of a name is Bobo? Did his mother name him that?"

"No, his mother didn't name him that," Mom replies, annoyed that I am not easily accepting a guest graciously to our family's Thanksgiving table. "His birth name is Bogart Beuchene," she says, as though the name is dignified.

Oh, that's better. I'll be sharing my mom's turkey with a bozo named Bogart. I roll my eyes as I leave the warmth of the kitchen with its smells that wrap around me like Grandma Jazz's great arms. But the smells waft with me into the dining room. The skin on the turkey is at the caramelizing stage and my old taste buds know the routine all too well. A roar emerges from my intestines. I begin searching for something to stick into my mouth and find the relish tray. I hover over it, plucking broccoli flowerets and dipping them into a ranch dip until I spot sliced baguettes all warm and brushed with garlic butter hiding under a starched linen napkin. I move on to the pickle dish and grab a stuffed Greek olive. I forget about old Bobo.

Mom has done her usual decorating for the holiday, a sign she is feeling her old self these days. The chemo treatments ended two weeks ago and most of her vitality has returned. Barb and Lori came early this morning to help her peel potatoes. Grandma Jazz has been here since before dawn putting on the turkey. Julie is more of a pest than a help—she's been on her cell phone texting endlessly since she arrived directly from the airport. Bob had tagged along with Lori and has been sitting on the couch watching the parades ever since.

I showed up right after Bob to catch the smells as they begin a journey from the oven to my fantasies. Barry is supposed to be here with the kids any minute. I sneak another garlic toast.

The dining room table is pulled out to its maximum capacity using all four leaves. I wonder who helped Mom get those leaves in the table since I wasn't around. Maybe Stuart helped her with it yesterday ... or last night. I shake my head to avoid any further thoughts about that. I look around but no sign of him anywhere. All I know is he'll be here for dinner. Him and his two grown children and ... Bobo.

Grandma's crocheted tablecloth is under the clear plastic Mom had rolled over the entire top of the table. Placemats Mom had cut out of orange felt in the shapes of fall leaves harbor the bone china plates with the little pink roses in the middle ... part of the 209-piece set Grandma and Grandpa Munson had given Mom and Dad for their wedding. The set never matched anything in our house but has graced our table every holiday and special occasion since I can remember.

Mine and Julie's fifth-grade art projects are placed side-by-side in the middle of the table on a bed of fake autumn leaves: two turkeys made from huge pine cones with feathers glued to their butts and brown pipe-cleaners for heads. Bob's and Barb's fifth-grade art projects hang on the front door: Pilgrims, a him and a her, made of construction paper and glue that is now wrinkled and cracked. Barb had written Happy Thanksgiving above her Pilgrim in orange crayon. Her Pilgrim stood on green ground under a blue sky with white puffy clouds. Bob's Pilgrim had nothing but thin air and one leg is grotesquely longer than the other. At least once each Thanksgiving someone will insinuate that the Uncle-Bob-O-Monster is going to pull someone's leg and then point to his old art project as proof of his capabilities. Barb's kids take it literally and squeal at the mere threat. One yank of a toe on a dozing kid is enough to keep us grinning the entire afternoon. These kids will someday need therapy. For now, they are *my* therapy. I relish family time; that's why I'm so irritated at having to share it this year with some guy named Bobo! I had met Stuart Millbrook once before and hadn't grown any fonder of the fact that he was boinking my mom. As soon as he and his entourage arrive, I walk over as enthusiastically as I can and shake his hands. He introduces me to the three willowy creatures standing next to him.

"My daughter, Cynthia," Stuart begins. "Cynthia is a veterinarian at the Wayzata Animal Clinic," he elaborates, as though this should impress me.

Cynthia's handshake is as firm as my dad's—and he is a construction worker—but I am able to conceal the surprise in my expression with a smile that exudes hospitality. "Nice to meet you, Cynthia." I've been trained in the art of people-stroking by the artful dodgers at Maugham Southerby and had decided I'd turn the day into a refresher session on people skills as a means to keep my discontent at bay. As salespeople, we must keep our emotions in control and use other people's emotions to our advantage. They taught us to use a person's name when being introduced and to look them in the eyes as we shake their hand to get a bead on their personality to give us a clue as to how to approach them. What I see in Cynthia's eyes is: 'Do not trespass! Keep out! Beware of attack dog!' I take a step backward.

"This is my son, Dicky," Stuart continues, smiling like a mannequin. Then he waits for my response.

How hard it must be for a father to introduce a son, yet know he's more like a daughter. I unexpectedly feel a little more compassionate toward old Stuart. He'd been dealt a tough hand and is still in the game.

"Dicky is an assistant caterer for Dominic's Italian Kitchen in Edina," Stuart offers enthusiastically, as though this proves merit.

But his name was still Dicky. I had to keep from busting out laughing. Dicky and Bobo. How am I supposed to get through this day? "Nice to meet you, Dicky," I say as I extend my hand and look him in the eyes. But the touching, or the eye-lock, or maybe it's the fact I'm suppressing a giggle ... something seems like a come-on to old Dicky because he lights up like a crepe suzette.

Bobo, whom I surmise by process of elimination, quickly steps between Dicky and myself, breaks our handshake and juts his own hand into mine. "I am Bogart Buechene, son of Lambert Buechene, the great Tarumi violinist famed for winning the Alois Kottmann Award in 2005," he declares, hacking up every phonetic like it was a hairball. He peers down his nose at me while he stands frozen in a stance of indignation.

Well, no humble pie this Thanksgiving. I feel like coming back at him with, "And I am David Yates, son of a beer-drinkin' ditch-digger who knocked up my mom a few times before he dumped us all to chase women"—but I want to practice my people skills instead. "Well now, that's mighty impressive, Bogart," I say. "Shall I call you Bogart or would you prefer I call you Mr. Buechene?"

Bogart blushes and glances at Dicky who is still staring at me. Then he takes another look at me, tilts his head back in approval and puts his hand on my shoulder. I don't so much as twinge let alone cringe. "Chew, my friend," Bogart begins in his exaggerated French accent, "chew may call me anything chew wish, but my friends call me Bobo," he says, emphasizing the last syllable and accentuating it by waving his index finger in the air.

He sounds like the cartoon character Pepe Le Pew, I think to myself. "Bobo it is then," I reply as I take him up on his offer of friendship. This guy is easier than Sally Weatherstrom was in tenth grade. Boy am I going to have fun with this dude today. Things are looking up.

Bob takes his eyes off the television just long enough to roll them, fold his arms, and cross his legs all at once. His body language tells me exactly what he's thinking. I give his shoe a purposeful kick as I walk past him to the kitchen with Bobo on my arm and Dicky trailing behind.

"You'll have to show us your tricks in the kitchen," I say to Bobo, who by now is bubbling, unnoticed by Dicky who seems overly intrigued with me for some reason. I hear Bob groan at my gall before the swinging door to the kitchen closes.

Dicky and Bobo fit right in with the girls. I take a stool next to the wall phone where I can observe without getting in the way. The decibels increase immediately. The entire kitchen sounds like one of Julie's bunking parties back when we were kids, giggles and all. I have never seen grown men giggle, but here they are … right in front of my own eyes. The girls don't even notice. How can they not notice? This is definitely a side of women's culture real men do not participate in. I squirm on my stool, resisting the urge to jump up and run out of the room, but I have to see more of this. It's like peeking into the girls' shower room in high school. Only this is my mom's kitchen.

"No, no, no, no, no, no ..." chirps Bobo as he waltzes to the chopping block ... and I do mean waltz. "We're not trying to murder them," he continues in his Parisian drawl. He lifts the knife from Julie's hand like a well-practiced passing of the baton in a relay race, then softly hip checks her aside to assume her position. "Like this, *mon amie*. Your hand becomes part of the cleaver. Keep the tip of it on the cutting board and rock your blade quickly. Rock it and chop it. Rock/chop, rock/chop, rock/chop ... that simple. This way you get a clean, crisp cut that releases the flavor of this lovely, lovely chive," he says as he whips a long green onion around like it was a feather and he was dusting the tops of everyone's head.

Gag me, I think to myself. That ought to get him tossed out of this circle. Who would dare tell a woman how to do anything in a kitchen?

"Oh," chimes Julie in a sing-songy way I've never heard from her before. "You are *so* good at this," she says emphasizing the word "so."

Then Mom chimes in. "Show *me* how to do that," she says as she dashes over to his side.

What in the world? This is creepy, I think to myself. No one notices me roll my eyes. They are all too busy learning how to become one with the cleaver. I have to leave or I will throw up.

Barry has since arrived with the rug rats. He is standing sentinel at the table ready to slap little paws, but his eyes are on the television and the Louisiana All-American Cheerleading Squad as they start strutting their stuff in front of Regis and Kelly. Nathan and Nicholas take one look at their dad and dig into the ripe olives with both hands. Twenty olives find new homes on the tips of wiggling fingers. I give the boys two thumbs up since I had been the one to teach them that. I glance at Barry, who is still mesmerized by the cheerleaders, then back at the boys who by now are waggling their olive-donned fingers at one another like monster claws. I push the swinging door to the kitchen open just enough to be heard. "Ma, ya better come out here," I tattle on the boys. She grabs the camera as soon as she sees them and snaps a picture. The boys run off giggling. Barry is still at his post, glued to the television. Mom refills the olive bowl.

"Gotta watch those kids every minute," I say to Barry as I pass him on the way to the couch.

"Got that right," he replies, never taking his eyes off the television.

I nudge Bob. He nudges me back harder. My stomach growls big time. When are we going to eat?

The couch is big enough to accommodate five people, but I find it curious whenever we have guests and any one person is sitting on the couch, that no one outside of another family member ever joins them. It is like the couch becomes one big single chair instead of a place for four people. Maybe that's why Mom sets up folding chairs around the living room whenever guests come. But it didn't explain why Cynthia chose to sit on the edge of the folding chair farthest away from the television and right next to an unoccupied overstuffed armchair. Legs not only crossed but entwined from the knee to the ankle and tucked slightly under the chair. Hands folded in her lap. Back straight. Neck—a skinny long neck—craned to view the parade over the top of Natalie's head.

I grab Natalie's arm and pull her into my lap. She's been standing there staring at Cynthia without getting any response. "How's kindergarten?" I ask Natalie who refuses to take her eyes off Cynthia in the same way people refuse to avoid looking at an accident scene.

Natalie's attention quickly turns toward me and her eyes light up. "I got to bring Dorothy home for the holiday weekend," she blurts out. I look about the room for someone who could be named Dorothy.

"Where is she?"

"At home in her cage, silly."

"Cage?" I ask incredulously. "Why is Dorothy in a cage?"

"Because that's where rats live," she explains as she cuddles up and begins twirling her hair with her fingers, presumably bored with the endless questions from her dumb uncle.

"Ah. Dorothy is a rat." I smile at Cynthia, wondering if rodents count as animals in her book, but she was ignoring the whole conversation now. I turn to Stuart instead, who *has* been paying attention. He just smiles.

Stuart's wife died of breast cancer at age twenty-seven and he was left to raise both their children himself. He didn't seem like the warm fuzzy sort of dad everybody hopes for, but then he didn't seem as self-absorbed as my dad either. I had heard him earlier ask Nick what he liked most about school and was impressed that Stuart paid attention to the answer. I wonder where old Stuart ate his turkey last year? Somehow, I can't imagine Cynthia doing anything but slicing open animals in a brightly lit room with a big garbage can in the corner. Then I thought about old Dicky-boy in the kitchen waving onions around with his little friend, Bobo, and decide those two bozos probably hosted. Yeah. That makes more sense. I smile at my ability to analyze the situation. It's my people-skills training. Just scouting out the terrain before I slip into a conversation about securities with Stuart. I don't know much about him but can tell by his hands he isn't a laborer, and seeing the way he is dresses surmise he has to have a few bucks. I look back toward Ms. Craneneck and wonder if she has any money. She might. Better not burn any bridges there just yet. But my bet is on Daddy-O for the big bucks. "Sooo, Stuart," I say, to attract his attention away from the Macy's parade, "how's business been?"

He looks at me a bit surprised, then inquires, "In what way do you mean?"

I turn a palm up and throw my arm out slightly. "I don't even know what business you are in. So tell me. I'm interested in anything you have to say."

He stares at me with reservation, trying to decide whether or not I'm sincere. I just smile. His eyebrows lift ever-so-slightly. I know he knows I'm a financial advisor. He's been prodded by a few FAs before. He leans ever-so-slightly backward in preparation of his rejection, but also realizes right this very second that he is in my mom's house and sitting in front of the guy who knows he's sleeping with her. His entire body tightens, eyelids freeze over the eyeballs, lips plaster against teeth in a forced smile, diaphragm ceases to move. Gotcha, I think to myself. He immediately opens up as though cracked under the brute force of Guatemalan interrogation. He's the HR director for Xerox. Survived the restructuring, but the whole ordeal burned him out, he tells me.

"Is that so?" I say, sitting forward as I give him my best smile. I send Natalie off to play. My bottom lip pushes against my top lip. My nose twitches. I smell money.

"You know," he begins in a tone of resigned surrender, "it was easier facing the day-to-day obligations of the job while the kids were growing up. There was purpose to what I did back then. I had to put a roof over our heads, food on the table, and pay for dance lessons."

Dance lessons? I look over at Cynthia who is still sitting straight-backed and ankles locked. Then a burst of giggles from the kitchen reminds me of Dicky. Oh yeah.

"But lately I can't wait for quitting time," Stuart continues.

"Why not retire?" I ask him.

"Need the benefits," he says.

Just as I thought. The guy's loaded or he wouldn't be so concerned about protecting his assets. He must have stock options, deferred compensation, a fat 401(k), I think to myself. I peg him for at least five mil, maybe more. He probably has a chunk of change sitting on the sidelines somewhere, too. My brain calculates the potential. I could be looking at $10 million or more. Mine, I say to myself and smile. Mine. "What if I could show you how you could retire now without putting your assets in jeopardy? Would you be interested?" I ask.

Stuart stares at me for a long while before he responds. I know what is going through his mind. Another stockbroker after his money. I raise my eyebrows and give him a little nod to encourage him to accept the offer. He's now wondering how he can decline without hurting my feelings ... the feelings of the son of the woman he's boinking. Yeah, buddy, let's not forget *that*. There's no way out, big guy. Give it up.

"Certainly," he finally replies.

Within seconds I have my pocket calendar out and arrange for him to come to my office.

"Dinner's ready," Barb announces.

Normally, I sit to the right of Bob who normally sits at the head of the table. But nothing is normal today. Stuart is given the honor of sitting at the head of the table. What's all *that* about? Bob doesn't so much as wince. He just slides into one of the chairs toward the wall next to his wife. I am told to sit opposite Cynthia. Dicky and Bobo sit next to each other, alongside Cynthia.

"Jule-a-monster," I say across the table to get Julie's attention. She scoffs at me. "Lookin' good today, little sister," I tell her. She is. When had she dropped the ponytail? College has changed her into a woman. Oh. I make a mental note to have a talk with her about boys. She sticks out her tongue at me, something that has turned into more of a loving gesture between us since we've both grown up. I reciprocate.

Mom is at her normal spot at the foot of the table. Grandma sits at the card table with the kids. We all fold our hands and bow our heads. Mom prays. "Dear Heavenly Father. We thank you for the food we are about to eat and ask your blessing that it might nourish our bodies, minds, and hearts that we might walk closer to you, Lord. Lord, we thank you for life ... the precious gift of life. We pray for safe journeys home from today's festivities for all those present at your table, and we pray for a safe journey home to you, Lord. Amen." I see tears in Barb's eyes when I look up. Her emotions are not usually this transparent.

There is a moment of awkwardness as we all look to Bob to cut the turkey, but since he isn't at the head of the table our eyes turn toward Stuart—but *that* doesn't seem right, so we all look at Mom. "Stuart, would you?" Mom asks.

All our heads turn back toward Stuart. He smiles weakly, then heaves a sigh. He picks up the long-handled, two-pronged fork with his left hand, and the carving knife with his right hand and briefly holds them both above the breast of the turkey. In one deliberate swift motion, he plunges the fork's sharp prongs into the bird a little above where the heart might have been and expertly slashes pieces of meat off the turkey and lays them upon a platter from which we will all eat.

Wednesday, December 5, 2007: 2:15 p.m. (CST)

As a favor to Mom, I had called Bobo. Supposedly, he had a question about investments. I got his answering machine the first time. I left a quick message and hoped I'd never hear from him. He called me a week later. He wanted to compare investment services, he told me. But when he explained his money was with Smythe Investments I had all I could do to refrain from hanging up on him. They are not even in the same ballpark. If it weren't for my mother, I wouldn't be having this conversation.

Today he insists I come see him at his apartment, right this minute. "Chew must come," he says into the phone. "It is wary important."

Against my better judgment, I agree. Initially, he was a novelty. Now, he's getting on my nerves. It is the first time I have agreed to meet at the client's place and not at the office. His unit is a small two-bedroom on the fourth floor of a six-story brownstone that overlooks Loring Park. It's a quaint area by day, but seedy at night. The building smells musty when I first enter ... or maybe musky ... I can't tell which. By the time I find his apartment I am ready to turn and run, but I remind myself this might be a way into the gay community. There's money there and less competition.

When he opens the door, it becomes all too clear what he really wants—more than my advice, for sure. He invites me in. His lair is uncomfortably bold and barren. I don't know what I had expected ...

pink frilly things ... doilies, maybe. This is very masculine—overtly so. Red carpet against stark white brick walls and fireplace. One giant bronze sculpture of two men embracing hangs above the mantel as a blaring and proud icon. The only furniture is a black leather sofa pit with a rolling leather ottoman that looks worn on one side. I refuse to contemplate how it got that way. There are no end tables or lamps. A sphere of green frosted glass is suspended from the center of the ceiling directly over the pit. Light diffuses through it like daylight through fog. Everything in the room is illuminated. The effect is hard and bold and overpowering. I feel exposed in some way.

We take seats in opposite corners of the sofa pit after he hands me a scotch. Up until now, I hadn't seen anything different in his eyes than I'd seen in Sally Weatherstrom's when she wanted something from me. The difference is with her I am usually ready to oblige. The only thing I'm ready to do here is punch this little cupcake if he crosses any lines, which he seems to sense. He tenses up, then flops back on the sofa and flips his head to one side, eyes closed while he contemplates the situation. Obviously this is not going as he'd planned.

"I knew you were an intelligent guy when I met you," I say to fulfill his need for flattery. The sooner I get the show on the road the sooner I can get out of here.

He immediately abandons his wounded lover act and smiles coyly. I can hear the wheels turning in his head right now: 'Intelligent. Yeah. That's me.' He's feeling the power of admiration. The corners of his mouth turn upward ever so slightly with new-found confidence. His eyes beg for more. To keep myself from bolting, I swallow another mouthful of scotch.

He relaxes and smiles as though he's in front of a camera, unfolding like a movie queen on stage. Every move flows with purpose. Every glance and flicker of his eyes is pregnant with intent.

Better nip this in the bud right now. "Of course, intelligence has little to do with making real money," I say. "I have clients who are PhDs who don't know their ass from a hole in the ground when it comes to investing."

He likes the analogy. Sits up a little straighter. Leans forward slightly as though he's intent upon my every word. His head turns almost completely sideways as he looks at me out of the corners of his eyes. It's the invitation to my next move.

"People think wealth management is working hard, paying their bills, and saving money," I continue. He nods to confirm what I am saying but something tells me he hopes I have other intentions. Hate to burst your bubble, little buddy, but I'm about to slam dunk you and hang you out to dry I think to myself as I smile at him.

He smiles back.

I lean a little closer, but just a *little*. "That's not how to *ever* become rich," I continue point blank. "I'm here to tell you how to really make money. How to make all the money you ever imagined." I sit back and take another sip of my scotch, swirling the cubes around in my glass and watching as his demons show up and surround him. His priorities shift right before my eyes. He wants more than just a conquest. His interest in me drops immediately. He now wants what he's always wanted: power to provide himself with everything he will ever want again. His dreams parade before him. His own limitations diminish as he begins to imagine what real money could bring him.

Within an hour I walk out of there with a signed agreement that will electronically transfer $250,000 in unqualified funds by the end of business tomorrow, and within a month will have rolled over three fat IRAs for a total of $550,000 in assets to manage for old Bobo. I could kiss him, but I won't. Instead, I kiss the paperwork as I hand it to the assistant on duty in the cage once I return to the office. I slap the granite counter and startle the little thing out of her wits. She looks up. She must be new, I think to myself. I don't remember seeing her before. "Get'er done, girl," I say. She nods and smiles. I break a grin that shows all teeth as I head for Crosby's office. It is gloating time.

After listening intently about how I closed on Bobo, Crosby leans over his desk and looks me in the eye. "This is what you gotta do next," he coaches in all sincerity. "Make this guy feel like a superstar in front of his friends. Stroke him—his ego, I mean. Get him and his little buddies to all start fighting over you for your attentions." He sits back and smiles. "They'll be trying to one-up each other in giving you their money. That's how to work it." He pauses in thought and smiles again. "You up for a blow job?" he blurts out before breaking into a belly laugh.

"Gotta do what ya gotta do," I reply.

We both burst into a hearty laugh, not knowing for certain if the other is joking.

THURSDAY, DECEMBER 6, 2007: 3:45 P.M. (CST)

Martin Bascomb is important. What he says is important. If you are lucky enough to be invited to talk to him you avoid genuflecting and you shut up and listen. Charlie and I follow him to a back booth at Monty's, away from the office crowd who are gathered near the bar.

Martin Bascomb doesn't just have a corner office within the branch; he has a separate wing with a private lunchroom. His group is the largest among all the Maugham Southerby offices in the Twin Cities, meaning it hauls in and maintains the largest book of business —it has over $800 million in assets under management. The group is officially called The Bascomb Wealth Management Group. It consists of two senior advisors, three junior advisors, and six assistants. On everyone's business card there are enough acronyms to baffle an English teacher: CFP (Certified Financial Planner), CLU (Chartered Life Underwriter) CSFA (Certified Senior Financial Advisor) CWM (Chartered Wealth Manager), (CRC) Chartered Retirement Planner), CMFC (Chartered Mutual Fund Consultant), CChFC (Certified Chartered Financial Consultant), CSA (Certified Stock Analyst). To render such services the Bascomb Group would need four times as many people and weeks to conduct the proper procedures on every client, so they don't. The credentials are merely another tactic to impress prospects. And it does. Everyone in this business knows that impressive credentials behind one's name gets prospects and clients to hand over their money faster than to those without.

Martin rarely shows up at Monty's. Martin rarely talks to anyone outside the members of his own client group. I wonder whether there's a particular reason he is here tonight and why he'd singled out Charlie and me.

Martin takes the side of the booth that faces the room and plunks down in the middle of the bench as an indication he doesn't intend to share his side with either one of us. He orders a scotch on the rocks.

Charlie tells the waitress to make it two.

I shoot a look at Charlie. No Mojito? I order a Heineken. "Not poured, in the bottle," I add, but nobody laughs—not even the waitress who just looks anxiously at Martin. Charlie shoots me a look that indicates I should shut up.

Martin gets right to the point. "How's it going?—and cut the skitsnack," he says to Charlie directly.

I look at Charlie, but he doesn't look back. I haven't a clue as to what is going down. The senior brokers pass us rookies in the office like we're invisible and now the top dog buys us a round at Monty's and is interested in our personal ambitions. Charlie shifts in the booth and looks down at the tabletop where he twirls a little square napkin.

"It's tough," Charlie utters meekly. "It's tough." He continues to stare at the little napkin as he pushes up his bottom lip then tightens it. He shakes his head in resignation. "A person's gotta have a class act to make it in this business, that's for sure." He lets out a heavy sigh and looks up at Martin.

Martin's eyes soften. He sits back. His head rocks back and forth. He glances at me but quickly turns his attention back on Charlie. The waitress returns with our drinks and he gives her a quick nod, which means for her to put it on his tab.

I tip my Heineken toward him as a thank you. Charlie verbally thanks him. Martin doesn't acknowledge either.

"Made it through any doors back on the east coast?" Martin asks Charlie.

Now I get it. Martin is licking his chops over Charlie's contacts back east. I look at Charlie, as eager for the answer as Martin.

Charlie shrugs. "I'm young and they already have brokers who are right out of New York," he explains. Charlie's been raking in the assets. His finesse opens more doors than a nugget did in a brothel during the gold rush. So why the sob act? I wonder.

Martin nods like he understands. Everyone takes a pull on their drinks, then he asks Charlie, "Got daddy's bucks yet?"

Charlie freezes.

Fat chance of ever getting daddy's bucks, I think to myself. Daddy isn't about to let sonny-boy manage his bazillions. What was Martin thinking? *Martin* isn't even in *that* category. The balls of this guy. I want to laugh, but I refrain.

"Got *anything* worthwhile out of *anyone* back east?" Martin almost begs Charlie to not disappoint him.

Charlie nods.

"How many?"

"Two clients and five viable prospects."

Martin turns up his bottom lip. "What do you have total so far?"

Charlie says, "$34 million, 21 clients."

163

Sweet, I think to myself. I compare that to my measly $18 million that I had to work out of twice as many clients over the same six months. Still, this has got to sound like peanuts to this guy.

Martin takes a long sip of his scotch and then leans in on his elbows. Instinctively, Charlie and I both lean in, too. "I can make things happen for you," he says with a wry smile.

I'm all ears. But he only seems to be talking to Charlie. What he lays out is a plan to help Charlie close on his friends out east to overcome their hesitation to do business with a rookie. He can offer Charlie some real credibility, he tells us. He wants Charlie on a plane out of here by tomorrow. "Get your nose where it belongs," he tells Charlie. "I don't want to see you back here for any reason. Keep your nose up their asses, you hear?"

Charlie nods.

"I'll fly out for every meeting you set up." Martin leans over the table and pauses as he looks Charlie in the eyes. "I don't want you to talk to anyone about investments." There's another long pause. "All you do is get the appointment. You hear?"

Charlie nods.

"Don't get any brainy ideas that you're a portfolio manager," he warns. "And drop the Modern Portfolio Theory. It's skitsnack." He just looks at both of us and sips his scotch. Word at the branch has it that Martin runs stock portfolios for all his clients with a few Index funds for bond diversification and international exposure. He uses stop losses on everything, but if you aren't careful that strategy can cost your clients a bundle. Either he knows what he's doing or he has his clients convinced of his methods to the point that they don't care.

Martin looks at me so quickly it startles me. "You," he begins with such authority I sit up straighter. "See compliance in the morning and get yourself licensed in every state Charlie is licensed in."

I nod but don't yet know what for.

"And get a good suitcase because you're going to be living between airports for the next few months if you plan on surviving in this business. "He stands up to leave, tosses a few bucks on the table for a tip and pats Charlie on the shoulder. He takes one last look at me and mutters, "You're lucky Charlie is your pal. We'll see if you're worth as much as he says you are. I have my doubts." Then he walks away.

Charlie waits until he is out of sight before he moves from the same side of the booth we're sitting on to the opposite side that Martin just vacated. Several minutes pass during which Charlie appears deep in thought while I wallow in confusion. Finally Charlie looks up and shakes his head. "You gotta love this business," he says as he takes a swig of his scotch.

I just smile and nod. "Did Martin just recruit us to his group?" I finally have to ask.

"Just an invitation to audition," he clarifies. Then Charlie chuckles and shakes his head slowly from side to side, deep in his own thoughts. I don't even have to ask the question on the table. My blank expression lays it out.

Charlie smirks. "Hang tight, little buddy. You are coming up on your lucky star."

CHAPTER 11: FLYING HIGH
NEW YORK, NEW YORK

SATURDAY, DECEMBER 8, 2007: 6:00 P.M. (EST)

Before I know it I'm waving goodbye to Charlie at LaGuardia and hailing a cab to Helice's where she is waiting for me with a martini in hand and naked under a see-through robe. I put the martini on the table and grab her ass. We don't get back to our martinis until an oil slick forms on the surface from the olives. By 10 p.m. we're showered, dressed to kill, and out the door for a quick dinner at Bergdorf's then on to a gala at a place I'd never been called the Rondo Club.

I pull out my Visa card for the cover charge and try to console myself that it will mean two thousand more flyer miles, but I still can't help but choke when I sign the slip.

The lobby of the Rondo Club is at the top of a vast marble stairway that flows into a room larger than a football field. My immediate gasp is drowned out by the chatter of what must be a few thousand people socializing. It is like a bubbling sea of heads and hairdos, some of which had been coiffed with plumes of neon-colored peacock feathers.

Once we are on the main floor Helice leans into my ear and tells me to follow her to the restrooms. You should have gone before we left Bergdorf's I think to myself, but I follow her obediently. We slither between people, rubbing bellies and asses with strangers until we reach a carpeted area at the far side of the room.

"Meet me here when you're done," she says anticipating me to visit the men's room. "But I don't have to go," I mouth to the back of her head as she disappears behind a door padded in black leather with a gold plate that says 'Babes' on it.

I look for another padded door and find one with a gold plate that says 'Dudes' about twenty feet down the hall. Inside the room, it is quiet; heavy metal music plays at low volume. The room is carpeted in deep red and gold. There are no urinals against the wall but rather stalls with doors made of frosted glass. There are two attendants. One is an elderly Caucasian man, the other a short Asian. The Asian attendant approaches and points to a stall toward the back. I walk past a long mirror-topped table around which there are several chairs upholstered in the same leather as the doors. Two men sit scraping a white substance into little rows before they bend down and sniffed them up. I look over to the attendant. He smiles politely and gives me a little bow. One of the guys looks up at me. He gestures for me to take a whiff.

I pause while I grasp the situation and conjure up a polite refusal. "Got to ..." I say holding up a finger and then point to a stall. The guy nods and goes back to his sniffing.

The inside of the stall is bigger than the efficiency I used to live in. It has both a commode and a urinal. I try to pee, but can't. Instead I just stand there with my dick hanging out wondering if I should try cocaine, or whatever that is they are snorting out there. I figure one hit can't hurt. I zip up.

As I come out of the stall, I notice a patron pay the attendant a ten spot. The two guys are done sniffing and they both watch me walk over to the sinks. I pass my hands under the faucet and warm water comes out. I pass my hands under another smaller spigot and foamed soap comes out. After I wash and rinse, I turn around to look for a blow dryer but the little Asian attendant is holding out a fresh towel for me. I place my hands into the towel and he dries them for me.

The two sniffers motion to me. Up close their nostrils look like they just got over a nasty cold. There are sweat beads on their foreheads. Their bow ties are askew. Their smiles are faint and their watery, red eyes are distant. I don't think I want to go to their party. I pat them on the shoulder and thank them for the offer then pull a ten spot from my wallet and place it into the little Asian guy's hand on my way out.

As I walk back down the hallway, I can't help but calculate ten times a thousand equals ten thousand! Those two attendants are clearing at least five thousand each on this crowd, and likely twice that much. Everyone has to pee at least once during the night.

"How often do these sorts of parties take place?" I ask Helice when she emerges from the women's lounge.

She looks at me with red, watery eyes and replies, "Every night."

I look back over my shoulder toward the men's lounge as we merge into the crowd. "A couple of washroom attendants in New

York," I mumble to no one. "Who would have thought they could pull down a million dollars a year at their job. Humph. I think of how little expertise one needs in this city to make millions.

We make our way toward the bar that spans the entire length of the room and has tenders every three feet. I see tens, but mostly twenty-dollar bills stuffed into tall glass jars at each tender's station. I'm in the wrong business, I think to myself.

It is nearly four in the morning by the time we leave. My pockets are loaded with business cards—leads, warmed up prospects, tickets to the big time. Once outside I shout, "Score!" Helice smiles smugly. We walk along West 54th Street. My head is spinning with possibilities. "We did it, baby," I tell her. "Am I going to rake the money in from the contacts I made tonight or what? Whoo-hoo!" I pat her ass with that thought in mind, knowing how she will show her appreciation later. I hail a cab to take us back to her place and we romp around till sunup.

It is after six in the morning before we close the drapes and bed down for some sleep that lasts well into Sunday evening. When I wake up I'm starving and head to Helice's kitchen where I open the refrigerator to find less than what I would find in my own. Nothing. Not even beer.

Helice slumps onto a stool at the counter and leans her jaw on the palm of her hand. She looks pale and sickly. Her red hair straggles down her back. There are dark circles under her eyes. A natural beauty she is not.

"Got anything to eat in this place?" I ask her. She doesn't respond. I keep searching in cupboards. The only thing I find is a can of stale nuts and a half a bottle of peppermint schnapps. I hold up the schnapps as a question to her as to why she has a bottle of schnapps in her cupboard.

She waves a hand. "Old boyfriend. I thought he was a Texas oil tycoon. Turned out he just worked for an oil company." She pulls herself away from the counter and flops on the sofa.

I take a pull of the schnapps. Not bad. I take another swig and swish it around in my mouth a little before I swallow. Sort of refreshing actually. I pop a couple of nuts into my mouth.

"We have to get going," she says. "It's past eight."

"Is food part of the plan?"

She stands up, puts her hand on her hip, cocks her head, and rolls her eyes—like I should know what that means. I don't. She walks away. I'm still wondering if we are going to eat soon.

By nine-thirty we are donned in our finest and ready to go again. New York, here we come!

MONDAY, DECEMBER 10, 2007: 6:30 A.M. (EST)

Charlie looks as crisp as one of Grandma Jazz's pickles early Monday morning when we meet on the concourse of the Broadmoor Building. He takes one look at me and says, "You look like crap."

"Time difference," I tell him. "Jet lag."

He shakes his head.

I follow him to the secured area. We show our identification and are scanned with wands by a uniform-clad security guard before we are allowed to proceed to a set of elevators. An older man in a gray suit carrying a three-ring binder stands looking anxiously up at the lights above the shaft doors. Must be a straggler from the current training class, I think to myself. I glance at my watch. Six fifty-three. He'll never make it. One demerit. I smile. We ride silently up to the sixty-first floor where the guy with the binder gets off. The rest of us continue to the sixty-eighth floor to the bond department where Charlie and I get off. We plan to engage with a few traders before opening-bell, intending to develop a professional relationship.

Bonds are the toys of choice for big players. Yields-to-maturity can be as high as 11 percent with little downside since anyone owning a bond can expect full payback at maturity or at least a guarantee they will have a place at the bankruptcy table should something really bad happen. A good contact in the bond department is imperative if you plan to be competitive as a broker. Being the first to buy an initial offering puts a broker ahead of the pack. There are fifty bond traders. There are 1,600 of us agents.

I can tell by Charlie's weighty expression he is in his zone, the part of his psyche from which he draws determination to become better than Cowen Bishop the Third. We all want to be better than our fathers. In my case, that's easy to do; but in Charlie's situation it's seemingly impossible to top that show. I'm betting he'll do it, however, which is why I'm tailing him so closely.

"Got your back, buddy," I say as we enter the bond floor.

Charlie looks over his shoulder at me with a look that begs to know what that's supposed to mean, but his attentions toward me quickly dissipate as he eyeballs the entire room.

Computer monitors are back-to-back without so much as a partition between them. I've been on the floor during trading. It's nuts. Traders wear headsets not only to save time but because it is the only way they are able to hear over the chatter of everyone else. The place is quiet as a mortuary at the moment, however. A couple guys stroll past us—one has a mug of coffee in his hand, the other has a bagel sticking out of his mouth. A few are leaning back in their chairs with their backs to one another but talking to each other, sort of like guys do when they stand around a car, kicking at tires to avoid eye contact. There are no windows. There isn't a female in sight.

Charlie walks up to a guy holding a coffee cup. "Lou Goldman?" he asks.

The guy points his cup toward a row of computers against the wall. I follow Charlie until we are standing behind a guy engrossed in whatever he is looking at on his computer monitor. It looks like a phone directory page. We watch him scroll down the list.

Then Charlie interrupts him. "Excuse me. Are you Lou Goldman?"

A mustache with a nose turns around and asks, "Who wants to know?"

"Charlie Bishop," Charlie says as he sticks out his hand. Lou stands up and grabs it. The two had talked over the phone several times but had never met in person. "Lou, this is a fellow agent, Dave Yates."

We shake hands, but Charlie quickly takes over. I listen for a few minutes before Charlie gives me a look that clearly conveys it is time for me to go hunt down a duck of my own. I slip away from the two of them and start looking for a direction in which to head.

I eyeball the same guy with the coffee cup who looks at me curiously as I approach and I ask him if he knows if Perry is in. I figure I'll look up the only guy I've talked to more than once, although I never found him to be all that helpful. It's a place to start.

The guy pauses as though he's giving me an out, then a smile emerges from the corners of his mouth and he points with the same cup, "That's him coming in the door," he says. "Hey Perry," the guy shouts. "Someone looking for ya who isn't wearing a white coat."

For just a second I wonder what he means, but my attention turns quickly to a guy walking toward us who makes it clear neither of us are his intention. He's a big guy who would look more suited to his environment in a hardhat holding a jackhammer; either that or a semi-automatic machine gun. He glances up before he passes us right by. I follow him a couple of steps. He glances over his shoulder like I am a stalker in a dark ally, then whirls around to face me and takes a step backward.

"Perry?" I inquire to make certain I have the right guy. He doesn't nod. He just recoils further. "Dave outta Minneapolis," I say to jog his memory. I stick out my hand, but he doesn't oblige.

A ray of light enters his brain, then finally lodges. He nods quickly and begins to walk away from me. I follow.

"In town on business," I say to his backside. "Thought I'd stop by and, you know … say hello."

"Hello," he says without turning around or breaking stride. Once he gets to his station he sits down in his chair, rolls it forward until nothing can get between him and the desk and puts on his headset.

Okay. So, that didn't go so well, I think to myself. I look over to Charlie; he and Lou are in an animated conversation. I turn to walk away, but Perry grunts. "You're too early," he says. "Don't have anything this early."

I turn quickly toward him. "Oh? Oh, I know," I hurriedly say, hoping to snag a conversation. "I'm not here to shop for bonds. Just hoping to talk to you a few seconds."

He spins around in his chair and pulls up the chair across the aisle for me to sit in, which I immediately do. He yanks off his headset and tosses it onto his keyboard, then leans his elbows on his knees and for whatever reason says, "It's about to blow up."

"Pardon?" A spasm on the very top of my head causes my eyebrows to shoot upward at his insinuation that the markets were about to crash. I look around the office and see we are basically alone. I lean in closer, inviting him to tell me more. I smell the starch in his plaid shirt. No tie. Rolled up sleeves expose muscular forearms with popping veins. His breathing is staccato. The whites of his eyes are bloodshot and cradle ultramarine blue irises that seem almost black. A chill runs up my spine.

"The whole ball of wax is about to go down," he says. The small muscles around his glassy eyes tighten. He leans closer. "CDSs," he says. He searches my eyes to determine whether I know what he is talking about.

I do. Derivatives are what they've filled the punch bowl with ever since the Commodity Futures Modernization Act (CFMA) deregulated the little devils back in 2000. Derivatives are financial instruments that are based on an underlying asset that can be anything from sports scores to weather conditions. They basically buy risk ... or provide insurance, whichever way you want to look at it. The popular girls at *this* Street dance are mortgage-backed securities. As quickly as mortgages can be sliced and diced and securitized, derivatives are created and passed around like condoms at a frat house on Friday. A team of math wizards at Maugham had created the super-extreme derivative—Credit Default Swaps, or CDSs. Using computer technology and historical data collected on corporate bonds they created a virtual risk-free derivative. The odds are similar to an insurance company that has sold insurance to every homeowner in America, but only pays claims if all the houses burn to the ground at the very same time. What are the chances of *that* ever happening? Genius. It is the greatest idea since bottled water. Investors love them. Brokers love them. Everybody loves them. The Street is one big orgy of derivatives with CDSs pulling everybody's pants down.

"The entire financial system is in jeopardy," he says, "including commercial banks."

Lighten up, buddy, I think to myself. It probably gets a little tense sitting in a windowless room barkin' bonds all day, but I cut the guy a little slack because if Charlie hadn't convinced me otherwise, I'd still be sounding just like him.

While a person can understand *some* things, they cannot understand *all* things relative to market movements, trends, world politics, and global economics that affect market movements every nano-second of every day, twenty-four-seven. Charlie finally made me realize it was preposterous for anyone to think they can outguess the legion of analysts who work for Maugham Southerby throughout the world. "Maugham Southerby is too big to do anything too stupid," he had said. "We're not driving this buggy. We're just the horses who sell securities at the crack of the whip. The only losers are those who aren't in the biggest race to riches in the history of the stock markets."

"We all have our jobs to do," I say, helpless to offer anything more meaningful to persuade him down off the ledge. Ignoring the temptation to believe anything he is saying, I still can't help but ask, "So, when will all this happen?"

"Any minute," he says without hesitation. "Investors own them, fund managers own them, the banks and the brokerage houses own them—they even own each other's, for Christ's sake," he whines as though he is pleading for his life. "The Street is overleveraged and they don't even know themselves how far their asses are hanging out."

Oh, and you do, I want to reply—but I don't. Seeing idiocy from this end is enlightening. No wonder Charlie nearly tossed me on my ear.

"It's so bad that if one goes, they all go." His eyes lock on mine. They are round and show even more bloodshot whites than they had a second ago.

My eyebrows rise at the same time my eyes roll at Perry's insinuation that Wall Street will fall like dominos. "So," I continue humoring him, "you think there are too many heads in the punch bowl?"

His expression changes from hope to disdain upon realizing I am not buying into his fear mongering. "Take it or leave it," he says as he turns his chair around and puts his headset back on as a gesture our conversation is over.

Some people don't deal with change easily. Wall Street is playing a whole new game these days. Maybe this guy can't handle the new rules. I turn and walk away, disappointed that I'd wasted my time on him.

There is more money being generated than ever before in the history of the stock exchange. Everybody can't be wrong. The guys at the top must know what they're doing, I reassure myself.

Charlie is lingering near the door, his conversation with Lou having ended too. We make our exit and once we are in the hallway, Charlie slaps me on the back.

"How'd it go?"

"Fine," I say.

Having a good contact in the bond department means we have access to fresh paper and can get a heads up on what's coming up for auction. I ask if Lou had mentioned anything about CDSs. Charlie replies he hadn't. I nod at my own thoughts. "Should have heard the monkey that fell out of the banana tree back there," I say, eager to vent Perry's prediction. "Says the world is about to blow up."

Charlie studies me, then shakes his head as he gets into the elevator. "Fixed income guys seem obsessed with impending doom," he says.

We laugh, but I can't help but ask, "What do *you* think?"

Charlie gives me a piercing look as though he is searching whether or not I still have any lingering idiotic notions myself. I give him the most confident expression I am able to offer to defy his insinuation, while still being solicitous of a response to a question that is within reason. "I think if you look hard enough for things to worry about you will find them," he says as he presses the down button.

By noon we are at the Four Seasons sitting at a round table with an impeccable linen tablecloth set for four. Each place has been preset with one goblet, two wine glasses, three forks, two knives, and three spoons. There were white linen napkins at each setting when we had been seated, but within seconds someone replaced mine and Charlie's white napkins with black napkins while leaving the other two white napkins in place.

"Lint," Charlie says in response to my wrinkled forehead over the napkin switch. "We're wearing black suits."

Another person in a long white apron and wearing white gloves silently fills our water goblets with ice water. A cocktail waitress in a calf-length black dress and unadorned by any jewelry other than silver hoop earrings takes our order.

"Iced tea for both of us, thank you," Charlie quickly tells her.

We are handed a single-page menu by yet another person, this one wearing a plain black suit and high heels. She jangles and spangles with gold bracelets on both wrists and a necklace like a Greek goddess, earrings to match. Her hair is strikingly yellow with deep streaks of dark brown, no bangs, long and straight down her back. Her lips are bright red to match her long fingernails. She smiles and greets us warmly, much more sophisticated than what she initially appears to be.

Charlie quickly grabs the menu from my hand and hands it back to her. "The penne pasta and sun-dried tomatoes, no salad for either of us," he tells her. "But wait until our guests arrive." She nods and jingles away.

"Got this planned to the detail," I remark, a little agitated that he ordered for me like I was a child.

"This is business. You don't want salad stuck between your front teeth, nor do you want to be working your food more than your prospect. Scoop, swallow quickly and be ready to talk at any given moment—without a mouthful," he instructs.

"Yes, sir," I salute. He ignores my gesture.

"You need to get more sleep," he reprimands.

"What are you, my mother?"

"I'm your ticket to the big time," he says matter-of-factly.

"And what am I to you?"

Charlie just looks at me. We both know the answer. I'm his monkey boy, his Hop Sing. I don't know if I like what is happening, but then I look around the room and realize I would never be here if it weren't for Charlie. A nagging irritation I cannot deny.

"How's the new car?" he asks abruptly. He isn't inquiring. He is merely changing the subject to calm the rising anger seething in my veins, as a reminder of why I am here at all. His motto is to always sell the benefits, never the product.

When I refuse to answer in an obvious attempt to control my emotions, he continues to brief me on the ensuing meeting insinuating he expects me to do as I am told. He'll introduce me as his junior partner in training. I should not have to say anything beyond cordial comments, he instructs. "Keep it that way," he commands.

The two gentlemen we are waiting to meet are co-owners of Montauk Boat Works, the largest marina for yachts and sailboats on Long Island, with storage services and a small shop that specializes in building canoes the same way the Montauk Indians had once built them. They cater to eccentric people all over the world who are interested in quality craftsmanship when price is no object.

Nice little lead list there, I think to myself. Let's see ... my contacts would be Maggie Swenson, Schmitty, Evie, Rick, and Vinnie. Yup. That's about it for my best contacts. I have to hang with Charlie. I have no other choice if I'm ever going to find the money pile.

"What are you pitching today?" I'm half-thinking bonds, munis, something along those lines.

"Just us. Nothing else." His eyes sparkle. He adjusts his tie and brushes his shoulders, checks his fingernails.

I rub the tip of my right shoe on the back of my left leg under the table and tug on my cuffs. We sit there not saying a word as we mentally prepare for the show that is about to begin. Then I remind myself it is not my show. It's Charlie's.

The real rub is Charlie's command. He needs me as much as I need him, but you'd never know it by his insinuations. My throat constricts. My jaw muscles flex as I try to calm myself.

I take a look around the room and start to relax once I remind myself of the perks of being in this business. It all still dazzles a guy like me who isn't far enough away from overdue student loan payments to forget what life was like in the poor lane. I shrug. It causes Charlie to look at me sideways. I ignore him with the same intent as I try to ignore reminders of my measly past. If money was supposed to make a person happy, why wasn't I happy? I ponder that for a moment until I realize that just thinking about how unhappy I am is making me more unhappy. I don't know and I don't care, I conclude. Life is pretty grand right now. That's all I know. That's all I want to know. Live in the moment. I smile and nod to seal that pact I just made with myself. Charlie looks at me sideways again, only his glance lingers a little longer.

The waitress brings our iced teas. She is followed by the Jingly One who is leading two gentlemen toward our table. Charlie rises. I follow suit.

"Gentlemen, I'd like you to meet my junior partner, David Yates."

"David," Charlie says addressing me directly as he introduces me to an elderly gentleman in a summer tweed sport coat with padded elbows over a blue oxford shirt complimented perfectly by a woven tan tie. "Mr. Sonnegan."

"Mr. Sonnegan," I say extending my hand.

"Oh, please call me Bill." Bill's hand is warm and dry. His grip is firm, but kindly.

"Bill," I accept and give him a firm jerk of my hand before we mutually end our handshake.

Charlie turns toward a stout man with several chins and a big bottom lip that seems perpetually shaped in a frown, who is wearing a three-piece gray suit with a watch pocket in the vest and is sporting a plaid bow-tie. "Mr. Arthur Albrecht," Charlie says as he introduces him to me.

"Mr. Albrecht," I say taking his hand. His fingers are chubby, clammy, and limp. He tries to smile.

"Mr. Yates," he replies politely, then withdraws quickly.

The three of them have known each other a long time. They quickly forget all about me.

I sit back and watch Charlie in action. He's completely at ease—accommodating, yet defines himself through differing opinions, but is never abrasive. Smooth. Polished. Manipulates every moment.

Throughout lunch they talk about boats, a little about the local politics on Long Island and of the State of New York. It's a mixed bag over Senator Hillary Rodham Clinton. Arthur clearly doesn't like her, but he offers no good reason as to why. Bill, however, applauds her.

"We need more females in office. She is a good politician and can open the doors for other females." The two men stare at each other. They've been down this road before. Neither goes any further.

Charlie motions for the Jingly One to see whether Bill or Arthur want anything more to drink. They've each had two bourbons. They accept another round.

It's Arthur that first asks Charlie what he thinks of the economy. It's a pointed question. He obviously thinks he knows something and wants to see whether Charlie is going to agree.

Both men lean way back in their chairs with their chins on their chests. Each had been anticipating that Charlie had invited them to lunch to sell them securities. They fend off brokers regularly, living so close to the financial district. Might as well get this show on the road. But neither look open to anything Charlie might have to offer. These gentlemen are in their late fifties and to them Charlie is like one of their kids—Charlie probably played with their kids while growing up on Long Island. Neighborly obligation and friendly nurturing instincts among men who want to see young lads make something of themselves brought them here today, and they weren't going away without paying their dues to society.

Charlie blows them away by saying, "Gentlemen, if anyone listened to me about what they should think about either our national or our world economy, we'd all be in trouble."

Their eyes nearly pop out.

Charlie laughs out loud.

They follow suit, but you can see by the expressions on their faces they were completely stymied by Charlie's comment. They were anticipating another pitch by a know-it-all stockbroker.

Arthur wasn't giving up. "Then you have some stocks or bonds you want to sell us?"

"No, sir," Charlie insists. He sits back and plays with one of the spoons left on the table after they'd taken our empty plates. Bill and Arthur just stare at Charlie. He smiles back.

Here they had thought they'd have to put the lad down gently but he isn't even asking them to buy anything. Their resistance dissipates entirely. But now they are confused. Why did Charlie ask them to lunch if not to buy something? They both begin to reposition themselves on their respective chairs.

Charlie puts the spoon down and sits as still as a cat watching a mouse.

I stop breathing.

Nobody moves a muscle until Arthur begins, "I wonder if I can ask your opinion on something." He carefully studies Charlie's face.

"Would it be in our best interest to offer a company retirement plan to our employees?" Before Charlie moved or could even answer, Arthur went on. "We have less than twenty-five employees, but we've lost a good craftsman recently on account we don't offer benefits."

Charlie doesn't move for several more seconds before he twists his head to one side and says, "I can't answer that for you."

They are now completely confused, as am I. What sort of a financial advisor was Charlie if he couldn't answer any of their questions?

"That advice requires a much more thorough investigation before anyone would know what's best for your company or for you as owners." It wasn't the answer they had expected, but it was one that resonated more than anything else Charlie could have said.

Nice, I think to myself, as I suck in a deep breath and lean back, eager to see and hear what else he has up his sleeve.

"I would never want anyone who does business with me to have anything less than the best and most thorough analysis and research done before making any major financial decision such as what you are contemplating. "

There is a long pause while the two men look at Charlie, then at each other. They could maybe trust this boy. He has access to things they want to know more about. Arthur finally leans forward and asks, "Is that something you can help us obtain?"

With subtle authority Charlie says, "Tell you what I can do. I'll have my best analyst meet with you tomorrow afternoon right in Montauk."

They both look at me as though I am the analyst.

"No," Charlie corrects. "I have a man in Minneapolis."

"What will it cost us?" Arthur asks while calculating the cost of plane fare and other expenses.

"Nothing," Charlie says.

"You'll have him come from Minneapolis for nothing?"

"He's coming anyway on other business I have for him. I can make sure you're on his agenda. I think I can have him freed up by 3 p.m. tomorrow. With the commute out of New York, how about I have him meet with you for dinner at 6 p.m. at ... say ... the Seafood Barge. In fact, I'll come with him—we'll all come with," he says, eyeing me. The atmosphere changes and becomes very light. "We'll all come out with him and have a nice dinner, enjoy the scenery, maybe even take a tour of your workshop." It was as though he had complimented the pair. They nod profusely.

Charlie looks directly at me and says, "We'll stay at the beach house for the night and head back into New York early Wednesday morning." He implies he's asking my permission to make spontaneous plans on the fly, but knowing Charlie he's rehearsed this part to perfection.

I smile.

Charlie looks between Bill and Arthur who are still smiling and adds, "It'll be fun."

We all nod our heads. Then, almost as an afterthought, Arthur asks, "What's the name of your ... your man?"

"Martin," Charlie replies.

My head snaps to look at Charlie.

Charlie smiles and adds, "Martin Bascomb."

SATURDAY, DECEMBER 15, 2007: 1:30 P.M. (EST)

I feel invincible! Immortal! Unstoppable! Everything I want is at my fingertips. It's as though I can reach out and take anything—just pluck it right off the Manhattan skyline while I stand here on the deck of the Staten Island Ferry.

"Which building do you want?" I ask Helice as we hang over the rail watching the waters part as the ferry slices through the steel-gray waters below. "I'll buy you whichever one you want." I am joking, but the idea plants in my mind like a seed in fertile soil.

"All of those," she says pointing to the complex of steel and glass towers that make up the World Financial Center.

"Why am I not surprised?"

"And of course, the Empire State Building," she continues in a full-fledged shopping mode. "That one," she says pointing to some building along the shoreline, "but it will need to be repainted. And, let's see ..."

I leave her to her own fantasy while I daydream of building Yates Towers—thirty-five stories, nothing too ostentatious, with a harbor view. The lobby will be a concourse of sport bars and restaurants and pool halls ... and a waterfall, no, a flume ... yeah, a flume. It'll have a jungle motif and a zip line, and an indoor amusement park. Why not? And a waterslide. Big screen TVs everywhere. There will be an elevator in the lobby designated just for my penthouse. The penthouse will have putting greens inside and out, a wet bar, and surround sound for a twenty-five-foot movie screen. Man, Super Bowl will be ..."

Ouch," I whine in response to Helice's fingernail being jabbed into my forehead to get my attention.

"And I expect to one day own everything along Central Park West," she says as though she means it, which she might.

"Wanna toss in a couple of cathedrals, too?"

"Can a person buy those things?" she asks in all sincerity.

We both laugh. She's alive and vibrant and exciting, unlike anyone I've ever known. I grab her around the waist and bend her backward to kiss those ruby, glistening lips of hers, but she's too fast for me. She shoves a hand in my face and pushes me aside while she turns her back to me, but I don't let her go. I love this woman. I haven't told her yet, nor am I ready to. I'm just going to let that alone for a while and enjoy the ride. I nuzzle my chin into her neck and peer over her head at the world at my fingertips. What a ride.

I've always felt like a nobody from Fiddlers Park. The Park is so small that people outside of Parkites don't even know it exists. That's maybe a better way to describe how living there had made me feel ... like I didn't exist. Moving to the condo in downtown Minneapolis was a start, but I realize now while we pass the Statue of Liberty on our way to Ellis Island that I belong here in New York. Just like my ancestors did. This is where I need to be. Energy. Movement. Power.

A cold blast of air tussles our hair. It is as though Lady Liberty just breathed upon us. Her eyes seem to follow us as we pass.

"Hey baby," I say to the monument of peace, but Helice looks up at me thinking I am talking to her. I lean down and suck her lips into my mouth, her tongue—I want to suck her all up right here, right now.

"Stop," she protests. "You'll ruin my make-up."

I snuggle her into my chest. I feel her hair against my cheek and breathe in the musky essence of her perfume. Together we huddle against the cool December morning and dream our separate dreams while the ferry moves us effortlessly along.

As soon as we dock, Helice begins to rattle on and on about her ancestry ... how she's related to Daniel Boone and General Lee ... how her Great Uncle Orman had been in the Battle at Gettysburg. A sharp chill off the water causes us to quicken our steps until we are off the dock, but I stop momentarily in my tracks to record in my mind the sight of a red-bricked mammoth of a building that spreads between two tall white-domed edifices—the first sight of America, the destination of the tired and poor who once trudged along this same pathway.

Inside the building our footsteps echo along with the fifty or so other tourists. Or perhaps it is the sound of the footsteps of the millions of immigrants I hear still echoing off these walls. The place is eerie with stories of the past, black and white photos, artifacts of a time long ago. I wonder what it might have felt like to just get off a boat from England in the mid-1800s not knowing a soul on this new earth.

"This is the exact spot where my great great granddaddy first laid eyes on my great great grandmother," Helice says.

"For real?" I ask with sincere surprise. I never imagined anyone ogling anyone else upon arriving in America for the first time.

"That's a fact," Helice claims. "Said it was love at first sight." She saunters away.

"Was it?" I trail after her, wanting the answer.

"Was what?" Her attention had already been drawn to another exhibit.

"Was it love at first sight?" I ask the back of her head.

She flaunts away as she flips her wrist. "Oh, of course not. There is no such thing as love at first sight."

"Oh yeah," I say trying to catch up to her. "What is there then?"

She turns to look at me squarely in the eyes. "There are common interests." She is frozen in an expression to remind me of the common interest *we* share.

"What about animal sexual attraction?" I whisper into her ear, then pull back to see her expression. She smiles, tilts her head, and bats her eyes. I feel my testosterone level double. She takes my hand and we stroll along the display cases and browse ancient artifacts.

"Whatever happened to your great great grandparents … the ones who met here?" I ask.

"He got her pregnant eight times and when childbirth didn't kill her he took her out west hoping Indians would, but instead she ran off with one and left him to raise the eight kids by himself."

Yikes, I think to myself. Quite the little lady.

"My idol," Helice adds with a wink.

She's such a vamp, I think to myself. I love that she is so unpredictable.

The next stop is Liberty Island, where we walk the perimeter of the grand lady of our great land and gaze up the folds of her gown as they fall over her huge toes.

"My granddad used to tell us kids stories about how his father had touched the very tip of the torchlight," I say, sharing a bit of our family lore. That comment quickly drew her attention, but she stares at me in disbelief. "Yeah," I assure her as we squint against the sunless sky. From our vantage point, we are unable to even *see* the torch. She strains her neck in a futile attempt. "Of course, that was when just the arm and the torch were on display at Madison Square Gardens," I confess.

She slaps me on the arm for trying to fool her. I look toward the torch and ponder the fact that I am standing within 151 feet of a spot my ancestor had touched in 1883. James Bodey had been just seventeen years old at the time and worked as a laborer for the City of Manhattan when enough funds had finally been raised to erect the Lady from France that would become the icon of America. Most of that money came from people who contributed only one dollar. I had heard the story all my life, but it had been just a story. Standing here now, looking up at her, I feel connected to James Geoffrey Bodey, my great great grandfather. Some foggy part of me finally turns into a substance.

"Come on," Helice pleads while she yanks on my sleeve. "I'm freezing to death."

Back at Castle Clinton we huddle together as we stroll up the long sidewalk that leads us across Battery Park.

"We can catch a cab at Broadway," she says with a gleam in her eye. "The old Algonquin Trail," she adds for enticement before she educates me on the history of Manhattan—things I should have learned in fifth grade, and maybe did but have now forgotten. Helice makes everything come to life.

She tells the cabbie to take us to Broad and Pearl Streets, then leads me into a quaint yellow-shuttered brick building. The façade seems unusual amidst the other buildings in Manhattan.

"This is where George Washington gave his farewell speech to his troops," she tells me. She had done a feature story on this place for President's Day last year, she explains. The place smells of stale beer and fresh French fries. I am glad to be in from the cold and close to a beer tap.

After we're seated and I've had a chance to look about, my first reaction is this would be a great place to break up with a girl. There is enough in the little museum to distract her, a gift shop where you could buy her a little something to remember you by, the meals are cheap enough you wouldn't have to invest much into a relationship that has gone south, and the atmosphere is a good lead into, 'Madam, as George

Washington once said, I must bid you farewell.' I chuckle at such ambiguity. Helice looks at me curiously.

I order a tall Heineken and dig into the bowl of nuts and pretzels. She orders a vodka martini up with no olives. As soon as our order arrives Helice smiles and says, "How about back to my place for a little wine and whatever comes up?"

I choke down a hamburger and fries while she nibbles on a salad and we are soon out the door before that little idea grows cold.

My head is still swimming with ancestral tales as our cab approaches the Washington Arch when one thought emerges as all-significant. "Stop," I order. "I have to stand under that arch," I tell Helice." Her lips curl in refusal. "It's where Beauregard Bronson Yates proposed to Beatrice Josephine Carnegie in June of 1886," I explain as my newly discovered ancestral past entices me. "Come with me."

"Just go," she orders as she stares out the opposite side of the cab, completely annoyed that I'd usurped her control over me. I hesitate, knowing I could blow the whole afternoon, but something still draws me to that edifice—something stronger than Helice's discontent and any consequence I might pay for not adhering to it. I leap from the cab and run across the street.

I stare upward as I walk toward the arch, trying to imagine what the area might have looked like back in the late 1800s on a warm June day. The trees would have been much smaller. For sure it would be green and lush, not bare like it is now in early December. While I'm gawking, I bump smack into someone whom I nearly knock over.

"Excuse me," I say emphatically as I grab her arm to prevent her from falling, but her case falls and papers spill out everywhere. "Oh, I'm so sorry, please forgive me," I say as I desperately grab for papers about to fly away in the wind. Having secured a handful of them I offer the bunch to the woman who is stooped and still situating things back into her tote. Then she looks up.

"Alison? What are you doing here in New York?"

She's just as speechless. "I … ah … ah … oh, my goodness! David!" she exclaims once she comprehends it's me. She stands up. Several rogue pages are swiped away by a sudden gust of wind. We come face-to-face and stare at each other before we awkwardly give each other a hug around all the books and papers.

She's doing research at the university she tells me as she points beyond the arch. "It's just on the other side of the park."

I look in that direction, but it's impossible to see it from this distance.

"And you ... what are you doing here?"

"Business."

"Oh, of course, you're working for Wall Street."

Close enough, I think. "Can we give you a lift somewhere?" She hesitates, wondering in what I might be offering her a lift and with whom.

"I'm with my ... ah ... a friend." I say pointing to the cab. "We'd be glad to take you anywhere."

"Well ... alright," she obliges.

Just as she is about to enter the cab she backs out and tells me to get in first. I sit between the two women and can't help but just smile from the joy I feel having run into her again.

Helice's eyes bug out in defiance—either that or annoyance—until I introduce them to each other and she realizes it is just an old friend from Fiddlers Park. Then she becomes so bored she resorts to looking out the window while Alison and I rattle on about how Mom is doing, how the Park hasn't changed, how Vinnie's pastries top any found in New York. I ask her if she'd care to join us for a show tonight, but she declines.

We drop her at the Doubletree at Times Square. I, for some reason, hate to see her go. Perhaps it is because she is a piece of home in such a faraway place. I don't know. "Take care," I tell her sincerely.

She raises a finger to reciprocate while she juggles her books and bags. The cab speeds away. She's disappeared into the crowd by the time I look back.

SATURDAY, DECEMBER 15, 2007: 9:10 P.M. (EST)

It is the second act of *Phantom of the Opera* when my cell phone begins to vibrate. I bolt from my seat, sidle over knees, apologize profusely, and head up the aisle toward the lobby.

"Hey, Charlie," I sigh with a note of disappointment, "You just caught me in the middle of ..."

But before I get the words out of my mouth, he cuts me off and gets right to *his* concern. "What was your bond guy telling you the other day?"

What the hell is so important that he has to call at this time of night and can't even say hello, is what I want to know. "Pardon me?" I ask.

"Your contact in the bond department," he demands urgently. "You said he mentioned something about CDSs. What was it?"

I'm getting a little tired of playing Charlie's fetch-dog. "Can this wait until tomorrow? I'm right in the middle of …"

"I'm sorry, Dave, it can't. If you are too busy just give me his number and I'll call him myself."

Wait a minute, I think to myself. You're not cutting me out. "What do you want to know, Charlie?"

He's right in the middle of a meeting with a banker in London, he explains quickly. Charlie knows bankers throughout the world. His London contact is a guy named Archibald Littleton whom Charlie calls Baldy. Charlie told me Baldy has his finger on the pulse of the world banking industry, which is why he went to see him.

"GIG insured $500 billion in mortgages," Charlie says while my brain calculates the five-hour time difference, making it three in the morning in London.

"Aren't they supposed to?" GIG is the world's largest insurance company. It can virtually underwrite any risk imaginable. Banks want insurance against loan failure. What's so unusual about that? I wonder.

"It's subprime paper," Charlie whispers into the phone.

"They insured $500 billion in subprime mortgage?" I ask to clarify what my brain is trying hard to resist. I try to recall what Perry had said … or what he had insinuated.

"What did your contact in the bond department say?" Charlie asks impatiently.

"That CDOs were being sold with abandon … that the Street firms were all overleveraged."

"Jesus." The tone of his voice is that of surrender. There is dead air between us for several seconds.

"Charlie?"

"Yeah," he confirms we are still connected, then adds in a voice so weak it is scarcely audible. "GIG is overleveraged."

"So is Citizens," I remind him. It was the reason Jonathan Baldwin had been asked by the board to step down. Charlie had ignored me when I first told him about the rumors. Now he's the one breathing heavy. "What's going on, Charlie?" I ask, meaning what do he and Baldy think they know that the rest of the world doesn't?

"Call you as soon as I get back," he says then disconnects.
A faint sound of applause from behind the closed doors penetrates the lobby where I'm standing, but the only thing that has my attention is the cell phone in the palm of my hand, which is dead silent.

SUNDAY, DECEMBER 16, 2007: 10:55 A.M. (EST)

Helice is a motionless lump under black satin sheets except for a nasally whistle that is slow and steady as a grandmother's rocker. I slip out from under her arm and stumble over shoes and clothes toward the door to the living room, but can't see a thing with the drapes pulled shut.

I fish around for my underwear. Finding them, I carry them out into the other room where the sunlight invades the east patio door and nearly blinds me on impact. With shorts still in hand, I fumble for the drapery drawstring and just before I pull the drapes shut I make eye contact with a gawking neighbor one story up in the adjacent wing. Hurriedly, I put on my underwear as though covering myself now will wipe out my embarrassment. I shudder as an odd feeling of vulnerability sweeps over me.

If Helice was a condo, she'd look exactly like the one she lives in. The walls are splashed red-orange—the color of her hair. Like mascara the black drapes outline pale green mini blinds the color of her icy, luminous eyes. A long, white, armless couch is perched like a naked model on brown carpet that is deep, plush and sensual. Just walking across the floor makes me feel like I am touching her. Above the fireplace is an abstract portrait of herself, physical features unrecognizable, but it captures her soul—passion pours forth through the vibrant reds, oranges, and pale greens. A visual masterpiece void of all traditional virtue and wildly exciting.

I pick up the copy of the *Sunday New York Times* lying outside her door. Charlie's call last night has me wondering just *what* is going on. Whenever I had brought up the subject of big investment banks being overleveraged in subprime debt, Charlie had always pointed out that it was not important enough to make headline news. I'm wondering just what *is* important enough to make the headlines, if it isn't the fact that half the investment world is likely overleveraged in subprime debt. I toss aside the variety and feature sections until I come to the financials, then spread it out over the steel counter top and park my ass on a leather padded stool the color of Helice's nipples.

The front page features an article on Ira W. Sohn, a trader who died of cancer at age twenty-nine. A mutual fund was developed in his honor, the Tomorrow's Children Fund. I lift my head and wonder whether this was Sohn's dying wish, or the brainstorm of a couple of fund managers capitalizing on a guy's early death. Anything and everything gets turned into money on the Street. I admonish myself for having become so cynical, but it is the only truth in this industry. Everything must make money or there is no need for it to exist.

I flip to the back to see where the markets wound up on Friday. The S & P ended down four basis points. Nasdaq finished down one. I search the mutual fund listings to check the Global Visions Fund ... up six basis points as of close of business Friday. Sweet. I sold a ton of that fund to people in Fiddlers Park.

A small headline catches my attention just as I am about to close up the section and make some coffee. I spread the section fully open and place it directly under one of the five chrome dangling lights above the bar. A glow of bluish light circles the article like a spotlight.

"Pendleton Hedge Fund Soars Prior to Nosedive." The London-based fund had averaged a 23 percent return since it was founded in 2005. It had achieved 43 percent in the third quarter of '07. Then abruptly its manager Hugo Rathbone found himself in a fate similar to that of Bastian McBeth, an American-based investment bank who bellied up in June as a result of leveraging gone awry.

I grab my cell phone and speed-dial Charlie.

MONDAY, DECEMBER 17, 2007: 6:55 A.M. (EST)

While I wait for Charlie to show up at headquarters Monday morning, I take a stroll through the office, hoping to eavesdrop at the mere sound of subprime debt—but nothing. Just the normal chatter. Business as usual.

Charlie sounded notably shook up Saturday night, but for reasons unknown he deliberately avoided divulging anything when I talked to him yesterday. I glance up at the row of clocks above the cage and spot New York time between Tokyo and London. 6:55 a.m., Eastern Daylight Time. "Where *is* he?" I mutter to myself.

When he doesn't show by 7 a.m. I join the others for Morning Call in a darkened conference room, but I no more than sit down and Charlie slides in beside me. He holds an index finger to his lips.

We listen to a parade of analysts and economists tell us what we ought to know for today. Other than one comment from a new economist about firms being *somewhat* over-leveraged, the only thing emphasized is that Bernanke just won't lower interest rates.

"What is he thinking?" grumbles one of the brokers sitting behind us, referring to Bernanke. The guy storms out of the room mumbling expletives.

I'm wondering why the drama about interest rates when there is real drama unfolding surrounding subprime paper. Why isn't everyone talking about *that*?

Charlie nudges me. I follow him to an empty client conference room where he tells me to close the door.

"What is going on?" I ask in a low whisper.

Charlie shrugs.

"What did Baldy say about GIG?"

Charlie replies satirically, "The world's largest insurance company slash investment bank slash commercial bank has insured more than $500 billion in mortgages." He smiles as though he's just delivered a punch line. Then he chuckles and adds, "Now isn't *that* a turn of the tables? Me sounding like you." Our eyes lock for just a second.

I feel the blood drain from my body while I contemplate the severity of the situation. To keep myself from passing out I quickly justify the devastating information with the fact that the largest institutions couldn't possibly be in that much trouble without anyone else knowing about it, without it being talked about all over the world—certainly talked about on the Street—and for certain we should have heard about it at Morning Call. It just can't be true. Can it? "What is the company worth?" I ask out of desperation to justify $500 billion of subprime debt on their books. But before Charlie answers, I quickly calculate that a debt-to-income ratio would require the company be valued somewhere around ... $2 trillion! I about piss my pants. "No shittin' way!"

Charlie nods in approval of what he knows I've just surmised.

My mind crawls back to denial, grasping for any morsel of comfort, and I find it in the fact Charlie and I are a couple of nobodies. "What don't we understand?" I ask Charlie in earnest.

189

He doesn't answer. He just chews on his lip and gazes toward the window, but I know he isn't seeing a thing either inside this room or outside in the sky.

"They wouldn't stand in front of *that* bus," I whisper more to myself than to Charlie. "Would they?" I am referring to the people who run GIG—the CEO, the board of directors, the shareholders. "Someone surely would see something like *this* coming. Wouldn't they?" It is a pathetically desperate plea.

"Now you're sounding just like me," Charlie concedes. Neither of us cares who the other sounds like at this point. The magnitude of what is happening on a global scale and the gruesome impact it will have on the lives of everyone alive is too real for either of us to engage in petty power games.

If GIG fails, two trillion dollars will vanish off the face of Planet Earth ... out of the pockets of investors, gone from the projection sheets of every business in every industry, diminished from the expectations of everyone currently alive who anticipates a steady paycheck until full retirement age. It will cause a domino effect that will make the Great Depression look like a nursery rhyme.

Even a slight increase in mortgage defaults could cause the whole thing to topple. Taking into account the influx of subprime paper, the over-leveraging that derivatives are causing, and the potential for some if not all of these mammoth companies getting caught with their pants down causes me to shiver at the realization it is no longer an *if* but a *when*.

Charlie just stands there staring out into thin air, deep in his own contemplation.

"There's no way the SEC would let them hang their asses out that far," I say, more just to hear some comforting words aloud than to converse in reality with Charlie. I am referring to the fact that there are regulations here in the United States that prohibit any investment company from acquiring that much debt to capital. "Yeah," I add desperate to confirm my trust in the regulatory system of the United States of America, the government of the people, for the people, and by the people. The Securities and Exchange hounds have their noses up our asses. Surely, they wouldn't let something this monstrous get past them, I remind myself over and over as I grasp for a morsel of relief.

"They did it mostly for European banks," Charlie mutters.

The realization they sidestepped the SEC rattles through my brain like a ground tremor in San Francisco. Goosebumps break out on my forearms.

"The real beauty is it enabled banks around the world to step up their leverage without raising new money because GIG had their backs," Charlie elaborates.

I can't keep my eyes from widening; they are beginning to dry, but I can't seem to blink. Mesh that with what Perry was saying about the CDSs and his accusations that the firms here are overleveraged, and at once the fixed income guys who'd been purporting impending doom seem like oracles.

"How can they get away with that?" I ask incredulously.

"The same way they got away with helping an Ohio medical parts manufacturer hide $22 million in losses back in 2004. The same way they got off with helping Midland Hills Mortgages shift $900 million in bad loans off its books in 2006."

I just stare at Charlie. We had both sat in the same training class when they taught us the consequences of not practicing the prudence of professional ethics. GIG was used as a bad example. It had paid $200 million in criminal and civil charges, and $25 million in a lawsuit filed by the SEC, not to mention a few white collars that had been exchanged for orange jumpsuits. I swallow hard. But Charlie's insinuation that GIG might still be up for a showdown doesn't make sense.

"GIG could be forced to pay out astronomical sums of money," I say. My mouth is so dry it gravels. I clear my throat. Neither Charlie nor I need to verbalize what that might mean.

"What if the hedgies get ahold of this?" Charlie says.

Hedge fund managers control the world. They systematically brought down Bastian McBeth back in June by pulling their brokerage accounts, buying insurance against the bank by purchasing CDSs— Credit Default Swaps—and then shorting its stock, causing investors to lose $2 billion. They're like black widow spiders who upon coitus devour their mates.

"Does anyone else in the world, besides Baldy and us, seem to realize how integrated the entire financial system is?"

"God only knows," Charlie sighs, sincerely summoning the almighty.

"This is systemic," I conclude as my mind still tries to grasp the mounting situation. Understanding the full ramifications of systemic failure is incomprehensible for *anyone* to imagine, but fear of the unknown grips my juggler and prevents me from swallowing.

We sit in silence, listening privately to the roar inside our heads. As real as it all seems, it is still highly unlikely Charlie and I—two rookies—would be the divine messengers of fate. There *has* to be something about all of this that we still don't understand. It just couldn't be happening the way that it looks to us. Billion-dollar companies aren't created on stupidity, are they? There *have* to be more answers than we can produce.

"Baldy doesn't know for sure what's going on. How can the rest of us?" Charlie rubs his forehead with his thumb and index finger while he puts his other hand on his hip and starts to pace.

"Should we be moving clients into cash positions?" I ask, fishing for justification to do the only sensible thing.

He mocks my suggestion with a forced chuckle. "And wind up in jail with hefty fines and our licenses jerked?" The fees that would generate from such action would be strong argument for incompetence on the part of an advisor—even under such market threats.

He paces back and forth once more before he turns and asks, "Besides, have you tried to talk anyone into putting money into U.S. Treasuries or cash lately?" That doesn't need an answer. Investors are driving this insanity. He continues pacing, then stops and stands at the window, looking out over the tops of buildings and lines of traffic as the early morning migration of humanity gathers momentum below. His arms are folded in front of him. He shakes his head every now and again but doesn't say anything for a long time. Finally, he turns around with a look of semi-resolve. "I don't know what is going on, but here's what we're going to do," he says.

We both open our briefcases and pull out the spreadsheet Charlie worked up as a business plan. I see Charlie has made a few changes on the copy in front of him. I pull out a pen.

The plan Charlie explains to me is different than the one in his head, of that much I am certain. But whether I know everything or just what Charlie wants me to know is irrelevant. What I *do* know is I have no other option if I want to make it on Wall Street. It's either Charlie's way or I spend the rest of my life snarling and scraping just to keep the big dogs away from my bones.

Finally, when we are through, he picks up his briefcase and pauses at the door. "People pay us to dodge bullets," he says. "There's no tolerance for gun-shy advisors." He yanks open the door and makes his leave before it swings closed.

I rap my fingers on the gleaming glass-topped table and leave perspiration marks.

THURSDAY, JANUARY 17, 2008: 12:30 P.M. (CST)

Charlie and I decide on the Metropolitan Club for lunch. Bryan—with a y—has taken it upon himself to be our personal table server since we started frequenting the establishment last summer.

"Right this way. I have your table all ready *just* for you," he tells us, insinuating he's been holding a spot for us even though he couldn't possibly have known we were coming until he saw us walk through the door. He doesn't bother to take our drink orders but rather scurries away to retrieve a Heineken for me and a scotch on the rocks for Charlie. No Mojitos for Charlie until late spring and only on unusually warm days, of which Bryan is fully aware. Amazing the benefits of good tips.

Our table seems to change every time we come, but it is always a prime location. In the summer it is on the veranda overlooking the cityscape. In the autumn it is near the window overlooking the garden. Since we are deep into January and we haven't seen the sun in days, Bryan seats us in the drawing room next to the fireplace. Its crackling embers warm us quickly. The books lining the walls insulate us further from the sub-zero temperatures outside.

Knowing we have a plan usurps my anxiety about the markets, and since no good ever comes from worry I've been focusing all my efforts on getting the job done before the whole thing blows.

"How was Glendale?" Charlie asks. Charlie is calling the shots these days. I'm the grunt man he sends to various ports to do everything from finding appropriate restaurants for meetings to picking up tickets to local sports and cultural events. All to influence a few pockets full of posies our way. Rarely do I even talk to prospects Charlie works until after the deal is closed. Then I act like Bryan—with a y—and cater to the new client's every need. Charlie tosses Manny a fish regularly to keep him dangling. I still don't know why Charlie's including him in all of this, but I've learned to keep my mouth shut. Martin Bascomb and his entire group don't yet know what's hitting them. Charlie is manipulating them to his own purpose with such perfection that not a soul in the office suspects a thing.

"Hot as a jalapeno pepper," I say in all sincerity regarding the temperature in Arizona. To a Minnesota boy, anything above 75-degrees Fahrenheit in the middle of winter just isn't right.

"Did you get the tickets to the Super Bowl?"

"Yeah," I reply. "Box with a full bar on the 50-yard line. L'Ultima Cena is catering. I got one suite and four double rooms at the Hilton Phoenix. There'll be a private charter waiting for them at the Montauk airfield. A limo will be there for them when they land. You and I are set to fly out of Minneapolis and hook up with the Montauk VIPs on Saturday in time to take them to dinner at Pablo's for a taste of local cuisine. Polish off the evening at a place called Soiree's—a top-notch girly club. Should be plenty ripe for game day by the time we tailgate out of the back of a limo in the parking lot at the University of Phoenix Stadium."

Charlie smiles and nods.

I haven't seen Charlie since I looked away from him at Times Square to watch the ball drop. By the time I looked up from Helice's lips, Charlie had disappeared into the crowd. We've been talking by phone ever since. Neither of us has been in any one place long enough for the other to catch up.

Bryan puts a steak sandwich with a pile of fries and a full bottle of ketchup in front of me and a steak sandwich with a green salad in front of Charlie, blue cheese dressing on the side.

"Suppose you're for the Giants," Charlie says.

"Of course," I retort with a mouthful of steak and Kaiser roll. "Just because the Patriots have had a perfect season so far doesn't mean there isn't hope for a wild card."

Charlie snorts at my optimism but quickly cringes in earnest at the sight of steak and lettuce protruding from my teeth as I pull my lips back as far as possible without food falling from my mouth in a big grin. He takes a fry from my plate and flips it at my head, but misses. It lands on the floor but only for a wink before Bryan picks it up and puts it into his pocket along with the other displaced crumbs.

I am so far from Fiddlers Park right now that I can't even describe my life to those who are still there. But I still feel guilty about telling Mayo I can't make it to his annual Super Bowl party. Every year Mayo and Ruthie fill their house with friends and family. This year is particularly special to them because they are in their new house and have room for twice as many people as before. I had told him I had to work. I couldn't bring myself to tell him I would actually be at the game ... in a box ... eating catered food ... drinking imported beer. It would drive a wedge wider than Grand Coulee between us.

"Everything set with the men in blue?" Charlie is referring to the corporate group at IBM he is scheduled to meet with in Rochester tomorrow. He's taking me along this time. He'll explain why on the drive down.

I nod while I take another bite of my sandwich. We always use the Kahler Hotel whenever in Rochester, the same place where the President of the United States stays and eats when he comes to the Mayo Clinic for his annual physical. We'll be initiating a relationship with the HR director, the Chief Financial Officer, and the Chairman of the Board to IBM. Charlie will introduce a service he developed in which he collaborates with a CPA tax advisor and an estate attorney to increase the personal value of the company benefits plans for highly paid executives that go above-and-beyond anything any company offers. He's already garnered executives at Ford Motor, General Electric, Cisco, and Pfizer who are all raving about the added services.

Charlie leans on his elbows. "Just a few more months," he says.

I look up. I stop chewing. I feel the closeness of achieving the dream. Something in my belly seems to take flight. The pinnacle is in sight. But my expectations are all a blur. I can't seem to visualize any one thing I'll acquire. After telling myself I wanted it all for so long, I can no longer identify what it 'all' is. *All* is something other than a thing, an item, an object. It is power. Like a living breathing beast stirring deep inside me, coming to life ... awakening. "Put this on my tab," I say to Bryan as he approaches. "It's on me," I say to Charlie.

Charlie nods a thank you and asks Bryan to bring him a coffee, black.

"Make it two," I add.

We pick up the remainder of our drinks and clink. It's happening. We polish them off before Bryan returns with two cups of dark roast.

"How's your mother?" Charlie asks.

While I silence a scream that shoots through me like an electrical current, I watch the steam from my coffee dissipate into thin air like a soul being sucked up into heaven. Rage flares inside me so strong I want to punch something, smash something. At Christmas she had been fine. She seemed fully recovered from the mastectomy she had last July. Go to New York, she told me. She'll see me when I get back.

Only I never got back long enough to see her. On the phone, she sounded fine. I should have known better. Barb should have called me. Grandma Jazz should have called me. Somebody sure as hell should have called me and told me my mom wasn't doing well … not well at all. But nobody said a thing. Everything is fine, they kept telling me. Fine my ass! It was a good thing I went straight from the airport to Mom's last night or I still wouldn't know a thing. It was obvious when I got there Barb had been staying with Mom day and night, sleeping on a cot they rolled in and set up next to Mom's bed. Why hadn't she called and told me? That's what I wanted to know. But Barb wasn't saying a thing and Mom was too weak to argue. "Fine," I reply to Charlie.

He nods and offers me ample time to say anything more that I might need to say.

I say nothing.

"How is everything?" Bryan asks cheerfully, appearing at the brink of our table.

"Fine," I shout. Bryan jumps as a result of the harshness in my voice; his eyes widen. "Everything was great," I say more calmly. Bryan bows apologetically and leaves.

Charlie just stares at me. He doesn't say a word or move. I look about the now-empty room. There's not a sound other than an occasional crackling of the fire and the beating of my heart. We drink our coffee in silence.

Outside our breath freezes in the airstream we leave behind us as we briskly walk to where I'd parked the car along a side street where it was less likely to be dinged, bumped, or touched. The leather seats yield to our bodies as we take opposite sides of the consul. It comes to life and I pull away from the curb. I pop the shift into drive and it purrs into first gear. The computer disengages and for a second the throttle drops back to idle as though it were a lady whispering what she really wants into my ear. There's a sudden lurch and we leave a streak of Michelin. I feather the throttle until we hit I-392. This baby hits 60 mph before we run out of ramp.

"What do you think of the credit crunch?" I ask, fishing for Charlie's take on recent evidence financial institutions throughout the world have been hoarding cash and are requiring ever-widening premiums before lending to one another.

Charlie runs his thumb under the seatbelt across his chest. Our eyes meet. "The big question is just how long can the Street suffer such capital hemorrhage," he replies.

Neither of us has the answer. Not that an answer from either of us would be anything more than a wild guess. See, the thing about the securities industry is that it is unlike any other business in the world. Every other business has a central product or service. The securities industry does not. It is based on absolutely every single action of every living soul on the face of this earth. If a third-grader in a public school in Ohio punches another kid in the nose and makes it bleed he affects the entire world: the legal systems that regulate federal funding to public schools based on that school's policies about fighting on the playground; companies like 3M who produce adhesive and sell it to companies like Pfizer who makes bandages using gauze made from cotton produced in Brazil; those are put into boxes created in Hong Kong and shipped on ships made in Seattle—all of which provide advertising service jobs for people in Bangladesh. Everything connected to life on earth affects the markets—natural disasters, political changes, health epidemics. Something as simple as someone reading a book influences the publishing trade whether they bought the book from a book store, a used book store, stole it, or borrowed it. They either contributed toward the commerce of the world or took something from it. Either way, the markets reflect it.

It is ludicrous for anyone to think any one person can predict what will happen in the next few minutes, let alone in a week or year. Past performance is just that ... *past*. Future projections don't mean a thing. In this industry it is difficult to differentiate the normal ebb and flow from a warning of something phenomenally serious. Large companies, such as Maugham Southerby, have a legion of analysts and economists who are paid to keep their eye on the world's pulse and to report causes for concern to us brokers in the field. A broker is only as good as his resources. It's what we've been telling ourselves for the past month as we feel the ground beneath us shake. But even with the best resources, the best analysts, the best economists it is still a crapshoot. The fact both Charlie and I know something sinister is going down doesn't matter in the greater scheme of things, because neither of us has the power or wherewithal to do anything about it. Our positions keep us nailed to this cross we must bear despite our hesitations. All we can do is waltz to this dance and hope we're still on the dance floor when the music stops.

We steady our nerves by avoiding all talk about the inevitable and stay focused on our goals—it's all we can do.

It's almost comical to listen to the so-called experts. For every economist that says one thing there is another who says the opposite. Seldom do analysts agree, and whenever there is any agreement it is on something so obvious no one would seek *expert* advice anyway. To sell advice in such an industry implies that all the activity in the world can be calculated with a degree of accuracy. This is why I hate our titles. They are bogus. But no one really cares. Everyone just wants to be able to toss the dice. So that's basically what any investment advisor does. We hand people the dice.

We both pause in thought … or, perhaps, dwell on our own justification for what we are doing. Since neither of us has been on the Street long, we have to trust everyone else's reactions to bank failures and hedge-fund bankruptcies, to a degree that has been making both of us increasingly uncomfortable. "Unless we want to throw our hands up in the air and run screaming into the night, there's not much else we can do but keep our wits about us and go forward," Charlie had once said—then added, "quickly," to which I agreed. We've been hustling ever since to put our plan in place and keep it on target, praying it all comes together before the lid blows.

Besides, what else can we do? If we aren't here to take people's money and tell them where to invest they will just take it someplace else. Might as well take our share of the pie. We're not doing anything the world isn't demanding from us. We're not breaking anyone's arms, nor threatening anyone at gunpoint to give us their money. Everything we do is legal. When we even suggest a more conservative strategy, clients bolt to the next advisor who will dazzle them with promises of bigger and better returns in this unprecedented market environment.

Brokers are little more than waiters who hop to the demands of the hungry—and boy are investors hungry for subprime debt obligations these days. Running right behind them are the firms dishing it out as fast as any of them can swallow. I have to wonder if the analysts know something the firms aren't letting them tell us because it would stop the money train before the end of the line—or are they are as oblivious as everyone else seems? Guess we will all know soon enough, when we run out of track. In the meantime, we carry on like rats in a maze. It sticks in my craw—the idea that the fate of us all hangs in the balance while idiot investors steer the world economy to destruction with their own greed.

But I have to ask, "What if we're wrong about the timing of things and the markets go south?"

Charlie snickers and pats the dashboard. "This little girl would soon have a new home," he says to my chagrin.

I slam on the gas pedal and we take the I-392 tunnel at 90 MPH.

CHAPTER 12: THE TRUE COST OF LIVING
FIDDLERS PARK, MINNESOTA

THURSDAY, JANUARY 17, 2008: 8:00 P.M. (CST)

"What do you mean you were trying to protect me? She's my mother, for Christ's sake. I have the right to know if she isn't well. You should have called me. I would have been on the first plane out of New York, or Glendale, or wherever I was at the time." I kick the leg of the coffee table and the plate under the cookies and the cups on top of the saucers all rattle. I continue pacing—or rather I continue going in circles because the room isn't large enough for me to pace.

Since when has Bob become the head of this family? is what I want to know. Barb said she wanted to call me but that Bob told her not to bother me. His way of protecting all of us, she tried to explain. He's just like Dad. Hide behind a facsimile of thoughtfulness only because he can't think any better than a doorknob.

I come home to find Mom is little more than flesh-on-a-stick she's lost so much weight; that she's used up all her vacation and sick time; that her job is on the line; and that her insurance is not covering as much as she thought they should so she's switched to County General—a county-funded hospital and medical center that is nothing but a death trap!

"I'm going to see to it that she has the best doctors in the country … in the world," I say pointing a finger at Bob, who is slumped on the couch as usual with his head down. I turn to Barb since she's the only one looking at me. "It's nonsense for her to go to County General." I shudder and look toward the bedroom where our mother is resting. Up until she left the room, none of us spoke except her.

"I'm fine," she had told us. "It is natural for people to not endure subsequent treatments as well as they did the first. I just need a little longer to recoup this time is all."

Mom's instinct to protect this house was foremost on her mind as soon as I walked in the door. Before she even said hello, she made me promise to never let anyone sell it, ever! She designated me involuntarily to be the one to make certain this house stays in the family indefinitely.

"Has anyone contacted Julie?" My temper is refueled. The fact they both suck in a breath and freeze is answer enough.

"Julie has a right to know."

"Why bother her?" Barb pleads.

My glare tells her why, and she backs off.

"Just because you two still live here in the Park you seem to think it is the Park against the world ... that anyone who doesn't live here isn't part of Fiddlers Park. At times like this we belong here just as much as you."

"We never meant to imply otherwise," Barb responds.

I know that. Really, I do. But she and Bob need to know that they can't go around making decisions for Julie and me. I walk over to Barb, bend down and wrap my arms around her. The tenderness causes her to sob uncontrollably from pent up worry, from regret for not calling me, for not knowing what to do. I lay my head on top of hers and let her cry for a long while. Bob sighs and uncrosses his ankles, then re-crosses them. It's our way of mutually apologizing and mutually accepting.

"Do you get a chance to see Julie at all?" Barb asks, her weeping beginning to subside.

I take a seat on the ottoman opposite her. "Yeah. Sure. I see her all the time. Went to a couple of her practices. She has her first performance coming up next month. I thought about flying Mom out to see it." I look toward the bedroom again where it is dark and lifeless. "She should be up to it by then," I say, trying hard to believe my own words.

"That'll be nice," Barb says with the same lack of sincerity.

There's a long pause; the sort of pause that can happen in a family—people with whom you are so comfortable there is no need for interaction to validate worth. Bob leans his head against the back of the couch. Barb slumps in the chair and turns her head toward the front window. I turn one of the dining room chairs around, straddle its back, fold my arms across the top, and park my chin there. We sit, listening to the quiet. Not a sound except for the drip of the kitchen faucet echoing through the dining room.

"I should throw in a load of clothes," Barb finally says, more to herself than either Bob or me.

"I'm going to get a maid to come in and do that," I tell her. "And maybe a nurse, too. Mom needs a nurse."

Barb jumps out of the chair. "Mom doesn't need anything of the sort," she argues. "We can take care of her just fine."

"You have a life, children, a husband. Bob has a wife, a job. You can't be here whenever she needs someone."

"We aren't," clarifies Barb. "A stream of people from the Park come and help. I'm just here tonight." Agitated, she gets up to go put a load of clothes into the washer to avoid saying things she will regret.

I look at Bob. He turns up his bottom lip and tilts his head, eyebrows raised, and gives a little shrug as if to say, 'What else did you expect?'

Mom emerges from the bedroom. I rush to help her to the couch. Her hair is a mess but she doesn't bother to smooth it. Bob retrieves her rinsed puke-bucket and sets it on the floor near her head. Together we wrap her in a blanket. She rests her head on a bed pillow that has found a temporary place here in the living room. Bob goes to the kitchen to get a fresh glass of water for her. Mom grabs my hand as I'm about to walk away.

I look down at her. She seems a shell of what she was only a month ago. Her eyes are sunken and dark. Her cheekbones protrude severely. Her skin seems to have doubled.

"How's Helice?" she asks.

"Fine." I think. I haven't seen her much this past month. We talked a couple days ago. I have no reason to think she's anything other than fine. I just haven't thought of her since I got here. I should give her a call. I'll call her after I leave here. Maybe I should stay here and let Barb and Bob go home. Yeah. I should just stay here tonight. I should stay a couple of days, maybe. My mind seems to be on a racetrack. I analyze the situation. I have to be in Rochester tomorrow morning with Charlie, but I could be back by 9 p.m. to stay the night with Mom. "I can work from home for a few days," I tell Bob and Barb when Barb comes back into the room.

"That'll be nice, won't it Mom?" Barb says as she plunks a stack of clean clothes on the dining room table to sort. I hear the washing machine whirring in the background. "How long can you stay?"

"A couple of days for sure, but I will see if I can swing it longer."

"I can take care of myself," Mom says.

Barb rolls her eyes. "We know that, Mom. We just worry when there isn't someone here with you. You don't want us to worry, do you?"

"No."

"I'll stay in my old room. Maybe go through some of those boxes," I pipe in, hoping to add reason to why I should spend a few nights at home. I try to sound nonchalant, like me sticking around would be as natural as butter on white bread. "I've been wanting to do that for a long time."

All eyes in the room roll to me except Mom's. She remains motionless in a prone position, then slowly she turns and peers at me over the top of her pillow.

"What?" I ask them all as they stare at me.

MONDAY, JANUARY 21, 2008: 4:00 A.M. (CST)

It's four o'clock in the morning. I stand in a tee-shirt and flannel bottoms, barefoot at the balcony window of my Minneapolis loft, staring at the freezing water of the Mississippi as it slithers like a snake between the two cities. The sky is still black as a witch's cat. The coffee maker belches from the kitchen nook while I search the empty streets seven stories below for any sign of life while I ponder mine ... and Mom's. She didn't look good. I thwart further thoughts about that. Instead, an overwhelming appreciation for the friends and neighbors who are taking care of her overcomes me. She'll be fine in no time, I try to convince myself.

I watch a cop car move slowly past the darkened storefronts below. The light from the corner street lamp falls on the icy pavement and glistens, giving the illusion of a sparkling lake on a summer's eve. A big rat emerges from somewhere among the shadows and scurries across the lighted pavement and back into the shadows on the other side of the street. I open the balcony door and a gust of frigid air engulfs me, but it feels refreshing.

While the coffee maker burps its last, I spread out the newspaper over the center island under the hanging light. I lean on the counter, belly against the edge, elbows propping me up. This is when I miss not having furniture the most. Headlines blare across the front page of the *Minneapolis Star Tribune*: 'Giants Head to Super Bowl as Wild Card.'

I left Mom with Lucy while I headed down to Schmitty's last night and met up with Petie to watch the playoff game—Giants against Green Bay at Lambeau Field. The only girls to show up were hardcore football fans, not the type looking for opportunities to parade their wiles, which is why I have this morning to myself. That and the fact I've been keeping myself just for Helice more and more these days. I wonder what she did last night?

If there are any Packer fans in Minnesota, they remain in the closet out of self-preservation, so the only fans at Schmitty's were Giants fans. Ever since seeing the Giants play in New York, I've been a fan. Whether it initially was because I could brag down at Schmitty's that I'd sat in Giants Stadium or the fact that the more time I spend in New York the more I seem to identify with it, I don't know. At any rate, my enthusiasm has influenced enough football fans in Fiddlers Park to where the Giants now come in second only to the Vikes.

It was a madhouse by the time I arrived, but soon bar calls were drowned out. At times I couldn't even get Suzie's attention to bring another round. When the Giants won you couldn't hear your own voice—it was sucked into one giant cheer.

The Giants will go up against the Patriots in the Super Bowl. The Patriots finished the only perfect regular season since the Dolphins in 1972. As crazy as it is, I feel in my gut the Giants can pull it off and win the Super Bowl this year. I feel an adrenalin rush just reading about the game in this morning's paper. Then all of a sudden the giddiness evaporates. If my gut instincts are any indication of how reliable my brain is in calculating outcomes these days, the Giants don't have a snowball's chance in hell. I fold up the sports section and pour myself a mug of coffee while I fish around for the business section. A headline causes me to spew my coffee.

'Citizens Says Boom To Run Into 2009.' According to the article Russell Miner is the new CEO of Citizens World Bank. It goes on to say Jonathan Baldwin had been asked by the board at Citizens to resign last November because of $11 billion in subprime debt found on their books. Minor was recruited from Morton Salzman and brings with him refreshing new ideas. It quotes Minor saying, 'The face of Wall Street is changing. The way money is made nowadays has opened new possibilities for every investor around the world. New state-of-the-art technology creates markets within markets we've never seen before now.'

He's talking about the derivatives market where bets on bets can be bought and sold for bigger returns than anyone can make on typical securities. These things can turn an investment firm into something that better resembles a bookie joint. A little deeper into the article it reveals why Miner so eagerly jumped ship. It says here Miner claims to have learned lessons from the struggle Morton Salzman just went through and brings new insight to Citizens.

Yeah, right, I think to myself. The only lesson Miner learned is how to save his own ass by first pushing everyone else off the life raft. If Citizens picked up Miner hoping he will bail them out, it's a true sign of how desperate the Street *is* these days.

Miner is further quoted as saying, 'Wealth is now at the fingertips of every person alive.'

He's right about that, I think to myself as I glance around my empty condo. I really do need to get some furniture.

The article goes on to say that under the guidance of Miner, Citizens plans to unveil a new model for its discount brokerage clients that offers day traders state-of-the-art technology that will allow them to be able to drop trades as instantaneously as the large institutional traders.

Yeah, now everyone can cut their own throats, I think to myself. He's just hoping if he throws enough bodies into the lake it will become shallow enough for him to keep his nose above water. I shake my head.

My eyes move to another headline lower on the page: 'Zellman Totters, Morton is Sold, GIG Seeks Cash.' I chuckle out loud over the irony of the story on Russell Miner as the new CEO for Citizens because it takes top billing over an article on Morton Salzman being sold. The bed where he slept is still warm while he trumps his own failure. In what other industry in the world could this happen?

The article confirms what I believe. Zellman is the biggest player on the Street, but because it dabbled too much in derivatives, short-sellers are literally going to sell it down the river. Morton Salzman had too heavy a foot on the derivative pedal and the company got yanked out of the life-sustaining maneuvers like a fish plucked from water back in September. Since then, like that same proverbial fish, it flopped on the dock until a buyer out of China finally came along. Meanwhile, the brains of this bunch are flip-flopping around to keep their heads above water—and above all stay in the game because the money being made is historical.

I shake my head and gulp the last mouthful of dark roast coffee from my cup. I savor the flavor while I stare into the space above the buildings across the street and watch the night sky being pushed from existence by the oncoming morning, digesting what I've just read.

I still can't believe Charlie and I were the only ones besides Baldy to know about GIG before now. Especially since we have the best market analysts in the world, supposedly. You'd think we would have heard *something* from our own people before reading about it in the paper.

I flip through the rest of the pages with irritation. My brain passes over headlines like a priest's incense burner over the heads of the wicked until I come to the second-to-last page. 'Liquidity Problems Lurk' reads a small headline near the bottom of the page. I read on. The comptroller general, a man by the name of Alhrik Ostness, had reported to a congressional committee his findings after investigating a developing market known as derivatives. 'Any sudden abrupt withdrawal from trading of any of these large U.S. dealers could cause liquidity problems in the markets that could pose risks to all other entities, including federally insured banks, as well as the financial system as a whole.'

I suddenly have to take a crap.

MONDAY, JANUARY 21, 2008: 6:00 A.M. (CST)

Charlie brought coffee and rolls for the three of us. He and I and Manny huddle around his desk. We are the only ones in the office.

Before Charlie says anything, he hops up and makes one last round through the darkened outer office then closes the door. He takes his chair behind the desk where Manny and I sit eating our rolls.

I avoid bringing up my discomfort with what I read earlier. I've learned by now to squelch all signs of weakness, especially around Charlie. You want to run with the big dogs, you can't pee like a pup. I have nothing to lose and everything to gain by keeping my mouth shut. Why shouldn't I take this ride like everyone else? After all, clients are begging me to make them money ... lots of money. My clients are making as much and more than I am. Even the little people with less than $100K in their accounts are pulling in percentages that exceed their wildest expectations. All I'm doing is satisfying their seemingly insatiable appetites for wealth, and being paid handsomely for my efforts. About time I get in on the fruits of capitalism. Besides, Charlie's ahead of the game. Everything will work out fine, I try and tell myself for the umpteenth time.

"Did you bring your account lists?" he asks, ignoring the last roll in the box while Manny and I glare at each other over it.

Charlie immediately begins to pour over our lists as Manny and I lick our fingers and slurp coffee and wonder whether Charlie is going to eat that last roll. I catch Manny staring at me like a gunslinger watching for the first sign of movement. Fat pig, I think to myself. Being the bigger person, I break eye contact to indicate I couldn't care less, that I am the better person by letting him have the last one. But Manny doesn't get the point. He smirks with childish pleasure as he takes a big bite. Jelly oozes out the side of his mouth.

When Charlie lays the lists on top of one another, grabs a pen from the inside pocket of his topcoat, and leans forward, Manny and I follow suit. Client by client Charlie goes through each list and strategically designates each to one of our three books of business. All the biggest clients will be transferred to Charlie's book since he already has the biggest clients. These are the accounts we will concentrate on moving to our new firm once we abandon Maugham. Accounts worthy enough to fight over will be transferred to Manny's book and used as bargaining chips during the anticipated legal battle that is bound to follow. I will take all the accounts we want to leave on the table into my book of business—accounts that don't have sufficient assets to warrant the time it takes for us to service them, or clients who require too much of our time to explain things. We must eliminate all potential drag. But most importantly, I will remain in full compliance of my non-compete clause by leaving my entire book behind, and *that* frees *me* up to contact Charlie and Manny's clients while their legal drama continues to plays out. Leave it to Charlie to find a way around the nooses dangling in front of us.

To avoid suspicion, we will transfer accounts accordingly over the next several months, yet collaboratively work clients to get them comfortable in dealing with any *one* of us. When it comes time for us to jump ship, we will do so on a Friday upon Closing Bell. That gives us about sixty-six hours lead time to transfer accounts to our new firm before anyone discovers we're gone. By keeping the transfers within that timeframe, we keep our asses in the gray area of the law enough to possibly work out a deal that just might prevent us from being forced to wear orange jumpsuits.

Charlie will set up the New York office and hire a team of assistants to prepare everything ahead of time: have all the overnight envelopes pre-addressed, put the courier services on stand-by, train phone operators with rehearsed scripts, and prime all the clients with instructions. "If all goes well, we should be able to move ninety percent of our targeted clients before Opening Bell on Monday."

Maugham will slap a cease and desist order on the three of us within minutes, but I will be cleared of any wrongdoing within days.

"It will be your show for a while, Dave," Charlie says with a smile.

The thought of running an international boutique capital management firm raises my testosterone to a whole new level. It is a glimpse of what Charlie is after. The fact I will be at the helm of his proverbial ship before him is also satisfying to know. *That* and the fact he trusts me with it.

Manny huffs and throws the donut box into the wastebasket noisily.

My mind evaluates everything Charlie just said. We aren't the first, nor will we be the last, to pull this stunt. It's all part of this wild game. If you don't play to win, you lose. It's that simple. The game is rigged to not allow anyone working a regular gig to stay in the game for long. You either keep your pile ramped up, or someone else becomes king of your hill. Soon our hill will be too big for anyone to take over. That's the plan, anyway. It all sounds good. We all nod in agreement.

That's when I glance at my list. It is made up mostly of people from the Park. I wince at the insinuation they are worthless; Maggie, Evie, Vinnie, Schmitty, Bobo and his pals. They'll be okay, I tell myself. They are in simple mutual fund strategies and are so small that any advisor assigned to them won't pay attention to them anyway. I'll come back and get them in two years, after my non-compete expires. They'll be fine until then, I assure myself. The thing that bothers me most is having to take Manny's crap while I hand over to him my best accounts: Stuart, Grandma Jazz, plus Walter and the entire Durkee 401(k) plan. It isn't so much my sense of competition, but rather a latent sense of responsibility that seems to be struggling its way into my conscience.

"Something the matter?" Charlie asks, recognizing my expression as foul.

A lot is the matter. Manny is the matter. The whole stinking idea that people are categorized is the matter. Questions keep popping up all over the Street, but no answers anywhere is the matter, I think to myself. "No," I reply.

Charlie searches my eyes before he continues.

I have all I can do to stay seated and not paste Manny in the face for reasons known, unknown, and borrowed for purposes I would deny in a court of law. But I refrain from showing further emotion. I am a professional, I remind myself.

Finally Charlie sits back in his big leather chair and sips his cold coffee. His face looks flushed, but his body goes limp. His eyes are red and glassy—evidence he's been awake nights planning this thing.

"I want you both in New York with me Thursday to transition accounts there," he says, glancing back and forth between Manny and me. Then he turns toward me and adds pointing a finger, "Then, you and I will head back to Minneapolis on Sunday to settle things here. By the end of next week, we'll be set to begin transferring accounts." His voice is resigned. His eyes, while they are still on me, are looking through me to somewhere in the future as he visualizes his dreams coming true. Then, as if he is swiftly pulled back into reality, he sits up and while he seems to be speaking to both of us he looks strictly at me and says, "We'll all be sharing one big book once we're set up on the other side." He pauses for reasons he assumes we know. "We're a team, right?" Charlie stands up and hovers over the now reassigned list of accounts sitting in the middle of the desk with a look that dares either Manny or me to disagree. Both Manny and I jut our jaws and glare at one another through narrowed eyes. Our heads nod reluctantly.

"Right!" Charlie slams his palm down hard with a note of warning which invigorates our nods. He surveys the two of us cautiously, somewhat regrettably. "You know what you need to do." His nostrils flare. His brow grows taut. His lips relax. His pupils dilate. "Do it."

CHAPTER 13: ROCKS AND BOULDERS
MINNEAPOLIS, MINNESOTA

TUESDAY, JANUARY 22, 2008: 9:00 A.M. (CST)

You have to be a stockbroker to understand how reducing your book's asset base for *any* reason doesn't sit well with the ego, which is why I am so pissed and which is why Charlie isn't.

Charlie and I are on our way to a meeting at IBM when he asks, "You okay with everything?"

With both the computer giant and the Mayo Clinic headquartered in the same city, he intends to eventually gain access to all the top echelons of Rochester, Minnesota society, and because he isn't taking any chances on blowing this initial meeting, he's taking an attitude check on me.

I don't answer him until we leave the metro area and I find open road on Highway 52 south. I drive a few more miles before I reply. "I'm fine," I finally say. I understand the plan. I just don't like being in such a vulnerable position. I mean, once we transfer our accounts Manny-the-slime-ball could walk away with mine if he chose to do so and there wouldn't be anything I could do about it. Just the idea that the people I care about will be subject to his discretion makes my skin crawl. Even though he isn't supposed to do anything with those accounts but harbor them, there is no guarantee he won't do something just to get my goat. I hadn't anticipated how vulnerable they would be for a period of time. It sticks in my craw to have to trust him, especially since the Durkee account is going to become part of his book, along with my own grandmother and half the high rollers of Fiddlers Park. It's Charlie's belief that their loyalty to me will draw those accounts back to us eventually, thus saving us the time and trouble to garner them while we face more challenging pursuits in the hours immediately following our abdication of Maugham Southerby. He understands how I feel. Even Manny understands how I feel. That's the scary part.

"Manny isn't going anywhere," Charlie says as though he's reading my mind. "It's necessary," he says. "I need you available to work the clients with me." Charlie looks out the window again. We ride in silence for several miles before he adds, "You know that, don't you?" He pauses, then continues. "Manny is nothing but a means to an end." We ride a further in silence. "Manny will come out of this alright," he says as if talking to himself. He nods his head up and down as he stares out the window, more so to assure himself of something than to assure me. "He'll get what he wants, and we'll get what we want."

"Yeah? Exactly what *is* that?" I mumble. Tensions have peaked. Emotions are raw. We're heading into the final stretch.

He gives me a long look. I glance over at him and in his eyes see doubt about me. I glower at him while I avoid taking a swing at him. How dare he question my worth. The look on his face is of complete bewilderment, but my current state of frustration is blinding me. All I see is his face is composure, his ability to always do and say the right thing. I grip the wheel and grind my teeth before I manage to spit out, "How about those Giants?" I either change the subject or I will be rearranging Charlie's face.

The talk immediately turns to the Super Bowl, with Charlie accepting the topic for the same reason I offered it. We've learned a thing or two about one another and this isn't my pretty side. When my dander finally settles back down, Charlie gets back to business.

"Got Martin to pick up the tab for the box, the airfare, everything in Glendale," Charlie says. It isn't about the money. It is about the power. Charlie is getting off on manipulating one of Maugham Southerby's highest rollers.

"Hotel rooms, too?" I ask, just to fuel Charlie's elation.

"The works," he replies.

I bust out laughing. My belly begins to convulse in spasms. The thought of Martin playing a bigger chump than I puts a whole new slant on the situation. Throughout the day I shake my head at the thought of Martin forking over the funds for Charlie to set up his business plan. By the time we head back to Minneapolis, I am no longer angry with Charlie. He is right. It is just business. We can't let emotions get in the way of our judgment.

The drive back to the cities is filled with talk of the upcoming Super Bowl, out of legitimate interest: how the Giants have a chance, how they don't; how the Patriots will go down in history, how the

Giants won't. It seems like it is always the same between us—Charlie on the winning side and me for the underdogs.

"You just never know, Charlie," I say with a grin. "You just never know."

TUESDAY, JANUARY 29, 2008: 4:15 P.M. (CST)

The edifice that used to scare the crap out of me as a kid still does. County General. It's a no-frills building built in 1935 funded by Roosevelt's CCC program. It was meant to put out-of-work men to work and to put a roof over the heads of doctors and nurses who were willing to work for little or nothing to save the lives of the poor. There is an emergency room bigger than most other hospitals because poor people brawl more and because poor people are more willing to do dangerous work that other people wouldn't think of doing for a living. It has a 50-bed maternity ward because poor people have fewer options for entertainment. There is a cardiac unit that is always full but has a high turnover. And a general ward where you go if you get food poisoning, pneumonia, whooping cough, or your temperature is so high they have to pack you in ice. There is no dermatology department. If you have acne you don't get as many dates. It would be a waste to have a dietician on staff to tell people to eat right when they can't afford to do so anyway. There isn't even a podiatrist. If you have a gimp you limp.

Blackened by a hundred years, or more, of smog, soot, and city crud the once-red bricks look black as tar. Some unidentifiable leafless vine remains frozen in its final death crawl in an arch above the entrance. I feel eerily dared by the devil to pass through.

I just happened to be in Minneapolis when I got the call that Mom had collapsed after her chemotherapy treatment and that they were keeping her in the hospital overnight for observation. Barb and Bob arrived just moments ahead of me and we all stare at each other upon converging in the lobby. We dispense with the obligatory hugs and scurry three-abreast toward the information desk. It is the first time any of us have had to come here since we were kids.

White and black marble tiles spread across the lobby to a black marble counter. As a child I used to think the big black counter had a voice that said, "Take a number and have a seat," but I realized when I got taller that an actual person was sitting behind the barricade.

I look about the room. Nothing has changed. The same poorly dressed people with crying kids litter the waiting room. A boy about six years old with hair hanging in his eyes is holding a toddler who is drinking something red from a blue plastic baby bottle the toddler is holding himself while their mother nurses an infant under a blanket she has draped over her shoulder for privacy. The blanket has green and yellow bunnies and is well worn. The six-year-old just stares at me without expression. His eyes convey a depth of wisdom uncommon for a kid his age. I force a smile. He doesn't smile back.

"What room is Donna Yates in, please?"

The desk nurse taps the keyboard of the computer, looks into its monitor, then tells us Floor Five, room 523 without looking at any of us.

The hallway to the elevator is flanked by people parked in wheelchairs and on gurney's, waiting their turn. I wonder if any are dead. The smell of Lysol mixed with odors of blood, urine, sweat, and medicine brings back the horrors of doctor visits. Nobody I knew ever went to the doctor for a checkup. You only went if there was something so terribly wrong Mom couldn't fix it.

I remember the first time Mom hauled me down this same hallway to the emergency room when I was five and Bob had bet me a nickel I couldn't swallow a straight pin. I thought they were going to have to slit my throat to get the pin that had caught sidewise in there out, but instead they stuck a long skinny tool into my mouth and made me say 'ah.' Then there was that time Mom got us all up in the middle of the night, bundled us up in snowsuits, and dragged us out in a blizzard because there was no one she could call to babysit at that hour and Julie was so sick Mom thought she would die if we didn't get her to a hospital. I still get shivers whenever I think about that night. Just about every year there was something that forced one of us to have to come to this awful place. Nothin' good ever happens in this hospital.

She wouldn't be here if it were up to me, but she's too proud to accept help from one of her children. "I am who I am and I refuse to be anything else," she had told me flat out when I offered to get her the best doctors in the world. Something about us all being born into circumstances which are our obligation to experience and become who we are meant to become according to God's great plan. Sometimes she just doesn't make any sense.

The fifth floor is carpeted and quiet. We all walk down the hallway and look for signage that will lead us to room 523. "What's that smell?" I ask. No one answers.

The room is a double, but there is no one in the first bed. The curtain between the two beds had been pulled back. There is a large box that displays quartz numbers. It reads: 129, then 131, then 128 ... A tall chrome bar holds a bag of something that drips into a hose that had been stuck into the arm of my mother. Geez. Barb pushes me in front of her as we near the bed. Mom's head turns on her pillow. The rest of her body remains dead still.

"Oh, they shouldn't have called you," she murmurs weakly upon seeing me. "Did you fly back on account of me?"

"I was in Minneapolis, Mom," I explain. Although I would have flown back from anywhere for her.

As soon as she gives us the details of what happened and an admirable attempt to assure us it is nothing out of the ordinary, the theme of 'nothing' prevails and it is what we talk about to avoid what is on our minds. Mom struggles to stay alert in spite of our requests that she sleep. We pull up chairs around her bed and offer small talk as a family incantation. It's our way of acting normal under abnormal conditions. Mom drifts off in a peaceful slumber.

"How's Julie?" Barb asks me.

"Great," I tell her. Julie is where she belongs. Being able to financially provide her the opportunity to attend the Julliard School of Dance brings comfort to my soul. But whenever I watch her practice, see her in her tights and whimsy skirts flowing around the room as effortlessly as fog rolling in from the sea, it almost brings me to my knees in gratitude toward a higher power, something outside myself I don't quite understand.

"How's Helice?" Barb asks, but quickly turns her head away as if it would pain her to have to listen to the answer.

"Fine," I say, wondering if Helice will ever fit into this family— or whether it matters to me that she does.

Mom stirs and we all lean forward. The clarity in her eyes materializes rapidly from the folds of slumber. The meds they gave her have worn off. She pushes herself to a sitting position and presses the button on her adjustable bed. Then she folds her arms across her chest and furrows her brow.

"What are you all doing here when you have more important things to do than stand around a sleepy old woman?" she demands. "Go home and take care of your families. I am just fine."

"What about me?" I ask. "This is the only family I have."

She smiles. "You can stick around and have dinner with me." I quickly nod in agreement while the others shrug acceptance of the idea.

As soon as Barb and Bob are done hugging Mom—and before I have to rip their fingers from her grasp—they leave and Mom and I are alone in her hospital room.

Soon we are picking through plates of Chicken a la King, trying to find the bits of chicken. "I shouldn't eat this," she says. "My hips are wider than a whale's."

"Enjoy your food, Mom. Enjoy life." We both look at each other. I didn't mean it the way it sounded.

"They have to let me go," she says of Cooper, Cooper and Zarembinski, Attorneys at Law. It is a small partnership in Roseville that handles estate planning and trust services, real estate and land titles, and a few simple divorces. They do no personal injury, workman's compensation issues, or criminal law, and they outsource any messy divorces. Donna Mae had gone to high school with Cheryl Cooper so when Donna needed a job after graduation, Cheryl's father let her come to work as an errand girl, making rounds to the courthouse and researching land titles. While Cheryl went on to become a lawyer herself and eventually becoming a partner with Mesham and Moyer Personal Injury Attorneys in Minneapolis, she had inspired Donna Mae to take an eight-month paralegal course through the local community college.

Completion of the course never gave Mom enough credentials to become a paralegal, but together with her typing abilities—130 words per minute—Donna Mae was promoted to legal secretary. It was supposed to be a temporary job until she and Dad could get on their feet financially. That didn't happen, and Dad left. We never got on our feet financially, until now. Now that I'm making big money, this family will want for nothing. I nod to myself out of determination as I shove in a mouthful of gravy-soaked biscuit. If only I could get her to realize that—if she wouldn't worry so much about money it would put her mind at ease.

"I'll be able to keep the insurance for a while yet," she replies with exaggerated optimism, unable to keep what's on her mind to herself any longer. "They've been so good to me." Her head drops as she contemplates the effort of others to help her. "Mr. Cooper told me he would do everything he could to hire me back as soon as I am able." She smiles broadly as though it were a conclusion to something she just said. When the expression on my face doesn't change, she adds, "I'll be back to work before the insurance ever runs out." She forces another smile for my benefit.

But I know better. Mr. Cooper isn't in charge. Circumstance is. The group rate drops immediately and she'll be lucky to find any affordable healthcare coverage with her pre-existing condition. And when she is hired back, the same insurance company will underwrite her condition right out of the plan. She's shit-out-of-luck and just doesn't know it yet.

But she has me. I can pay for everything, insurance or no insurance. If she'd only let me help her, she wouldn't need to worry about money ... about saving the house ... about anything! The only thing she needs to concern herself with right now is getting better. If only she'd accept my help, I'd get her out of this dump, get her the best care ... better food, I think, trying not to look at my next mouthful. My head involuntarily wags back and forth out of frustration before I have a chance to catch myself.

"What?" she asks, aware of my emotional discomfort.

Now I have to answer her, or else. I try to stall to gather my thoughts. Logic isn't worth a thing in this argument. Death isn't an incentive where Mom is concerned. I haven't yet figured out what is, but she insists I have to learn something about life that she claims I haven't learned yet. Something important. Something more important than her life, evidently. "Mom," I say, still stalling for words. "I love you."

"I love you, too, dear," she instantly replies.

"Mom," I start again, "We *all* love you."

She stops chewing and gives me her full attention. She knows there is nothing I can say to influence her about where she accepts healthcare. We've had this conversation several times already. She knows I want the best for her, but she won't hear of me paying for it. However, she would never discourage me from standing up for what I believe. Therefore, she gives me her undivided attention as though I were still in kindergarten and telling her about my day.

I suck in a breath. "It's because we all love you that we want you to stay alive."

She pooh-poohs me. "I want to stay alive, too," she exclaims. "But that might not be what the Lord has in mind for me. We all have to be ready for His plan, David. God's in charge."

I'm in charge, damn it! Or at least I would be if she would let me, I blurt to myself. But then I realize I can turn this around. "Exactly!" I stand up for effect. "You are always talking about accepting our role in God's plan, right?"

She nods.

"*I* am part of God's plan!" I jab my chest with my index finger so hard that I think I just bruised myself.

She just looks at me.

"I'm your son. God gave *me* to *you*, right?"

She nods. This is good. I continue. "So, if *I* am part of His plan, then His plan is for you to have the best doctors in the world, because *I* can afford to get them for you."

There is an initial look of surprise in her eyes, but it quickly turns to resolve. "You are a good boy," she says. "I know you mean well, but I don't want to be a burden to my children. Parents provide and protect. They do not sponge off their children."

"It's not sponging, Mom," I whine in exasperation. She gives me *the look*. It is meant for me to get my emotions under control before she has to get them under control *for* me, only she forgets I am a grown man now.

How can I convince her that I can financially take care of her? Knowing she will think I'm lying if I tell her how much money I make, I tell her far less—a figure she will believe yet large enough to convince her I can afford to take care of her without it ever being a burden on me.

She doesn't answer immediately. Instead she contemplates while she looks out the window, which at this time of night only reflects the images inside the room against the cold hard glass and the black universe outside it. All she sees is a view of herself sitting in a hospital bed with blinking and dripping apparatus all around her. "We don't need to worry about anything just yet," she says in a whisper.

"Yeah," I tell her. "Sure." I gratefully accept her *maybe*. We take a few more bites in silence. "Here," I say holding my fork up to her mouth. "I think I found a piece of chicken."

She takes the bite. She chews it thoughtfully, then replies, "Must have been a rooster." We both make a sour face.

"How's your gelatin?" I ask her.

She takes some in her spoon, turns it around, aims it at me and, using her finger, pulls back on the tip and lets it go. I duck and red slime splats against the green ceramic tile and slides down the wall. We point and laugh until Mom falls back against her pillow too exhausted to do anything other than smile and bite her lip. Her eyes twinkle with renewed life. "That's one for my list," she sighs.

She's been making a list ever since I can remember of what she calls her death-bed wishes, things she would love to do just one more time before Jesus takes her to the promised land. Things like pet a puppy, blow bubbles, feel sand between her toes, feel a snowflake melt on her tongue—and now she wants to add fling food from a spoon to her list.

I don't want to hear any last wishes any time soon.

CHAPTER 14: RUNNING WITH DOGS
NEW YORK, NEW YORK

THURSDAY, FEBRUARY 14, 2008: 1:20 P.M. (EST)

I'm on flight out of LA to New York in time to take Helice to dinner. Got reservations at the Four Seasons and rented a limo for just the two of us. Called Tiffany's and had some gal there pick out a set of rocks for Helice's ears. I told her to wrap it and keep the doors open until I get there to pick it up. A dozen red roses should have been delivered earlier today. Check, check, and check. I'm feeling pretty proud of myself for remembering to do all the little things women get their thongs in a knot about.

"Sir," the flight attendant says softly as she places another Heineken in front of me along with a fresh bowl of nuts. The old guy sitting next to me smiles, then goes back to his laptop. I munch on nuts and dream about the future while I eyeball the legs of both flight attendants in the first-class galley.

Aside from having to put up with Manny, everything is coming together nicely. We could be ready to jump ship as early as August. Charlie's lined up Certified Public Accountants and estate attorneys in every major city in which we do business to prepare to initiate a full-service investment service in each. He's got a couple of his old college buddies pulling together a hedge fund strategy using some of the tactics he pilfered off Maugham Southerby. It will be the bait we use to lure clients to get them to suck on the new nipple once we go independent. Since unemployed securities personnel are like debris after a street dance, he had no problem hiring a compliance officer who is handling the licensing and regulation requirements on the sly.

Charlie told Manny and me to prepare to go without significant commission for a month. Afterwards, we'll be raking in millions, nine million the first year by his calculations. But we're to keep four million in the pot for business growth and development. Each of us are to take only two million our first year. Our financial projections are still unfathomable to me, a kid from Fiddlers Park. "Unbelievable," I whisper to myself as I lay my head against the back of my chair and gaze out the port side of the plane while the people destined to fly coach stream past.

Two million! I can't comprehend such income yet. That's over $165,000 a month! I have to chuckle at the thought of owing nearly $60,000 a month in taxes! Or will I? Charlie has already connected me to the CPA firm in Minneapolis that he uses to advise his high-income clients. I've been learning how to shelter my income from excessive taxation and the real reasons behind the platform of the Republican Party ... to keep Uncle Sam's mitts off our money.

I've been a Democrat since before I was old enough to vote. Mostly because my family is Democrat. The only thing I heard throughout my childhood was how we need to take care of each other and that the Democrats are big on that idea. While that all once sounded good coming from Mom, who relied on food stamps to feed her kids, it just sounds pathetic now that I'm standing on the other side of those tracks. I hated the fact we were on food stamps. While not everybody in Fiddlers Park received public assistance, every household with school-aged children qualified for the free lunch program at school—all except the Rasmussens who made it known to all the rest of us that they didn't take handouts.

I pop a handful of mixed nuts in my mouth and chase it down with a swig of beer.

If people want equality, then let's start with taxes. Why should people who make $50,000 a *month* have to pay any more taxes than a guy making $50,000 a *year*? Like we're going to use more roadway, or send more kids to public schools, or need more soldiers to protect our borders because we make more money than the next guy. Let them pay for all the federal programs they want by raising their own taxes and leaving those of us who will never use any federally funded program alone. I take another pull on my beer.

A 1 percent increase in taxes to a guy making $50,000 a year is a measly $500 bucks. But to a guy like myself who makes $2 million, it pushes my entire tax obligation $20,000 higher! C'mon! Is there anyone who can't see the inequality in *that*? I scowl at the guy next to me. He glances up from his laptop and smiles, once more.

I nod like we mutually agree on something. Perhaps we do. He's riding first class, too. I look around the cabin. My bottom lip begins to curl over my top lip as my assessment assures me that I am no longer second class *anything*. I rest my head against the back of the seat and let the confidence and power of money sweep over me like fairy dust. It's not that I wish anyone anything less than I have, but they should go get it themselves, not expect those of us who found our fortunes to have to pay for those who didn't. I don't mind seeing my tax money go toward industry because more industry means more job opportunities. If someone isn't willing to work then they shouldn't expect a handout. We're supposed to be a capitalistic society, aren't we? The Democrats are nothing but a bunch of socialists who should all move to China if they like it that much.

I look up, smile and shake my head at the flight attendant holding a plate of warm chocolate chip cookies in front of me. She smiles back and politely removes the plate of cookies.

Within two years I could be pulling down ten, twenty, thirty million. The sky's the limit. While Helice won't have to look any further for the man who can fulfill her dreams, I'm going to have to do things to protect mine. That starts right now with supporting my local Republicans. I make a mental note to find out who they are as soon as I get back to Minneapolis. Meanwhile, to hell with what's his name ... Obama. I'm getting on the McCain bandwagon.

WEDNESDAY, MARCH 12, 2008: 1:10 P.M. (EDT)

"What are *chew* doing with my money? I am goink to lose it all," Bobo exclaims excitedly through the Bluetooth stuck to my ear.

I am dodging the crowd on the mezzanine of the Broadmoor Building in New York, juggling a pastrami on rye I'd just picked up at the deli. "What's happening?" I ask, not certain what he is talking about.

"Eet es go-ink ca-razy! The markets are go-ink ca-razy!"

A bolt of adrenaline shoots through me as I contemplate the possibility of the bottom dropping out of the Markets. "Let me call you right back, Bobo, as soon as I get to my office," I assure him.

"Chew better hurry," he threatens—or warns, which I don't yet know.

I bustle back to the office but when I get there nothing out of the ordinary is happening. I walk back to the lunchroom and find the usual gathering calmly discussing the merits of GIG's new variable annuity.

"Pays seven for seven," I hear Manny comment, meaning the annuity will pay a trailing commission of 7 percent for seven years to the broker. Sweet, I think to myself as I head back toward the visiting broker's office I had commandeered the past few days. GIG can't be in too much trouble if they are offering a little number like that, or their hides would be tacked to the wall at the SEC. They wouldn't dare, I think to myself. Course, if Manny thinks it is good, I better check it out more thoroughly. That slime-ball would be pushing dope if he didn't already have a securities license.

I had left the monitor tuned in to the closed-circuit Bloomberg channel, so once I close the door, I quickly slide into the leather chair with a mouthful of pastrami. Rose McKinney is interviewing U.S. Secretary-Treasurer Sharon Gerber about recent accusations of incompetency due to huge amounts of subprime debt found on the books at Fannie Mae and Freddie Mac. "This current situation, while cause for concern, should be viewed in retrospect to the subprime debt we are finding throughout the lending community," Gerber tells McKinney.

My brain is numbing to the sound of subprime. The term is everywhere. I flip the channel to the Maugham Southerby monitor of the markets and watch the little orange and green lines flicker for a while before I determine that while the markets will likely close down today, there doesn't seem to be anything earthshaking going on.

The mounting frenzy on Main Street is likely what spooked Bobo. I call him back to calm his fears while I pull up his account stats and change his rating to B2. Charlie had rated all our accounts A, B, or C according to the amount of assets; then using numbers 1, 2 and 3 to identify how well clients do what we tell them without questions. When the time comes for us to make our move, we won't have one minute to waste on anyone who might slow us down in reaching our goal.

"Chew know best," he says with renewed confidence. "I will do whatever chew say." But it's too late. Bobo just got demoted.

He invites me to his St. Patrick's Day Costume Party this coming Saturday. The thought of a bunch of gay guys in green tights makes it easy to decline. Bobo doesn't know it yet, but his future is the cutting-room floor. Just a few more months until blast-off, I remind myself.

"How ees your mother do-ink?"

"Just great," I tell him. After completing the last set of chemo treatments in February she's recuperated completely and is in full remission, I happily report to him. Then, remembering all the medical bills I have to yet pay, I pull up his accounts once again and take a closer look.

"You know, Bobo," I begin, "I'm just looking at your portfolio and I think we could spice it up a little. What do you say?" The jingle in my pocket just got louder.

MONDAY, MARCH 17, 2008: 8:50 A.M. (EDT)

Zellman Barclay, the largest investment bank on the Street, opened down Thirty-five percent this morning. It is down forty-eight percent by the time I step into the lobby of Maugham Southerby headquarters in New York less than an hour later. I have my carry-on still slung over my shoulder and am holding my briefcase, having just arrived by cab from LaGuardia. I took the first flight out of Minneapolis earlier this morning.

Most of the brokers throughout the branch have left the solace of their private offices and migrated around the television in the outer lobby, much in the same way people in the Midwest come out of their homes and look up at the sky during a tornado warning.

About thirty brokers stare at the wall-mounted monitor tuned to CNBC. A harried reporter on the trading floor looks pale in the lights of her adjacent cameraman. She holds a microphone out to one of the traders but is ignored. She pulls the microphone back into her chest and begins to help viewers make sense of the chaos we see on the trading floor behind her.

"Zellman's stock is dropping on news that some of its largest hedge funds are pulling out ..."

We stand around mesmerized by the velocity of the trades as we watch the numbers flash across the bottom of the screen. None of us dash to our phones to call clients. We're not causing this and don't yet know who or what is. United only by confusion, we stand around with mouths open while emotions swirl within us as our brains attempt to find the horizon. What is happening? To whom is it happening? Who is causing it? Should we do something? What?

"It's the shorts," someone finally shouts near me. "That's what's going on. It's the short-sellers."

The fed is still bolstering fallout from the demise of two large hedge funds that short-sellers caused last year. Short-sellers seem to be behind every rock lately, I think to myself. This guy might be right. Then it dawns on me that *that* was what Perry's been saying all along. If Perry and this guy are right, the short-sellers are already in the bell towers. The whole world is behind this eight ball. With the Street below littered with money—trillions of dollars being made trading collateralized debt obligations, credit default swaps, BISTROs, TIGRS—it is in a frenzy of greed from which no one is willing to look up no matter how many bodies fall next to them. Fingers just keep reaching out to grab more money. Could this actually be happening? I wonder, fearing the obvious conclusion.

Just then the reporter on the trading floor announces that Moody reaffirms it is giving Zellman an A-1 rating and that Maugham Southerby announced it would trade with Zellman all day. The selling frenzy immediately turns into a buying frenzy. The brokers make a run for their offices.

"Push as much Zellman as you can," Charlie says as he appears from nowhere. "Get on it," he orders and is gone. He means for me to contact clients from our shared book of business, but I'm jumping on my own pile of bones first. Just a little something to pad my landing should anything go wrong with Charlie's plan.

While short-sellers pull their triggers, it will be several more months before they spill enough blood on the Street to horrify anyone. By then it will be too late and the snipers will have gotten away with murder. But for the moment, adrenaline is pumping through the veins of brokers across the nation ... around the world. Investors are being intruded upon from bedrooms to boardrooms. It's the smell of fresh meat. It's the kill!

I punch in the number twenty-two on my cell phone to speed-dial Willard Rybach while I head to a row of offices reserved for visiting brokers. I am surprised to find Manny sitting in the one I usually use when in New York. When did he get here? Manny looks up, the phone stuck to his ear.

"I figured you'd be calling," Willard says as he answers his cell phone from somewhere in Miami. "It's all over the Bloomberg Channel."

"How much do you want?" I ask, getting right to the point.

"As much as you can get for under $30 a share up to a million," he tells me. But before he hangs up, he tells me he just closed on another condo in Miami right on the beach. The decline in real estate is nothing but another buying opportunity, he tells me.

"North end or south?" I ask.
"South," he replies. "Want me to hold one for you?"
"Not today," I say.
"They'll be gone by noon," he tells me. "Easy money."
He has no idea how easy money is on the Street. While Willard thinks he's making it big in real estate within a few weeks to a month, it is nothing compared to what I can make in minutes. I press twenty-three on my cell phone to speed-dial the next investor in line to make the same offer.

Before anyone answers on the other end, Manny pokes his ugly mug around the door to the office I am sitting in. "How about *that* one?" he asks as he slaps the door jamb with an open hand. "Old Felton," he begins with a sinister smile, "just lost $92 million before the markets even opened today!"

George Felton is the CEO of Zellman. Stock holdings of CEOs are made public. It is no surprise that Manny's pursuit of happiness runs parallel to other people's misery, but it isn't the real reason he's hanging at my door. What he's doing is using this as an excuse to give me the rub ... to remind me of the fact he is here in New York at Charlie's personal request and I am not.

"Oh," I say with satirical surprise, "it's *you*." I pronounce the word 'you' as though it were a piece of Limburger cheese. Then I offer as phony a smile as I am capable of portraying and add, "I thought I was looking at a hog's ass."

Manny's lips pinch together while he struggles to come up with something clever to say in retaliation, but I know from experience he's too lame. He gives me the finger and leaves.

"Gordon," I say to a raspy voice on the other end of the line, "sorry to wake you, but I can get you Zellman for under $30 a share. Are you in for a thousand rounds?" Gordon Nash is a real estate developer from Charlie's book who is intended to be left behind because he doesn't follow orders, but he's been listening to me pretty carefully lately, which might put him back on the taker list. Gordon understands I am asking for the number of round lots he wants. A round lot is a securities normal unit of trading which is usually 100 shares. A thousand will cost Gordon three mil. He's in.

One man's loss is another man's gain, I mumble as I enter the trade and speed-dial yet another investor. Within twenty minutes I accept and place over $25 million in trades. I make over $200,000 in commission. But I'm just a pup in this pack of dogs. The commissions that will be made by some will make Felton's loss look like chump change. But the real beauty is that the fallout lands on the shoulders of the investors. You just got to love this game. No one is going to bump *me* from this roster; not Manny, not Charlie ... no one!

Zellman rallies late morning and closes up 46.23 percent, the biggest one-day gain in the stock since it went public in 1999. Felton's only out a few million by the end of the day. I shake my head slowly back and forth, amazed at how much money is made on Wall Street ... amazed at how much *I* am making. Not bad for a kid from Fiddlers Park, I tell myself. And Willard thinks he's picking up the candy at the parade.

By the time I finish after-hours trading, I am pumped and ready for some serious drinking. Charlie rounds up Manny and myself and suggests we join some of the other brokers who are heading to Four Seasons for a little celebrating.

Three limousines are waiting for us by the time we leave the building. Chauffeurs stand next to open doors. I purposely avoid getting into the same one as Manny and Charlie. Instead, I pile in behind an elderly man impeccably dressed and extremely reserved amid the hyped-up younger brokers. "Dave Yates," I say extending a hand once inside the limo. He leans forward. His eyes are keen and observing, equally as reserved as his mannerisms ... perhaps calculating.

"I know who you are, Mr. Yates," he says to my surprise. He extends his hand. "Conrad Dorn."

"Mr. Dorn," I say with a tone of respect. Everyone in the industry knows Conrad Dorn for his success on Wall Street. This is the first time I've laid eyes on the living legend. Before I even know what I am doing, I blurt out, "So what do you think about Zellman?"

Conrad's forehead flattens, his chin raises, and his eyes narrow ever-so-slightly. "Anyone can build a house of cards," he replies. "I prefer something more sound." He looks outward and upward. "How do you like our little city?" he asks, directing my attention to the architecture of many of the buildings as we pass, explaining their period, history of occupants, and a little about the architect who designed them.

"How is it you know so much about New York?" I finally ask.

"Only a fool beds a woman without knowing her strengths and weaknesses."

I relax at that analogy and concentrate instead on his finesse. He is exactly like the brokers I remember watching from a distance during training ... the ones I had wanted to become. Here I am sitting among them, I remind myself. I look around the compartment. The guy next to me slaps me on the shoulder and offers me a drink from the little bar.

"Earned it today, didn't we," he says.

"And never broke a sweat," someone else adds.

We all lift our glasses in a unified cheer, except for Conrad Dorn, who isn't drinking anything. He just smiles.

We step out of the limousine and onto a carpet that rolls across the sidewalk and up four steps. As we enter the lobby of the restaurant, our voices pare down as though we are stepping into a sanctuary. Only the muffled sound of our footsteps on deeply cushioned carpet is heard over the muted burble of water as it slips down a two-story wall adjacent to the entrance. To the right are four more carpeted stairs that lead to a Picasso painting fifteen feet high and thirty feet long. The door to the dining room is to the left of the massive painting. The door to the bar is to the right. We take the door to the right and follow one another in single file. The room's expanse includes living trees amid round tables, two bars at each end with several bustling bartenders preparing for the evening rush. Our lead man heads toward an empty row of tables and we all follow.

Three waitresses take our drink orders as we arrive. While others take their seats, I pause to avoid sitting within arm's length of Manny for fear I might not be able to restrain myself. Again, I find myself taking the seat next to Conrad Dorn.

The talk explodes about what happened on the Street today ... every possibility from terrorist-attack to short-seller-intervention. Manny gets everyone hooting about the heavy loss Felton took on his own shares. Charlie remains quiet.

I turn to Mr. Dorn. "We did it today," I say.

"Did what, Mr. Yates?"

I look at him, wondering why he is being facetious. He looks at me as though I should know. "We made a shitload of money today," I reply, losing decorum.

"Oh," he says as his eyes drop to the lowball before him hosting two fingers of scotch. He begins to turn it slowly with his thumb and index finger and asks condescendingly, "Was that your intention?"

What is with this guy? I think to myself. "Yeah," I reply. "That was my intention."

"One must always understand their *true* intentions. Your fate is determined by them." Then, as if to clarify further, he adds, "The desires of your heart, Mr. Yates. Do you know them?"

We stare at each other. He is waiting for my reply. I'm deciding what that will be exactly. "I want money and lots of it," I finally reply. He waves a hand. "Your answer is foolish." He leans toward me. "What good is an oar to someone who lives in a desert? If you do not know exactly what you need, you will wind up with things you do not."

"Okay ... then, I want enough money to buy anything I want anytime I want it." That should cover it, I think to myself as I watch intently for his response.

He repositions himself on the chair as he prepares to take another approach. Why he has engaged me in a philosophical conversation amid this celebration is beyond me, but he intrigues me.

"When a person says they want money, they either are running *from* something or *toward* something, Mr. Yates." He pauses to let that sink into my brain, then continues. "When a person runs *from* something it can only mean one thing: something oppresses them, they are afraid. These people run with their hands over their eyes. But if they try to run away from a bear in the woods, it will kill them." He pauses again. "If they are running *toward* something it, too, can mean only one thing: they want power, they are angry. But these people run with fists. Mother Teresa ran toward poverty. Hitler ran toward humanity." He pauses once more and stares into my eyes with anticipation of witnessing a rebirth of cognitive perspective.

I'm not sure whether I fulfilled it, however. "You make your point, Mr. Dorn," I concede. "I'll have to give this more thought."

"You do that, Mr. Yates," he says. "Your life is like a great canvas, much like the one in the foyer," he says, referring to the Picasso. "Desire is what paints your picture. Not well-laid plans. Not good ideas. Desire, Mr. Yates." He smiles and takes another sip. "Best to always know your innermost desires." This time he doesn't wait for a reply. He stands up and pulls a fifty from his wallet, places it under the drink he didn't finish, then leaves.

An hour later I have no doubts about what my desire is. When I tell Helice how much money I made today her eyes light up like cherry bombs on the fourth of July. She exhibits her admiration more than I am able to withstand and by 4 a.m. I have to cry uncle for the first time in my life.

"Baby," she coos into my ear, "money turns me on." She's straddling me and her hair hangs down around us like a tent.

I look up into the dark shadows where her face must be and beg, "Mercy, mercy."

She jumps off me so quickly that my dick slaps against my stomach. I groan as she bounds into the kitchen for some energy she says that she has for me in her purse. She returns within seconds with a small mirror, a razor, and something in a little plastic bag.

CHAPTER 15: THE SHADY SIDE OF THE MONEY TREE
MINNEAPOLIS, MINNESOTA

SUNDAY, APRIL 6, 2008: 5:40 P.M. (CDT)

Zellman surged 46 percent in the days that followed and managed to remain erect while under scrutiny. InterCon Bank, GIG, even Maugham Southerby are now under investigation for accounting errors and mismanagement due to suspicions surrounding over-leveraged subprime debt. Fannie and Freddie fell under severe pressure by the feds. The Street turned frantic when several other big players toppled.

Lending between investment banks has tightened faster than a waistband at a Thanksgiving Day feast. But nobody leaves the table. Short sellers sit like dogs in the dining room as they bet which belly will burst first. And *I* am busy in this kitchen scarfing up the scraps along with the rest of the rats.

Reporters are having a field day exposing wages and bonus packages of the big boys. Every day the carnage continues to mount but the show goes on!

"Step right up ladies and gentlemen and get your ringside seat! It's Master Greed and Madam Fear playing under the big tent! Greed enters the arena and starts the show while Fear crawls under the bleachers. As soon as all eyes are on the center ring a match is lit. The sawdust ignites. Greed disappears like magic, replaced by Madam Fear! The crowd stampedes for the exits and all are trampled to death. Screams reverberate within the canvas walls. There is crying and wailing and the sound of gnashing teeth. But wait! What do we see rising from the bodies that are stacked up? Greed. Greed is alive! Everyone runs back to their seats around center ring for the next act of the greatest show on earth!"

What once was cause for my concern is now the norm. I dance to all the songs the short-sellers are playing at this—the biggest Street dance in history. People are lining up to get in on the fun. Some who'd never invested before in their life are now banging on my door and begging me to take their money.

John and Dorothy Metzger, who when I'd first met them last October had told me they were God-fearing people who consider themselves stewards of the money the good Lord sees fit to place in their possession. Then they had given me five million dollars to invest into a conservative income strategy. I assumed his other three brothers had received equal inheritances, so began to work my way toward meeting the family, but it wasn't until two days ago that I finally got that chance.

The meeting had been held at the family farm now run by the eldest brother, Ernest and his wife, Agnes. Weak coffee and snickerdoodle cookies had been placed on a round oak table in the middle of the kitchen where all the men had been seated, including me. The women had either stood ready to retrieve something for the men, or sat on a chair next to and slightly behind their spouse with hands folded in their laps.

I figured $15 million was on the table. I nearly crapped my pants when they divulged $100 million, and they were not interested in any conservative strategy. They wanted to know if I could get them into a hedge fund or commodities.

How did they know about hedge funds and commodities trading? I asked.

Minnie Metzger had stepped forward meekly. "Commodities are king," she had said in a voice sweet as a church choir soprano. "Oil is at $140 a barrel and Russia is pumping out millions of barrels a day."

Seems the youngest brother's wife had found a way to keep herself occupied lest the devil find her mind idle. It was she who investigated investment options through the internet. With an overwhelming number of hedge funds and futures and options to choose from, they felt they needed some guidance and John had suggested *me*, since he was the only one of the three brothers who had an actual financial advisor.

"Now why would a nice family like all of you want to risk $100 million playing the stock market?" I had asked them in all sincerity, but they all snickered and giggled. I could have made enough commission on $100 million to make myself very happy putting them into an income strategy with U.S. Treasuries and municipal bonds, but they wouldn't hear of it. Their sights were on something much bigger.

Their answer: "To make thirty million more."

"But you realize that this is not a savings account that pays interest. This is Wall Street, where fortunes are made and taken away as quickly as an up-tic or a down-tic."

"Easy come, easy go," they had all said in unison, including their wives. The smiles around that table seemed like one long white picket fence. Their eyes froze open awaiting my response.

So much for God. The devil's got this one, I had thought. I walked away with $100 million in assets to invest and $255,000 in commission by the time it was all over. I should be reveling in my good fortune; but every time I feel a glow, the conversation I had with Conrad Dorn creeps into my thoughts. I catch myself wondering what my true intentions are—if not to put Julie through college, pay for Mom's doctoring and living expenses, pay my mortgages, buy a bigger car, have a little fun with Helice. Am I supposed to want more? Or am I *not* supposed to want so much? Or did he mean that I was supposed to *know* why I want what I want?

I still keep coming back to the same response. I want money and lots of it. I'm no different than anyone else. I'm just no hypocrite. I've heard people argue that there are more important things in life than money. Yeah? Show me *one*, I say. Money gets us what we want and need. There isn't a person on earth who wouldn't take more of it if they had the chance. This is *my* chance.

A few weeks ago, Helice told me to look at a one-bedroom apartment on Central Park West listed at $5 million. Before I balked at the price tag, she mentioned that Callie Sampson, one of Maugham's fund managers just bought a townhouse for $33 million on the Upper East Side, and that while she knew I wasn't yet in *that* league, I was certain to be soon.

Whether it was her sly smile, the glint in her eye, or the fact her cleavage was particularly low, I couldn't resist. I let her babble on about how she can no longer stand to be so far from me, but all I could think about was what it must be like to be able to afford a $33-million-dollar anything—and how I can't wait to find out. Besides, I know that what Helice can't bear to be apart from isn't so much me as it is my money. It's the only reason she comes to Minnesota. She's like a poodle dancing on hind legs for a treat. It's a show I'm not about to stop. I enjoy watching her jump for whatever biscuit I hold above her head.

By the time we are rolling around on the floor of my still-empty and furniture-barren river loft, things are in motion beyond my control. Within sixteen business days, I will close on a $6 million one-bedroom apartment in New York City. Helice already has my credit card and an appointment with her interior decorator. Zero-down, interest-only mortgages are said to be a fool's paradise, but you'd have to be a fool not to buy anything and everything you can on such terms. Free money.

What could possibly go wrong? Either sell it for a profit or let it go. It is what Willard has been trying to tell me for months. But it wasn't until I bought a condo on South Beach at his prodding that it began to make sense.

Now I buy real estate without spending a single penny of my own money. Then I take out lines of credit on the property and invest those funds into the stock market. So far, I have $21 million in mortgages, $15 million in equity lines of credit on the underlying property for a total of $36 million in debt with zero down. In case you haven't been following, I deposited $15 million which, as of market close today, is up 22 percent! That's a $3.3 million gain! Also, I can take a margin loan for up to 50 percent of the equity in my investment account—that's millions of dollars more available just for the asking.

Even if the real estate market drops, I figure I stand to make as much as $20 million on the investments made by using the equity lines of credit alone, which has been gyrating between $21 and $55 million in market value daily—and that's not even mentioning the money I'll make when I sell the real estate, which has already more than doubled in market value.

Wall Street is a place where money is handed out as easily as candy is on Halloween. I no longer need to wait around for Charlie's plan to materialize. Maybe I won't. That's *his* thing. He's the one looking for power. All I want is money—and I've found it. I revel in the freedom this much money brings a person like me, then realize it is why Charlie needs so much more. Conrad Dorn was right. We all need to know our true intention. Which is why I decide to stick it out with Charlie. He's my friend. He'd do the same for me. Makes me feel his equal, finally. I like the feeling.

I look at the naked back of Helice, her red hair cascading over her shoulders, her hip bone protruding from her side, and wonder how she can lay so still and not be dead. She and I are a lot alike. We're both simple, unlike Charlie; all we need is money to keep us happy. I have so much money at my fingertips I don't know what to finger first, but

Helice comes to mind. I grab her by the waist and roll her back on top of me.

"What?" she asks playfully.

"Give it to me," I demand.

The look in her eye is sly as she slithers on top of me and coos, "You're getting everything you *deserve*, mister."

TUESDAY, APRIL 29, 2008: 3:30 P.M. (CDT)

Tuesday is Lady's Nite at Monty's, but I'm not as eager to get a ringside seat for the big parade as I once was, so I finish up paperwork and trade orders for the day before I head to the elevators. I no sooner step into the elevator than I hear someone holler to hold it up. I reach over and press the 'open' button, then want to slice off my own finger once I find it's Manny I'd been holding the doors open for.

"Haven't seen you much," he says.

"What's that supposed to mean?" I ask.

"It means I haven't seen you much." He repeats himself.

I know what he means. He means to remind me he is sharing the turf with Charlie in New York more than me these days, as though that makes him better than me. Not that I ever needed more reasons to hate him, but he does such a nice job of providing them. I knew he was the type to steal scraps from the dog in front of him the first time I laid eyes on him. He's a piece of shit. No set of clothes or manicure can clean him up. He's slime. "Yeah," I say.

"We're up over five mil so far this month," he says, like I didn't know it—which I didn't.

"I know," I lie. I'm not going to let him think Charlie isn't telling me the details. Just wait until I talk to Charlie next time though.

"Then you know we sunk old Nelson," he says.

"Who?" I blurt out before I can stop myself.

"Nelson Albrecht," he says, purposely withholding information that he wants me to beg for.

"Oh, yeah, Nelson Albrecht," I say, pretending to know who he is talking about when we both know I don't.

"Yeah," he says with a wry smile, enjoying the agony he is putting me through. "Arthur's brother," he says in answer to the question on my face that I can't seem to hide. He stops abruptly to focus on my expression while it sinks in.

I don't disappoint him, much to my chagrin. Arthur Albrecht is *my* client ... part of Montauk Boat Works, part of Charlie's and my joint book of business. Any brother of his is *my* prospect by anyone's ethics.

"Don't look so wounded," he says. "We're all one big happy family."

One big happy family, my ass.

"You'll be happy to know Nelson landed us another $3 million."

I feel my face muscles tighten, but I force a smile.

"Oh, and by the way, I ran into Helice last night." He pauses and looks at me out of the corner of his eye. "Quite the lady." His eyebrows go up and down rapidly while I wonder where he ran into her. I thought she went back to New York on Monday. "She really, *really* enjoyed hearing how I got old Nelson to give us all that money." Manny gives me a cheesy grin as he leaves the elevator.

I want so bad to belt him, but instead I say, "Good. That's good." The elevator doors close between us and I stand there smoldering in frustration. Then, the doors re-open with me still standing there.

"Shouldn't you be getting off?" Manny asks facetiously.

"No," I retort and push the 'up' button. I ride the thing all the way to the top before I push the 'down' button again. I still don't have a grip on things by the time I reach my car. I leave two years worth of tread on the cement in the underground garage before I blast past the gate and onto Seventh, then weave around traffic on my way to Schmitty's. To hell with Monty's. To hell with Manny. To hell with Charlie. To hell with ... I speed-dial Helice.

CHAPTER 16: SAVORING THE SPOILS
NEW YORK, NEW YORK

SATURDAY, MAY 24, 2008: 1:20 P.M. (EDT)

Mom, now fully recovered, accepted my offer to fly her to New York for Julie's final performance of the school year. It is the first time she's been on a commercial airline and she frets over the silliest things.

"What should I wear?"

"Clothes would be good," I told her.

"Do you think I should bring one or two crossword puzzle books?"

"None. Just enjoy the trip."

"Will I need a pillow? Maybe I should bring my pillow."

She about drove me crazy before I got her on the plane. Once settled in our seats I tell the steward, "A Heineken and a Bloody Mary."

"In the middle of the day?" Mom asks with a note of disdain.

I grab the in-flight magazine from the back of the seat in front of me, open it up randomly and begin to read. Mom examines every person that boards, the cabin stewards as they tend each passenger in first class, and now she is straining to see into the cockpit to check out the pilots. Every few minutes she pokes me with her elbow to look at someone who catches her attention. A man full of tattoos. A woman with so much hardware in her face it is surprising she can hold her head up. A baby swaddled in a pink blanket. I get rapid multiple pokes when an attractive woman my age walks past.

I roll my eyes. "Mom."

"All I'm doing is looking ... like you should be doing," she says without moving her lips, as though she is concealing what she is saying from someone who might care.

"Aren't mothers supposed to teach their children to avoid strangers?"

She looks at me wide-eyed and apologetically for an instant before she catches herself. Then she bops me gently on the arm with her fist.

When the steward sets a Bloody Mary in front of her she just stares at it. "What is this?"

"Mom. Drink it."

Her brow furrows as she gives me a sideways glance, but she softens up quickly to the idea of a midday cocktail. My faith in miracles renews!

I toss my head on the back of my seat and close my eyes. This is going to be a long weekend. To be so close to Helice and not be able to be as close as I want will be a real test of my fortitude, and hopefully a test of hers.

"Your father was going to take me to Hawaii once," she says out of the blue. "On a plane," she clarifies, as though there is any other way to get there in the time my father would have had accumulated in vacation days.

There's a lot of things my father was going to do and never did, I think to myself.

"Stuart said he'd like to take me."

My head pops up. She's staring at me while she sucks on her Bloody Mary through the little straw. The whites of her eyes cradle her faded blue irises. I lean over and kiss her on the forehead.

"You in a muumuu with a lei around your neck sitting on a beach next to Stuart is a fabulous image."

She smiles and gazes out the window as we prepare for takeoff.

While growing up, I don't remember Mom being anything like other guy's moms who would have fresh baked cookies after school, would drive a van full of kids to the beach in the summer, and host parties in the middle of a school week. My mom was the gatekeeper to happiness my whole life. It was clean your room before you go play, eat your vegetables before you leave the table, do your homework before you watch television. Mom never had a tan, didn't wear fingernail polish, and rarely had anything more to her hair done than a cut. She was the cause of embarrassment on several occasions, like my wrestling banquet when she came in the same dress she wore to my baptism; and when she made all the macaroni salads, ham sandwiches, and even baked the cake herself for my graduation open house when everyone else had catered food at theirs. She never did anything worth bragging about. She was just a mom. My mom. I lift my head from the back of the seat and look at her.

Then there were the things she did, like when I was in third grade and she made me take a roll of toilet paper to school. All I needed was the roll it was on, but she handed me the whole roll while I raced out the door to meet the school bus. Before I realized it, I was standing on the bus in front of all the other kids holding a full roll of toilet paper. And the stink she made to my pee wee football coach for not playing me enough during games. Everybody knew I couldn't carry a ball near as well as the other kids ... except my mom. *She* even swore me to never tell anyone that she had wrapped store-bought cookies in plastic wrap and passed them off as homemade at the church bake sale. But after nearly losing her this past year, I look at her and see an entirely different person.

"What?" she asks.

"Nothing," I reply, then put my head back on the seat and close my eyes.

She's never had much of a life. Married right out of high school, she was never able to go to college to fulfill her dream of becoming a teacher. She never traveled—never even went anywhere outside of taking us kids to Duluth once to see the draw bridge at Canal Park and to the Iron Range to see the taconite mines.

Lately, she's taken up reading the classics, says she's always admired literature but never had the time to read until now. But I know better. She spends her time looking for work. I've told her she doesn't need to go back to work, that I can take care of her for the rest of her life. She won't hear of it. Says I've already done enough. Says she wants to pay me back. Says she can take care of herself, that she doesn't want to burden her children. What she can't comprehend is that the money she thinks she needs to live on for a year, I make in less than a day. While I'm glad she feels good enough to want to go back to work, I wish she'd just find a hobby ... loosen up and enjoy life now that she has a fresh new lease on it. I'd love for her to go to Hawaii with Stuart. It would be good for her. Maybe get her to realize there's more to life than duty and obligation. "We'll check out Macy's for muumuus," I tell her.

She smiles and asks if I'm going to eat my almonds.

As we shuffle off the plane and into the terminal, Mom is overwhelmed with people bumping into her as we make our way to the baggage claim area, so she hangs on to me tightly. As soon as we step from the terminal, however, she sees the yellow taxi cabs lined up along the curb and involuntarily gasps with glee.

"New York!" she exclaims. "New York City!" She whirls in a circle and if she'd been wearing a hat she would have tossed it into the air.

I tell the cabby to take us through the financial district for a little tour. Mom marvels at the tall buildings, is elated when I point out the Broadmoor Building, and gasps at the statues of the bear and bull. But she was awestruck when we pulled up to my Central Park West condo and the doorman opened the cab door for her. Upon stepping from the cab, she held out her hand to shake the doorman's hand instead of accepting his assistance. Once outside the cab she gave a little bow to both the cabby and to the doorman.

She nearly tripped getting into the elevator because she couldn't take her eyes off the polished gold doors. She was so overwhelmed with the luxury that by the time she walked through the threshold to my apartment I thought she was going to faint.

"This is *yours*?" she sighs in disbelief. "You *own* it?"

"I pay the mortgage if that's what you mean." I'd have to call an ambulance for her if I told her what my actual debt load is.

Her fingers linger on the back of the chair designed by British designer Robin Day, which Helice and her interior designer said I couldn't live without. The chair that cost me as much in shipping as its price tag. While I watch Mom's eyes widen in appreciation, I wonder if interior designers get a commission on shipping.

"And the furniture. It's lovely." Her voice softens in intimidation. She is just realizing who and what her son has become. He's no longer her little boy, the guy from Fiddlers Park who lives over the Curl Up and Dye Hair Salon. She's just learned her son is now wealthy and has taste in furnishings and—besides the river loft in Minneapolis—he owns an apartment in New York, a condominium on South Beach in Miami, and a beach house in Malibu. She stares at me as though seeing me for the first time in her life.

"Mom," I say to jolt her from her perplexity, "what's mine is yours. You can come here anytime you want. The condo in Miami is even nicer. Right on the beach. You want that one? It's yours. Or do you want the beach house in Malibu, to take up surfboarding? No problem. Or ..." I twirl around the room with my arms flung out, "how about this one? You can have any one you want. Which one will it be?"

She shakes her head adamantly. "I have a home."

My shoulders slump in defeat. What is so important about the house in Fiddlers Park that she can't even imagine living anywhere else? The expression in her eyes turns to suspicion, as though I might force her to live here against her will one day. "You can have the bedroom," I tell her. "I'll take the couch." I roll her bag into the next room.

Helice isn't able to make it at the last minute, so I call Charlie to see if he wants the extra ticket to Julie's dance repertoire. He does and suggests he take us all to dinner first.

Mom is not used to the crowds, the lines, the waits, the cramped feeling of a major metropolitan city. She has never been outside Minneapolis where downtown restaurants host bigger tables, higher ceilings and wider isles than supper clubs here in New York. Her comprehension of New York is that it is the epitome of a downtown, so therefore she is expecting bigger better restaurants than anything she's been in so far in her life. So, when the cab pulls to a fenced off sidewalk crowded with little tables and patrons in front of a restaurant the size of Vinnie's bakery, she is a bit taken aback.

"Welcome to Benetti's Little Italy," says the maître d' as he rushes toward us from his outside waiters podium. We follow him inside single file and sidle our way to a small table near the middle of the room. Mom takes the chair being held out for her by the maître d', but for the first several minutes all she does is clutch her purse and adjust her chair every time someone walks by.

I just smile and take the liberty of ordering for her and tell the waiter to bring her a plate of *pappardelle* with chicken and porcini. She stares wide-eyed at me, still clutching her purse to her chest. "It's chicken and mushrooms, Mom."

When they place a plate of risotto with squid and garlic butter in front of Charlie she can't take her eyes off the little tentacles curling among the pasta. She asks to taste what was placed in front of me, however, without hesitation. I stab a scallop, wrap it in porcini, dip it into cream sauce and put it into her mouth.

"Oh," she coos, "this is delicious."

"Now eat your own food," I chide her.

"What is it again?" she asks, lifting a strip of chicken from the pile in her bowl with the tip of her fork.

Julie was reluctant even to come to dinner with us, worried she couldn't eat before a performance. However, she seems to have no trouble scarfing down a plate of *bavettine* with smoked salmon and arugula. "I need it for energy," she explains. She avoids the wine and sticks to water—without ice.

"Disciplines of the master Take," Charlie acknowledges for the rest of us on her behalf.

Julie's head snaps toward him. "You know of Take Ueyama?" she asks.

I chomp my food while my brain twists trying to understand what I just heard ... something about taking something for you and me. What are they talking about? I wonder to myself while Charlie nods intelligently.

"Takehiro Ueyama is a master at blending Eastern and Western nuances that are inspired by nature. A perfect match for such a natural beauty," he says directly to Julie.

My eyes dart between the two of them, but neither is looking anywhere but at each other—with some sort of renewed and intense interest. "Time to get going," I say abruptly. "Julie has to be there early."

"I'm not finished with my ... my ... what is this again?" Mom asks.

Charlie jumps up. "Why don't I get Julie to the theater and meet you there? I'll take care of the tab on my way out. You two stay here and enjoy the rest of your dinner."

How am I supposed to enjoy my dinner when you're running off with my sister? I ask myself.

"That would be wonderful," Mom replies as she pats Julie's arm. "Break a leg, dear."

Julie kisses Mom on the top of her head and she and Charlie disappear into the crowd. Mom and I sit alone. She finishes the rest of her meal. I drink the rest of the wine and fume over the thought of Charlie and my sister together ... alone.

By the time we arrive at the Irene Diamond Building, Charlie is in his seat waiting for us. The orchestra is tuning up. The curtains are closed. I put Mom between us and give Charlie my best stay-away-from-my-kid-sister look, which he ignores.

He instantly engages Donna Mae with information about the theater's unique design with its open ceiling, its wood-paneled walls, and wooden seats all created specifically to enhance acoustics and vibration. "Part of the experience," he tells her.

Oh really, I think to myself. Is that what's making your seat vibrate?

Then he starts spouting off like an expert on dance repertoire as though he knows the choreographer personally. I sit back, shake my head, and think to myself—maybe he does.

"Did you know he once was a baseball player?" he says to me, but before my mind wraps around that far enough to ask questions, Charlie is explaining the choreographer to Donna Mae.

"Take is a nickname for Takehiro," he tells her, spelling it out for her as though she will remember. He opens the playbill and points to the name.

She nods eagerly despite the fact she hasn't a clue as to what he is talking about. Then she notices Julie's picture in the program he is holding in front of her. She grabs the playbill from his hand and stares at the photo of her daughter right there on the page of a program right here in New York City.

"He calls his dance group TAKE Dance," Charlie continues, but Donna Mae is no longer listening. The playbill has her full attention until the lights flicker and begin to dim, then she nudges me and points toward the stage as a means of getting me to pay attention to what I'm supposed to be paying attention to ... as though I'm still a kid. But my attention is all on my mom right now. Emotions nearly overwhelm me while I watch her as she anticipates seeing her daughter dance across a New York stage. The fact she is no longer ill, has her hair back, her smile back, her attitude back, and is finally outside Fiddlers Park makes me happy beyond belief. A sense of warmth engulfs me, but this time it is not for her being the only person in the world who loves me in spite of myself. I smile this time because I realize how much I love *her*.

She pokes me again and points once more to the stage. She clutches my sleeve with a rolled-up tissue held in her fist. She is about to burst with anticipation as the lights lower and the crowd hushes into silence.

The orchestra opens with a clarinet solo that calls our souls like a pied piper. A male dancer, naked from the waist up and barefoot, walks poetically to center stage and poses arms above his head, back arched. The room goes black. Then a blue light shines down from the ceiling above the dancer's head and drapes him in a glow. Slowly he lifts one leg, then leans and twists until his leg is outstretched from his body and his arms circle his head. His head drops. He freezes. The lights raise ever-so-slightly.

Two more dancers appear. This time females, their bodies draped in flimsy material that wraps and unwraps as they flow about the male dancer who is now frozen in a pose like a statue in a garden, head bowed. The first female bends down and peers up curiously at the male's downturned face, but he does not stir. The second female comes to see what the first female is looking at, only she kneels before him and stares upward. He stirs ever so slightly. She turns away. They all freeze, suspending the anticipation of the audience as though balancing it upon the tip of a needle before they unfold from their rapture with the grace of a feather floating from a cloud. The trio begins whirling. Slowly at first, then more and more rapidly until they are twirling and intermingling with one another joyfully, freely. They leap through the air. They grab onto one another and effortlessly form contortions beyond our belief while the music soars and pulls our hearts upward. As the trio finds comfort with one another, the music descends slowly until it becomes entirely inaudible. Julie appears stage right.

Both Mom and I are breathless upon witnessing Julie fulfill every hope we've ever held for her. Mom leans forward, captivated. The plight of the dancers now summons all our senses for the next hour and fifty-five minutes until the velvet curtains close.

We jump to a stand and clap our hardest and longest. The entire room erupts in a standing ovation. Finally, the lights come on and people begin to leave their seats, but Mom sits back down and stares at the stage as though Julie might reappear any moment. Charlie and I exchange glances over the top of her head. We both watch her stare at the closed-curtained stage. He and I pinch off smiles, then sit back down, willing to wait with her. "Take all the time you want, Mom." I heave a sigh of relief at the fact she has more time to enjoy life. "Take all the time you want."

CHAPTER 17: CELEBRATE AND CONTEMPLATE
FIDDLERS PARK, MINNESOTA

SATURDAY, JUNE 14, 2008: 9:20 P.M. (CDT)

It's the one-year anniversary of Donna Mae Munson Yates's successful mastectomy. Half the people from the Park are expected to gather at Rick's Nick's for a potluck to celebrate. My plane was delayed from New York so I am late getting there, which is why there is no place to park. I leave my car in Mom's driveway and walk the three blocks, earning a little sweat since it is 86 degrees and the humidity is still near 90 percent. I didn't have time to change clothes so I'm still in a starched white shirt, only I pulled off the tie and left my topcoat in the car.

The room behind Rick's Nick's only holds thirty people, but during the summer Rick puts up a fence around the back parking lot where I've seen as many as two hundred people easily gather. Must be more here tonight, I think as I approach from the alleyway.

"Hey," Mayo shouts as soon as he spots me coming. "About time you got here!"

I start to explain that my plane had been delayed, but before I get a chance, Mom finds me and admonishes me for being tardy to her celebration, to which Julie turns all smiles and chirps "neener-neener." She's been home for days.

I hug Mom, make fun of her all-pink outfit, and pinch Julie. Julie squeals louder than the pinch was worth. Mom slaps me playfully. It's good to be back among family and friends.

Grandma Jazz is sitting in her pink lawn chair, which she hauls everywhere she goes since she bought it in support of breast cancer awareness. I pay my respects and let her brag a little about her grandson 'the stockbroker' to her friend Minnie who is sitting in a matching lawn chair. Someone hands me a beer in a pink plastic tumbler. I smell corn on the cob being roasted on grills brought in from every back yard within carrying distance. Music from the sixties and seventies wafts above our heads. Must be Maggie at the sound station, I think to myself.

"Get me another beer," Grandma Jazz says as she hands me her empty. I exchange hers with my full one before I am ushered into the back room by Barb, who is insisting I get something to eat before I starve to death.

"Don't eat the rhubarb pie," Barb whispers in my ear as we enter the back room. "Mrs. Knutson never knows when to pick it. It's woody," she warns.

The back room is brightly lit by strings of white Christmas lights. Spread on tables are every kind of hot dish imaginable, along with a huge tub of coleslaw and eight gelatin salads, followed by twenty or so different kinds of bars and breads and cakes, all frosted pink. I slap Petie's hands from the potato chip bowl as a greeting. He pulls his hand back in earnest before he realizes it's me.

"You old son-of-a-gun," he says. "Where ya been? Haven't seen you in a gopher's age." He slugs me on the arm. We spar a few minutes before I wrap my arm around his neck and draw him in for a knuckle rub on the top of his head. He smells like gym shorts. He always smells like gym shorts, I think to myself, and smile at the little turd. I never thought I could miss Petie, but it is awfully good to see him. "Schmitty's ain't the same without you, man," he says. "When ya coming back?"

I look around the crowd. I see Pastor Mic from Our Saviors Lutheran sneak a sip of beer, but it's no secret to anyone here. Evie has taken charge of trash cleanup and is wandering through the crowd with a Hefty yard bag. And there's Maggie, just like I suspected, inserting the CDs into Rick's sound system—this time it's a Merle Haggard country western. I shake my head.

"Oh," Mom sings out. "Look who's here!" She rushes away and returns with Alison in tow.

Alison and I immediately embrace. After running into her a couple of times this past year it is like we are old friends again. She kisses me on the cheek. I smell her hair, jasmine or lotus flower—whatever it is it is nice, really nice. I hold her just a little longer than I should. It is good to see her. Mom's shining face is what I see when I look up from hugging Alison, but someone who seems vaguely familiar appears over her shoulder.

"Oh," Alison says pulling herself from my arms and wrapping hers around the bulging bicep of a guy who seems irritatingly familiar.

"You remember Guy," she says, then offers to my blank stare, "Guy Everett. You met him during the McBrindle debacle." She looks up at him and the expression on her face is oddly familiar. He is taller than me, but weighs about twenty pounds less ... leathery face, jaw a little too big for his face, but it matches his brow that is softened by a thick mane of dark brown, sun-streaked hair pulled back into a ponytail at the nape of his neck. Tufts of chest hair pop over the buttons of his khaki shirt and his legs are equally hairy from his shorts to his sandals. Looks like he's ready to jump a crocodile or something wild. I glance at Alison.

I don't remember this dude at all, but the rest floods to mind. Alison's academic advisor was using his influence as the world's expert on climate change to sway the gas and oil markets while he scarfed up on Wall Street. It had been my input that put Alison onto his scheme.

"Whatever happened to Professor McBrindle?" I ask?

"Jail. Fifteen years."

"Enough," Guy interrupts. "It's the reason we're going to Peru—to get away from all of that." He clutches Alison close to him as he looks down on her face. "She saved the world. Now it is time for her to rest."

"Since when does resting mean working on a research team?" Petie's expression exudes both shock and confusion.

Guy explains they are part of a five-person special task force being sent to Peru to track the life of microorganisms being researched for possible harvesting for the purpose of waste decomposition here in the United States. "It's a welcome diversion from normal pursuits for nerds like us," he adds with a chuckle. "This trip is a breath of fresh air for us both." He looks down at Alison and adds, "A whole new start."

Alison pokes Guy in the side playfully, then adds, "Guy and I are engaged."

Mom frowns but quickly recovers and grasps Alison in her arms like she will never let go. "I'm so happy for you," she utters over Alison's shoulder.

Guy blushes through his tan like someone flipped a switch.

"Yeah. I'm happy for you, too," I say to both, but since Mom is still clutching Alison, I toss my arm around Guy's shoulders. Instantly, I realize that wasn't such a good idea. He stoops to compensate for the difference in our height. I pull away and give him a light punch in the upper arm. I sense a discomfort between us. Alison must have told him she and I once dated, that I was her high school sweetheart.

"Thank you," he replies. "And how did you and Ali come to know each other?"

"I'm her ... er ... I'm Donna Mae's—the guest of honor here—I'm her son," I utter lamely, pointing to Mom. Then as I try to regain my dignity I add, "Alison and I went to school together ... grew up together." I want to tell him she was *mine* first, but I don't. His eyes are searching, but they are on Alison, not me or Mom or any other living soul on earth. "So," I begin reluctantly and perhaps a little too sternly. "When's the big day?"

"Not for another year, at least," Alison replies. "We won't begin making plans until we're back from Peru, and I still need to complete my graduate work."

A sense of relief washes over me for reasons I can't identify.

Guy turns the focus back onto Donna Mae and says, "Alison and I are truly happy for your recovery."

Mom's eyes melt as she replies, "Thank you." I can tell she likes him. I hate that.

Just then, they bring Donna Mae a piece of cake with a candle in it and we all sing, "for she's a jolly good person." Parkites have long adopted a tradition of any celebration to simulate a birthday party. Whoever is the guest of honor, for whatever reason, they get a piece of cake with a candle in it and get to make a wish. Mom looks straight at me and smiles. Then she blows out the single flame.

The immediate family is ordered to squeeze together for the photo ritual. Grandma Jazz stands behind Mom, who sits in the middle. Bob grabs Nathan and lifts him to his shoulders. I do the same with a giggling Natalie. Nick tells his dad that he is too grown up for that "baby stuff." Barry shake's Nick's hand and welcomes him to manhood.

"Say 'cheese'." A blast of light and the special event is recorded for posterity. The photo will hang on the corkboard at Rick's Nick's for all the world to see until another layer of images obscures it.

Once the photo shoot ends, I search the sea of heads for Alison, but she is nowhere to be found.

"Let me shake the hand of the world traveler," Tom Garrison says in his tenor voice—the voice that two churches in the Park had vied for when Tom first moved to the Park in 1989. Our Saviors Lutheran Church won out and their Christmas concert has drawn the biggest crowd ever since. Tom is the local tax preparer. "I was hoping to run into you tonight. Was hoping to get your opinion on something."

While my eyes are still searching for Alison, Tom and I stroll away from the crowd toward the rear of Rick's Nick's and find an empty sidewalk table along the front of the store. Teens have been gathering here on hot summer evenings since Mom's day and age, and tonight is no exception. The teens that have gathered here tonight all look at us, anticipating we will break up their fun; but once we engage in our own conversation, they go back to doing whatever they were doing.

"I've been asked by Smythe Investments if I'd care to open a securities shop here in Fiddlers Park," Tom says. "Sort of a side business to tax services."

I sip the beer I had carried with me from the party.

"What's *your* opinion? Should I get into the stock market business?"

"What are you asking me for?"

He looks at me as though I should know. I do know, but what I don't know is how to answer him when he thinks he's just asked an intelligent question. I don't want to be the one to burst his bubble and tell him Smythe Investments is not the "stock market business," albeit it sells mutual funds and variable annuities. The firm markets to small communities and targets people who only have a few hundred thousand in investable assets, which is appropriate for this area. It has no seat on any stock exchange so it cannot offer initial public offerings where the real money is made during lateral trends, nor does it engage in futures, options, commodities, or anything that is currently making the Street rumble and shake these days—but then there aren't any people in the Park with enough money to warrant such strategies. "You want my opinion on what to do with your life?" I ask incredulously.

"I want your opinion on whether or not you think *now* is a good time to sell stocks and stuff."

I wince at his reference to securities as 'stocks and stuff,' like it is chips in the middle of the table at a friendly game. He is too naïve to know he's talking about car keys and deeds, perhaps birth rights. It is an indication of his vulnerability. If he had any money, I'd love to work him as a prospect, but Tom is too small-potatoes for me these days.

My head tilts as another thought occurs to me. Instead of leaving most of the Parkites on the table once Charlie's plans materialize and we terminate our relationship with Maugham Southerby, I'd rather refer them to someone like Tom. But I hesitate to suggest to anyone to get into selling securities, at least not right now.

"I hear a lot of things in the news and it sounds like there is trouble on Wall Street." Tom's eyes are clear and bright and intent upon my response.

"There is always trouble on Wall Street," I snicker.

"I just don't know if it is the right thing to do right now. What do you think? I know I can trust *you*."

I am flattered, sincerely, that someone thinks of me as a purveyor of truth and worthy of their trust. I sit up straighter and search my soul before I answer. I think I've tried to always do what is right and have always told the truth. Sometimes it feels like I am a sleaze-ball, but I don't think I've ever purposely misconstrued the facts or lied to anyone. What should I say to him? "I don't know, Tom. That depends on what you want to get out of the deal, I suppose."

"I just want to help the people here in Fiddlers Park. They need retirement and college savings plans and all they have is the bank, savings accounts, and bank CDs. Just being able to offer them an IRA account to save a buck in taxes would be better than nothing. The Park needs a local financial advisor. What do you think?" Then, as an afterthought he nervously adds, "I wouldn't be cutting into any of your business. Promise."

I look into his eyes and see one of the most honest souls I've known—a guy I've seen carry groceries home for neighbors, hold people's dogs on the sidewalk while they do their banking next door to his office. He lives five blocks over and rides his bike to work each day and leaves it unlocked leaning against the wall outside his office. He's lost several bikes that way, but he never reports them stolen. His way of donating a bike to a kid who needs it more than he does, he once told me.

"I think you're too nice a guy to get tangled up in the securities racket," I say.

"It's tough, is it?" His eyes are searching.

I just sip my beer and lean back in my chair, hoping something will interrupt this conversation. For the first time, I realize how much I've changed. There was a time I was as naïve as Tom. Look at me now, I think to myself. Is it so great where I'm at that I'd tell someone else to climb aboard? If they want to make a lot of money, yes. But Tom is looking to help others. I wonder who I'm looking to help? I polish off the rest of my beer.

"Say," he says energetically, "why don't *you* open a securities office here in the Park? We could share office expenses—there's plenty of room in my office ..."

I hold up my hand to stop him before he goes any further. The last thing I want to do in life is wind up back in the Park. I am so far gone from here I ain't *ever* coming back, I think to myself. I search for a more tactful way to decline his offer. "That all sounds mighty good, Tom, but I already have a job," I remind him.

He slumps a little as though the wind was just knocked out of him then replies with admirable resolve, "Then will you help me get started? Show me the ropes?"

I smile at his willingness to put himself out there for the sake of his little community. "They ought to make you mayor," I jest.

"They're about to," he says as he reaches in his pocket, pulls out a campaign button, and flips it to me. "So, what do you say?"

I catch the tin button, turn it over and read the words printed across the front in bold blue: Trust Tom to all our Tomorrows." I close my eyes, grin, and slowly shake my head from side to side. I open my eyes to his eager expression waiting for my response. "I say you are crazy for wanting to get into this business, but if I can't talk you out of it, then you can count on me to help any way I can." I give him my card. We shake hands. "Good luck on the election," I add. "You'll make a good mayor."

Just then I see over the top of Tom's left shoulder something going on that shouldn't. "Cindy Milner, go home or I'm telling your mother," I shout into the shadows. There's a loud groan. "Now," I reiterate the order.

A blond ponytail bounces defiantly down the block while I stand and watch to make sure no one struts after her. Then I turn to the goons still milling about and call them into the streetlight. Jake Rasmussen, Luke Thompson, and Ronny Miller. I either played football with their big brother or danced with their older sister. "Alright you guys. Come with me." They follow reluctantly to the back of Rick's Nick's where I point them to the dessert table.

"Thanks, Mr. Yates."

When did I turn into *Mr.* Yates?

FRIDAY, JULY 11, 2008: 8:00 P.M. (CDT)

"We all have to die sometime," Mom says, as though she were deciding whether or not to bake white cake or chocolate for the church bazaar. "I'm not afraid of dying; but I refuse to burden my family." She stands up for effect.

I strain my neck to look up at her from where I sit on the sofa. What is she talking about? I wonder to myself while I try and figure out why we all were summoned here in the first place. I look over at Julie, who should know. She's staring back at me with the same blank expression. We both look to Barb. Barb's eyes are on Mom as Mom paces around the living room. I can see Bob in my peripheral vision and he's in his usual position—head down, harboring his emotions. What is going on?

Dr. Lundblad ordered tests after Mom's last appointment. They came back positive for yet another strain of cancer.

"But it can be cured, right?" The apprehension in my voice is magnified as everyone leans forward. Our necks stretch while the whites of our eyes attempt to pluck the answer we prefer from our mother's foreboding expression.

"The insurance has run out, my savings is nearly depleted, and I can't find work—never mind the fact that even if I do, all the insurance companies will exclude me because of my preexisting condition," Mom finally says with a note of despair. But only for a second does she hesitate before she continues to say as she points a finger at every one of us to command our attention. "And I won't have my children burdened with a debt they can never pay off for as long as they live." She straightens herself with resolve and swallows. "I have decided to cease further treatment."

We all blink. What did she just say? It takes a few seconds for the thought to sink in. For the next several seconds the room is void of all sound as we psychologically cling to one another out of some unidentifiable fear that makes the thought of living without each other unbearable to the point none of us are able to breathe. Our thoughts meld in unison—without further treatment Mom will die!

"You can't do that, Mom," Barb says. I take it to be her way of expressing a thought we all share, but Barb further explains that the laws in the State of Minnesota don't allow a patient to withdraw from life-saving treatment.

Mom just stares at Barb. We all stare at Barb. I feel strangely relieved.

"But it costs more than I have," Mom cries, throwing her hands into the air.

"No, no," Barb begins. "Medicaid will provide what you need. You've paid your taxes your whole life. You have four children who are all paying taxes, too. You're a citizen of the United States. We don't park our citizens beside trees to let them die just because they run into a bit of trouble. We take care of our people," Barb says as she leans in to look deep into Mom's eyes. Seeing something more in them than the rest of us do, she continues. "You helped make this country what it is today—you are a good tax-paying citizen who is entitled to medical care. None of us kids will be burdened by any of your treatment or hospital bills," Barb explains.

Mom still isn't convinced.

Barb continues her argument more adamantly. "This is the very reason we pay taxes, so families like ours aren't in jeopardy of situations like this." Barb is now on her knees before Mom, who is unwilling to accept what Barb is saying.

Keep talking, Barb, I think to myself. Keep talking.

"But the house ..." Mom looks over the top of Barb's head at the rest of us, as though she is pleading with any one of us to understand.

The forlorn look in her eyes makes me to want to jump up, grab her, and hold her in my arms ... to protect her from whatever is causing the fear I see rising in her expression. Instead, I sit frozen in denial that all this is even happening.

"They will take the house," she pleads.

Barb shrugs. She feels the same way about the house as the rest of us. It's done its job. Mom is the only one who still wants it. The rest of us want her to move to Florida and play gin rummy on the beach with her friends. The only important thing is that she continues treatment until she is well again. Isn't that the most important thing? Why doesn't Mom understand this?

"But the house," Mom sighs again and slumps into the overstuffed chair. She covers her mouth with her hand. "I never thought it would come to this. That *I* would be the one who would lose daddy's house." She turns to look at us. "He built this house," she says pleadingly. "Your grandfather built this house," she expounds, as though it is the first time for any of us to hear this. "He built this house and made sure it stayed in the family so no one would ever go without a roof over their heads." She looks each of us in the eye to make certain we all understand the significance. Had it not been for that, there might not always have been a roof over ours. Her brows scrunch tightly as she surveys the plaster walls, the hardwood floors, the lead-glass windows, the solid oak front door. Then, as though someone pulled a plug from her toe, her spirit drains from her like water through a sieve. "It's a good house," she sighs in resignation. She slumps back into the chair and begins to weep. "And I've gone and lost it. Lost it forever."

Her muffled sobs overcome my thoughts. I've tried offering to pay for her treatments a dozen times before, but she continually refuses my offers. "Parents provide and protect their children. Not the other way around," she would reply each time I suggested it. Unable to tolerate her distress any longer, I plead with her once again. "Let me pay for your treatments." My sudden sternness causes everyone to look at me, even Bob. I kneel beside mom. "Mom," I say in a softer tone, "let me pay for your treatments."

"Do you have any idea how much we are talking about?"

"It doesn't matter. Money is no object."

Everyone reacts as though the air has been sucked out of the room. No one in our family ever uttered such nonsense. Bob even sits up straight. But before anyone else can move, Mom's eyes narrow as she wonders just how it *is* I make so much money it no longer matters.

"It's all legal," I assure her before her eyelids turn to slits. Our eyes lock while she searches the depths of mine for the truth. Finally, she accepts it.

We all exhale in unison. Bob falls back into his chair. I get up and walk to the front window. I look out across the street to where the Morrissette girls are sunbathing on the front lawn. The wind whisks a spray of cold water from the sprinklers next door. The girls spring to their feet giggling as they run a few feet away then return and again spread themselves thinly upon their beach towels under the beating rays of the sun. I wonder just how much it *will* cost me for mom's treatments. Then I remind myself that what I told her *is* the truth. I don't have to worry about what it costs. Money really *is* no object. I'm no longer part of the 98 percent who has to worry about such things. I work on Wall Street not Durkee Box Manufacturing. I can cover anything my family needs. My mom gets to live ... *and* keep the family homestead.

Now that I am in charge, I insist she return to the Edina Cancer Clinic and to do everything they tell her to do. No more going to

County General for anything. I also tell her in no uncertain terms that I'll be picking up her cost of living as well.

"But you already are paying for Julie's tuition. Won't it be too much for you?" she asks.

I just look at her.

I tell Julie to collect all the bills, that I'll take them with me before I leave today. I'll have my assistant, Becky, take care of everything from my personal accounts. I tell Mom she should keep what's left of her savings to buy her grandchildren presents and to go out to lunch with friends, and when that runs out to let me know. I am now in charge of this household. Whatever they need, I will take care of it. "Is that understood?"

Everyone nods, including Mom.

"Now that that's over, is there anything to eat?" I ask.

TUESDAY, JULY 22, 2008: 8:45 P.M. (CDT)

My old room hasn't changed since I left it, other than the fact Mom's sewing machine now sits on the card table in the middle of the room and quilt patches are strewn around on top of the bed. Since she won't be doing any quilting until she's feeling better, I carefully fold the material, box it up and bring it to the basement.

Mom's platelets were too high last Tuesday for her to receive treatment. When she still wasn't able to receive treatment on Thursday, Julie called me. She was upset and worried. I was able to calm her then, but when her platelets were still too high this week, Julie became unglued and begged me to come home. I agreed and came prepared to spend a few nights, as much out of my own concerns as Julie's.

The folks of Fiddlers Park have been taking care of everything here at the house, including Julie—who does little else but concentrate on her exercise and dance routines. She is scheduled to fly back to New York next month in time to get ready for classes that start September 2. She's reluctant to return to school what with Mom's health and all, but I've assured her everything will be fine. "Besides, I'm here and will stay as long as I'm needed," I told her. Lucy—who had brought over a hot dish and was sticking it into the oven—had overheard our conversation and agreed. I'm not certain which of us was most persuasive but Julie finally relented and that's all that matters. It would only upset Mom more if Julie didn't go back to college. Besides, a lot can happen in two weeks, I tell myself with as much optimism as I'm able to muster.

It feels weird to be back in my old room. I walk around and look at all the stuff still here. An old baseball glove in desperate need of mink oil. A box of BBs. Manchester steel BBs made in Hannibal, Missouri. I look around for the BB gun. I wonder where *that* went? Probably one of Barb's kids. An old Outkast poster is still taped to the wall above the desk. "Get Up, Git Out ..." I move to the beat in my head. It had been my theme song. Then I realize—it came true. "I'm up and I'm out," I tell the poster. "Well, in all actuality, anyway. I'm back just temporarily," I explain to the inanimate object on the wall just so there is no misunderstanding. "Thanks," I add.

Julie pokes her head in the door. "Are you talking to someone?"

"Never mind," I tell her and kick the door closed.

I open the closet door. My letter jacket hangs there wrapped in blue plastic with the dry-cleaning tag still on it. I shove it aside and hang up my garment bag with the two suits I brought, along with ties picked out by Maurice, my personal fashion coordinator at Macy's in New York. I remove my shoes from the zippered pocket and place them on the floor of the closet. The rest I leave in my luggage bag, which I set on top of the desk.

I take off my tie and pull out the cufflinks from my cuffs and set them next to the suitcase on the desk. Out of curiosity, I pull open the top drawer. There's an eraser that is so hard I could use it as a skipping stone. A few rusty paperclips, a dried-up fountain pen, and an unopened pack of gum. I shake it. It rattles. I toss it into the trash.

As I remove my clothes, I hang everything neatly on hangers, all except my sox, which I stuff into the laundry compartment in my suitcase. I've been living out of it so much lately it feels a bit like home. I spin one of the little coasters on the bottom of the luggage case. "Home on wheels," I say, then quickly look at the door. No one heard me. I wonder if I talk this much to myself when I am alone? Then shrug.

The boxes Mom has been harping about are stacked in the corner and marked in big letters: 'For David To Go Thru.' The walls seem to close in on me. The strongest memories I have of this room are of wanting to get out of it. Dreaming of the day I'd leave Fiddlers Park and never come back. Yet here I am.

I flop on the bed and stare at the ceiling for a long while. The glow-in-the-dark planets and stars are still there from when I initially stuck them to the ceiling back in fifth grade. I flip off the light and obsess on the big dipper until I doze off.

I wake with a start. The old quartz clock says 11:15 in red numerals. Where's Mom? I wonder. Did anyone check on her before we all went to bed? I pull on my sweatpants and tiptoe down the stairs. I listen at her bedroom door. I hear her steady breathing. I exhale and head to the kitchen in search of something to eat.

There are three pans of cake on the counter. I grab a plate and cut a chunk out of one and with my fingers devour it in two bites, then scoop a second piece to take back upstairs to eat while I give Helice a call.

"What do you mean you can't come to New York this weekend?" she complains as soon as I tell her I had to move back home for a few nights on account of Mom's health. "You'll miss the party."

"What do you want me to do?"

"Hire her a nurse."

I stuff the piece of cake into my mouth.

"I'll just find someone else who'll go with me," she says in her best vamp voice, the one she uses whenever she wants her way with me. I love it when she does that, only we've always been naked whenever she has said that before—not one thousand four hundred miles apart. An angry dread surges through me.

Her raspy voice fills my head long after she hangs up. She's just kidding, I tell myself. It's her little way of teasing my interests until they are about to pop, which is right about now. I do a few push-ups before I crawl under the covers. A restless sleep soon overcomes me. I find myself wandering in a fog but don't know where I'm going. Something shiny is up ahead. It keeps sparkling in the distance, drawing me toward it, but something is holding me back—a rope around my ankles ... no it is a snake that begins to wrap itself around my torso squeezing the life out of me slowly. I gasp for air, the shiny thing glistens more brightly, I try to run toward it but can't. I struggle to pull the snake off of me but it only gets tighter. Instinctively I bolt upright in bed. I am sweating profusely.

The rest of the night I lay waffling in and out of consciousness. My thoughts are all over the place and move with such rapid speed I don't seem to complete any one thought before I am on to the next. At times I even wonder if I am awake or sleeping and don't know which. If only I knew what to do. About what? I wonder. What had I been thinking of, and what was it that I didn't know what do to about? I close my eyes again. I can't hear you, I mumble. Awake again, I wonder who can't I hear? I raise my head from the pillow and listen intently. Had I actually *heard* something? Hearing nothing I assume that I hadn't, that I'd just imagined I had. I lay my head back down on the pillow and stare once again at the glow-in-the-dark universe I once created from innocence—and wonder what I am creating now.

THURSDAY, JULY 31, 2008: 6:30 P.M. (CDT)

"I'll finish up here," I tell Lucy as she fills the dishwasher with the stack of plates she's brought in from the dining room table.

"It's no bother, Davy," she says. "I've been coming here nearly every day for one reason or another since before you were born. This kitchen is as comfortable as my own." She shakes her head at the thought of just how long it has been since we've been neighbors. "Gives me great pleasure to help your mother after all she's done for me and my family."

What was that? I wonder, not remembering when Mom ever went next door to make supper for Lucy. But I decide not to ask. I'm too wrapped up in my own situation to have room for anyone else's right now. I let Lucy clean up the kitchen while I go help Julie position Mom on the couch.

"You go right ahead," Mom is saying to Julie as I enter the room. "You need to maintain discipline if you are ever to be what you are meant to be."

"And what's that?" I ask teasingly. "You mean to say Julie is supposed to be something other than the little bratty sister she's always been?"

Julie slugs me in the upper arm. I tussle the top of her head until her long blond hair covers her face. She blows hard and her hair lifts from her forehead just enough to expose her eyes, which are sparkling with laughter. She throws her arms around me and gives me a hug. "I'm so glad you're here."

She bounds out of the room.

"Where's she going?" I ask.

"To the gym to practice," Mom replies.

"What should we do tonight?"

Mom looks up at me as though I've never asked her that before. Maybe I haven't. I take a seat at the end of the couch by her feet and begin to give them a massage, the way I used to when she'd come home from her second job as a waitress when I was still a kid. I haven't given her a foot massage in years. She leans her head against the pillow and closes her eyes.

I listen to the clunking of dishes in the kitchen, smell the aroma of Hungarian goulash still hanging in the air, and hear Julie moving about upstairs. It's all so oddly familiar. The living room is exactly the same as it's always been since I can remember. Same gold drapes, same avocado carpet, same matching ceramic lamps, same fake oil painting on the wall of a stormy sea coast. The grandfather clock ticks loudly as its pendulum swings back and forth slowly, rhythmically, as it has for over a century in this same house.

"Are you afraid?" I ask before I even consider what I am saying.

"No," she flatly replies.

I turn to look at her. She doesn't stir a muscle. Her eyes are closed. "How can you remain so positive through all this?"

"All what?" she asks, but it isn't a question. "Life?" She rephrases my question. "How can I remain positive throughout life?"

That wasn't exactly what I was asking. No. I was talking more about the fact she has cancer; that she's been in and out of hospitals and treatment centers, and has lost control of nearly every aspect of her life, including her health. I stand up and begin to pace for no apparent reason.

Her eyes open but her head remains upon the pillow. "I am content to serve the Lord." She stares at the ceiling as though she is looking into heaven and talking to God himself.

"Where did *that* get you?" I mumble and slump into the overstuffed chair, tossing my legs over the arm and hanging my head over the side. I don't fit in this thing as easily as I once did, I think to myself, then try and adjust in it better.

"What did you say?" she asks.

Finally, I just stand back up and examine the chair to make sure it is still the same one it has always been. It is. Then I turn toward Mom who is still prone on the couch, eyes closed. I don't want to repeat what I said. Not to her. Not right now. So I decide this is where the twain must separate on this issue. I walk over to her, bend down and kiss her forehead. "We all can believe whatever we want."

Her eyes pop open. She grabs me by the sleeve and pulls me toward her. "You're not being disrespectful of the Lord, are you?" Our eyes meet and it feels like she's trying to crawl right into my brain through my pupils.

"Mom," I say as I try to pry her fingers from my shirt sleeve. "You are entitled to your beliefs. I'm entitled to mine." I free myself from her grip. Her arm remains outstretched.

"Over my dead body," she says adamantly.

We both look at each other intensely then immediately look away, not wanting to consider the real possibilities of that for a moment longer.

"Rats," I think to myself, knowing exactly what is coming next. Her same old lecture about how each person ever born either contributes toward or takes something from 'the great fabric of all mankind' ... that should so much as one weft or warp be severed how the entire fabric becomes vulnerable ... that we all are equal in creation ... that it is the most obscure threads which hold the pearls in place ... that it is just as honorable to be the thread that holds up the hem as the one that forms the lace about the collar ... and that all it takes is one tiny snag to ruin an entire garment. If I've heard it once, I've heard it a million times.

She props herself up on an elbow and points her finger at me as though I am still five years old and says, "You're going to heaven whether you like it or not, mister. I didn't waste my time being your mother to have you just waltz off and think whatever you want. I was put here to raise you up to follow the Lord, and by God, that's what I'm going to do if it is the last thing I do on earth."

In an attempt to settle her down I explain I was only inquiring how she was able to maintain such resilience throughout her entire ordeal—that I admire her for her spirit, that I respect her beliefs. "That's all I'm saying, Mom."

"Then you listen to this." The look in her eyes dares me to comprehend what she is about to say next. "Praise God in *all* things."

"Even this?" I ask incredulously, meaning her sickness—cancer, although I don't actually say the word.

"Even cancer," she adds, as though she can read my mind.

She's nuts, I think to myself. The treatments have fried her brain. I can't imagine thanking God for giving anyone cancer, let alone my own mother. In fact, it fuels more reason to doubt God altogether.

"I'm the one paying for treatments to make you well and you're praising God for giving you cancer. I don't get it."

"You got *that* right," she says.

I shake my head.

Lucy bustles into the room, declares that the dishes are done and asks if there is anything more she can get Mom.

A little sanity, I want to say, but instead I thank her for all she's done and tell her she can go home.

Julie bounds down the stairs with her gym bag over her shoulder. Together she and Lucy leave by the back door. I listen to their voices dissipate as they part ways.

Silence fills the room. The noise inside my ears increases while the thoughts in my head get the best of me and I blurt out, "How can you choose a God who gives you nothing but strife?"

"God is not a genie in a bottle. He doesn't grant wishes like *some* people seem to think."

"What is he then?"

"I can't answer that. God is incomprehensible to the human mind."

"And yet you choose to follow a God you don't understand."

"Well, what sort fool would want to believe in a God no wiser than himself?"

Buddhists come to mind. They believe the human mind can alter destiny. Perhaps I should give that a try since Christianity isn't providing any spiritual comfort. Helice claims yoga is her source of power. That's a better argument than Mom's right now. "I don't have the same capacity for faith as you," I finally sigh.

"Nonsense. You prove otherwise every time you cross a bridge."

"Like the I35 bridge," I remind her. "The one that collapsed, killing thirteen people last year." That's a better argument for my side, I think to myself.

"Exactly," she retorts. "You put faith in things that fail all the time. Put that same faith in God and I'll see you on the other side." She smiles.

How does one do that, exactly? I wonder to myself. I stare at her until she seems to fall asleep. The house is quiet but for the hum of the window air conditioner in the corner. I notice her Bible on the end table near her head. It is in a pocketed quilted carrier that is worn and stuffed full of notes, along with a pencil, two pens, and a yellow highlighter. I reach over and grab it. It opens to James, Chapter One. I begin to read.

"...Consider it pure joy my brothers whenever you face trials of many kinds because you know that the testing of your faith develops

perseverance. Perseverance must finish its work so that you may be mature and complete, not lacking anything."

It is highlighted, underscored, and there are two hand-made asterisks in the margin. I look back at my mother. Must be her motto. I stare at the words without reading. I wonder what my testimony is? I know it is not my faith in God. I seem to be having an argument with Him of late, but the grudge goes back further than that. I think I stopped believing in God when my prayers were overlooked one too many times. That's when I became determined to do something about my own life. It wasn't as though I stopped believing there was a God altogether. It just became more of a back-up plan— sort of like if all else fails I hope to hell there is a God.

Look at her—battling death without complaint. The fact that there is nothing I can do for her overwhelms me and I feel a depressing darkness invade every inch of my being. I am bereft of all hope. My brain pounds the inside of my skull for answers that will not come. But sitting here in the quiet of the home my grandfather built—watching my mother slumber upon the couch, knowing there is cancer inside her that I have no power to eradicate—I am humbled by my own incapability and mortified at the thought there might *not* be a God. If I only ride my mother's coattail into heaven, I find a degree of comfort knowing that might be all that's between me and hell.

Tuesday, August 12, 2008: 8:00 p.m. (CDT)

"Don't you think twice about it," Mom assures me as she pours brown gravy onto her second helping of roast beef. "I couldn't be better." Her treatment had gone well earlier today and we are all surprised at her renewed resilience, including Mom herself. She is scheduled to have another on Thursday and while I intended to forgo my trip to New York this week, she now insists I go.

I really need to be in New York, if for nothing else than to keep an eye on Manny. Lately the three of us have been acting like a pack of hyenas—circling each other with caution while we yank pieces off the main carcass. With Charlie's plan materializing in less than a month, we are all on edge.

The scheduled jump date is Friday, September 19 at exactly 3:01 p.m., Eastern Daylight Time. Imagining it all keeps me going these days. We'll be standing at the helm of Providence Capital Management, Inc., the materialization of both our dreams. In less than three days we will have transferred the majority of our books of business from Maugham Southerby to Providence where it becomes the basis of our future empire.

Headquarters for the new company is already up and running. Charlie found an affordable suite of offices on Chambers Street in lower Manhattan, right in the financial district. Two people have been hired and trained to set up the office and to prepare the necessary paperwork to transfer the accounts. Our assistants here at Maugham have all agreed to come with us. Some of their family members have already moved to New York, found places to live, registered children for the new school year, and found employment there themselves. While Charlie and Manny work more often from the New York office, the rest of us must remain in Minneapolis until the final hour so as not to raise suspicion. Being designated the primary visual for the three of us has kept me in Minneapolis more than my comfort level can tolerate.

The entire operation is a multi-billion-dollar move, and billions more are riding on it. It is all about to happen I think to myself as I shove down the last mouthful of mashed potatoes on my plate.

"Besides," Julie pipes in, "I'll be here until you get back on Monday. My flight isn't 'til Tuesday."

I wipe my mouth with my napkin, smile, and nod. I feel a weight lifted off my shoulders. The time worrying over Mom's health this past week has seemed like an eternity. Now that she is well enough to take treatments, It will be good to get out of this house, get back to New York, see Helice—who hasn't returned any of my phone calls for the past two nights. I need to find out what's up with that.

Eager to get out of the past and into the future, I book a ticket on the first plane out in the morning.

CHAPTER 18: GETTING THE BUSINESS
NEW YORK, NEW YORK

WEDNESDAY, AUGUST 13, 2008: 7:00 A.M. (EDT)

Manny is at the New York branch by the time I arrive direct from JFK. He is sitting in one of the offices reserved for visiting brokers, the one I usually use. He smiles smugly while I linger over the threshold with my leather carry-on slung over my shoulder, a copy of *The Wall Street Journal* under my arm, and a Starbucks coffee in my hand. "All dressed up and no place to go," he says.

Since the other complimentary offices are taken, I begrudgingly trudge to the bullpen. I plop my stuff on the floor and log onto the server as I try to ignore the beating my ego just took. I open my emails. The first three are from Perry and all say the same thing in the subject line: Auction Today.

There's no auction today, I think to myself. I open up the first email. There is no message in it. There is no message in any of them. Knowing Perry this has to mean something in itself. I call him.

"Go short," he says and hangs up.

My adrenaline skyrockets. I gaze around the office for signs of agitation. Nothing.

Perry's prediction of doom is that the financial systems will virtually implode as a result of the hedgies leveraging subprime debt to the point they are driving down interest rates even further, which has sparked a colossal buying frenzy among common consumers who are scarfing up everything their little hearts desire from mini-mansions to motorhomes—which has exacerbated normal envy into some sort of exhibition of false wealth to a degree never before witnessed by mankind. People are maxing out their credit cards with abandon beyond figures that once would have bought a three-bedroom home in the suburbs. But despite personally witnessing this phenomenon from Bob's construction business boom to Julie's pals' shopping sprees, nothing has happened. Adding further to my doubt is the fact nobody else in this industry seems too worried that anything will. Topping that is the fact there are no headlines from this nation's trusted sentinels of truth—the free press—nor word of anything to worry about from our nation's regulatory bodies, or any of the institutions designed to keep an eye on the kings of *this* hill, such as the SEC, SIPC, and FDIC. On the contrary. The Treasury-Secretary of the United States issued a statement in a national press conference saying, "It will all be over soon."

Outside of a few articles on the inside pages of a couple of trade journals, there hasn't been any noise about any toppling of the world financial systems other than Perry, and my gut. Charlie's back to his original conclusion that if anything serious was happening our analysts would let us know. Meanwhile, he is taking advantage of all the power given him as a licensed representative of this industry and has advised me to do the same.

So to hell with Perry. My gut is taking orders from far more serious things these days, such as my mother's health and Charlie's plan that is about to unfold. I don't need some nervous bond trader distracting me from what I need to do. So what if the markets are unpredictable. That's the way it is. That's all. Nothing more than that, I tell myself.

I force a chuckle. It comes out sounding more like a goose honk. The rookie in the next pen looks my way. I shake my head and wave my hand to imply he should ignore me. I'm not about to tell him I am laughing at myself for ever thinking all it takes is a couple of guys like Perry and me to be able to notice the toppling of the global financial systems. I bust out with another chuckle; this time I don't bother to thwart attention from anyone. My belly starts to shake with laughter.

Like the CEOs of the largest investment firms in the world aren't aware of what's on their own balance sheet. Right. Like there aren't enough laws to protect the good people of the United States. Right. Like there aren't enough chaperones at this Street dance. I scoff at my own stupidity.

Keep your domino theory, Perry. I'm all done with you and anything that might hold me back from doing what I came to Wall Street to do … what I now *have* to do. Medical bills, tuition payments, property taxes—and in less than a week I'll be coasting without income until everything is up and running under our brand. I smile, but the euphoria laces with anxiety as I contemplate the proximity of our blast-off date. Soon, I think to myself. Soon. Then, I delete Perry's emails.

Saturday, August 16, 2008: 9:50 p.m. (EDT)

"Hey, Jule, you caught me right in the middle ..." I was going to lie and say a Broadway show because I didn't want to have to tell my little sister I was boinking Helice, but before I get a chance to say anything she bursts into tears on the other end of the phone.

"Mom's in the hospital," she wails, her voice cracking.

"Why? What's wrong?" Treatment has been going well and she was fine just a few days ago. So now what ... an accident? "Is she okay?" I jump from the bed and stand naked in the darkness. Helice flips on the bedside lamp and groans as she rolls over.

"No," Julie says adamantly. "She's in the *hospital*," she cries again. "I'm so afraid she's going to die."

A pang of fear slices through me. Then I realize I am talking to Julie. Julie's drama is starting to irritate me. "Is Barb there? Let me talk to Barb."

"Barb's in with Mom."

"Where are *you*?"

"I'm in the family lounge; they won't let both of us with her at the same time."

That doesn't sound good. "Who else is with you?"

"No one. Come home, Davy. Come home," she cries.

I'm on the red-eye out of LaGuardia by 10:30 p.m. I take a cab straight to Mom's house where the family has gathered and is spending the night. Everyone is asleep except Barb by the time I arrive. We sit at the kitchen table with just the light over the kitchen sink.

Barb looks tired. She's in Mom's bathrobe. The neon light deepens the crevasses around her eyes and mouth and if I didn't know better, I'd swear she was Mom.

Barb had told me everything she knew over the phone while I waited to board in New York. Julie had found Mom doubled over in the bathroom and called the ambulance. They ran tests and gave her a hypo. She underwent another battery of tests. We'll know more tomorrow.

Barb ordered me to come straight home as soon as I landed, not to go to the hospital. "She is sedated and resting comfortably at County General," Barb had assured me.

I shudder to think of Mom lying in that horror chamber. I hate hospitals. I hate *that* one. We have to get her out of there and back to Edina as soon as possible, I think to myself. If only I'd been here, I never would have let them take her to General. General is for poor people. We're not poor. Mom's not poor. Why can't anyone around here understand that?

She'll be fine once we get her back to the Edina facility, I try to convince myself. We can take her down to Mayo if we have to. We *should* take her to Mayo. Get a second opinion. My mind is racing. My emotions run rampant.

"Dr. Lundblad has been wonderful," Barb says more calmly. "He said he'd come by to meet with you personally tomorrow afternoon." She looks away. "He met with each of the rest of us individually this evening. He stayed late to do so. He's wonderful," she says again, almost as an afterthought.

"Afternoon? Why can't he see me first thing in the morning?"

"It's Sunday. He told us he'd come by the hospital right after church."

"Mom's more important than church."

"Let me make you some tea," Barb says, ignoring my comment.

"Why did he meet with everyone individually?" I ask with curiosity. That doesn't seem right. Why wouldn't he have just talked to everyone at once? What did he say to Barb that he didn't want to say in front of Julie? I stand up and walk over to the stove and whisper needlessly to Barb as though there is someone other than the two of us in the room. "Did he tell you something that he didn't want Julie to hear?" That must be it, I think to myself without waiting for her reply.

She elbows me aside in the same manner she would any other time. Oddly, the gesture lowers the pressure in my head. "Go sit down," she whispers loudly to exact an order.

I sit. Okay. I get that I'm a little irrational. I need to control myself. But my head is spinning with the thought of her lying in that hospital—there's probably bums sleeping in the doorways. I shudder again. I thought I'd made it clear the last time this happened that I didn't want her to go to County General under any circumstances. "How did she wind up back in that hellhole?" I ask in exasperation, unable to control my impulses any longer.

"In an emergency you go to the nearest emergency room," Barb explains adamantly. Then in a whisper, she adds, "Mom was unable to take her last treatments because her platelets were too low again."

"Why didn't anyone call me?" I demand.

The steam inside the teapot wells into a furious hiss. Barb whisks it off the burner before it whistles and wakes the whole household. She pours hot water into two mugs with little white tags dangling from the contents. She sets one mug in front of me while she clutches the other. Blowing lightly across the top, she sips.

    I slurp the boiling brew in staccato bursts to disrupt the daunting silence between us. We stare at each other. Something has changed and neither of us is certain how to deal with it.

CHAPTER 19: UP IN FLAMES
MINNEAPOLIS, MINNESOTA

SUNDAY, AUGUST 17, 2008: 11:44 A.M. (CDT)

I *hate* this place, I think to myself as I stare at the top of the receptionist's head. "Where is Dr. Lundblad?" I ask for the umpteenth time. "Is he on this floor? Is he somewhere in this hospital? Is he even on this planet?"

The nurse behind the desk continues to ignore me. The first couple of times I demanded to know where the doctor was, she gave me some bogus excuse he is making his rounds. Rounds my ass. His rounds can wait. My mother is in there dying. She needs a doctor. Now!

I pull my phone from my pocket and push 411 for directory assistance. I ask for the number to St. Mary's Hospital in Rochester. I'm taking her out of this stinking hole and I'm going to get her decent medical attention, one that has doctors on staff who attend to emergencies. Directory assistance automatically connects me. A voice answers. I explain that my mother has collapsed and that she needs immediate medical attention. The person asks if I've dialed 911 and what the address is, then tells me to remain on the line.

I ask the nurse behind the desk for the address of the hospital, but she just stares back at me. "I don't know what the address is," I tell the person on the other end of the phone impatiently. "It is County General in St. Paul. She's here. My mother is here. Come and get her."

"Sir," the person on the other end of the phone begins, "we cannot remove your mother from County General without an order from County General. I'm sorry, sir, but you will have to speak with the doctor on duty there to find what is in the best interest of the patient. We can't help you."

"Sir," the nurse behind the desk says.

I look at her.

"Dr. Lundblad will see you now."

I look around but don't see anyone.

273

"He's in your mother's room with her now."

I snap my phone shut and race down the hallway. Julie is standing outside the room crying. I clutch her in my arms. "It's going to be alright. It'll be alright," I attempt to assure her. She buries her head under my chin.

I hear footsteps running down the hall. It's Barb. Her eyes are frozen open and searching. "The doctor is in with her now," I explain to Barb.

Julie releases her grip on me and falls into Barb's arms. I pace back and forth in front of the closed door to Mom's room, tempted to just bust it down and go in there. What is taking so long? What is happening in there? Why won't they tell us anything?

Julie's whimpers are muffled by Barb's shoulder.

After what seems like an eternity the doctor emerges and motions for us to come into the room quietly. Just then, the elevator doors open and Bob bursts onto the floor. He scurries down the hallway and follows us into the room.

Mom is motionless, her head placed perfectly in the middle of a fresh pillow, a blanket pulled to her chest and turned down expertly, her arms exposed and parallel to her body, the tips of her toes together causing a tent-like protrusion near the foot of her bed. She is much shorter than the bed, however, and she seems miniaturized even more by the machines and tubes surrounding her.

Dr. Lundblad stands opposite us on the other side of the bed. His expression is serious, but not grave. He waits until we are all in the room. There is no other sound but the wheezing of the machines and a clicking noise.

"Your mother is in a medically induced coma. She is in the final stages of life. She could remain in this state for several days, perhaps weeks. We are forced to release her since there is nothing more we can do here at County General. You will need to make arrangements with a terminal care facility of your choice and let our staff know by noon tomorrow. Are there any questions?"

"Wait, wait, wait, wait, wait, wait just a minute," I stutter. "My mom is what?"

"Your mother is in the final stages of life," Dr. Lundblad says for the second time.

"Final stages. When was she in the first stages?"

"This is the first we've seen her for this issue. Upon examination, we found a tumor affiliated with an aggressive form of cancer that has spread. Surgery is out of the question. She is beyond treatment. All we can do is make her as comfortable as possible."

"That's not enough," I shout. "There must be something someone can do for her."

"There is nothing more we can do for her here at County General," he replies.

"Then where?" I ask.

The doctor shrugs. "You are free to take her anywhere you wish. But you will get the same answer. I will sign the release forms immediately." He pauses then asks, "Are there any further questions?"

Damn right there are questions. What do you mean you are going to release her? How can you release a person when they are dying? Aren't doctors supposed to save lives? Why the hell aren't you saving my mother's? That's what I want to know. But I say nothing. I'm getting her out of this place. Then we'll get some real answers. To hell with everyone here.

"When will she regain consciousness?" Barb asks.

"In a few hours," he tells us.

"Thank you," Barb mumbles.

"For what?" I ask in Barb's direction, but quickly turn back to the doctor. "For telling us there is nothing you can do to save our mother?" I lock eyes with the doctor. What I read from his expression is sincere regret, but I have no one else to blame.

MONDAY, AUGUST 18, 2008: 12:44 P.M. (CDT)

Once word got out in the Park that Mom needed an in-home nurse it was a matter of minutes before I got a call from Lucy. Mary Perkin's daughter, who lives in Falcon Heights, is a nurse and she has a friend who just retired, is still licensed, and who is willing and available for immediate hire.

By noon the living room has been rearranged to accommodate a hospital bed that I bought new, which Rick and Petie picked up from some warehouse on Hennepin Avenue. The main floor study has been turned into quarters for the nurse, whose name is Nellie Matthews. She still wears the traditional white dress and thick-soled white nurse's shoes. No cap though. Grateful for her readily accepting the position, I ask her if there is anything I can do.

"Stay out of my way," she tells me.

An ambulance delivers Mom. Two EMTs amble around the living room furniture with the stretcher, then lift her expertly onto the bed. Mom vaguely grimaces, then grabs the forearms of the technicians to get their attention. "Thank you for bringing me home," she tells them, her eyes crescents upon her cheeks. She swells with delight as though she is looking into the eyes of a long-lost lover as she gazes about the room.

Nurse Nellie immediately begins to take Mom's blood pressure, while Barb bustles around the bed tucking in the blanket and positioning the pillow. Julie all but sucks her thumb while leaning against the wooden archway to the dining room to which she's clung as though it were our mother's apron. I walk over and put my arm around her. My eyes follow the EMTs out the door. Bob should be here any minute with the oxygen machine. Pastor Mic is on his way. Julie whimpers into my shoulder.

After making a scene at the hospital, I was able to coordinate an ambulance to take Mom directly to the Edina Cancer Clinic this morning where she'd been receiving treatments and whose care she is still officially under. The team of doctors there reassured us that while Mom has an aggressive form of cancer, there are available measures they believe might prove effective, although no guarantees.

Hope is good enough. Mom's spirits are good. She's coherent. Things seem back under control now that we're back home. Everything will be fine, I tell myself. Everything will be fine.

Nurse Nellie takes over the entire household within minutes, which is somehow comforting. I cancel all engagements for the next two weeks. With Charlie's plan coming together, there are fewer things on my schedule these days anyway.

Julie also wants to cancel her flight back to New York tomorrow, refusing to return to school.

"I can't leave her, Davy. I just can't leave her right now." It isn't for Mom's sake as much as it is for her own that she is refusing to leave our mother's side. "I'm going to cancel my flight and that's all there is to it." She pulls out her cell phone and begins tapping into the search bar.

"You'll do nothing of the kind," I say as I grab her cell phone from her hands and hold it above her head. "It would only upset Mom more to think she was standing in the way of your education."

"What's going on in here?" Barb asks as she bursts into the kitchen.

"Nothing," Julie and I lie in unison. We remain frozen with arms above our heads, mutually tugging on the cell phone.

Barbs eyes flick back and forth between the two of us. Julie and I straighten up. I hand Julie back her phone. "I'm going to cancel my flight back to New York and stay here with Mom," she tells Barb.

"You'll do no such thing. Mom would rather die than come between you and your dance instruction," Barb admonishes. "Stop thinking about yourself, for once."

I give Julie a look that implies 'Told you so.' Then I grab her and give her a hug while Barb stomps out of the room, irritated at the both of us for the disturbance we caused. "You were only thinking about Mom. I know that," I say to take the sting out of Barb's words.

She looks up at me, her blue eyes now red from crying, her cheeks glistening with tears. "We need to cut Barb a little slack right now," I tell her while I rub my thumbs across her cheeks.

We sit down at the little table opposite each other. Our eyes saying everything to one another that needs to be said, but which neither of us is able to utter.

Wednesday, August 27, 2008: 7:45 a.m. (CDT)

The office no more than opens and half a dozen clients have called to make certain they are making as much money as their neighbor, or uncle, or whoever else told him they were making a killing in the markets lately. I tried to talk some sense into a few, only to be dumped for another broker who made them bigger promises. If there were no johns there would be no prostitutes, I think to myself for reasons I try hard to ignore. Charlie is right. If we don't give it to them, they will get it somewhere else. I tell Becky to hold my calls.

With Mom's medical bills starting to pour in I would be bankrupt inside a week if the money stops. Where would that leave her? Instantly I am flooded with anger over the injustices of world values. The thought of any human being having to die on a doorstep in this day and age because they don't have money makes me sick to my stomach. Especially after watching trillions being traded daily as some sort of game. It's time someone took some of the chips off the table and did something humane before we blow ourselves to kingdom come and have to answer to God Almighty for what we've done—or didn't do when we should have.

I stomp a few self-righteous circles into my rug before the truth of the matter stops me in my tracks. I'm no better. I'm just like the rest of these slugs scarfing up whatever chips I can in this God-awful game. I fall into my chair and smack my fist into my palm to thwart the urge to smack something else.

At what point does greed consume good sense? My mind reviews my choices. Either continue to conduct business as usual, meet my quotas, and make Maugham Southerby happy, or follow my instinct—which tells me to sell everyone out and stick them all in a cash position until we know what is going on. To put everyone into cash without clear and reasonable evidence is like a foot soldier yelling retreat against orders to advance in the middle of a major battle. Am I cracking under typical investment pressures, or is it really the right thing to do? I don't know. I don't know anything for certain. That's just it.

Nobody seems willing to stop the madness. Brokers are taking recent news about impending doom as business-as-usual. I seem to be the only one with an urge to … well … duck. That's all that comes to mind. Duck. When bullets are flying all around and no one knows who is shooting or why, the best advice I have is to duck.

I snicker to myself while the probable repercussions of taking such action materialize in my mind. I can hear the conversation between me and the judge now:

'So, you had an urge to, in your own words, 'duck;' is that it, Mr. Yates?'

'Yes, your honor.'

'And this urge to 'duck' caused you to advise your clients to move to cash, is that correct, Mr. Yates?'

'Yes, your honor.'

'By moving your clients to cash you caused great tax consequences as well as the loss of potential capital gains which are estimated into the millions of dollars. Do you agree with these figures, Mr. Yates?"

'Yes, your honor.'

'And by advising your clients to … ahem, 'duck'… you made a shitload in commissions. Is that right, Mr. Yates?'

'Yes, your honor.'

Yup. That'll get me a pillow in the penitentiary alright. I slump further into my chair and search the walls for an answer. Most people in the Park are my clients, people I've known my whole life. I know they no more understand the risks they are taking with their money than a kid about to plunge off a high bridge on a bungee cord. The thrill of risk is impervious to good judgment.

I'm between the devil and a speeding bullet. I either take it in the head—which will kill my own mother and destroy all my aspirations—or I become another Wall Street god.

I watch the imprints of my sweaty fingers accumulate on the sheet of glass that sprawls across my desk as I tap nervously. If a person does something wrong for the right reason is it still wrong?

I begin to finger one of my business cards, twirling it around, flipping it from one side of the desk to the other until it lays face up. I snicker at what it says: David D. Yates, financial advisor. I belt out a cynical laugh at the fact the only reason we brokers can insinuate that we know anything is because the rest of the world knows nothing. It is ludicrous to even suggest that anyone can possibly know enough about what is happening in every sector, every business, every consumer market, in every political arena, and in every terrorist group everywhere around the world, and be able to predict what will happen in the next minute, let alone the next uptick or downtick. Such is the basis of the so-called investment *advice* we give. Then it dawns on me as to what the card doesn't say. It doesn't say 'David D. Yates, purveyor of Charlie's advice, or Maugham Southerby's stock analysts' advice. The only advice I can give is my own.

For a long time, I sit in silence, thinking beyond words, just emotionally responding to a growing awareness of truths that seem to be swirling inside me, fighting each other like the demons of Armageddon.

I'm still slumped and sulking in my chair when Charlie whirls into my office. He and Manny flew in from New York late last night. The two of them have been in a meeting behind closed doors since early this morning. Supposedly they are wrapping up paperwork on the spoils of their most recent acquisitions.

"Ten-point-two-million," Charlie says with a smile and a celebratory rap of his palms on my desk. "They can't live without us, Dave. Everyone in the Hamptons is clamoring for our services." He tosses the forms I am to take back to New York in the morning. I don't bother to pick them up or even look at them.

"You sound like you believe your own bullshit," I tell him.

He slams his palm down again, only this time it is in anger. "You have to stop this attitude, or you're going to leave me no other choice than to cut you out."

We've had several conversations about the markets lately, by phone and in person. Each time Charlie's logic has won out. Each time I've been the one to back off, tuck my tail between my legs and move to the back of the pack. Each time Charlie's patience has grown thinner. So has mine.

"Is that what you were meeting with Manny about?" I ask. "You're planning to cut me out? Is that it?"

Charlie exhales. The veins near his temples are protruding more than usual. His face is flushed, but he is still composed, under control. It bothers him that I'm not.

It bothers me that he is.

"You need to calm down," he says.

"You need to fire up."

We stare at each other for an uncomfortably long period of time.

"C'mon, let's go for coffee," he says, trying to dial down the intensity of the situation.

I'm not going anywhere until he listens to me. "It is one thing to get drunk on the punch, Charlie," I begin again. "It is another to not realize the punch is what gets you drunk."

There's another long pause. I don't take my eyes off his even when his lids close, tighten in frustration and reopen only to avoid mine. He looks toward the floor and, without looking up, he says in the same calm tone a statistics and probability professor might use and pronounces each word singularly to begin his usual lecture, "Investing is what we do ..."

"Don't give me *that* crap again," I butt in to cease another one of his parables about how we advisors are like captains of every client's ship. "Captains go *down* with their ship," I retort. I stand up and lean over the desk. Charlie backs up. My voice lowers to a whisper and flows between clenched teeth. "Are you willing to go down with yours, Charlie?"

"Our advice is what keeps ships *from* sinking," he says defiantly.

"Your advice worth a million bucks, Charlie? Huh? Is it? Stand there and tell me to my face that you believe the advice you give is worth a million bucks. C'mon. Say it if you mean it."

A darkness comes over his eyes. This is where we draw the line in the sand. To a person like Charlie, who has grown up with everything imaginable, there are no limits on a person's worth. It is a matter of entitlement. Charlie's always been in the right place at the right time. To a guy from Fiddlers Park it is a whole different story.

"What do you think?" Charlie's eyes dart from the floor to my eyes for a moment, then out the window. "That we're just rolling the dice here? Nonsense. We make educated decisions."

"You are too full of yourself, Charlie. What we do here *at best* is make educated guesses, which is just my point. We should be out there educating ourselves as to what is really happening in the markets, because even a dumb shit like me knows *something* is happening. We just don't know what, yet."

"So what do you want me to do about it?"

"Wake up."

"And do what, Dave? Run and hide because the world is rumbling? This is what we get paid to do. It's your job to go out there and find stable ground on a moving horizon. I shouldn't have to tell you that."

"And I shouldn't have to tell you that something is going on that is very different from the normal ups and downs in the markets. Something serious."

"And you know all of this after being in the business, let's see now ... how long?" He shakes his head and looks away. He's frantic to patch the crack I am causing in his plans. Being this close to fruition has made him blind to everything else.

"I am just as qualified as any broker out there, and you know it. My point is none of us are qualified to deal with what is happening out there," I argue. "Nobody seems to know what is happening. That's my point. We haven't heard a word from the analysts in New York that make any sense and sure as hell nobody around here is talking like there is anything unusual happening, but are you going to stand there and tell me you really don't see anything out of the ordinary?"

"That's because ... just maybe," Charlie says with a jeer, "there isn't anything unusual happening."

I step in front of him to get his attention. "And that opinion is based on ... let's see ... how long have *you* been an FA?" The taste of his own medicine doesn't sit well judging by the look on his face.

"A couple of money markets failed. They do that, Dave. A few CEOs get a better offer somewhere else. They take the job. An investment bank gets bought out by some conglomerate. It's business." He turns to look directly at me. "It's business *as usual*." He pauses then adds, "Maybe that's something you just can't get used to." He rushes toward me until the ends of our noses nearly touch. "Maybe I had you pegged all wrong, Dave." He says my name like he just bit into something bitter and is trying to spit it out.

I grab him by the throat before he realizes what is happening—before *I* realize what is happening. He takes a swing with his right arm, but I instinctively block him with my left and lay one on him square in the nose. He falls back, blood everywhere.

"Not on the carpet," I cry. "Not blood on my carpet," I complain, like I care about the carpet. "Aw shit, man," I wail as Charlie pulls himself to a stand. Even holding his nose with blood oozing from his fingers he can command a situation better than I. Our eyes lock and everything that doesn't need to be said is conveyed clearly before he turns his back and walks away. I stare at the bright red spot in the middle of my office.

Becky whirls into the room, sees the pool of blood and screams.

CHAPTER 20: FATE FINDS A WAY
MINNEAPOLIS, MINNESOTA

FRIDAY, AUGUST 29, 2008: 7:00 A.M. (CDT)

Charlie stands in my doorway. He and I have been avoiding each other since the altercation in my office. He had convinced everyone it had been a mere nosebleed, to avoid suspicion. Charlie is still in Minneapolis for one reason and one reason only—I've become an obstacle he can't afford to leave lying in his path to power.

Charlie steps inside and closes the door. We stare at each other several long seconds before he blinks and looks away. He shakes his head then lets it hang. His shoulders slump in exasperation.

The same thing is going through both our minds. I've waited my whole life to get this far, and with Mom's life now hanging in the balance I have more to gain—or lose—than he does. What went wrong with our plan?

I just don't know if I can do it on the backs of everyone I know. The fact I am still here says more than I'd like to admit.

"You're unpredictable," Charlie utters under his breath.

"We stand in the eye of a storm as unpredictable as the hour of the Rapture, yet you want predictability."

He leans over the top of my desk until he hovers like a vulture over its prey. Having ignored what I just said he glowers and tells me, "We both need to cross that finish line for either of us to win."

It isn't a statement. It is a demand. He wants guarantees. I can't give him any. I jerk my head to the right, then to the left as though I'm a dog trying to get loose from the chain about its neck.

"You got nothing to lose and everything to gain," he says, purposely using my personal philosophy to try and convince me to drop the jitters.

What he doesn't realize is that I'm not worried about myself. I'm worried about the people I've known all my life, whose money I have under my management, whose accounts are destined for the cutting room floor according to Charlie's plan and which will be the first to blow up and the last to be patched up if the markets blow—if I leave them here to fall into neglect. They are part of the 98 percent of society who need authentic financial advice the most, yet will never get it. They are vulnerable bait for salespeople, from bankers to insurance agents, not to mention securities brokers. I should know. I'm part of the scam. "I have my integrity to lose and millions to gain, don't you *really* mean, Charlie?" I clarify.

He smiles and says, "Same thing."

God, I hope not, I think to myself, genuinely pleading to a higher power for protection for everyone I know and care about—and for those I don't.

He leaves my office assuming he's made his point, and that I'm still on board.

I'm not so certain.

TUESDAY, SEPTEMBER 2, 2008: 6:55 A.M. (CDT)

Benny wasn't at his newsstand this morning. *The Wall Street Journal* was sold out at Starbucks. I am waiting for my computer to boot up, sipping a Grande French Vanilla Latte with a heavy sprinkle of cinnamon and wishing I'd just ordered black coffee for some reason when the phone rings, startling me out of my mundane routine.

"It isn't just Fannie and Freddie who are in trouble." Perry is breathless on the other end of the phone. "GIG is exposed to $1 trillion concentrated among twelve financial institutions." I can hear his throat tighten as he speaks. "If GIG goes, we all go." He hangs up.

"Satan has landed," I mutter as I look around the office. Only a few brokers are in this early. I head over to Charlie's office. I barge in. He looks up. "What has your guy on the bond desk told you lately?"

"Nothing. Why?"

I tell him what Perry just told me. Charlie listens, but when I am through, he just slowly shakes his head.

"What if they nationalize Fannie and Freddie?" I ask, my old wheels turning once again.

"That won't happen. They wouldn't dare." Charlie's face tightens. He is angry.

So am I. "I have a bad feeling in my gut about this, Charlie." I persist to get him to fully contemplate the facts of this mounting situation.

"Then take a dump."

"Stick your finger up your ass," I retort before I stomp back toward my office.

I grab the lobby copy of *The Wall Street Journal* off the receptionist's counter as I pass. The headlines: "Standard and Poor Downgrades GIG." I read the article. Analysts who had kept a buy rating on GIG since May are all of a sudden concerned that a distressed sale situation could cause a catastrophe.

"Now they tell us," I say aloud to no one but the walls of my office. Stiff demands for performance make it impossible for any broker to perform the research necessary to determine the degree of risk on every bond they sell and still keep their job. We rely on rating services. If they are no longer reliable, this shitshow just got shittier. I know it. The firm knows it. I wonder if investors know it.

I throw down the paper and begin to pace in the four-foot area of my office. I take one step and have to turn. It's like I am going in circles.

I leave my office and head to Crosby's. He's the manager. He ought to know something the rest of us brokers don't. He looks up when I barge into his office and plunk myself in the chair across from him. He sits back and sighs. While he's been more tolerant of my questions since I've been hauling in the assets, he still gets irritated whenever I pose questions for which he never seems to have the answers.

"See the headlines about the miscomputation by the illustrious credit rating experts?" I toss the paper onto the desk.

He doesn't move. He doesn't even look at the paper lying before him. He grins as though he just got his wish.

I don't give a shit what he thinks. I want answers. I want direction from this damn company, the one who purports to be a leader in the investment world. "What are we supposed to do?" I ask him, knowing full well he hasn't a clue. But I have nowhere else to go at the moment except to my own den of iniquity, which I am trying desperately to avoid.

"It's your call," he replies casually. He thinks I am inquiring as to how to keep my own ass out of trouble. It's the broker who will be hung out to dry if a client decides to sue, not Maugham Southerby.

Maugham only provides each broker with the means by which to sell securities. Each broker bears their own burden of what they sell and to whom, and how they manage such assets. Clients sue when they lose principle *and* when they don't make the expected returns. I know what he means.

"Will the firm back me up if I put my clients into cash?'

He just looks at me, smiles, and shrugs.

"This isn't just another stormy day at the beach," I say.

"You got that right," he replies.

"What I want to know is whether you or anyone else in this firm knows the difference between the signs of a tropical disturbance and a Tsunami?"

He just stares at me blankly, then laughs. "I knew you couldn't cut it."

I bolt from his office. My teeth clench. The office ceiling lights start to come on. Workstations begin booting up. I walk in a daze for a few more steps. Then I pass Manny's office. The little worm is in there fidgeting with his monitor. Martin Bascomb enters the office and slowly and purposefully saunters toward his private suites. They are all so cavalier, so certain of themselves. What do they know that I don't?

I head back to my own office, unable to avoid doing so any longer. I stand in the middle of the room staring at the wall, alone with nothing but my thoughts. Thoughts about systemic failure of a magnitude too wide to fully comprehend. Thoughts about responsibility and obligation ... the great fabric of all mankind. Wondering how insignificant one grain of sand really is—or isn't.

My cell phone vibrates indicating a text message. It's from Helice. She's booked a bed and breakfast for us up the coast for Friday night. Pick her up at eight. Check your emails, her message says. She just got out of the shower and thought I'd want to see something. I sit down in front of my monitor and grab the mouse eager for the distraction. I open her email, but before I get the attachment open my phone rings. This time it is Julie.

"I'm just heading to class, and Davy ..."

"Yes?"

"I just want to thank you for all you're doing ... for giving me the opportunity to study dance. You are the best brother in the whole wide world. You've made my dreams come true. Every tear I ever cried as a kid over not being able to dance is all worth it now that I get to go to Julliard."

"Yeah, sure," I sigh. "My pleasure." My voice is weak and barely audible.

"And when I think about where Mom would be if it weren't for you, Davy, why ..." her voice catches, then she continues, "she wouldn't even be alive." There's another pause. "I just can't thank you enough." Her tone is calm and sincere. I hear sounds around her enough to know she is on the Plaza at Lincoln Center. "Love you! Gotta go."

"Bye," I say into the phone, but she's already hung up.

Forgetting to open Helice's attachment, I head to Morning Call, anxious to see whether headquarters has anything further to offer about the failure of the rating services. I take a seat and listen, but the only mention of it is that ratings have been lowered on some bonds. Not even a word of caution in accepting such ratings. I leave before Morning Call ends.

Becky catches me in the hallway.

"Our business cards and letterhead came yesterday," she whispers, looking about nervously. "I had them delivered to my home." Then she shows me the samples she has concealed inside the file folder she is carrying. The letterhead reads Providence Capital Management, Inc. Just underneath the name, the address, suite number, phone number, and website address stretch across the page in small block letters. It's happening for real.

"We have a website?" I ask.

She nods. "It is scheduled to be published at exactly 3:01p.m." She then pauses, and with a gleam in her eye and a smile as wide as I've ever seen on her face she continues, "September 19, Eastern Daylight Time." She accentuates the word 'eastern' to insinuate that at that very moment we will all be at our work stations at the Manhattan headquarters about to launch a strategy which will make all our dreams come true. Her excitement would be contagious if it were not for the fact I am drowning in second thoughts.

She's about to walk away when she remembers to remind me she's scheduled an oil change for my BMW at the dealership in Bloomington.

"Thanks," I tell her.

I stand in the hallway, alone and unable to take another step. What seems like an eternity passes while only my brain moves, flexing more than sanity might allow. People disburse from Morning Call and pass me without comment, as though I am nothing more than a figment of their imagination. Perhaps I am. I know one thing— nothing is the way

I ever imagined it. I once thought wealth brought freedom. Freedom to buy whatever I want, go wherever I want. I never imagined for a minute the responsibilities that come with wealth ... only the irresponsibility of spending it with abandon. I used to think I would be willing to do anything to be a millionaire; now I'm not so certain I am willing to do anything to remain one.

How did I get into this predicament? Where had I taken a wrong turn? I need answers and I need them right this minute. I am frozen in indecision; either that or numb from the only real possibility. Afraid to take action. Yet more afraid not to. I stand motionless in the hallway while thoughts swirl in my head. I'm not at all concerned that my legs won't move, and even less concerned whether or not I am breathing.

Manny swings around the corner and we come nose to nose. The sight of him jolts me from my enigma. It's a contest of wills to see which of us will back away. Manny finally breaks into a smile and saunters off. I avoid sucking in air to avoid ingesting so much as the scent of his after-shave. I force what is left in my lungs to exhale before I walk away.

Back in my office I close the door. I call Becky and tell her to hold my calls. I turn off the lights ... all but the desk lamp. I flip on CNBC and divide the screen monitor to watch both it and the trading floor activity on closed circuit at the same time. Then I take a seat for what is bound to be a long day.

By the close of trading I switch off the monitor and call my assistants to come into my office. I tell them to run a list of every client, the breakdown of every portfolio, and the emergency phone numbers for each client, and to plan to stay late.

In less than an hour they are standing in my office with the list. Both are wide-eyed for fear of what they know I am about to do.

WEDNESDAY, SEPTEMBER 3, 2008: 7:45 A.M. (CDT)

"What did you do?" Charlie asks in a hushed whisper as he closes the door to my office. He doesn't bother to take a seat, just stands at the door with his hand against it as though he is keeping the mob from entering. There is no one outside my door.

I look up at him briefly and continue shuffling paperwork, more as an excuse to not have to talk to him ... hoping he'll go away. I know why he's here. But I don't need to justify my actions to anyone. Charlie doesn't own me. I am still a full-fledged registered rep and independent of anyone else.

"It's all over the office that you put all your clients into cash. Do you realize what sort of lawsuit you are facing if you are wrong?"

"And if I'm right?" I look up. Our eyes meet. Neither of us blinks for an unnervingly long time. Finally, Charlie shakes his head and looks away.

The monitor on my desk is broadcasting more of the same. The volume is low, but audible enough to hear Maria Bartiromo tell her audience that she hasn't seen anything like this before. But it is nothing but background noise to what is going on in my own head. Somewhere between making people money and fattening my own pocketbook it got fuzzy. But it is clear as a bell now. I'm out. All done. No more gold ring for me. Charlie gets to keep all the marbles. And I have to go home—back to Fiddlers Park.

Charlie just hangs his head. He doesn't need to tell me that he's moving forward without me. We both know that. Maybe we both knew it all along. Maybe Manny's been nothing but my stand-in.

"What are you basing your actions on?" he finally asks, unwilling to accept that anything could justify putting every single client on the sidelines. It is like going to a Rolling Stones concert and telling ticket holders to go home because there's no guarantee that they will like what they hear. On top of that, in this case, I am like the Stones' manager who just turned major revenue away and put a dent into the public's confidence in the act itself. What would make a person do such a thing is what he wants to know.

"Unanswered questions. Things that go bump in the night. Boogiemen under the bed. Chains rattling in the attic. What else is there to base my actions on?" I throw my arms up into the air. This isn't the answer he expected. Or maybe it is. Either way, it is all I've got. "They don't tell us anything," I say of our illustrious band of economists and analysts back at headquarters who roll out daily suggestions for us to take into the field. "I'm supposed to make sense of some biased opinions about the markets given to us from highly-paid economics students fresh out of college and dazzled by the big city lights and even bigger paychecks?" I kick myself away from the desk as far as the chair will roll before it bangs up against the credenza. "Or should we be listening to the other half-baked advisors who parade across television screens who are put there to boost program ratings? They are nothing but the Trojan horses." I whirl to a stand and lean toward Charlie.

"Even the general public knows enough to pull back. Not one client protested when I told them to go to cash. Some even sighed in relief."

"The only reason no one in your book protested is because they aren't authentic investors. Why do you think we stacked them all into one book in the first place?" He pauses for an answer, but then adds, "To rid ourselves of them when we leave. They will never understand."

But it is Charlie who doesn't understand. He'll never understand what it is like to work every day of your life, hoping for something better while knowing it will likely never come. He'll never understand the amount of trust it takes to hand over your life's savings to an advisor. Charlie will never understand how a house can be your most important possession. He can't possibly know what it feels like to be part of the 98 percent of a society who never seem to have or do as much as the 2 percent who do. I do.

He rubs the back of his neck, then turns with renewed resolve. "What's done is done. Nothing else needs to change," he says. "You'll just go to New York a little sooner than planned, oversee the staff there, get ready for the rest of us. This could all be for the better. In less than two weeks none of this will matter."

"There's just one thing," I remind him. "The real reason I put everyone into cash."

"Oh. Now we're back to that again." A look of exasperation comes over his entire body. "Wall Street thrives on market swings. Why do you persist on playing as though you are some hero riding in to save the little people?"

I pelt from my chair and lean so close to Charlie our noses nearly touch. "These *little people* you refer to," I begin, emphasizing the term he uses every time he insinuates there are lesser beings in this world, "are hard-working people who pay their mortgages and save for retirement and hope their kids make it through college." I throw a pen down with such velocity it bounces off the stock reports on my desk and careens against the wall.

"These people," he says, clarifying *his* definition of clients holding accounts with less than half a million, "are investors." Our eyes lock in defiance of the other. "Stop coddling them." He sits back down, anticipating he's made his point and that the discussion will now resume with more civility. "They don't belong on Wall Street in the first place. If you are so worried about them, why don't you stop acting like the oracle of doom and get out there and make them money with all your infinite wisdom?"

"I can't do that."

He throws his arms out wide in reaction to the question which neither of us has been able to answer, but which he can't help but ask once more. "Why not?"

His question is valid since I am a trained securities agent whose job it is to maneuver in all sorts of economic climates, but all I can say is, "When you know in advance there aren't enough lifeboats for everyone on board, at what point do you get into one?"

He shakes his head. He raps the tips of his fingers on my desk. We sit in combative silence while he mulls over his next step. I've already taken mine. He's just unwilling to accept it, but no more than I was at having to make it.

MONDAY, SEPTEMBER 8, 2008: 2:50 P.M. (EDT)

We had spent the weekend together and I tried to make it as special as I could. Rented a Porsche and took a drive up the coast to Boston with the top down. Stayed at a bed and breakfast where they served us lobster omelets in bed. I knew I had to tell Helice before she found out from someone else that the money flow had stopped, but only temporarily; that as soon as the crisis is over—whatever crisis that now looms—once it is over I would build back up again. I'd once again make all her dreams come true.

I didn't find the courage to tell her until the final hour. We had gotten back to town around five o'clock on Sunday and went to Sardi's for an early dinner. I reached my hand across the table for hers, which she placed gently into mine. Her green eyes were searching. She sensed a seriousness. I felt her hand withdraw slightly. "I'm not proposing," I quickly assured her. She relaxed and smiled once again. "But there is something I have to talk to you about." Her hand remained relaxed while my palms began to sweat.

Once I finished explaining what I'd done to my book and what might happen, she slowly withdrew her hand and looked down for her handbag. She pulled a small silver compact from it and flipped it open. Then she put on a fresh coat of lipstick and looked around the room as she closed the compact. Without saying goodbye, she rose, tossed her linen napkin on her plate of unfinished lobster cakes, and sauntered away from the table.

As fate would have it, Manny showed up and was among the post-matinee crowd standing at the top of the stairs to the dining room. His eyes met mine. Evidently my dejection showed because he began to look about the room instinctively in search of the reason, but looked right over the top of Helice's head as she climbed the stairs. Before he could process what was going on, she mounted the staircase and came face-to-face with him. His look of surprise quickly turned into a smug smile as she whispered into his ear. She grabbed his arm and spun him around. As she pulled him toward the door, he looked back over his shoulder, gave me a sleazy smile, and flipped me the finger. Helice never looked back.

"Headin' to Monty's for a drink at the bell," Charlie says, yanking me back into the present. "Want to join us?" He stands in the doorway to my office while he considers my response. It is his way of saying he is accepting my decision graciously and still wants to be friends. His fingers drum against the door jam. "Manny won't be joining us," he says to let me know I wouldn't be facing humiliation if I took him up on his drink offer. Manny took no time at all letting people know Helice was now his.

"I don't think so," I reply. I think I'll head down to Schmitty's instead, I think to myself.

Charlie takes a seat. We look at each other for a while.

"Everything still a go?" I ask knowing full well it is.

He nods an affirmation. "What are your plans?"

That's all I've been thinking about lately. How I'm going to pay for the rest of Mom's treatments, come up with Julie's tuition, keep Mom's house off the auction block. Yeah, sure. I got plans. Plans to go down the toilet. "I think I'll just take some time off for a while," I tell him.

He nods, knowing full well I don't have any plans.

There's a long pause between us while each of us wonders how it will work out for the other—him with more hopes than I at the moment. I've tried to kid myself, but the truth of the matter is there is no future for me here at Maugham Southerby after what I pulled—or anywhere else on Wall Street where they shoot Chicken Littles on sight. I'll be blackballed.

"Closing in on the big move?" I ask in an attempt to occupy my mind with anything other than my own financial demise.

Charlie looks over his shoulder before he answers. He leans closer and talks softly. If anyone found out Charlie's plan he'd be escorted to the door before me. The fact he's telling me anything means he still trusts me.

"You can still come with us," he offers.

I shake my head. While I doubt the sanity of my actions as much as Charlie does right now, I have to follow my instincts. Truth be known, I hope to hell I *am* wrong, for God help us all if I am right. "Maybe you're right. Maybe I'm not cut out for this business."

"Give it a little while—once things quiet down—you'll give it another go, I'm sure of it."

"What makes you think it will quiet down?"

He smiles broadly and replies, "Because it always does."

I hope Charlie is right. And I sincerely hope he gets what's he's after, for two reasons. One, because it means humanity will have avoided a financial meltdown so great it will never recover in my lifetime. And two, because I still like the guy and call him friend. Charlie is not doing anything wrong. In fact, he's doing everything the way clients of his caliber expect him to do. It's just that we are not cut from the same cloth, and my people aren't anything like his people.

Maybe, if I didn't have nearly all the assets of everyone in Fiddlers Park in my book, I might be willing to put everything on the line too. I don't know. I don't know what I don't know anymore and I doubt everything I thought I did know.

"How's your mother?"

"Fine, thank you." Guilt immediately drags me into the darkness like a demon that's come to claim my soul. I have been able to bring myself to verbalize the fact she might die as a result of my decision. I'll soon be out of money. It is what poor people do when they can't afford healthcare. They die.

WEDNESDAY, SEPTEMBER 10, 2008: 3:10 P.M. (CDT)

Crosby waited until today to threaten to fire me even though he was the first to know I parked my clients on the sidelines and that it was just a matter of time before my stats would drop to the termination point. The delay is his way of sending a message to indicate just how far I've dropped on his priority list. By the time he calls me into his office, my ego is sufficiently deflated. For the first few minutes, he just smiles and soaks up the joy. He's now one dog up.

I'm not about to give him the benefit of watching me squirm. I sit as relaxed as I can appear, hands folded in my lap, gazing right at him, head cocked, and chin up. Take your best shot, I'm thinking to myself. Bring it on.

He gets out of his chair, walks around to the front of his desk and parks his ass on the edge of it, then looks down at me over folded arms. "We don't sell boxes here," he says, purposely demeaning my former trade.

"That's for *damn* sure," I mumble, more to myself than as a response.

He bends down and leans into my face. He grins at me and smacks his cheek, then returns to his seat, leans back, puts the tips of his fingers together to form a little pyramid and tells me if it were up to him, we wouldn't be having this conversation—that he has seen something in me nobody else saw.

He stands up rapidly, leans over the top of his desk, narrows his eyes, peels his lips back so tightly every tooth in his mouth is exposed, then says between clenched teeth, "You never belonged here in the first place." He sneers smugly. "I can *always* tell a loser. You have until Friday."

We both know I'm not about to raise my stats by Friday—which is the only way I can keep my job—but there is nothing more he can do for now. Standard Operating Procedure requires him to issue me a warning before taking action. He dismisses me with a rapid flick of the back of his hand as he turns his head, like he can no longer stand the sight of me.

Once I leave his office, I just keep walking. Outside the street is busy with people in suits and high heels moving about with purpose. I take a seat on one of the empty benches along Nicollet Mall and watch the street vendors sell bagels while I await my own fate. The mid-morning sun threatens it will be another scorching day of high heat and humidity. Summer just won't let go, and there's no sign autumn is anywhere near. It seems the season will never change. I loosen my tie.

Right now I have no answers to anything. My head feels like a vast wasteland with tumbleweeds blowing aimlessly toward a dusty horizon. I could be the biggest dumb ass around.

My cell phone rings. It's Lucy. My heart rate increases until I hear her tell me Mom is alright. She is calling for another reason. She thought I'd want to know Alison had been in an accident down in Peru.

I jump off the bench, eyes wide, mouth open, stammering, "Wha ... how ..."

Guy was killed. Alison is in a Hospital in Lima. "Beings you two are such good friends I knew you'd want to know right away."

The truck they were in lost its brakes while they were coming down the mountain. They went over the cliff. Alison was found inside the wreckage with Guy wrapped around her like a cocoon. His body was the only thing that prevented her death. She is in critical condition in a hospital in Peru. They are doing everything they can to save her life.

The helplessness I feel is unbearable. My back teeth grind. My jaw muscles ache. My clenching fists cause the veins in my forearms to protrude as though they are snakes beneath the surface of my skin, crawling their way to my heart. The thought of Alison lying in a lowly hospital in Peru makes me want to jump out of my skin and go get her.

"What's being done to get her back to the United States?" I ask.

"Nothing we know of," Lucy replies. "I don't think there is anything her parents can do."

"There must be something we can do."

"Even if there is, it is not our place to do so," Lucy reminds me.

If frustration is a demon it just swallowed me whole.

Embittered by the injustices of life, I stomp back to my office with resolve to do what I can with the time I have.

I see Manny heading in the direction of the men's room and follow him in. We need to have a little private chat since the mid-morning rush for the john is over.

"I want my accounts back," I say to his back.

He turns around, startled. Then snickers as soon as he realizes it's me. "Beg me," he says with a grin smeared on his face.

"Listen you little worm," I tell Manny, "the only thing I'm begging for is a reason to paste you in the nose."

"You need anger management classes," he says with a smirk.

I lunge at him. He turns and runs into one of the stalls and closes the door.

I reach over the top, grab a wad of his hair, and bang his head against the metal door. I don't let go.

He yelps in pain. His fingers try prying mine from his curly locks, but I have them entwined to my advantage. "Are you going to give me back those accounts, or are we going to have a little more fun here?"

"You can't make me. They are mine." He tries to free himself, but the more he twists the more I pull.

I bang his head again, this time harder.

He yelps again. "C'mon man. This hurts. Let me go. Let me go, or I'll ..."

"What? What are you going to do, Manny?"

"I'll sue. I'll sue your ass," he threatens.

"Go right ahead," I tell him. I have nothing to lose, I think to myself.

He tries kicking me, but only bangs his own shins on the bottom of the door.

I laugh out loud. I let him struggle awhile longer before I let him go. I lean my back against the wall outside the stall and silently wait.

When he tries to peek over the door, I smack him hard on the top of his head with one knuckle protruding from my fist, certain to ring his bell some. "Don't try peeking over that door again," I warn him. "I don't want to see you're ugly mug unless it is attached to your ugly body and both are walking out of that stall."

"I'm not coming out 'til you leave."

"I'm all done talking here, Manny. I'm not saying another word. I'm just going to stand here and smack your head every time I see it rise above that door until you come out, you hear me?"

He doesn't answer.

I tip toe out of the room.

It's after lunch before I see Manny again. He's carrying the same newspaper I saw him take into the men's room with him this morning. When he sees me he picks up his pace and heads in Crosby's direction.

"Crosby ain't gonna save you," I yell as I run to catch up to him.

He slams his back up against the wall and holds out his arms to prevent me from getting any closer. I grab his hands, twist his wrists and bend his fingers back until he stoops over, then I clunk him with the edge of my hand on the back of his neck. He goes down like a sack of potatoes. Crosby steps out of his office and looks at us.

"Oh, look here," I say with an audacious tone of sincerity. "Manny fell over his own feet," I tell Crosby. "Here, Manny, let me help you up," I say as I reach out to grab the little weasel. Before Manny has a chance to speak, I have his arm bent behind his back and am leading him in the other direction.

Crosby goes back into his office.

Once inside Manny's office I shut the door with my foot and throw him into his chair. "You're going to give me back those accounts," I growl as our noses touch.

"Okay, okay," he relents. "I'll give them to you."

"Agent-reassignment-forms. On my desk in a half hour," I demand through clenched teeth. I slam the door behind me.

I go back to my office but no more than sit down when it dawns on me—I can't trust Manny any more than a horny guy in a pick-up bar. I bolt toward his office, but he's gone.

"Where did he go?" I ask Adeline at the reception desk.

"He didn't say. He just said he won't be back."

My brain contracts like I've just sucked an ice cube. My cell phone vibrates. It's a text message from Manny. "Gotcha."

I call Grandma Jazz, but my call goes into her voicemail. I dial two more times before I catch her. She is about to leave for her luncheon at the senior center and she insists there is nothing more important than getting there on time.

"Just ask your friend, Manny," she tells me after I tell her we need to make some changes to her investment accounts. "Whatever needs to be done he's already taken care of it," she tells me. "I just go off the phone with him right this second," she explains, then adds, "He's such a nice young man. Talk to Manny. I have to go, dear." She hangs up.

Great. Now I have to explain to my own grandmother that her accounts are little more than a chunk of cheese on a rat trap, but I have to wait until after lunch to do so.

By now Charlie's game plan has changed. Instead of using the accounts in Manny's book as a distraction, he's intending to leave them on the table so they both can concentrate on the bigger fish in Charlie's book. The accounts in Manny's current book are good for only one reason now—to antagonize me—and are doing a fine job.

I dial Rick's number at Rick's Nick's. "Manny was just here," he says. "He said you'd be calling, but I'm supposed to tell you for him that he's got what you need."

When I call Vinnie, he praises me for helping him make his dreams come true. Since he'd never retire from the bakery without doctor's orders, his hope was to have enough money to be able to travel with the missus before they got too old. "We just booked ourselves on our first European cruise," he says. "I am so grateful to you that I created a new dessert bar and named it after you. David's Delight. It's a good seller," he says with a song in his voice. "Everyone in the Park is just as happy with you as their advisor, too. They buy a piece just because it has your name on it."

When I tell him I want to drop by and have him sign some papers, he tells me the same story Rick just told me. "Your friend was just here," he says. "He's on the ball, that one." Then he shares that he's named a muffin after Manny because he is such a good friend of mine. "I call it the Manny Muffin." He pauses expecting me to say something.

"That's nice," I choke out. "I'm sure he appreciates that."

"Oh, ya. He said it was a real hoot. I gave him two to take back to the office with him ... one for him and one for you. He told me to tell you when you called that he can't wait to give it to you."

"Touché," I mumble to myself.

Friday, September 12, 2008: 4:00 p.m. (CDT)

While Naomi Oscarson, the branch compliance officer, searches the contents of my pockets, my wallet, and frisks me, I remove both office keys from my key ring and drop them onto my desk ... *the* desk. My former office will be locked until she has had an opportunity to go through every drawer, search my electronic files and emails, and gather for storage any notes and pages from my Daytimer and drawers to keep for potential legal reasons before I will be allowed to pick up my personal possessions.

"Can I take my souvenir paperweight?" I ask, more as a reason to maintain some sort of control over the situation. I bought it at the New York Stock Exchange during my training period. It has NYSE engraved in silver. It's a good paperweight I tell myself in an attempt to justify my ridiculous actions.

"Nope," she tells me.

"How about a roll of mints?" I persist as I open the drawer to reveal the pile which has mounted over the past year.

She takes pity on me and says I can take one—but just one—roll.

Together with one other member of the clerical pool, in accordance with Standard Operating Procedures, she escorts me to the outer office door. Crosby never shows his face. I thought I saw Manny in the shadows, but everyone else stayed away for fear of contagion. Adeline is the only person to wish me farewell graciously. She offers me a ceramic mug with the Maugham Southerby logo on it.

I take it. That's it. That's all there is. My tenure at Maugham Southerby is over. I'm out. Washed up. Raked over. Shoved over the edge. Alright. Enough, I tell my rumbling thoughts.

I push the down button outside the elevators. The doors open. I step in. The doors close. I just stand there in that suspended chamber, holding an empty mug in my fingers, twirling a roll of breath mints in my pocket, and listening to music softly waft around me that I've never noticed before.

With no place else to go to lick my wounds, I go back to my river loft. The place smells stale since I haven't been here in nearly a month. I open the balcony doors, but quickly close them again as hot humid air sweeps into the room. Instead, I adjust the thermostat to cool the place down and freshen the air.

The refrigerator is empty but for one bottle of beer. Good enough, I think to myself, but that's all I'm capable of comprehending. I sip the beer slowly, savoring it ... hoping I can make it last longer than it will. But before I take the last sip, my cell phone rings. Durkee pops up on my screen.

"David," Walter's big voice fills my ear. "I wonder if you would be so kind as to join me for a drink after work this evening."

Walther's *never* asked me to join him for a drink. "Certainly," I reply. "You name the time and the place and I'll be there."

I meet him two hours later at the Old Spaghetti Factory. A Charlie Chaplin movie plays on the screen above the main dining room. Walter asks the hostess if we can sit in a booth. He asks if he can buy me dinner.

"Of course."

We chat about the box business, how Mom is doing, how Julie's dancing is coming along, how summer just won't give up to fall. We slurp up a plate of spaghetti and gobble a few meatballs, share a bottle of Chianti.

When the waitress finally clears our plates and we've ordered two cups of coffee, his tone changes. He sets his elbows on the table, twines his big stubby fingers together, and leans his broad chin upon them. "How are things going for you, David?" he asks.

"Great," I reply.

His pause indicates he isn't buying it. "I know you've been let go," he says.

"Who told you that?"

"Manny called me." He waits for me to tell him more.

When I don't, he tells me Manny implied I had been fired as a result of some indiscretion. "We all make mistakes, David. I'm here to help you. Will you let me?"

"Manny had no right to say that to you," I tell him.

Walter waves a hand in defense of Manny. "Manny meant no harm. He did the right thing to tell someone who he thought might be able to help you. It is what friends do." He leans forward even more so and looks sincerely into my face. "I don't know what you did, David, and frankly I don't care. All I care about is getting you back on the right path. Will you let me help you, please?"

What can I say? That Manny was never my friend, that I just told him that to get him to accept Manny as the newly assigned plan administrator to the Durkee 401(k) plan because we needed to restructure our books to use the Durkee accounts as pawns? That I've jeopardized him and all his employees, but that if he'd just *trust* me now that I will do my best to get him out of harm's way—but that I can't guarantee I actually can?

"Sure. I'd appreciate that," I reply.

He lectures to me for an hour before he makes me promise to eat right, get at least eight hours of sleep per night, and tells me he expects to see me in church on Sunday. "Priorities, boy," are his last words. "Keep your priorities straight."

"Yes, sir," I reply with all due respect. That is exactly what I intend to do, I think to myself as I watch him walk away. And the first thing on my priority list is busting Manny in the chops.

Saturday, September 13, 2008: 2:50 p.m. (CDT)

Mom was asleep by the time I got to her house last night. I sent Lucy home and went directly to bed. Still staring at the ceiling when the pre-dawn light swallows up the glowing universe above me I realize I have a load of energy that needs to get out of me—now!

I jump from the bed, pull on jeans and a t-shirt, and head down to the kitchen to make coffee. Before the old percolator is done, I have donned a tool belt and am measuring the outside eaves over the back door. That eave has been warped since I can remember. Every good rainstorm and it swells up and drips. That little problem is going away today, I think to myself. Next, I pull up the carpet in the front entranceway. It is ragged and torn and an accident waiting to happen. I cram the carpet pieces into the trash bin and roll the bin to the curb.

Mom gets up around seven, but after I hollered back from the basement that I am fixing things, she goes back to bed. By 9 a.m. I have a list of things I need and head down to Stan's hardware.

Saturday is a big day for the local hardware store. Folks around here do most of their own repairs and maintenance. Stan offers coffee and donuts on Saturdays, and always sets out a few extra chairs. The place is busy by the time I get there and all the chairs are taken. I quickly wave at everyone and head directly to the back of the store to where the paint and varnish are located. When I return to the front everyone seems to be leaning in toward one another. They straighten up as soon as they see me approach.

I place my items on the counter. Stan rises from one of the chairs and comes behind the counter. He begins to ring the items up. I feel everyone staring at me and when I turn around, they all look away. I look up at Stan. Our eyes meet for just a second before he looks away.

"Alright," I say to everyone in the room. "What's up?"

Nobody speaks. Finally, Joe Dungan stands up and walks over to me. "We want you to know we're here for you."

"Here for me? Why?"

He shrugs and waggles his head as though he doesn't want to say what he thinks I already know.

I don't know.

He leans in as though he doesn't want everyone else to hear what he is saying as he tells me what everyone here knows except me. "We heard you got ... you know."

"No. I don't know," I reply. But now I *do* know. I know exactly what they all heard. That weasel Manny has called them, too. But then it occurs to me—since Manny will be gone from Maugham Southerby himself by the end of next week, the ball is as much in my court as his. Two can play this game. I stand up straight, stick out my chest and reply, "Oh, you mean you heard I'm moving back to Fiddlers Park."

His eyes widen. No. That wasn't what he had heard at all.

"That I'm fired," I say, purposely using what I presume were Manny's own words, but with an overly positive tone.

Joe's eyes first jump to life, then just as quickly turn into a look of confusion. But before Joe or any of them can remember Manny's exact words, I fill their ears with new ones. I jump into the middle of their circle and lean into each of their faces as I tell them, "I'm all *fired* up about coming back home, to *my* people. Isn't *that* what Manny told you? And he told you right because I am *fired* up." I shout the word 'fired' and pound the air with my fists.

All eyes are on me while I tell them I am partnering with Tom Garrison ... and Manny is too. Using Manny's own momentum, I tell them we're coming here to provide the good people of Fiddlers Park with the sort of financial services they deserve. "In fact," I say, "there's no sense wasting time. Let's all go down to Tom's office right this minute and get on board. Grab your coffee and donuts." I look up at Stan standing behind the counter and ask, "You don't mind do you, Stan?"

He shakes his head and waves a hand and tells us, "Take some donuts and coffee down to Tom."

Tom is behind his desk when I arrive with a crowd behind me. He is stunned until I walk around the desk, put my hand on his shoulder and introduce us to the crowd.

"Meet your new full-service financial team. Insurance, annuities, securities, IRAs, trusts, and financial planning services, including tax advice and preparation. Everything you need right in your own backyard."

I look down at Tom. "While you sign them up, I'll swing over to my 'other' office," I say, implying I am still operating out of the Maugham Southerby office. "I'll get everyone's account information and be back before you get the initial paperwork completed." I bop back to the house and return in minutes. Did anyone really think I would leave Maugham without my client list and all the information I'd need to transfer their accounts?

The process goes so smoothly that we have them back at Stan's before their coffee gets cold. Once the last person leaves, Tom sits back in his chair and expects an explanation of what just happened. I try and come up with one as much for myself as for him. Moving back to the Park is the last thing on earth I ever intended to do. I only insinuated as much to avoid Manny getting the best of me once again—but I just dug the hole I was in a whole lot deeper. I am not so certain, however, my subconscious hasn't processed something during the heat of that moment that my conscious mind has been too afraid to admit: that going into business with Tom is the only option I have left. Unable to deny it any longer I surrender to the inevitable— I am moving back to Fiddlers Park. "Is your offer still open?"

"David," he says, "you are the answer to my prayers."

Chapter 21: Day of Doom
Minneapolis, Minnesota

Monday, September 15, 2008: 10:00 a.m. (CDT)

Adeline tells me to take a seat; it will just be a minute. It is awkward for both of us to have her treat me like a visitor in my former office. She turns up the volume of the monitor, which is tuned to CNBC, to offer us both a distraction. The humility I am feeling is quickly usurped by shockwaves as I listen to the television newscaster.

"Zellman, an icon of the industry for the past 158 years, filed bankruptcy in the early hours of this morning ..."

Why is there no wailing from the masses? Why hasn't traffic stopped? Why are people going about their normal business? Don't people know what this means? I scream silently in my head.

Adeline brings me a cup of coffee. "Here you go," she says, placing it on the table next to me.

After an hour of suffering humility as the other brokers arrive and walk past me with little more than a nod, Naomi finally arrives carrying a box of my belongings. I take it from her. She tells me my last commission check will be cut tomorrow, first thing in the morning, and confirms my correct address. I tell her I'll pick it up, instead. She has nothing further to say. Neither have I. She turns and goes back into the forbidden area, having completed Standard Operating Procedures for ridding the premises of scum.

Failure screams from the recesses of my mind as I press the down button and stand in front of the elevators, holding my box, waiting for the doors to open. When they do, Helice waltzes out, much to my shock. Her red curls bounce defiantly when she stops once our eyes meet. Manny peers over her shoulder. They both smile as though they just got the last gumball in the jar.

"Oh, David," she says through ruby lips, "so good to see you." She blows me an air kiss. "Just stopped in on our way to New York from Lake Tahoe where we had a simply marvelous weekend," she accentuates the word 'marvelous.' There is a gleam of mischief in her eye that is all too familiar. "Manny has to get his things," she sing-songs. Her eyebrows raise ever so slightly as she turns her head and looks out from under half-closed lids, a devious smile on her lips.

Manny nudges her aside, swings his head in both directions to make sure no one else is within earshot, then says hurriedly, "Sorry we won't be seeing each other *ever* again." He waggles his eyebrows at me. "I'll miss all the fun we've had."

So this is Manny's final hour here in Minneapolis. I consider going back in there and announcing it to Crosby, letting everyone know Manny is jumping ship right before their eyes. But I can't do that to Charlie.

They turn their backs and saunter through the threshold of the Maugham Southerby suites as though they own the place. I watch Helices' ass. It is a really nice ass.

Unable to stand on the same floor as the two of them, I take the stairs and listen to everything in my box juggle with each step I take on my way down. By the time I get to the underground garage, I am feeling sweaty and desperate to hang onto something ... anything.

I call Perry. I know it's a pathetic attempt to cling to something that is no longer mine, but I can't help myself. I just need to feel part of something bigger than myself ... and a box!

"Perry is no longer here," someone on the other end of the line casually explains.

"Where is he?" I ask.

The guy chuckles cynically before he replies. "He said he was going to Tahiti and there was no reason for him to ever come back." There's another chuckle just before the receiver clicks in my ear.

Perry is the canary in the coalmine. If he's gone ... I head to Tom's office and can't get there fast enough.

The clients I abandoned to Maugham I had positioned for any storm. But Tom, who was taught little more than how to sell mutual funds during his brief orientation as a new agent of Smythe Investments couldn't possibly know how to prepare investors for a major downturn in the markets, no matter how good his intentions.

Uncertainty as to how much time we have causes an anxiety worse than anything I've ever felt. After I explain to Tom what needs to be done we work fervently, calling everyone he had brought on board that hadn't been put into cash positions yet. Together we fax forms back and forth between us and the back office of Smythe

Investments where the exchanges and trades are placed. I run courier all around the Park until it is finished several hours later.

Tom and I stare at each other with looks of exhaustion mixed with great satisfaction.

"There's a lot I don't yet know about the world of securities," he says.

And if you're lucky you'll never need to, I think to myself. Having purported dubious credentials thus far in my career, it felt redemptive to apply myself legitimately. It will take a lot more before I am able to wash my hands of *this* mess, however.

Knowing Manny is about to abandon all the accounts we stacked in his book of business gives me a window of opportunity to contact these people before Maugham even knows what I am up to—and long before they are likely to serve me with a cease and desist order.

I dial Grandma Jazz, then Stuart, and all the rest and tell them exactly what to do to if they want to keep their hard-earned money. When I slip my Blackberry back into my pocket I whisper, *"tueri innocentem"* (protect the innocent).

Tuesday, September 16, 2008: 8:10 a.m. (CDT)

Benny hollers at me from behind the counter of his newsstand as soon as he sees me. He rushes toward me with a copy of *The Journal* held up. The headline spans the entire six columns in double the normal point size: "CRISIS ON WALL STREET AS ZELLMAN TOPPLES, MORTON IS SOLD, AND GIG SEEKS TO RAISE CASH."

I nearly choke on my saliva as I bolt for the elevator. *Now* it becomes headlines! As the elevator climbs to the eleventh floor, I read with fervor, hoping to find it isn't true—but it is. More headlines blare: "American Financial Engineering Falters," "Hedge Funds to Pull Accounts from Maugham."

By the time I reach the Maugham office suite, brokers are abandoning their posts and migrating toward the waiting area where the volume on the closed-circuit monitor to the New York Stock Exchange mounted above their heads has been turned up. We huddle together and look upward like innocent birds awaiting regurgitated worms from the beak of our parent. I join them as though I still belong. No one suggests I don't. Something just sucked the entire human race together into a catastrophe too impossible to fathom.

Upon Opening Bell we remain transfixed on the drama unfolding before our eyes on the trading floor of the New York Stock Exchange. InterCon Bank announces plans to cease all loans to McDonald's franchises. McDonald's stock drops like a rock from a tall building. Painful sighs and moans emit from gaping mouths. Morton Salzman's stock plummets to $12 per share from $69, where it had already fallen from $155 per share earlier this year. Another round of gasps.

"Wall Street is on the brink of epochal devastation," reports a wild-eyed reporter from the trading floor.

Some of the people I am gathered with close their eyes in disbelief only to open them again to find they are still in the nightmare. Others cover their mouths to squelch a gasp. Some place a hand over their heart. Everyone feels it. We unite in the horror of those words, even though we cannot fully understand the impact this moment will have on the lives of everyone in the world. Together we feel the doom.

Maugham Southerby's stock dives ... down 28 percent. Eyes dart back and forth among the thirty or so brokers now standing like a herd of sheep. More gasps. More sighs. Phones begin to ring.

"Short-sellers seem to be driving these markets," says the same reporter. "Why the Feds haven't stepped in is the big question on the minds of Morton and GIG. It's too late for Zellman, but our sources have it that George Felton, CEO of Zellman, had pressured the government to no avail for a mandate on short-selling in the hours prior to its filing bankruptcy."

All the ticker symbols rolling across the bottom of the screen are followed by red down arrows.

"Eminent danger of a domino effect related to the dealer, hedge fund, and buy-side activity could virtually wipe out Wall Street as we know it today." The demeanor of the harried reporter changes to a mournful resolve as she comprehends the meaning of her own words. She stands solemnly in front of the camera that zooms in on her face. Chaos continues behind her. As though oblivious to it all, her eyes stare past the lens and into every viewers heart as she says, "The golden era of investment banking is in a death roll."

The iconic firms of Wall Street had created the vehicle of their own demise—the derivative, little more than a wager on top of a wager. Only this time the house didn't win. The short-sellers did. Trillions of dollars vanish from the face of planet earth within minutes.

Martin Bascomb is the first to leave the gawking group. His pace is quick and determined. His two junior partners and three assistants follow him without uttering a word.

Half a dozen people begin to migrate back toward their offices. Everyone seems in a daze. Minds are working hard to make sense of what can't yet be comprehended.

Charlie walks up next to me. Together we stare at the screen. "Where are the Feds?" I ask Charlie, who hasn't yet uttered a word. "Why didn't they bail Zellman out?" They bailed out Fannie and Freddie, I think to myself. Surely *they* know what will happen if a tightening of credit occurs between big lenders throughout the world. Well this is it, guys. It's going down. Where are you? You better stick a finger in this dike soon or we'll *all* drown.

This is genocide at the hands of greed. Everyone—from the kid whose mom opened him a bank account to save his birthday money, to the retiree living off the income from the investments in his retirement account—is about to lose it all if Wall Street isn't saved. Most people will never come to understand what just hit them.

I can just imagine the wide eyes in the Oval office right now. How are they going to explain this to the American taxpayer? Convince the average voter—Democrat, Republican, Independent or Libertarian—that unless one out of every four Americans is willing to give up their job and live on what they've saved thus far for the rest of their life, that Uncle Sam is going to have to break their piggy bank to clean up this mess. Okay. I get it. Who wants to swallow a bitter pill just so others can keep the cookie in their mouth? Besides, denial has been rampant to the point of confusion. The only people who seem to know what is going on are the short-sellers who've capitalized on the pending mayhem, and a few guys in plaid coats and bow ties who have been filling gaps in the roster on financial talk shows that nobody has listened to—and a scarce few of us who did. But surely I can't be the only person here to have paid attention. I look about the room. Maybe I am.

My cell phone rings. "Chew lost all my money! It is gone!"

"You didn't lose a dime, Bobo," I say to calm him. "You're all in cash, remember. Safe as a baby in the arms of its mother."

I catch Charlie's glance in my direction.

"Chew are my hero," Bobo sighs. "I love you. I love you. I love you. Chew are the best financial advisor!"

I hang up but before I pop it back into my pocket the phone rings again. "What the hell is going on? I want to know, buster, right now!" It's Gordon Nash, originally one of Charlie's A3 contacts. He is a developer with projects up and down the west coast from California to Washington State. He has the money but doesn't do what his advisors tell him without long drawn-out explanations. Charlie planned to leave him on the table, which is why I had him in my book. I doubled his money on options trading, but when I told him to go to cash, he refused and told me I didn't know my ass from a hole in the ground. That's when he demanded another advisor, which I gladly gave him—Manny. Now his original $5 million investment that soared to $10 million under my advice is, no doubt, below $4 million at the moment and still tanking—but he's barking up the wrong tree.

"I'm sorry, Mr. Nash, but I am no longer your advisor, remember?"

"You listen to me, you little bastard. I don't care who I'm talking to at that fucking firm, you have my money and I want it back."

"You need to contact your advisor, Mr. Manny Vulpine," I tell him calmly.

The phone disconnects. Gordon is about to get even more angry if he tries to reach Manny right now—because if I know Manny, he isn't taking any calls.

Charlie motions for me to follow him. We go back to his office where we watch the fallout for the next two hours. Charlie tells his assistants to take messages, that he'll call them back as soon as he can.

I call Tom Garrison on my cell phone and tell him he can assure everyone who calls they are safe on the sidelines with nothing to worry about.

Charlie particularly avoids looking at me.

By noon trading is halted on The New York Stock Exchange. The world has gone crazy. Everyone needs a slap in the face, a reality check. It won't open again until tomorrow morning. Go home and sleep it off, is the message.

Within minutes an eerie quiet overcomes the office. People are stunned, energy is expelled, they are frozen in fear in spite of the denial they desperately cling to—that somehow they will wake up tomorrow and things will be back to normal. But the world will never go back to the normal everyone expects. They just don't know that yet.

"I need a drink," Charlie says.

We head to Monty's, which is filling with patrons wandering in off the street like zombies and migrating around the bar where they can be closer to the television monitors to listen to reports still coming in from Wall Street. There are no smiles, no jokes, no friendly jostling and jabbing, no sounds of whirring blenders whipping up Mojitos or Cosmopolitans. Just a stream of people who look tired and drained.

Charlie grabs the last two stools at the end of the bar. We sit in companionable silence, mesmerized by Mitch as he dunks glasses in some sort of sudsless clear solution, gives them an experienced shake and lines them up on a rubber mat under the bar to allow the grime to slip down the sides and eventually reveal the crystal-clear containers which will be once again righted and filled. Mitch sees us and soon sets a scotch on the rocks in front of Charlie and a bottle of Heineken and a fresh glass in front of me.

People begin flowing into chairs at nearby tables. No one wants to get too far from the television. People who have never met take seats at the same table without asking permission, as though we all belong to one another. We are all comrades. We are all in this— whatever *this* is—together. People grip their drinks and cling together in silence as they listen to CNBC on the television monitors, hoping to hear something that will change what has happened... give them back what they had.

Charlie and I sit for a long time without saying a word. What can I say ... I told you so? I would rather be the crackpot than to have been right about this one. Besides, I still feel like a piece of shit for the part I played in it all. Neither anyone on Wall Street nor Main Street is yet capable of fully understanding what is happening. It will be months ... years ... before any of us begin to make sense of it. But one thing is certain: every single person in the world will feel the effects of what is happening on Wall Street this day, at this moment in time.

Neither Charlie nor I can look each other in the eyes. We stare into our empty glasses. Charlie motions to Mitch for another round for the both of us. Mitch obliges like a machine. In one motion he grabs two dry glasses from the row under the bar, jams one into a mound of crush ice and quickly uprights it on a little rubber mesh mat, yanks a bottle of Cheviot's Scotch from the rack while he sets the other down in front of me and with his now-free hand pulls a bottle of Heineken from the cooler—all the while holding the neck of the bottle of scotch like he's milking a cow for the exact amount of time to pour two jiggers before he gives the bottle a quick upward motion to break the stream of liquid before he drops the bottle back into its slot, then reaches for a napkin, slides it under the bottle of Heineken before it hits the mahogany, picks up the glass he just filled, slides another napkin under it before he sets it down in front of Charlie; and as he withdraws he takes our empty glasses, runs them through the clear solution, then turns them upside down under the bar. In one swift motion it is done.

Tuesday, September 16, 2008: 6:30 p.m. (CDT)

Lucy planned an intimate dinner just for immediate family to celebrate Mom being well enough to eat at the table. We've been praising God for small miracles these days. We're going to need a big one now, I think to myself as I sit down next to Bob.

"That's too bad, dear," Mom says in response to me telling her the global financial markets collapsed today, that Wall Street is gone, and that nothing will ever be the same in any of our lives again. "I'm so sorry your day didn't go well." She picks up a bowl of food and passes it to me, "Here, have some of Lucy's garlic mashed potatoes. They are just wonderful. You'll feel better after a good meal."

"Might as well enjoy dinner," I say as I plop a mound of potatoes onto my plate. Could be our last, I silently contemplate.

Barb stabs a piece of roast beef from the serving platter and places it next to my potatoes without prompting. Bob reaches for the bowl of corn and empties it onto his own plate. If Julie were here it would be just like old times.

Nellie has taken the night off. The fact she believes the three of us can keep our own mother alive until she returns in the morning is saying a lot. Nellie hasn't left Mom's side hardly at all since she came over a month ago. It is the first time the family has had a chance to be by ourselves.

"Did you see what we have for dessert?" Mom asks.

I look around.

Barb grins as though she knows what it is.

Bob shovels food off his plate and into his mouth, oblivious to what's been said.

"David's Delight," Mom says with pride. "Vinnie brought some for us when he came to visit this afternoon."

"Vinnie stopped by?"

"He does every week."

That's nice, I think to myself.

Bob finishes his plate and looks about for more.

"In the kitchen," Mom tells him.

He returns with four plates of David's Delight. Double chocolate layers of brownie with a cream cheese frosting and little sprinkles of something or other. I place my hand over my stomach and say a little prayer at the idea of saving room for dessert, then keep eating.

"Vinnie told me you are now working for Tom," Mom says with a note of indignation. "Why I had to hear it from Vinnie and not from my own son is something a mother should know, don't you think?"

"I'm not ..." I begin to protest through too big a mouthful of spuds, but before I can swallow and finish what I am trying to say, Mom says something that makes me choke.

"Now you won't have to go back to that empty apartment anymore. You'll stay right here where you belong." She smiles, then adds, "forever."

"So, when did you decide to work for Tom?" Barb asks.

"I'm not ..." I begin to say again, but this time Bob butts in.

"If you needed a job why didn't you come and see me? We're hiring construction workers. We can't keep up with the demand for new homes."

If anything, he'll be the one looking for a job. They got it all wrong, but I decide to keep that to myself for the time being. What has happened is beyond their ability to comprehend anyway. That's not saying it is comprehensible to anyone else just yet either. So why shake them out of oblivion just yet? I think to myself. That will come soon enough. There's nothing to be done now except wait for the fallout. What that might mean to our family only God knows.

"Thanks," I tell Bob. "I'll let you know if I ever need a job again."

Bob nods and sits up a little straighter. He gives me a sideways glance as he shovels in another mouthful of Lucy's garlic mashed potatoes.

With Mom on the rebound and Julie's tuition paid through December there is a brief and welcome respite from the emotions of the day. Either that or it is the calm before the storm. I'm not worried, though. I don't expect much more can happen that hasn't already shaken my world to bits. Moving back to Fiddlers Park would just be the cork in the skunk's butt. No way could it ever be permanent. Life isn't *that* cruel, is it? I shove my plate aside. I've had enough. My belly begins to gurgle with indigestion.

"What's wrong with you?" Mom asks.

"Nothing is wrong," I assure her. "What could possibly be wrong now that you are getting better?" I scoot my chair closer to hers and steal a piece of David's Delight from her plate.

She slaps my hand away. I pretend to tickle her rib cage, but due to the fact she's grown sensitive to touch lately I avoid actually tickling her. She responds, however, as though I did. It is good to see her giggle again. Some things still take precedence over even a world catastrophe.

"Uncle, uncle," she cries to beg me to stop. Her laughter subsides due into a notable sign of exhaustion.

Barb helps her back into bed in the living room, turns on the television, and hands her the remote. A special edition of the nightly news is being broadcast to cover the debacle on Wall Street. Mom flips the channel to see what movies are on. Barb begins to clear the dishes. Bob belches loudly and begins picking his teeth with a toothpick.

I shake my head in response to their oblivion.

WEDNESDAY, SEPTEMBER 17, 2008: 4:15 P.M. (CDT)

The desk next to Tom's is mine. We share a wastebasket. Depending on immediate need, we share the client chairs too. Tom's wife, Hannah, is the part-time assistant who files and processes some of the paperwork. The rest we do ourselves. It can work, I think to myself. It will have to.

Before I'm even able to try out the chair and inspect what is in the drawers, Evie pops in to tell us they just picked Alison up at the airport.

"Lock it up and we'll meet you at the Bly's," she tells us. Then out the door she goes.

I look toward Tom for what is going on, but he just grabs his keys and begins locking the file cabinets. Then, looking over his shoulder, he realizes by my expression I must not have heard Alison was scheduled to arrive home sometime this week. But because the Bly's don't have cell phones, he explains, the communication between them and their nephew Mark—who had flown down to Peru to get her and bring her here to Fiddlers Park—had been sketchy.

"But she's here," he says. "That's all that matters now." He flips the 'in' sign on the front door to 'out' and we're gone.

I haven't seen the Bly's or been in their house since high school. Sugn, who everyone calls Sunny, had a stroke the year we graduated from high school. Alice was at his side diligently for the next several years. While Sunny eventually regained most of his dexterity abilities, Alice had lost a few of hers. Now, what one can't do the other can. Together they make a whole.

"Mom would be here if she could," I tell Mrs. Bly as we are ushered into the back door.

"You tell her she's in our prayers daily," she orders of me.

I nod in obedience.

The kitchen table is filled with food. Maggie is bent over by the oven, pulling out a roaster. So many smells mingle that I can't distinguish one from the other, but the dog is intently trying. Requests for manpower emit up from the basement, so Tom and I descend to help set up chairs around the pingpong table which has been topped with a sheet of plywood then draped with two tablecloths that don't match. Lucy sets out paper placemats as quickly as we set up chairs. Just before the last chair is opened and set into place, there is an eerie absence of sound. We all stop what we're doing and strain our ears while our eyes search each others' for an answer. Then suddenly we all get it. Alison has arrived. We shush each other while we bumble up the basement stairs. There are so many people at the top that all I see is a crescent of ash-blond hair roll past waist-high. My neck strains to get a better glimpse, but she is gone from sight.

The line was more fortuitous than Alison's energy, so by the time I reached the living room they are taking her to the bedroom for rest. Whoever didn't get a chance to greet her yet would now need to wait.

"There's food in the kitchen," I am told. "Maybe in an hour or so."

I take a seat on the back steps where the dog had been dispatched. The mutt seats himself next to me as though I'm his owner. We've never met. Border collie and shepherd mix of some sort, I guess. His coat is another story of confusion, brown and black with gray patches, but the gray isn't from age.

"Shouldn't you be barking or something?" I ask the dog. My fingers dig into the long fur around his neck to find his tags. His name is Buddy. "Figures," I tell him.

His tongue drips on my pant leg while I try to ignore him, the house full of people behind me, and the humidity brought on by the stubborn summer. While engulfed in this invisible torture, my thoughts go back in time and trace every pathway Alison and I ever walked, everything we had once said to one another, every dress she ever wore, every flip of her ponytail—they didn't go unnoticed by me after all. The magnitude of information I possess about Alison that surges forth from the recesses of my memory is overwhelming. Her laughter, the way she sneezes, the funny way she runs, the anger that seems to pop out of her like a jack-in-the-box at any injustice, the way her hair never held a curl past the first dance. Just the thought of her being snatched away in a second causes my skin to shiver despite the unbearable heat of a relentless sun.

My head falls into my hands and suspends between my knees. I stare at the concrete between my feet and vow to protect her from all harm from this day forward. "Nothing will ever hurt you again," I whisper.

Buddy licks the tears that roll down my cheeks while I watch the ones he misses spatter upon the pavement.

Friday, September 19, 2008: 7:35 a.m. (CDT)

Matthew, Charlie's brother—who had initially orchestrated the events which led up to what will become known as the greatest financial disaster in the history of the world—was just appointed CEO of Citizens World Bank. Having proved his ability to demolish all obstacles in his way, the board of directors led its stockholders to a unanimous decision within hours of the crash. Now free to mop up, Citizens is swallowing up the fallen angels of Wall Street like a Kirby vacuum. It just became the largest wealth management institution in the world with the biggest branch network, and the largest issuer of credit cards, auto loans and home equity loans, according to this morning's edition of *The Wall Street Journal*.

"Try and trump *that* one, Charlie," I think to myself as I realize that my old pal is not only up against father-envy but some pretty stiff sibling rivalry.

I fold up the rest of the paper and leave it on the table to join Vinnie, Evie, Stan, Rick, and Maggie who are standing in front of Vinnie's old Zenith television trying to get it to work. Stymied by the new technology, the four of them grumble about how nothing is the same anymore, and leave me to examine the cords and cables. After tightening the cable to the converter box, the picture pops to life.

"There it goes," they all say in unison.

Vinnie's, being the closest thing to a coffee shop here in the Park, is an intimate affair early in the morning when just the local proprietors gather before opening their own doors. Now that I've joined those ranks, I start my day there along with the rest of them.

The only coffee on the menu at Vinnie's is the same coffee Vinnie has made for his customers since I was old enough to drink it. There is no fancy name. It's coffee. The flavor doesn't change. It's dark and rich and so thick you can use it as syrup. There is no decaf available. If you don't want the jolt he'll give you a glass of water, fresh out of the tap.

Our little group huddles together as we listen to early morning reports about the ebbing financial crisis. "Zellman gone, Morton Salzman gone, GIG and WorldBank on the brink. Icons of the industry collapsed on September 16, largely as a result of overexposure to securities of packaged subprime loans and credit card debt. A number of bank failures in Europe and sharp reductions in the value of equities and commodities have since occurred worldwide. This is the biggest financial crisis since 1929 ..."

"Be darned if I know what der takin' 'bout," says Stan. "Maybe you can 'splane it to us," he says to me.

My eyes scan the five of them while they each take a bite of donut or a sip of coffee, anticipating I can bring them up to speed on events they've paid no attention to up until four days ago. "To Stan, here," I begin addressing the small crowd, "it means he better stock up on exterior paint and ladders, but cut back on ordering carpet runners and birdbaths."

I turn to Evie and put a hand on her shoulder, "You, my dear, should line your bookshelves with more 'How To' books than books on global travel for the next several years."

I point a finger at Maggie. "Better cancel that appointment you have with the banker and put a hold on any big ideas about adding another chair to your salon for the time being."

I pause when I come to Rick. He's a bright guy. People will always need cough drops and bandages, he's thinking. What he isn't thinking about is what will happen once people lose their jobs and their insurance benefits run out. "As a pharmacist," I tell him, "you may be all that stands between life and death for some. Bone up on signs and symptoms of critical illness and disease." His eyes grow wide in disbelief.

"And Vinnie," I add, leaning over the counter, "plan to make more donuts and fewer expensive éclairs."

They all stop chewing and just look at me. The television blares in the background. Why should they change the way they do business because of what is happening on Wall Street? they are wondering. Because the human race will survive, and only those who anticipate *how* the human race will survive will thrive. I want so badly to explain it to them. Every single business plan should be re-evaluated and adjusted because the world as we once knew it no longer is. In less than a few months the world will need new products and services to meet the needs of the new society we all became just four days ago, whether anyone realizes it yet or not. As much as I want to tell them all of this, they are not ready to believe it nor are they capable of understanding it. So I tell them the only thing that will calm the concerns I just exacerbated.

"Tom and I are right next door. You come to us when you have questions and we'll help you make good financial decisions." I find some comfort in knowing these people, at least, won't face an uncertain future alone.

They all smile and nod. *That* they understand.

"It is goot you came back home," Vinnie says with a nod so intense it bends his whole body. One arm shoots above his head as he flips his wrist in a gesture the locals long ago termed 'the Sicilian salute.' The rest nod and look toward the floor while muttering, "Yeah, yeah," and "You bet" as they disburse to their respective businesses.

I remain standing in front of the Zenith. It blares: "Still no word from the White House. If ever there was a need for a bail out ... this is as serious as it gets."

"You got that right," I say aloud to the inanimate monitor. Amid references to the Crash of '29, the ground continues to rumble throughout the nation. Yet assembly line workers from Silicon Valley to Detroit will put on their hard hats and go to work today as though nothing has changed. They don't realize that the leaders of every major institution of commerce in every single sector have the reins in their hands and are poised to hold the horses. Talk of a U.S. government bailout is the only thing holding up that show. But taxpayers—who are fed up having already doled out $85 billion due to such shenanigans—will more likely cut off their nose to spite their face by protesting any further bailouts.

Exacerbating matters are the carpetbaggers—Manny being one of them I've heard—who are stealing clients away from faltering firms, causing them to falter further. This is a time when nobody should be holding heads underwater with their foot, but instead should be helping each other out of the drink before we all drown. My own thoughts of what should have been are as difficult as a bad booger to shake—but the idea Manny is still flying high on other people's misery sticks in my craw.

"Me, too," Vinnie says.

"Pardon?" I reply.

"I can tell by your expression dat you feel the same," he says.

"About what?"

"About what I just said."

"What did you just say?"

Vinnie stops shoving a tray of chocolate éclairs into the display case and looks over the top at me. "Maybe you didn't hear me."

I shake my head. I must not have.

"That Alison is going back to Washington today."

I'm halfway down the block before the door closes on the bakery. Tom waves frantically for me to come into the office from the other side of the plate-glass window as I fly past; instead, I ignore him and hop on his bike and peddle toward the Bly's house. I don't know what I'm going to say yet, but something that will keep Alison here a while longer—like forever.

Just as I am running up the steps to the Bly's back door my cell phone rings. It is Lucy.

"David ... your mother ... collapsed ... ambulance ... " Her words intermingle with the screams in my head to the point I am unable to hear everything she is saying, but I don't need to.

I peddle toward the wail of the siren. By the time I reach the end of our driveway it is filled with neighbors who are gathered around the ambulance. The paramedics have Mom on a stretcher and are about to bring her through the front door when I reach her side.

"Mom," I whisper.

"Please sir," one of the paramedics says to me. "You may ride along with your mother if you wish, but we need to get her to County General."

Can't this thing go any faster? I think to myself as I crouch in the back of the ambulance near the door while they work furiously over

Mom. As soon as we come to a stop, she's whisked away immediately while they order me to go to the admissions desk.

I am met by a mousy brown head of hair with a crooked part. "Insurance?"

"No," I reply.

She looks up partially, eyes peering out from under lids that aren't about to open fully for such tedious matters. "What sort of payment guarantee can you provide?"

"I'll guarantee payment," I tell her.

"And how might you do that, sir?"

I pull out my VISA credit card and toss it at her.

She picks it up and holds it between her thumb and index finger as though it was a turd.

I toss Discover, American Express, and CitiBank cards at her, all the rest. "Take all the numbers down. There should be a couple million right there. Is that enough of a guarantee?"

Her eyes widen, but more from fear of having to confront another deranged person than being impressed by credit cards. She's seen it all. This is nothing new to her.

"Call it in if you don't believe me." I pull all the bills out of my wallet and dump them onto the counter.

By now two more staff members have protectively gathered around her and I see someone else in my peripheral vision approaching quickly. I turn and a nurse in a dark blue uniform and Reeboks is rushing toward me.

"Are you David Yates?"

"Yes," I answer.

"Follow me."

I snatch the card from the fingers of the woman behind the desk and grab my money and the rest of the credit cards, cram them into my pockets and follow quickly after the nurse who is now halfway down the hall.

"Wait just a minute," the person behind the desk protests to our diminishing backsides.

We keep walking as quickly as possible without breaking into a run. She takes me into an oversized elevator and up several floors, then down a long hallway. She pulls back a curtain. There's Mom. I rush to her side and grab her arm. Her eyes flutter open for just a second then close again. Her lips are slack.

Dr. Lundblad is standing on the other side of her. "She is in a drug-induced coma for the moment," he explains. "Talk to her," he orders of me. "She was asking for you, so let her know you are here."

I glance at Mom then back at him.

He nods. "She can hear you." He nods again.

"Mom, I'm here," I tell her. "Everything is going to be okay. I'm going to stay right by your side. Just sleep, Mom. Just rest. I'm right here."

The doctor's head moves up and down slowly in approval while he continues to read the machines and monitor the drips going into the tubes running into the back of her hand.

She has days ... two weeks at best. We should feel lucky she's made it this long, they tell us. But I'm not feeling the luck. Death is too ugly and harsh and *mean* to feel anything other than what an untrained rock climber with finger cramps might feel three-quarters of the way up a steep cliff.

Tuesday, September 23, 2008: 7:35 a.m. (CDT)

I pick at a crack in the plaster of the wall next to Mom's bed in the living room while I listen to her breathe. Her breaths come in spurts, laboriously and shallow. The rest of her is as still as a mountain and has been for the past two days since we brought her home from the hospital to die. She is rarely conscious—Nellie making certain she isn't by injecting all the medication necessary to block her pain.

The only sound, besides my picking and her breathing, is the subtle tick of the pendulum of the grandfather clock while it stands in the afternoon shadows like the ghost of an ancestor. It has been the background to everything that has happened in this house since the day the clock was delivered and set in that exact spot.

My memory lingers over the stories drilled into my head. Joseph John Munson, the youngest son of a poor blacksmith, had been put on a boat to America with nothing but a bible and a second pair of socks. He found work on a Manhattan construction crew and quickly learned English and how to build most anything—an exemplary example of fortitude.

He married Muriel Parker, a waitress he met at a lunch counter. They raised four children in a one-bedroom apartment, the eldest being Iver Daniel Munson.

When World War I broke, Joseph was too old and Iver was too young to serve. While others went to war, Iver began going to work with his father, learning construction and high-iron work at the age of nine—a perfect example of humility and obedience.

The construction company expanded into single-family homes for the returning World War I vets. Iver was sent to Minnesota as a crewmember to build homes along Summit Avenue—the governor's mansion being among those he helped construct.

A tree nursery located between the two campuses of the University of Minnesota also had been cleared for home construction to accommodate the influx of professors. It was there that Iver decided to build his own home. Until the area became a community of homes it was unofficially referred to as Rose Hill, the name of the former nursery. Later the community would adopt the name Fiddlers Park. The land serves as an example of God's benevolence to those who evolved from a man with but a Bible and two pairs of socks.

When the stock market crashed in 1929 both Joseph and Iver maintained employment, fulfilling work orders still under contract. As the nation's economy deteriorated over the next several years, both Munsons were promoted to foreman positions over the new hires who could afford little more than their worn-out suits. An example of God's grace.

The clock had been sent as a wedding gift from Joseph to Iver. The family folk lore goes that it represented something about tenacity and patience the true meaning of which only the two of them shared. It was placed on the north wall of the living room next to the fireplace where it has presided as master of the minutes and sentinel to all those who have resided here for the past seventy-eight years.

It was Iver who had watched the hands of this very clock while awaiting the birth of his first child, recording the moment at exactly 1:01 a.m., December 4, 1931; a day this family still celebrates along with Grandma Jazz, who continues to count the years of her beloved as though he is still alive. I try now to imagine what the wail of a newborn might sound like from this spot—then realize my own initial wails had been heard from this same spot. My eyes roll upward as though I can peer through the ceiling while curiosity consumes me about all the stories we hadn't been told that suddenly seem important. Little things, like which bedroom had been Mom's when she was a kid? Mom's room had always been the master bedroom while I was growing up.

I look over at Mom. She is still and her face is peaceful. She knows she's home, I think to myself. She knows.

The clock strikes at the top of the hour. One chime shimmers from its cherry wood casing and echoes off the plaster walls throughout the house. I hear Nellie in the kitchen placing dishes into the sink. Then the house goes quiet once again as my eyes follow the gold pendulum back and forth as it resists the afternoon sunlight—instead reflecting it effortlessly as it dutifully repeats itself in a precision known only to God and clockmakers. How many times has it swung? How many more times will it swing? Who will be here watching it swing a hundred years from now? I wonder.

Mom stirs. I jump to her side.

"Nellie," I call out.

Nellie pushes through the swinging door between the kitchen and the dining room and rushes to my side.

"Barbara?"

"No, Mom. It's me, David."

"Where's Barbara?"

Mom closes her eyes and becomes exceedingly still. My head snaps toward Nellie. Nellie's expression assures me Mom has just drifted off. "This is good," Nellie assures softly. "She'll no longer need to remain in a coma. She'll be conscious more often," Nellie explains as she takes Mom's blood pressure and twists the valve on the tube going into her hand. She raises the end of the mechanical bed, slightly elevating Mom's upper body.

A few minutes later when Mom opens her eyes and sees where she is, she closes them once again in pure joy. Her lips fall into a smile as though someone is massaging her neck in just the right place. Home. She's home.

I pat her hand gently. She tries to respond but is physically too weak. "Everything is going to be okay," I tell her. "Just rest. I'm right here."

She opens her eyes and looks at me groggily. "You just said that," she says, as though I repeated myself once too many times.

Then I realize it is likely the last thing I *had* said to her before she fell into a coma days ago. "Yeah," I affirm. "Everything is going to be okay."

Barb and Bob show up sometime after dinner. I leave them alone with Mom while I go up to my room. The vigil has been mentally draining and I need a break, time to be alone.

I wander around the room picking things up, twisting them around in my hand, looking at the bottom as though I'm searching for the price tag or an expiration date. It's all junk. Why she hasn't thrown it out before now is beyond me. A wooden token from a local carnival, a glass canning jar full of marbles, my old baseball glove. My hand no longer fits into it.

I open one of the boxes stacked in the corner. A near-deflated football, the jock strap I wore in middle school. Why is she saving this stuff? Then, my eye falls on something I'd long forgotten. I reach into the box and gently pick up a sterling silver locket now tarnished and blackened by neglect. Recognition causes a tickle of adrenaline throughout my chest. My eyes widen. My mouth opens with glee. Then just as quickly the feeling turns to dread; an oily slime begins to clog my veins, prevents me from being able to swallow. I hold the evidence of my sin in the palm of my hand. How could I have forgotten? What harm have I caused?

It was Alison's. My memory of when she gave it to me rushes to mind. A precious heirloom, she had told me. At one time it had been a gift from a young man to a young woman who had not yet spoken the words of love to one another, but who were about to be separated by war. The locket held their pictures ... and had been engraved. I turn the locket over in my hand. My thumb rubs gently over the words: *'fata viam invenient.'* "The fates will find a way," I whisper aloud.

It had been tenderly fastened about the young woman's neck only moments before the conductor's whistle blew and the young man was forced aboard. As the train began to pull away, she ran along the station platform until at the last second she ripped the locket from her neck and thrust it into his outstretched hand as he reached out to her from the window of the train. "Bring it back to me," she had cried amongst the billows of steam and the roar of the engine. She could no longer see him, but his words rang out: "I promise." During the darkest moments of war, her picture had given him hope. With his life he protected that moment, when he knew he would return to her and keep his promise, and offer her one more promise. They were married within a week after the young soldier's return.

Alison's grandmother had given the locket to her with the intent it would bring her everlasting love. I remember how glassy-eyed Alison was as she told me the story of her grandparents. She wanted me to keep the locket while we both went off to college. She had placed our pictures over her grandparents.'

"Accept this locket only if you really love me," she had requested softly, with hesitation.

I accepted the locket and kissed her reverently as a token of my sincerity.

"Promise you'll give it back if ever you don't," she had whispered in my ear while I held her in my arms.

Her words repeat in my head over and over while I try to stabilize adolescent emotions that have somehow found their way back into my being. I never intended to forget. I never intended to let her go. I loved her even then. But things got in the way. I open the locket and stare at the photos of Alison and me, cut from a photograph taken at our senior prom; the curl in Alison's hair had relaxed by the time they took our photo and the bowtie beneath my chin had gone askew. The sight of us summoned an old emotion that burbled up from my soul.

My hand clasps around the locket, tightening until it becomes a fist. I walk to the window and look out toward the street. I must return this to her, I think to myself. The locket belongs to her. It is a family heirloom. I have no right to keep it. But how can I give it back ... now? Besides, I think to myself, she's gone back to Washington— left before I had a chance to even say goodbye. Who knows when she'll be back? She might not ever come back. I can't just send it to her. But the excuses seem as hollow as I feel.

Standing at the window contemplating my options, I watch the last rays of light ebb from the autumn sky. The earth turns another degree and instantly there is darkness. The emptiness of the room engulfs me and penetrates to my core. Here I stand. The guy who was going to have it all, come home with the prize, show everyone how to live. Now all I have to show for my life is what remains in a few boxes at my feet and what I hold in the palm of my hand. Memories harp inside my head of what I've done and of what I've left undone. The sound becomes a ringing in my ears, escalating until it drowns out all silence. I clap my fists to my ears. "Stop," I cry out, demanding the demons crawl back into the recesses of my soul.

I force myself to think 'onward.' I look outward toward the distant heavens. There, beyond my windowsill, the infinite universe stretches beyond anyone's ability to fully comprehend, yet completely within the realm of realization. Stars fill the sky like endless possibilities. "What on earth can stop me?"

THURSDAY, SEPTEMBER 25, 2008: 11:45 P.M. (CDT)

With Mom asleep and Nellie in charge, I walk to Schmitty's as much for the fresh air outside as the familiar stale air inside once I get there.

I take the stool next to Uncle Billy. Only a handful of locals are still here. Petie waves from the pool table. Junior pauses in mid-shot as they both stare in my direction. Schmitty sets me up with a Heineken. No one says anything. We just glance back and forth, each of us knowing how to read the other with shrugs and glances. Sorry about your mother. Thanks, appreciate your concern. They don't know what to say. Neither do I. It is the language of men when things get serious. We sip our beer.

I no more than take the last gulp and Schmitty sets another down in front of me. It is a suggestion to stick around a while; that hanging with pals is what they all think I need right now. The rest of them pause at what they're doing, all eyes still on me. I glance around the room at the four of them. I grab the bottle and take a long pull.

Junior finishes his shot and makes the corner pocket. Billy turns sideways on his stool to face me, to indicate he is all ears for whatever I want to say.

I say nothing.

He sighs heavily. "It's the shits," he finally utters.

"That it is," I reply.

Billy comes every day to see Mom. I realize it is just as hard on him as it is us, but he is still our pillar. Julie flew in last Saturday. She was released from her classes due to hardship and has canceled the rest of the quarter. Grandma Jazz stays overnight most nights. We practically have to force Stuart to go home and get some rest. We are all reluctant to finish this final chapter in Mom's life, because we know how it ends.

I never anticipated this—that I would witness life being pulled from the body that gave it to me. If I had, I would not have imagined the experience to be what it is. It is nothing like waiting at all. It is more like having to clean out a drawer that I've tossed junk into for years and never organized before. Initially, there is a sense of comfort in seeing what lays exposed in my proverbial drawer. It is *my* junk. No one else's. I have power over that, to decide whether to keep or toss. As I pick through the junk, small things conjure up great meaning, scraps remind me of the whole. I pause to process things I set aside long ago as though I am discovering them for the very first time. Nostalgia and regret then seem to wage an internal war until things are put into their proper place. Only then do frustration and reluctance meld into a peaceful-like surrender as I become able to let go of things both extremely important and not so. It is all just a little too much to fully comprehend, let alone verbalize. It is a relief to be sitting among people to whom I don't need to verbalize.

Uncle Billy and I both swivel around and place our elbows on the bar, hunkering over our beer bottles. I blow softly across the top of mine. It makes a soft foghorn sound. Schmitty sets a bowl of peanuts in front of us. I munch. Uncle Billy pats his protruding belly. I remind myself of our shared DNA and push the peanuts aside.

A strong yearning to talk to Alison pervades my thoughts, accompanied by a flood of emotion, all of which I keep in check, all of which confounds me further. She left days ago. No one expects to see her back here anytime soon. "Ever take the wrong path?" I ask Billy.

He smirks and winks. "More often than not."

"No, seriously," I urge of him. "I mean where you *really* took the wrong road, one on which you never belonged on in the first place."

He pushes back from the bar and groans confidently. "Yup. I bought a brand-new red pickup."

I look at him hoping he isn't about to tell me his buying the Ford Ranger was his big mistake in life. When I don't respond, he nods.

"No way," I refute.

"I was trying hard to be something I wasn't and it cost me everything. Got to showing off so much it went to my head. Liked all the attention I got. Pretty soon I was giving pretty girls rides in my new pickup. Didn't sit well with Linda Malcomb. She dumped me. Course, at the time I told everyone I dumped *her*. Said she wasn't classy enough for me. That hurt her pretty bad. Half believed it myself. I wanted girls who would swoon over me. Found out those types swoon over the next best thing that comes along. Learned the hardest lesson of my life. Yup. I know all about doing dumb stuff." We both nod our heads in camaraderie.

Interesting how relationships can seem so unimportant at one point in your life and mean everything at another, I ponder. Then something dawns on me. "Why did you give it to me if that truck brought you such bad luck?" I'm feeling a little irritated at that thought.

"Probably shouldn't have, should I," he remarks. "Never thought about that at the time. Just knew you wanted it, so I gave it to you." He takes a swig of his beer, then swings his head in my direction. "Why? Did that truck ruin your life too?" A worried look comes over his face. I pause to think about that for a second. "No," I assure him, but I am not so certain it didn't. "I'm a big boy," I tell him. "If I screwed up my life it wasn't on account of you giving me that truck," I add, reminding myself of the truth.

He heaves a sigh of relief and takes another pull of his beer.

We are who we are. Figuring out who we ought to be is the difference between success and failure. It has nothing to do with who has the most toys or the fattest checkbooks. That much I've learned. I still have the rest to figure out.

"So, did you?" he asks.

"What?"

"Screw up your life?"

Wednesday, October 1, 2008: 6:00 a.m. (CDT)

Last night was the third time I had come here intending to pack up my stuff to move it back to Fiddlers Park, but haven't yet found the fortitude necessary to admit such defeat. It is hard to let go of expectations despite having no other options. The silence of the loft rings in my ears, but is soon drowned out by my thoughts, which loom about me like bad breath.

The central banks in England, China, Canada, Switzerland, Sweden, and the European Central Bank followed suit to match the United States in lowering their funds and discount rates. So the rope around everyone's neck now is the American citizens, whose lack of understanding about sophisticated financial systems jeopardize the entire world should their big mouths prevent a bailout. Socialists—who oppose our American philosophy of power-to-the-people—just might make their point if the people in this country don't shut up before it is too late.

The proposed stimulus package—a corpus to purchase $700 billion of distressed assets—is the only thing between people facing a financially challenging few years or fighting over a handful of beetles. What the average American doesn't understand is even *this* may not be enough to stop a financial meltdown of an unfathomable magnitude.

Angrily, I slide open the plate glass balcony door and step over its threshold to the cantilevered appendage I trust it as easily as I once did the systemic structure of the entire financial industry. From this vantage point, I survey the city like a general returning to the battlefield to count the wounded and dead—all the slumbering people who don't yet know they've been thrown into a mad dash for job security, financial self-sufficiency ... every type of economical means to an end. The majority will wake up and go on about their day as usual.

Steam from my coffee mingles with the morning mist. October had crept in overnight like a sick child, clammy and pale with a disquieting fever. Fog looms around the spindly downtown buildings like a smothering mother obscuring visions of a lost horizon. The ominous waters of the Mississippi snarl silently along the levee below while I continue to fathom the future.

While a small percentage of the wealthiest are already re-structuring their ambitions, and while an ever-widening group of people capable of surviving without as many millions as they once had are bracing for the worse, the greater portion of humanity will never know what hit them—yet will be forced to bear the brunt of this single event for decades.

I step back into the warmth of the loft; but while I can close the door against the harsh air, I can't close my mind to what is happening. You don't have to be a psychic to predict the inevitable. Everyone's piece of pie just shrunk beyond their wildest imagination. Everything from literal shares of securities to equity values and opportunity have been snatched from everyone alive. Most just don't know it yet. And no one is going to sit still for it once they do.

A dark pool of mingled thoughts swirl in my head as I attempt to grasp it all. After seeing what greed did to people on Wall Street, it occurs to me that people on Main Street are no different. How long will it take for us, as a nation, to veer from the age of enlightenment? Will we turn away from intellectual and philosophical reasoning and once again embrace our former primitive sentiments of racism, anti-Semitism, and ethnic cleansing? I shudder to think. But the reality of such is imminent. When resources diminish, survival instincts kick in. Initially nations will growl over waning resources—but what happens when their scraps are gone?

The irony is that the safest place to be when all this unfolds is still going to be the United States—the nation that started it all.

"Awe, man," I shout aloud at the audacity of us Americans. I don't care what time of day it is—I need a beer. The last two bottles rattle as I pull open the door to the refrigerator with more gusto than necessary. I swig a third of the bottle before I come up for air while that last thought lingers.

It is only a matter of time before the poorest of this world will be at the doorsteps of every industrialized nation begging for help. The sentiments of this nation's great lady will soon be put to the test when the tired and poor huddle in masses along our borders. But it has become the American way to hoard the spoils. They should put it on a plaque: "Give us everything you got and go away."

I recall the documentary I watched with Mom in which the soup lines caused by the great depression broadcasted the severity of that economic downturn which enticed an out-pouring of empathy and generosity. Government humanitarian programs came about as a result. But today no one will see the soup lines, which exacerbates the illusion that all is well when it is not. Out of sight, out of mind.

And the question still remains—will we, the citizens of the nation who plunged the world into economic turmoil, own up to what we did? I don't need to wait for congressional hearings to know there is no mastermind on Wall Street who created this mess. Wall Street is a symptom. It is not the cause. People like Walter and Grandma Jazz all across this nation are what propel Wall Street. Merely depositing funds into a checking account or swiping a credit card through the gas pump is what sets the financial world into motion. Never mind the mortgages and student loans, credit card debt, and automobile financing people rack up. It all becomes fodder for Wall Street. Apathy and ignorance are the deadliest of culprits.

Since advanced technology was the knife that cut our throats, should we blame the technicians and programmers who created the systems that tracked the trades at such lightning speed accountants couldn't keep up? I can stand here all day and point blame, but the fact is every living soul is to blame, in one way or another, for either what they did, or left undone. This is a perfect storm and illustrates only one thing: human nature. This great fabric of all mankind just tripped on itself and fell into a shithole. Whether we will get up and brush ourselves off as a unit, or whether we will rip and tear ourselves apart is all that remains to be seen. But one thing is certain: this is where it has *already* begun. Life as we know it is gone. Gone!

It's just shy of 7 a.m. when I polish off the rest of my beer and go looking for another.

There is solace in the expectation that people will adapt, because people always do. They will determine new values, create new norms, and survive—some better than others—but the species will go on.

I flip on the television. It's all about the impending presidential election. The beer I've drunk has gone to my mouth. "What now Mr. George W. Bush? Who's going to put Humpty Dumpty back together again? John McCain? Some guy named Barack Obama?"

Whoever he is, it will be like taking the helm of the *Titanic*, becoming captain *after* it struck the iceberg. "Keep us all afloat, Mr. New President, whoever the hell you turn out to be." That's what the good citizens of the United States are sure to cry, I think to myself, then add, "But whatever you do, don't ask us to make any concessions."

Matthew comes to mind. Charlie's brother. The mastermind behind the deregulation of big banks. I chuckle aloud at the echoing pleas from those same banks—now lying in rubble—that once thought themselves too sophisticated to let anything like what happened in 1929 ever happen again. "Huh!"

"What a mess," I groan as I shake the bottle to see what's left in it. While the Feds may have dangled free money in the faces of predatory lenders, the buying frenzy was born of common consumers' greed that ballooned private debt from credit cards to mortgages. The most desirable being subprime, which the investment bankers turned into the most sought-after securities in trading history. "What a ride," I remind myself.

Having finished my last bottle of beer, I survey the premises. I look about the room. Not much more than what I moved in with over a year ago. Still just a sleeping bag—for a bed, for a place to roll around in with Helice. Stop, I tell myself. Don't go there. That's history, not my future. Move forward, I keep trying to tell myself as visions of Helice scamper about in my head. I mumble a few expletives in protest of my dreams going up in smoke. But somehow, I really don't feel as bad as I am trying to make myself believe. It is all so confusing. I look at the near empty bottle of scotch sitting on the kitchen counter. "Maybe this will clear things up," I tell myself.

That's the last thing I remember until my cell phone jars me awake sometime in the afternoon. Tangled in my sleeping bag, I struggle to find it. My vision is blurred by sleep—or maybe beer and scotch—but I make out the number to the landline at the house. My heart jumps as I take the call and a surge of adrenaline replaces the fog. "David, you better come home," Nellie says calmly.

CHAPTER 22: THE BATON PASSES
MINNEAPOLIS, MINNESOTA

SATURDAY, OCTOBER 4, 2008: 7:00 A.M. (CDT)

An emotional numbness seized me the moment I heard Nellie's voice on my cell phone. The frenzied drive back to Mom's had seemed surreal. I felt choked by a scream that would not release until she took her last breath. With her fingers still entwined in mine, I had felt the power that pulled my mother's soul from her body, its potency unnerving yet its presence immensely reverent. While others had broken into wails at such loss, I felt no abandonment. Instead, it was as though something had been passed to me ... like a baton during a relay race ... a race which I now must run toward a finish line, yet knowing there is none.

I learned later that while we huddled in grief over Mom's bed, the financial markets around the world had collapsed further and sent shockwaves of a different nature. As our family and friends fell into each other's arms for comfort, world investors sought safe havens in the U.S. dollar and Japanese yen. Both my worlds dissolved simultaneously. I will never be able to think of one without the other. But it is clear which one is more significant. Perhaps it is Mom's final blessing—a permanent reminder of priorities.

This morning I step outside and breathe more deeply than ever before; suck in the autumn air, smell the pungent aroma of decaying leaves and drying grass, feel the warmth of an inferno perched in infinity 93 million miles away, all while my mind struggles to grasp the imponderables of life on earth and the universe in which it floats.

I watch as a brittle wind rattles reluctant leaves from the tops of trees and carries them gently to the ground before it sweeps them around the base of perennials to protect roots from the impending winter. I'd feel like a new man if it weren't for the fact my iniquities are like rocks in my socks. But I guess there's a stone in everyone's shoe. We must all be careful how we step.

I take another deep breath before starting off on a morning jog—a new habit I'm developing as a means to preserve my new-found appreciation of life. Maybe today I'll stop off at Vinnie's for a scone, or stop by Schmitty's to see if he needs any help stacking empties.

They had shut the Park down yesterday for Mom's funeral. Every store, including the library, closed for the morning. A parade of people gave personal eulogies and each told how she had affected their life, what she had meant to them, how wonderful she had been, how they would miss her. If a person's worth is measured by the number of people they touched while alive then Mom was a multi-millionaire.

The sermon Pastor Mic gave at Mom's funeral has been rolling around in my head ever since. "We are all significantly insignificant," I say aloud, repeating his words to the morning star as it lingers in the eastern horizon, summoning a reluctant sun—and to the rodents that are scurrying to their burrowed nests, and to the frogs ... where do frogs go for the winter? I wonder.

"Hey, Davie," Lucy shouts from her doorstep.

"Beautiful morning," I reply.

"That's exactly what your mother would say." She smiles.

I stop in my tracks and look at her. Her words bring peace to my soul and lend comfort through our shared knowledge. "Thank you," I tell her.

She nods, picks up her newspaper, and goes back inside.

Wednesday, October 15, 2008: 1:30 p.m. (CDT)

Bryan—with a y—hurriedly rushes toward me, menu in hand, a smile on his face, shoulders bent slightly in a mini bow.

"So good to see you, Mr. Yates," he says and leads me upstairs to a table just inside the veranda. "Will Mr. Bishop be joining you this afternoon?" he asks as he sets the menu down in front of me.

"Yes," I tell him.

Bryan rushes away to get me a Heineken.

Charlie's uncanny ability to always be at the right place at the right time parallels my apparent destiny, only in reverse. One week's delay in initiating his plan and it was back on track while I still don't even know if I have a plan.

With amateur hour over for self-proclaimed investors and others fleeing firms whose agents are little more than a possum in headlights, it is a virtual cakewalk for Charlie as he scarfs up debris in the wake of denial. Maugham's corporate counsel being engrossed with more important matters than a couple of agents absconding with accounts left the road wide open for Charlie, who was gassed up and ready to go when the markets collapsed. Providence Capital Management, Inc. is on track for first month earnings despite a global financial meltdown. That's the difference between Charlie's world and mine.

Tom and I have our hands full just stabilizing asset value in client accounts, and if we aren't forced to deliver pizzas at the end of the day just to pay the office rent we consider ourselves ahead of the game.

"Sorry I'm late," Charlie apologizes as he takes a seat opposite me.

Bryan is right behind him and sets a bottle of Heineken in front of me and a scotch on the rocks in front of Charlie even before Charlie sits down.

Charlie and I smile at one another. I haven't seen him since the funeral. It has been only a few weeks, but in view of the changes that have taken place in each of our lives it seems an eternity has passed since we last were together.

"How have you been?" Charlie asks.

"Not nearly as good as you," I chuckle.

Charlie sips his scotch and remains silent for an inordinate length of time, allowing me the opportunity to express myself over matters dearer to my heart than a couple of thugs getting together for lunch.

"I'm fine," I assure him in answer to the questions revealed in his eyes about how I am doing after the loss of my mother, and adjusting to having moved back to Fiddlers Park. It's been good. Julie is back at school, working as a teacher's assistant until next quarter when she can resume a full class schedule. I go to Barb's nearly every night for dinner and to tickle the kids. Bob and I started hanging out together more. He's helping me repair and remodel the house. The new norm. Been far more satisfying than I'd ever have guessed. But Charlie wasn't put on earth to ever understand such things.

It is good to see him. There is an appreciation for having spent time with someone in ways I will never again share with anyone else. I will miss our friendship, as it will no doubt fade into the sunset now that our paths seem to be parting. He will always be someone I admire.

"It's been a wild ride," I say as I tip my bottle in a salute.

"Still is," he adds, eyes gleaming with something more. He leans forward on his elbows and lowers his voice. "Come back to New York with me." When I don't say anything, or even breathe, he continues. "I need you now more than ever."

What for? I'm wondering, but my lungs are still paralyzed at the thought that everything might still be within reach.

"You have the instincts."

"Harrumph! Now they are instincts. At one time they were babblings from an idiot, but now I'm an oracle." I laugh out loud.

"Something like that." Charlie sits back in his chair and twirls his drink. "You had the tenacity to follow your intuition." He takes a sip and looks about the room with no apparent focus. "I felt the rumblings, too, only when I didn't find the answers I went with the flow." He leans in on one elbow and his eyes grow narrow. "I learned my lesson. *Never go with the flow.*" He sits back again, and while his eyes bounce around the room without focusing on any one particular thing, he tells me his intention is to never get caught with his pants down again. "Ever!"

I remain in repose, listening—and wondering what he has up his sleeve.

"We need to be proactive," he says, accentuating the first syllable of the word proactive. He goes on to explain the details of his revised business plan, which includes in-house analysis. It is why he is here. "We need you ... your gut instinct." He smiles at the fact that in the past my so-called 'gut' hadn't been treated with the respect it is now being given. "Head analyst," he offers. "Come back with me. We'll take it all the way to the top, you and I. Come with me." He cautiously examines my eyes. Now it is his turn to hold his breath.

It is all still here. Nothing has changed. He's right. The current environment is ripe for such a strategy. It is an opportunity to build a fortune ... an empire.

"Fifty-fifty," he adds for further incentive.

Our eyes lock.

"What about Manny?" I murmur.

"We'll talk about him next." He sits up in his chair. "What do you say?"

Thoughts pass through my mind—such as I won't have to sell the condos in a down market just to pay off the medical bills and keep Julie in school. I'd be part of the pack again. I swell with exhilaration.

They say the mind can process 700,000 thousand words per second. It must be more than that because everything I've ever considered—from wanting to find a way out of Fiddlers Park to winding up back in it—comes to mind. Things I can't comprehend and explain are understood by some internal translator I was unaware I possessed until this very minute. It is all so clear and certain. Every part of me resonates with this new-found truth of who I am, what I am capable of doing ... what I must do.

"Sorry, Charlie. I can't," I reply flatly.

"What?" Charlie reels in response. He's wondering how I can turn my back on everything I've purported to want since he's known me. He's wondering why anyone would refuse becoming one of the wealthiest people in the world. He particularly is wondering how I can possibly think there is any future for me in a shared one-room office as an agent of Smythe Investments.

So am I.

Bryan places a steak sandwich, a plate of fries and a full bottle of ketchup in front of me and a steak sandwich and a salad, blue cheese dressing on the side, in front of Charlie. Whether he asks us anything further or whether we say anything more is a blur since Charlie and I have all we can do to restrain our thoughts. Bryan senses the tension and quickly leaves us alone.

"Why?" Charlie finally blurts out in a hushed whisper when Bryan is out of earshot.

"There are people who rely on me, Charlie."

He takes that to mean I am talking about my family's needs in the aftermath of our personal loss. As he sits back, a look of relief washes over him. He exhales and a smile pulls at the corners of his mouth as he apologetically tells me he never meant to imply that I should shirk my obligations to my family right now. Of course, I should take time to grieve. He'll handle everything in the meantime. "Take all the time you want," he tells me.

"It's not that," I interrupt him hesitantly while my mind scrambles for the words to explain the difference between his world and mine.

His eyes are steady, mouth relaxed. There isn't anything I can tell him he doesn't already know, he is thinking.

I envy Charlie. He is the perfect specimen of a human being. Well-adjusted, kind, generous, intelligent, thoughtful, entertaining, athletic, and accomplished. He isn't a typical rich kid ruined by indulgence. He is the poster boy for the epitome of what everyone ever born wishes life to be. But there's a little more to it than DNA. Nurtured by the best nannies until he was old enough to follow in the footsteps of his highly accomplished parents; encouraged to reach his full potential at the finest educational institutions in the world; influenced by some of the greatest minds of the century over dinners in the privacy of his parents' homes ... plural, that is, all of which are fully staffed; then to start on his own in life given a Cessna to help him spread his wings and a Lamborghini to explore uncharted territory in search of his destiny—all of which just might have contributed something to the well-rounded young man he is today and the self-made man of tomorrow.

Charlie has never had to scrape garbage off the bottom of his shoe because he has to take out the trash to earn the right to put his legs under the dinner table; never had to deliver papers in the rain to make money to pay for college; and never had to wonder if a person can actually die of boredom. So how am I going to explain that where I come from it takes a community just to give a kid a fighting chance; that letting out your attic could mean the difference between someone making it through college or not; that sometimes all that is between a person buying a gun or getting a job is someone making an employment opportunity where there was none; that it isn't how fast your car can go but how many people it will hold? How can I expect him to understand when I am just beginning to understand it myself? "Destiny isn't something you go looking for where I come from, Charlie. It is what you are given at birth."

"What do you mean?"

"I mean I have to stay here. At least for now."

There is a long pause while he digests what I just said. Meanwhile, I douse my fries with ketchup and stuff a few into my mouth using my fingers, take a pull on my beer, belch a bit and swallow.

"In Fiddlers Park?" he asks, to clarify his understanding, which is apparently as hard for him to believe as it is for me to digest.

I nod in the affirmative and continue to eat what's on my plate. I nearly finish before he says another word. I can only imagine what is going through his mind ... that my cheese has slipped off my cracker ... that I'm delusional, perhaps depressed. After all that has happened in the last month, it is not surprising he'd think such. Watching a beloved parent fade from life, losing my job, my girl—both girls actually, although he doesn't know anything about Alison—all four condos will soon be in foreclosure, and I've been humiliated in front of everyone I know. I still might need to yank the dance floor out from under my little sister's tap shoes, and that's not to mention I share a wastebasket with a guy who rides a bike to work. What more does a person need to justify jumping off a cliff? But it just isn't the case. It is *because* of all these reasons that I am refortified to stay here and help people fight adversity in the wake of what could possibly be the world's greatest financial catastrophe in the history of mankind. While the world is yet unable to fathom this, I am not. If I'm right about what is coming down the pipeline, the folks of Fiddlers Park will be like babies on a beach without sunscreen in the middle of August—helpless against elements they know nothing about, which could affect their lives permanently. Until I see otherwise what choice do I have?

"Are you okay?" he asks cautiously, assuming I am in some sort of psychological distress.

"I'm right side up," I assure him.

Our eyes engage while he searches mine analytically. Once he's certain he doesn't have to call the crisis line his face contorts into a grimace as comprehension sets in.

"What on earth are you doing?"

"That's exactly what I've been asking myself lately. The answer to that question is not a hell of a lot for anyone but myself."

"And ..." he asks leadingly as though there is nothing wrong with taking care of oneself—in fact, it is the preferred state of adulthood and all.

"It is no way to live," I tell him.

He just looks at me. Whether he is contemplating his own motives or mulling over mine is hard to tell. "And by staying in Fiddlers Park you will be doing something for someone besides yourself?"

"Something like that."

He scoffs loud enough to cause the people at the next table to turn in our direction. "The only thing you'll be doing is leaving a bigger piece of the pie for Manny and me. Is that your plan? Because Manny is going to love you for that."

That thought seethes through me like a seltzer in water and I have to take a pull on my beer to keep from foaming at the mouth.

"What do you hope to accomplish by staying here?"

I shrug. "Help folks get through the next few years."

"What? Don't tell me you're intending to be the local financial planner?"

"Yeah."

He laughs again. "These people don't have enough assets to warrant what a financial planner costs. I've seen those accounts. I have half of them in my book yet that I dragged over from Maugham for your sake." Then his eyes widen with what he now realizes. "You're going to stay here and give away your advice free, aren't you? That's it, isn't it?" He doesn't wait for an answer. "These people won't even know what you're giving them," he says intending to dissuade me. "Come back to New York where people really do need what you've got ... and where you can get paid for it. You can make enough money in New York to support every man, woman, and child in Fiddlers Park until the day you die!"

"That's not the point."

Exasperation fills his eyes as they beg for explanation, but I offer none.

"What are you trying to prove?"

To be brutally honest, the only thing I've been trying to prove my whole life is that I am better than Dad. Well, I certainly proved that, didn't I? If screwing up my life in record time beats Dad, then mission accomplished. How I ever thought messing with more women, buying bigger toys, and rejecting the love of my life meant anything other than following in my father's own footsteps, I don't know. But there it is. Like father, like son. And while I made it out of the hole in the earth called Fiddlers Park in less time than it took him, I'm right back in it deeper than ever before. So Dad is still the champion in this corner, but I am no longer competing for the title. Game over.

"Impiety can be defined by what is left undone," I say to Charlie with enough introspection to surprise us both.

"What?" Charlie asks.

"Nothing," I reply. "I'm not trying to prove anything," I say in answer to his first question.

Charlie shakes his head and finally begins to eat his food. I mop up the rest of the ketchup on my plate with the last of my sandwich. Each of us has a mouthful when Bryan steps up to the table and asks if there is anything else he can get for us. We both shake our heads.

Self-absorption is the American way—the constant pursuit of happiness. But what is happiness? I look at Charlie who is about to surpass his father's expectations, think about Mom when she was still lying on her death bed, see Julie dancing across a stage, Helice on Manny's arm, Alison sliding down a hillside in a broken-down bus. Happiness is relative. If you chase the wrong ball you get run over. If I am beginning to realize anything it is that to fall prey to social standards is to be consumed by other people's values and not led by my own.

By the time Bryan brings our coffee Charlie's posture relaxes as he finally accepts my decision. "So, there's nothing I can say to change your mind. You're going to stay here and serve the good people until they erect a statue in your name."

I turn up my bottom lip. Not a bad idea, I think to myself. Not a bad idea at all. I can just picture a bronze monolith of grandpa Munson in front of the library steps with a plaque that proclaims him the founder of Fiddlers Park. I make a mental note to check into that.

"Since I can't convince you to come back to New York as my partner, can I at least get you to take a seat on my board of advisors?"

My eyebrows lift. I cock my head. "Yeah. I'd like that," I tell him—if for no other reason than to have an excuse to stay in touch with Charlie. Perhaps that's the only reason he's offering the option.

"There will always be an opening for you in the firm when ..." Charlie catches himself and corrects what he is about to say, "... *should* you ever decide to come back to New York."

That's nice to know, I think to myself.

We sip our coffee in silence a few minutes before Charlie sighs. "What more can I do?"

He means with regard to convincing me to change my mind, but I take the opportunity to tell him what he really can do.

"You can reassign all the Fiddlers Park accounts back to me," I tell him.

"Done," Charlie replies without hesitation.

"Including Walter and the entire list of Durkee accounts."

Charlie nods. "And about Manny ..." he begins. He explains his initial intention of bringing Manny into his plan was only to use him to distract the legal beagles off our scent while he and I secured clients into the new firm. He always intended for Manny to be fairly rewarded, but he never intended on making Manny a partner. The fact Manny assumes such reveals the fool that he is. There is no further need of Manny. Charlie looks at me over the rim of his coffee cup with mischief in his eyes. "Board members decide on who's in and who's out."

My eyebrows lift and my mouth crests in response to the daunting possibilities now running rampantly through my mind with distinct appeal at what Charlie just suggested.

Charlie winks.

Saturday, October 18, 2008: 11:00 a.m. (CDT)

It started as a plan to replace the bus lost in the accident in Peru, but once the good people of the Park learned of the dire conditions in the small village where Guy lost his life, efforts turned to more serious endeavors. Stan and Joe designed a ferry they can make using indigenous materials that would be strong enough to transport cattle and sheep across the Hurbama and Yavero rivers. They are scheduled to leave the end of this month to engineer the project. Evie is organizing a group of teens to go down during spring break and bring the textbooks she will donate. Boxes of clothes and toiletries have already been sent. Parkites won't stop until the village has everything from a school to a hospital, and is economically self-sustainable. Then my guess is they will do the same for the next village, and the next. Peru won't know what hit them.

Everyone would understand if I didn't feel up to fulfilling the role of Master of Ceremonies so soon after the funeral. They will manage somehow without me. I should take all the time I need for myself, I've been told. They all worry about me too much. I'm fine. And besides, there is no place I'd rather be than with people who knew my mother … who know me. It's why I am here today.

Fiddlers Park Middle School is the Park's conference and event center when Rick's Nick's parking lot isn't serving as such. The faculty lot is full and about a dozen or so cars are parked in the bus zone by the time I arrive. Inside, my lone footsteps echo between the lockers and cement block walls as I follow the sounds to where everyone has congregated in the gymnasium-slash-lunchroom.

Silent auction tables wind around the room and display everything from nail polish kits donated by Maggie to Weber barbecue grills donated by Stan. The smell of pulled pork and steamed buns permeates the room as people waft in from the outside and begin wandering around.

I head to the boy's locker rooms to change into my tuxedo. Uncle Billy follows me in.

"Going to put your Beemer up for auction?" he asks.

My head snaps around to see whether he is serious.

He is.

The expression on my face, should be answer enough, but it doesn't deter him from pushing the matter further.

"Going to let all the people in Porte de Dios suffer just so you can drive around in a Beemer?"

Ouch, I think to myself. That's just plain mean. I glare at him before I pull the shirt off my back and notice the one on his—a white undershirt spray-painted with two large number fours with a dash between them. I purposely avoid asking him what it means.

I heard about the eBay auction he and a few of his cronies are conducting this afternoon in conjunction with the silent auction. Seems some of the guys, being guys, thought it would be more fun if there was a competition to see which group could raise the most funds. Since it all goes to a good cause it's a good way to burn off some testosterone without causing injury—that is, unless someone comes between me and my car.

I glare at him between searching the front of my shirt for all the tiny buttonholes.

Uncle Billy picks his teeth with a toothpick and watches me but he says nothing further. He's hoping my conscience is saying it all for him ... that I'll cave to guilt and cough up my keys.

Think again, buddy, I think to myself as I give him the meanest glare I can muster.

He twirls the toothpick in his mouth complacently and smiles.

"No," I finally tell him verbally. "That's final." I grab my duffle bag, stuff my old clothes into it and I am out the door of the locker room, but he's right on my tail. Once inside the gymnasium I quickly lose him among the crowd, or so I think. While I'm looking backward, he pops up in front of me and before I know it our bellies bump.

He smiles and points to the corner of the room where three of his pals sit in the center of a circle of laptops. The sign above their heads reads: "4-4-the Money." Ah, I think to myself. That explains the shirt.

"It's a $60,000 car, for Christ's sake," I plead under my breath through clenched teeth.

"All the more reason we need it," he replies. "And it is."

"What is?" I ask.

"For Christ's sake," he replies with a smirk.

He walks away before I can belt him for his gall.

Evie grabs my arm and jabs note cards at me. "Here's the eulogy for Guy the Blys wrote—they want you to read for them." She bustles away.

I look down at a stack of note cards carefully numbered and clearly printed with words describing a kind and generous young man who had been struck down in the prime of his life, and how forever grateful the Blys and all the rest of us here in Fiddlers Park are for his heroism and for giving his own life to protect our beloved Alison. I had agreed to read it on their behalf because they were certain they would not be able to do so without crying and making a scene. But now I'm not so certain I can either. I swallow hard as I tuck the cards into my tux pocket with a firm pat.

The junior high string quartet is playing under the direction of Ms. Brost, the mother of our local fire chief who gave up a promising career as a symphony violinist when the Park was unable to contract a music director for the middle school. She came as interim. That was forty years ago. I smile in admiration of her relentless struggle to instill the spirit of great musicians into the dense minds of seemingly unyielding youth. She'd be proud to know that I recognize the piece her students are trying with difficulty to play as Handel's *Water Piece: Suite in D* as a result of the trumpet lessons she once gave me. I smile as I pass and wonder whether she ever got anyone to play Rachmaninoff to her satisfaction.

On a screen above the stage, a slide show featuring Guy revolves. Images of him as a child, a college student, and many images of him in Peru. I pause in stride at the sight of him and Alison together. They made a striking couple. Full of health and vitality. A close up of them reveals something in their eyes as they look at one another. Love. Adoration. They had found what some search a lifetime for and never find. As I begin to imagine what it would be like to lose such a thing, an ache forms in my heart for both of them that I'm certain will never leave me.

A few minutes later the quartet ceases playing and everyone's attention is snared with a blast of feedback from the sound system as I tap the microphone. "Welcome everyone to the Guy Andrew Everett Memorial Fundraiser," I begin solemnly. "Let's open in prayer."

The room falls silent and becomes surreal as words flow through me from a higher power and deeper understanding than that of which I am capable. If I have ever felt the presence of God, it is during the next half hour while I unwaveringly give a eulogy for a man I never knew, but whom now will never forget. I am humbled by the time I turn the mike over to Tom, who is to give a PowerPoint presentation on the five-year projection and proposed costs of the projects initiated by the good people of Fiddlers Park for the benefit of the people of Porte de Dios.

"Thank you, Mr. and Mrs. Bly, for that wonderful tribute," Tom begins, giving all the credit justly to the Blys. "While Guy wasn't from Fiddlers Park," he continues to say to the somber crowd, "I think I can safely say Guy belonged here. I know many of you will remember him forever as the man who saved our Alison." Then as an afterthought, he adds, "And perhaps a village in Peru!"

The crowd erupts in applause and whistles.

He proceeds to present an elaborate presentation complete with colored graphs on the cost of each project and the timeline to establish infrastructures for the village, including an exit strategy to avoid financial dependency and to promote economic self-sufficiency for the tiny village.

The crowd turns to one another when he is through and mulls over what he's proposed.

Tom lifts his head to address the crowd in the back of the room. He steps closer to the microphone so no one will miss a word he is about to say. Then in his best tenor voice, he harks, "Ladies and gentlemen, we plead your benevolence on behalf of less fortunate people in our world. This is your opportunity to help give others in this world a fighting chance."

The crowd falls silent.

Cindy Milner pipes up in her junior high cheerleader voice, "Give me an 'f'."

The crowd responds.

"Give me an 'i'."

She spells out Fiddlers Park, then finishes with, "Go team go! Fight, fight, fight!" The crowd chants along, fists pounding the air.

Tom beams and begins clapping in applause for the audience who are the ones who will make it all happen. Soon everyone is clapping and cheering.

Once the crowd resumes their anything-but-silent auction and eating, I help Tom dismantle his laptop and projection equipment.

"You should pitch this to people with real money," I tell him, thinking of some of my former clients, people on the east coast. "I can get you in touch with people who could make this happen in one afternoon."

He pauses in what he is doing and gives me his undivided attention. "It's not about the money." His eyes search mine. Our eyes lock. It's as though he is tethering his brain to mine and transferring data and information, like we are a couple of cell phones. "We only have so many opportunities in life. Givers are the true recipients of blessings. I'd never take this opportunity away from these people." His attention lingers intently on me for a few seconds longer before he goes back to packing up his things.

I sit myself on the edge of the stage, legs dangling while I ponder Tom's words. I look out over the sea of bobbing heads. It really is one great fabric of all mankind.

Uncle Billy squeezes off another blow on the foghorn from his corner to indicate another milestone has been reached. The crowd parts and Uncle Billy bounces his belly all the way to the podium where he announces, "Another $15,000 was just made on the sale of Stan's vintage Airstream motor home."

The crowd shouts with joy.

"Only $75,000 to go," he belts out.

He's nuts, I think to myself. "Are you crazy enough to believe you can raise $75,000 in the next two hours?" I ask him as he jumps down from the stage.

"With your Beemer we could." He smiles and winks.

"No friggin' way," I tell him.

On his way back to his corner he grabs Cindy Milner's cheerleading megaphone and shouts through it as though he is speaking to the entire room, but I know he intentionally means me.

"Is there anyone here who has ever bought something they thought would bring happiness and found it didn't? This is your chance to turn that selfish act into something good. Give it up for the people of Porte de Dios!" He looks directly at me. Our eyes lock.

Someone from the crowd shouts, "Take my wife!"

I reach for my key ring, remove those for the house and the old van, and clutch the last of my dreams in the palm of my hand before I toss it into the air toward Uncle Billy's outstretched hand.

He toots the foghorn and announces to the crowed what I've just done. The crowd erupts in song. "For he's a jolly good fellow, for he's a jolly good fellow, for he's a jolly good fe-el-low ..." and as I sheepishly shake my head, someone whispers into my ear, "... which *no one* can deny."

I turn to see who it is. Alison! She sits down beside me on the edge of the stage and smiles. "Thank you for what you are doing," she says as she pats my forearm.

I'm dumbfounded. "I ... thought you'd ...   gone back to Washington," I stammer.

"I did, but I just couldn't stand being alone. I flew in early this morning. I need to be here ... home ... I need it for a while longer."

That's good, I think to myself. Not just for myself, but for her. It is good she is back where she belongs.

"I had no idea this was taking place," she says of the fundraiser. "When I got to the house and no one was home I called Mother on her cell phone and she told me to come here. I was astounded when I walked into the gym, saw the banner, and heard you giving Guy's eulogy."

"Your parents wrote it. Every word. I just read it."

She pats my arm again. "You did a nice job."

"Your parents didn't tell you about the fundraiser?"

She shakes her head. "I haven't been able to talk about anything related to Peru. I'm sure they thought it was best I didn't know." She lays her head on my shoulder. "Glad I was able to be here for it, though." She begins to sob. "It is so wonderful what everyone is doing."

I put my arm around her and pull her to my chest and hold her tight to help calm her tremors.

She pulls away and looks up at me. "I'm so sorry," she says with heartfelt regret. "Here I am going on about my loss and you sitting there with your own sorrow. I am so sorry to hear about your mother. How are you ... how is the rest of the family?"

"It isn't over. We're all still processing our grief, but we're getting through it," I assure her. "Thank you for your concern," I tell her.

"I would have ..."

"Mom wouldn't have expected you to attend her funeral under your own circumstances. You know Donna Mae well enough to know that, don't you?"

She leans her head against my shoulder. We sit for a while and watch the mulling menagerie of people. They all belong to us and us to them. We are part of a haven of humanity, as Mom always put it. My inability to squelch a smile at that thought seals my acceptance of something Mom had pounded into my head for as long as I can recall. I kiss the top of Alison's head. Then something occurs to me. "Hey," I say nudging Alison, "this is where we had our first dance."

She lifts her head from my shoulder, smiles, and looks about the room, then replies, "This is also where we had our last."

Ms. Brost has since dragged the piano to where her seventh-grade orchestra students sit in a semi-circle. With a scowl on her face, she plunks the keys in an effort to synchronize them, but only grimaces further.

"Would you care to dance madam?" I ask Alison.

She looks up and wipes her eyes. Together we rise and face one another. Wisps of hair dangle from her temples, no longer in bondage to the ribbon at her neck. Paled by a long journey, eyes still swelled with heartache, cheeks streaked with tears, she is the most beautiful woman I've ever seen. I hesitate out of respect to even approach her, but she steps toward me and I take her into my arms once again.

Our bodies come together, tentatively at first, then begin to move in harmony to the clumsily played notes of Rachmaninoff's *Rhapsody* as it twines with the cacophony of sounds around us: Walter's intermittent bellows, an occasional wail of a toddler, Uncle Billy's foghorn, Lucy and Evie's voices rising over the clinking of dishes from the kitchen area, the soft thumping of Ms. Brost's foot against the wooden stage floor as she prompts her students to rise to the capabilities she believes is in them.

My heart soars. Something in my throat catches. A sob—which I stifle. A strange and wonderful sensation engulfs me as though the great fabric of all mankind just wrapped around me in beautiful music easily recognized by my soul. Home.

EPILOGUE

While this story and its characters are purely fictional, it reveals truths about how the greatest global financial collapse in history unfolded. Theoretically, if all the so-called financial advisors in the world had been as astute as David Yates (the main character in this story) the entire real-life debacle could have been avoided. But that's hindsight—or is it? Since there were significant signs that something was awry in the financial systems as early as 2006, the question has to be asked why it went undiscovered until it was too late.

The fictional characters in this story were created specifically to portray the very real aspects of the mentality shared by people from Main Street to Wall Street who played a part in bringing the world to its knees. From innocent bystanders to the wolves of Wall Street, readers get a glimpse as to how it all came tumbling down, and why so many failed to prevent the disaster while they could. For certain, it raises questions about the value of professional financial advice which one should take seriously today.

History has now recorded that the initial plunge happened on September 16, 2008, followed by a deeper plunge in the markets on October 24. The Dow fell another 680 points in December. The stock markets were in free-fall until March of 2009. By then, everyone was fully aware of what was happening but no one yet knew why. $27 trillion vanished from world economies due to this one event. Often compared to the Crash of '29—which impacted only the economies of major industrialized nations but plunged the U.S. into the Great Depression—the 2008 event affected *every* nation on earth and *every* single person alive at the time and born since. Its aftermath, both positive and negative impacts, will be felt for generations, if not indefinitely by some. New norms will emerge and replace life as we once knew it. But many will remain oblivious to it all.

It wasn't until after the congressional hearings that we learned the cause. The financial failure wasn't the plan of an evil mastermind on Wall Street. It was the result of innate human behavior. But who is the most to blame? Should we blame investors who demanded low-risk/high-return securities? Or should we blame Wall Street for creating such investment vehicles to meet their demands? Should we blame banks for offering zero-down, low-interest mortgages, credit cards, and automobile loans? Or should we blame the debtors who accepted those offers? Should we blame the government for lifting regulation that prevented big banks from causing such a financial disaster? Or should we blame the voters who elected representatives that lived up to their campaign promises to support deregulation?

Those who never knew what hit them in 2008 gave power to those who did. So long as there are people willing to play the roles of either puppets or puppeteers, and so long as there are enough people in the audience who find benefit in such acts, the world will continue to revolve in exactly the same way. Here again, we can turn to the fictional characters in this story to help us understand how seemingly-innocuous intentions can lead to such disastrous results. That said, the moral of this story is *no one* is to blame because *everyone* is to blame. We are all part of the great fabric of all mankind.

—Susan Joyce

"This is a once-in-a-lifetime crisis, and possibly the largest financial crisis of its kind in human history,"

Charles Bean,
Deputy Governor
of the Bank of England

October 24, 2008

ALSO BY THIS AUTHOR:

Real Women Manage Wealth
Financial Security
Once and For All and Forever

And an accompanying workbook to the above:

Personal Finance
NOTEBOOK
Real Women Manage Wealth
Step-by-Step Guide

Available for purchase at

Sweet Reads Books and Candy, Austin MN: 507.396.8660
The Homestead Boutique, Albert Lea, MN: 507.421.5368
and
www.amazon.com

Women are natural-born wealth managers, yet, the entire financial industry has failed to provide women with the products and services they need to manage one of their greatest resources—money. The book reveals the reason women lack interest in wealth management, identifies what women really do need, and the workbook shows them step-by-step how and where to get it. Once women start managing wealth like a Real Woman, instead of trying to managing it like a man, they are able to live their lives more fully and with greater purpose.

A must-read for every woman.

www.BooksBySusanJoyce.com

Made in the USA
Middletown, DE
06 January 2022